The Limits of Dishonor

A Novel

by

Thomas Hofstedt

Table of Contents

From infancy on, we are all spies; the shame is not this but that the secrets to be discovered are so paltry and few.

John Updike

Prologue

"This isn't right!"

The words were shouted and angry, but the wind absorbed them. She turned to me. "He spent most of his miserable life in grubby little rooms in grimy cities, convincing pathetic little people to betray themselves and their friends for petty causes. Why should he be entitled to *this*?"

She swept her arm in an accusing arc that encompassed the entire magnificent cove, including the chapel, the rocky cliffs, crashing surf and gnarled cypress trees. I thought, *she's right, it isn't fair*, but what I said was, "He's dead, Magda. We're not. Your notion of what's fair is irrelevant."

She wasn't listening, or maybe she was and just wanting some small measure of revenge for the wrongs he had inflicted on her … and through her, on others far more innocent. She said, "You should have left him to rot in the sun, something for the dogs to pick at."

It wasn't sunny, and there were no dogs. But he knew he was going to die, and why. And because of that knowledge, it was not a pleasant death. Not unpleasant enough for Magda, of course, with her old-world views of how personal grudges should be settled, with fire and sharp knives.

We were early for the service and had walked out to the highest point of the promontory that formed the northern arm of the cove. From there, we could look back at the chapel. It was all glass and curved redwood beams, with angled walls that seemed perfectly natural within the tree-studded rocky landscape. It was a structure that celebrated nature rather than any particular god, something suitable for a Druid ceremony perhaps. According to the plaque near the entrance, the Oregon Department of Transportation had commissioned it at a time when the state had one of its rare surpluses. Just off of the most remote stretch of the coastal highway, it had few visitors and these days it was rented out for weddings and other ceremonies, although this was surely one of the more unusual ones.

Schmidt's sister had made all the arrangements. She'd met me at the airport, standing alongside the hearse that was parked among all the luggage carts, between the refueling tanker and the airline's catering truck. Not much of a hero's homecoming but then he wasn't much of a hero.

The sister's name was Vera. She was a severe-looking woman, so devoid of warmth or grief that I suspected she had been bribed – like me – to play at being a mourner. I could see nothing of Schmidt in her except for the watchfulness. I had prepared a story for her, a non-verifiable completely fictitious tale of a fatal incident that was nobody's fault and led to a merciful quick death, the sort of story that an estranged relative could hear without experiencing any reflected guilt. But I didn't need it. She showed no curiosity about either his death or that vast part of his life that she obviously knew nothing about.

"Thank you for bringing him," was her greeting and I think she would have been content if our conversation ended there, but I was curious. He had never mentioned a sister, the state of Oregon or any part of his past.

"Did he grow up here?"

"Yes."

"Are there other family members?"

"No."

"When did you last talk with him?"

"Long enough that I can't remember." She turned away, saying, "We weren't close," leaving me to watch a pair of longhaired baggage handlers slide the plain metal coffin into the hearse. *The dead American soldiers coming home from Afghanistan and Iraq are received at Andrews Air Forec Base by an honor guard, with pomp and ceremony.* The thought depressed me only for a second or two. *Schmidt would have said, 'But they're still dead, aren't they?'*

I had a few hours before the service so I walked around the small town. It told me nothing that fit with my concept of Schmidt's formative years. It was a town that hadn't changed for a long time except to get emptier and poorer. The main industries – logging and fishing – were far along in the long slow process of disappearing and I guessed that the only viable businesses were the pot farms back in the hills and the craft shops. About every second storefront on the three blocks of the main street sold quilts, candles, watercolors or homemade jewelry. In the end, I came to view it as a place that would be easy to walk away from.

"It's time," Magda said, so we walked back to the chapel. There were only six rows of redwood pews, so highly polished that they seemed to magnify both the quantity and the quality of light that flooded the small sanctuary. I could not help contrasting it with the vast dark interiors of the great European cathedrals and wondering how many times I had used their dim spaces for a purpose that no religion in the world would have condoned. Here, there was far too much light and openness.

There were four people in the first two rows. Two men and two women, each separated from their neighbors by enough space to clarify that there was no emotional connection between them. Magda and I slid into the third row. The space in front of the pews was completely unadorned, as though to emphasize the view through the twenty-foot high glass front that looked out at a single magnificent wind-carved cypress tree and, beyond it, at the surf striking against the rocks. The only object in the space was the casket on its trolley. The unadorned metal box had been replaced by a gleaming casket, seemingly of the same wood as the pews and heaped with flowers.

His sister – Vera? -- may have been unfamiliar with his life, but she had given a lot of time and attention to scripting his funeral. And money too, given the apparent quality of the casket. As was the case these days, unbidden videos began to run in my head, of bodies thrown into shallow graves and hastily covered with dirt and whatever rocks could be scrounged from the surroundings. *It's odd ... those graves were scattered across two decades and four continents, but there were never enough rocks, except in Afghanistan.*

I didn't realize that music had been playing until it stopped. A relatively young man in a dark suit with a purple scarf draped around his neck came up the aisle, stood alongside the casket with his right hand resting on it and began to speak in soft unctuous tones. He used neither notes nor gestures, speaking in the faintly apologetic way of one encountering grief in strangers. The title for his talk could have been 'A Eulogy for a Man That I Never Met But Presume Was Good in Ways That I Do Not Know.' He talked only for seven or eight minutes and never referred to Schmidt by his proper name.

There was a vague religiosity to what he said, although it was probably more pagan than Christian. I definitely heard references to a gender-free god that was omnipotent and omniscient and yet perversely unwilling to intervene in human affairs while retaining the right to judge the outcomes and – in the end – to accept you despite your faults. He made his vague deity sound like a Little League coach saddled with all the town's athletic misfits and speaking at the annual awards banquet.

Schmidt would have enjoyed it. For the irony if nothing else, because he was as atheistic as they come. It was yet another part of him that I never understood: how a man that did not believe in *anything* could care so much about causes that were, if not hopeless, so flawed as to be unworthy. It was as if his disdain for the truly existential questions enabled him to suspend both his critical judgment and his conscience in equal parts.

I acknowledged but did not pursue the obvious corollary: that whatever Schmidt had done or had been, I was his avatar, the means by which his imperfections played themselves out in the lives of ordinary and innocent people.   I wondered how I could have allowed that to happen.

The Start (1985)

You have to think of your career the way you look at the ocean, deciding which wave you're gonna take and which waves you're not gonna take. Some of the waves are going to be big, some are gonna be small, sometimes the sea is going to be calm. Your career is not going to be one steady march upward to glory.

Alan
Arkin

Job Offer

I met Schmidt almost twenty years ago. Reagan had just declared the Soviet Union to be the 'Evil Empire,' but even then *nobody* appreciated that the entire communist system was hanging on by a thread and would soon come crashing down. If some sideshow fortune teller had told me that I would spend the better part of my adult life committing reprehensible acts to bring that about, I would have admired her creativity and suggested she should look for more gullible customers, and failing that, another line of work.

I was twenty-five years old with a brand-new graduate degree in journalism, forty-thousand dollars in student debt, a lone job offer from a right-wing newspaper chain based in Texas, and an inflated view of myself that did not fit with any of those realities. It was a natural turning point in a life that, so far, had been more drift than purpose.

The man who approached me in March of 1985 looked nothing like my concept of an espionage agent. He was perhaps forty years old and bulky, like a one-time college football player – a guard, maybe, that hadn't quite kept up his conditioning routine. He had dark features – eyes, skin tone, thick black eyebrows and a beard that may have been just a decision not to shave that morning. His nose was slightly bent and he did not smile. He was wearing khaki trousers and a V-necked sweater over a plaid shirt. He could have been anything or anybody, so I guess he may have been a good spy.

He pulled out the chair opposite me, uninvited. I was sitting at a plastic table in a corner of the student union and waiting for the blank laptop screen in front of me to suggest a career path more appealing than the one I had blundered into through a series of default decisions made possible by my tendency to avoid hard choices. *You like to travel. Why not carom around Europe for a year? You're good at writing. What about journalism? An undergraduate degree doesn't get you much these days. You should go on for the master's.* But I'd played out the string; there were no more options.

So Schmidt's timing could not have been better, although I would learn that he was a genius at picking the right moment, whether it was for a show of anger, compassion or any of the other influencers that he used so well. He slid a business card halfway across the table and said, "Mr. Mahoney" in a tone that made it clear he knew who I was. "My name is Schmidt. I'd like to talk to you about a job."

"I have one." I did not look at his card or say the words "Go away," but they were strongly implied. In those days, I was trying to be 'cool,' and I was pleased by the way that I responded. No trace of curiosity about his 'job' or who he was. The reality that I had no intention of actually accepting the Texas job offer did not even occur to me until later.

He said, "Yes, I know. With the Armstrong Media Group, in Texas. That's not a problem." It was the first of countless times that he would surprise me by demonstrating how thoroughly he saw through me. He reached out and pushed the card closer. I looked down at it and read, "Samuel Schmidt, Intelligence Directorate, Langley, VA." There was no title, phone number or any other information, but it did have a very official-looking logo. Given what I knew about the Central Intelligence Agency at the time, the image could have been lifted from a cereal box and I wouldn't have known the difference.

I dropped the 'cool' act. replacing it with genuine curiosity. "You're recruiting for the CIA?" It set off a rapid-fire string of questions and answers, as though each of us was determined not to show weakness by responding fully.

"Yes." ... "Me?" ... "Yes." ... "Why?" ... "You fit." ... "How do I fit?"

He didn't answer that last question. Instead, he took a pen from his shirt pocket and wrote a phone number on the back of the business card and pushed it back toward me. "You don't like your options and think you can do better." He stood up.   "Work for me for six months and I'll pay off your forty-thousand dollar student loan as a bonus. Call me if you're interested." Then he simply walked away.

I spent a week ignoring his offer, pretending that I was offended by his invasiveness. *What right does he have to know about my job offer in Texas or excessive student debt! What makes him think that he has any idea how I feel about my options!* When I began to tire of my own petulance, I used the rest of the week convincing myself that working for the CIA would be a sellout of some sort, but I finally admitted that I couldn't identify exactly what part of my ill-defined value system I would be offending.

So I called the number. A woman's voice said only, "Please leave your name and number for a callback."

The same voice – a female of indeterminate age -- called twenty minutes later. "My name is Marshall. Mr. Schmidt has authorized me to speak for him. Are you interested in his offer?"

"I'm interested, but I have many questions." *Like your use of personal pronouns. Schmidt said, "Work for me." And this voice asks me if I'm interested in his offer. Maybe they think of the CIA as a human? Like how the navy calls its ships 'she.'*

"Of course. Mr. Schmidt will answer them for you. He will meet you at 1052 Fielding Street at 10 AM on Saturday." The call terminated before I could respond.

Years later, sitting in a hospital in Germany, I asked him, "Why did you pick me? In 1985?"

The question surprised me even as I heard myself ask it. It was one of those off-limits topics, too personal for everyday conversation between employer and employee, but – apparently – permissible in settings where dependency and mortality were omnipresent.

We were in a post-operative recovery room. He had just come out of a six-hour-long surgery to remove a piece of shrapnel lodged near his spine. It had been there for years, long before I knew him, but had shifted enough that it was now causing continuous pain and the threat of paralysis. He was still coming out of the anesthetic fog and I think that was the only reason he answered my question.

He didn't respond for a long time. I presume he was trying to decide if I could handle the information.

Finally, he smiled and said, "I didn't pick you. No one did. It was an algorithm."

"You recruited spies by using a *formula*?"

"Why not? Look at what happened to the Brits, with their 'good old boys' and pipe-smoking 'grey eminences' in tweed suits identifying the likely candidates."

George Smiley. John LeCarre's master spy. Recruited out of one of the Oxford colleges. But he was fictional.

Schmidt was going on, as though tracking my thoughts. " ... handpicked their intelligence agents from the best and tbe brightest at Oxford and Eton. They got Kim Philby, Burgess, McLean ... all of them highly productive double agents for the Soviets. We thought we could do better ... protect ourselves with mathematics. So we tasked a couple of our PhD's in the Analytics Group to develop a model. They were excited about the possibilities. I think they used some of the research from the early work on personality types and the career choices of college graduates."

It was a long speech for Schmidt, especially in his post-operative condition, and he closed his eyes when it ended. I asked, "What were the variables that they built into the model?" but I wasn't sure that I really wanted to know. *Even after all this time and the ample evidence to the contrary, we still think that we are unique beings, not something that can be reduced to parameters in a mathematical model.*

"The variables? Mostly codified common sense. Citizen, no criminal record, spent time outside the U.S., graduate degree in selected fields – journalism included -- multiple languages but some Russian for sure, unmarried, financially insecure and – don't ask me why – an only child who played sports on a varsity team in college."

"So, that first day –"

He raised a hand to interrupt me. The pain was ramping up again. He was clenching and unclenching his hands and his forehead was developing deep furrows. He finally reached for the morphine pump and pushed it three times.

"They said they hacked into resume files in college placement offices and ran thousands of them through their model. Their algorithm identified thirty possibilities. I talked to each of them. And twenty-three of you showed up. You know what happened next." His voice was slowing, but I still had to ask the important question.

"Did it work? The algorithm?"

He looked at me, puzzled.

"Were we good spies? Did you get what you wanted?" *And are those even the same question?*

I watched the blankness seep into his eyes and the tension flow out of his muscles and I envied him his narcotic haze. And my question was entirely rhetorical in any case. *We all know the answer to that question. At least, those of us still alive.*

Casting Call

I was at 1052 Fielding Street at 10 AM on the designated Saturday. There was never any real question in my mind as to whether I would show up or not. It had taken Schmidt four minutes, using bribery and innuendo, to set the hook. I would learn the technique and use it for the next twenty years to recruit prospects for treasonous purposes, but it took me a long time to accept that I was as susceptible to it as any dissatisfied civil servant in a depressing third or fourth world country.

In those early days, my concept of the life of spies came almost entirely from the novels of John LeCarré . By 1985, he had published nine novels and his protagonist George Smiley was an old and invisible friend, one that I would subconsciously try to please for approximately the next two decades, until I reached a tipping point in Tikrit, Iraq.

One of the many ironies was that, because of George Smiley, I knew more about Britain's MI6 than I did the American CIA. So I did some elementary research. The internet was in its infancy, so I mostly read old newspaper articles about the agency. Most of them were highly critical, with in-depth treatments of the many failures – the Bay of Pigs, the hamhanded overthrow of Iran's government, Vietnamese bungling, the smuggling of dope and arms, and a litany of dirty tricks. More recently, it was clear that the agency was deeply involved in helping the Afghan mujahedeen in their bloody war of attrition against the occupying Russians and in staving off Mr. Reagan's creeping communist threat in Central America.

There was also some glossy CIA recruiting literature in the university's placement office that tried to put a public face on the agency, making it sound like a cross between General Motors and the French Foreign Legion. My only real takeaway from any of my research was the conviction that Schmidt was operating on his own clandestine agenda, hence those personal pronouns.

What does one wear for a job interview as a spy? Figuring that 'blending in' was important for undercover work, I went with corduroy slacks, no tie and a sport coat. I would have 'blended in' with a tea party in the faculty lounge, but that's about all.

1052 Fielding Street was an ordinary looking two-story office building in a mixed-use neighborhood, sandwiched between a car dealership and a four-story apartment building. There was a bright red 'For Lease' banner draped from the rooftop and a woman in blue jeans and a sweatshirt just inside the entrance door. She was holding a clipboard and when I gave her my name, she made a checkmark on her sheet and said, "Room 101. To your right. Coffee is in the room."

"I'm meeting Mr. Schmidt."

"Yes, I know." She repeated, "Room 101. To your right." Her obvious indifference and the low hum of voices coming from Room 101 were the first signs that I was overrating my importance to America's intelligence community. There were a couple of dozen individuals already there. It was a large room with three ragged rows of hard wooden chairs facing a single high stool in the front. The back half of the room was empty except for a table with two coffee urns and the individuals clustered in awkward small groups. It reminded me of my first day of college, walking into freshman orientation, and I felt the same kinds of uncertainties. I made a slow job out of filling a Styrofoam cup from the coffee urn so that I could get a reading of the group.

Nobody knows anybody else. About half of the individuals were standing by themselves pretending to look out the windows and those who weren't stood in tense groups of two or three people, not talking very much and clearly uneasy with one another.

The second immediate impression was, *we've got a lot in common.* Everybody seemed to be within four or five years of the same age ... late twenties, I guessed ... and had the same indefinable aura about them that I had imputed to myself – surprise that I was not alone and the inevitable sense of competition that went with it. There were three women and they all stood together, looking just as uncertain as the rest of us.

I think all of us were relieved when Schmidt walked in and said, "Please take a seat." He went to the front and sat on the high stool, one foot on the floor and his hands folded. As far as I could tell, he was dressed exactly as he had been when he approached me in the student union. Once all of us were seated, he made a four-second speech.

"You're here because you are interested in working on behalf of the American intelligence community. I'm here to answer your questions." Then he sat waiting.

We were expecting more and the room was dead silent for twenty seconds or so. Then feet began to shuffle and covert glances were exchanged between those sitting next to one another. I began to suspect that we were being watched, that some oddball behavioral scientist with a hidden camera was looking for reactions that would separate the valid candidates from those who merely wanted a job. But it was only Schmidt and he just sat there waiting, oblivious to our confusion.

"Who are you and what exactly do you do in the CIA?" It was an aggressive question, expressed in a hostile tone, coming from one of the three women.

"My name is Samuel Schmidt and I work for the Director of the Central Intelligence Agency. I do special projects. This is one of them."

A man in the third row stood up to ask, "Are all of us being interviewed for the same job?" Something in the way he asked the question told me that if the answer was "yes," he would walk out.

Schmidt said, "First, this is not an interview and, second, I can hire all of you, none of you, or anything in between." The man sat down again, slowly, and I suspected that he had planned his response assuming he would get a 'yes' or 'no' answer to his question.

The next question came from me. "What *is* the job – *the special project,* as you call it -- exactly?" I did not raise my hand or stand up and was careful to keep my tone absolutely neutral.

Schmidt was amused by the question. "*Exactly?* I have no idea. What it is *generally* is the gathering of intelligence that will further U.S. interests. The exact means by which that intelligence is gathered will be highly contingent on your particular skills, who our enemies are at any given moment and what particular opportunities may be presented."

"So, we shall be spies?" This from a tall man at the far end of the third row. He was nearest the only door into the room and sitting – almost reclining – with his arms crossed and his legs stretched out in front of him. It was a posture that would be deemed offensive in an ordinary interviewing context.

Schmidt seemed to consider him before answering. "Yes, although I don't like that word. But only if you complete the six-month training course." After a few seconds, he added, "Most people won't."

"Assuming I complete your six-month course, what will I be doing?"   The man asking the question was wearing a suit and held a pen poised over a pad of paper.

"I think I answered that question. But if you need more, I can tell you that the work is incredibly important, deadly dull, intensely lonely and very occasionally dangerous. There will be lots of travel and you will encounter more than your fair share of unpleasant people, some of whom you will be dependent on."

The Q&A went on for another twenty minutes, gradually dying out as it became apparent that Schmidt would answer only in generalities. Finally, he stood up from his stool and said, "For those of you who wish to continue, Miss Marshall – the woman at the front entrance – has a quite lengthy application form that must be completed within the next three days. In one week, you will be notified of our decision. If accepted by me and you agree to join, you will go through a six-month training/orientation course.   At the end of that, you will have the one-time option of continuing or stopping, without prejudice on our part."

With that, he walked out of the room, leaving us in the same awkward silence that we started with and me with what I thought was a plan. *I'll sit through his six-month long training program, take his forty thousand dollars, and then exercise my option to walk away.*

Over the years since then and in many contexts, I have learned and relearned that decisions are different than outcomes or, as Riley put it with his usual eloquence, "You don't always get what you want." But, back then, in 1985, I was young and principled, unable to foresee the sins that I would commit and the massive regret that I would feel for what might have been.

Training Program

I really met Riley and Magda for the first time three months later, in June 1985, although all three of us had been in that office building on Fielding Street on that first day. Riley was the one with the 'fuck you' reclining posture and Magda the woman who posed the first and most hostile question to Schmidt. When I expressed disappointment that neither of them remembered me from that meeting, Riley said, "That makes you the superior spy ... bland and unremarkable is good."

There were nine of us entering that six-month program -- eight men and Magda. And Schmidt, of course. There would always be Schmidt, even when he wasn't there.

I now know that he lied to us continuously for those six months. He lied about why we were there and who we worked for, beginning with that first morning when the nine of us were gathered in the same place. He also lied about how well-trained we would be when we finished 'the program.'   In fairness to Schmidt, we were highly susceptible ... as in gullible ... to being lied to, except for Riley, and he never called out Schmidt or any of our instructors when they lied to us about how good we were.

"This six month program will give you everything you need, wherever you are, whatever you're doing." Schmidt said it with a straight face, a statement that proved so categorically wrong so soon that we should have immediately gone back to civilian life. However, he also told us that we were special even though we didn't know it. That turned out to be true, but not in a good way. The lies worked because he told us things about ourselves that we wanted to believe were true … how *special* we were.

Certainly, the training program was special. Unlike our six-month program, I learned that a 'regular' CIA recruit entering through normal channels would undergo an 18-month program called 'the Clandestine Service Trainee Program' at 'the Farm,' a not-so-secret CIA facility. The curriculum was extensive and continuously evolving, part of the vast infrastructure needed by an incredibly bureaucratic organization that operates globally and requires diverse talents to carry out its often ill-defined missions.

For all but the last week of those six months, we lived on a working farm about fifty miles outside of Washington DC and nowhere near any CIA facility. It had dairy cows, goats, chickens and horses. The buildings – the rambling and ramshackle house that we lived in, an enormous barn with complex milking apparatus, and several outbuildings – were surrounded by cultivated fields, and tractors and other specialized machinery would be at work most days.

Within the first week, I decided that the training regime was a strange blend of a Marine Corps boot camp and an English public school. Our six months were necessarily far more focused than today's CIA recruits in their 18-month long program. We saved a lot of time by ignoring all of the administrative material required of employees in a vast Federal bureaucracy. There were no "This is Your Benefits

Package" or "Cultural Sensitivity" or "Embassy Protocols" classes. A much more serious difference was our very abbreviated self-defense education. Schmidt's philosophy was that if you found yourself engaged in hand-to-hand combat, the mission was hopelessly lost in any case. "All that Kung Fu shit," he said, "just messes up your hands."

Each week had six twelve-hour days, with homework each evening. Our Sundays were nominally 'free,' although none of the nine of us ever went anywhere and I slowly became aware that we shared a tendency toward aloneness. All of us were only children and I think that we all were indifferent to family and had no 'significant other.' The forced isolation caused us to be close, but all of us knew that it was a temporary condition. Schmidt had chosen carefully.

The curriculum was highly concentrated. The first part of every day was intensive physical training and, after the first few weeks, that became the most enjoyable part. Then there were the languages. We all spoke reasonably fluent Russian, so they drilled us on Arabic, German, Spanish and Chinese. Toward the end, it was exclusively Spanish. The middle part of the day, including a working lunch, was devoted to Russia … its history, culture, politics and economics. All the remaining time was on 'tradecraft,' an area where my extensive knowledge of the LeCarré novels actually gave me an advantage over everybody except Riley.

The instructors lived with us. Schmidt introduced them as 'Arthur, Benjamin and Carlee' in a manner that clearly signaled that they could just as easily be called Wynken, Blynken and Nod. "Their names are not important. What they will teach you, however, is vital. Pay attention."

Arthur was physical training, with an emphasis on aerobic conditioning, as though long distance running would be routinely called for. Each session included some elementary self-defense techniques and, late in the program, weapons training with handguns and rudimentary explosive devices. Benjamin schooled us in all things Russian, requiring us to recite entire Pushkin poems at random intervals during the day. Carlee taught us 'tradecraft.' She was the antithesis of what I expected a female CIA operative to be like. She was old, in her sixties, matronly and vocally intolerant of mistakes. We came to fear her disapproval.

"She reminds me of my drill sergeant in basic training," said Riley. "A truly mean perfectionist and ever unhappy. Carlee could be my Sergeant Lowe after a sex-change operation."

"You're military?" I asked. *That would explain the weapons proficiency.*

"Ex. Marine Corps ROTC, then three years in Naval Intelligence."

Schmidt was nearby and overheard. "That's not for sharing, Riley. Personal history is irrelevant. The idea is to make you invisible and facts like that just get in the way. And Mahoney here doesn't care anyway." He was wrong, of course. I craved to know more about the personal lives of my eight fellow-students, figuring that such knowledge would tell me something important about myself.

Carlee liked games and most days would feature a puzzle of sorts.   They could be simple technical problems, as in 'Contrive a simple code using the map of the London tube system" or tests of your observational powers, such as "Here's a street scene photograph of several pedestrians in Warsaw. Identify those who are not Polish." The worst -- or perhaps the best -- ones were moral dilemmas.

Riley and I were sitting at the kitchen table drinking coffee and practicing our German.   Carlee came in, placed a very old Webley revolver in the center of the table and said, "You are in East Germany.   The Stasi knows you are Western spies and has the house surrounded. They will enter in force very shortly. The pistol has a single bullet.   What should you do?"

The correct answer – according to Carlee -- was "Use your single bullet to kill the one of you who knows the most and then charge out of the house waving the empty gun. The Stasi will do the rest." We, of course, were still naïve and recommended drawing lots to see which of us committed suicide, allowing the other one to surrender and do his pathetic best to resist torture.

On the last day of the third month, the three instructors and Schmidt closeted themselves in the farmhouse kitchen for three hours and when we assembled for physical training the next morning, there were only six of us. No mention was ever made of the missing three, but the training regimen shifted slightly and each of us began to meet one-on-one with various individuals who would appear for a two-hour session late in the day. We were 'building our cover' as Carlee put it. It turned out that one of the ways our little group was 'special' was that our training was designed to turn out a very particular profile. In today's terms, it was a little bit like prospective parents using genetic manipulation to create the specific child they wanted, instead of relying on the randomness of an unsupervised pregnancy.

Aside from Magda, Riley and myself, our group consisted of Peter, Roger and Alex. We were all different and yet all the same in some ways. We were told that personality is a handicap, that individual differences are quirks to be eliminated and, if that's not possible, to be suppressed in the interests of a greater good. Our faculty would have been severely disappointed if they knew of the bonds that would form between the six of us. In their world, mistrust and competition were the core values, and they did their level best to instill them into the human receptacles that filed into the bleak classroom on that first day.

Even with Schmidt's prohibition against sharing biographical data, we knew a fair bit about one another. Not the back-stories nor any real facts, but the physical proximity and the intensity of the training revealed much about a person.

Riley and Magda were the unofficial leaders within the group of six, a position defined solely by their shared cynicism and the deference the rest of us showed them. Magda was tall, dark and intense; a gypsy-like presence that switched from brooding to effervescent instantly and without any apparent cause. Her cynicism expressed itself as hostile questions to

Schmidt, always asking "Why?" as though we had a right to know.

Riley's cynicism was turned inward, a trait that made him mysterious and exotic.   He exuded a world-weariness that implied past tragedies or the presence of secrets that would – if revealed -- explain why he carried out acts that he thought wrong. I think that, even then, in those early days, we all knew that eventually he and Schmidt would have to confront one another.

I knew the others less well. Peter was quiet, almost brooding, and intensely competitive with a quick temper.   Roger talked a lot, often to himself and usually in some language other than English. Alex was a perfectionist and I often wondered how he could exist in a world where everything was gray and there were no absolutes. It turned out that he couldn't, but it would take him fifteen years to find that out and almost cost me my life.

One of the ways that we were special was that our cover was prearranged, unlike the usual CIA trainee. Schmidt had selected us in part because each of the six of us had already established our bona fides. Riley and Magda were consultants, Riley as a security specialist and Magda as an advisor to NGO's. I knew less about the other three, although Roger had been to medical school, Peter had something to do with high-end computing systems and Alex was always reading obscure academic journals involving art.

At first, we watched each other, seeking some form of advantage in what we thought was a contest for Schmidt's attention, like a covey of ninth-graders hoping to make the varsity team. Except for Riley, of course. He needed no reasssurances about his position. I think we all had in mind the early morning disappearance of the other three recruits and feared that we would be the next to go.

Schmidt was waiting for me in my room. With him was another middle-aged professorial looking man. My first and panicked thought was, *He's going to tell me to leave ... that I'm not good enough for the program.* It wasn't until that moment that I realized how badly I wanted to stay.

But it wasn't that at all.

"This is Daniel," was how Schmidt introduced my particular career counselor and mentor. "He's going to be working with you on how to be a journalist and a spy at the same time."

I'd been thinking about this for a while. "Uh, Schmidt? There was this little thing called the Church Committee ..."

Neither Schmidt nor Daniel seemed very alarmed. They just looked at me like I had said, "The sky is blue." So I quoted. "Effective immediately, the CIA will not enter into any paid or contract relationship with any full-time or part-time news correspondent accredited by any U.S. news service, newspaper, periodical, radio or television network or station."

They continued to stare, so I went on in a slightly sharper tone. "That's a 1976 quote from the then CIA Director George H.W. Bush, responding to

Congressional complaints about the agency's nasty habit of bribing journalists and editors."

Schmidt shrugged. "Well, I think we can arrange to stay within the letter of the law." He didn't mention the spirit of the law.

Daniel began, "In your role as a correspondent for the Armstrong Media Group –"

"Wait. I never accepted their offer." AMG was the Texas-based holding company for a chain of local newspapers in the southwestern U.S. They were my lone job offer before Schmidt wandered into my life.

"Oh, but you did. Here's a copy of your employment contract." And he handed me a sheaf of papers, complete with my very authentic-looking signature on the cover page and a date from four months in the past.

"But I haven't written anything for them."

Daniel had the good grace to look slightly embarrassed. "Ah, but you have. Here are copies of the articles and columns you've written in your brief time on the job. Quite a lot actually." He handed me another and much thicker sheaf of papers. I leafed through them quickly, seeing my byline atop stories ranging from the sorry state of the Rio Grande watershed, to an El Paso School Board election, to a police shooting in Tulsa.

"Who wrote these?"

Schmidt looked disappointed in me. He said, "You did." When I just continued to look at him, he went on. "OK. A sixty-five year old retiree in Abilene who needs the money to pay for his wife's chemotherapy. Once upon a time, he was a major stringer for the Dallas Morning News, so he's quite competent."

It was a wonderful story, calibrated to appeal both to my compassion – the chemotherapy bit – and my ego – 'my' stories being written by an authenic and reasonably noteworthy journalist. Like much of everything else that Schmidt told me over the years, I would learn that it was a lie, albeit one of the more harmless ones.

Daniel chimed in, right on cue. He sounded almost apologetic when he said, "The publisher and editor want you to take on more international stories." *No surprise there! Not much need for highly trained espionage practitioners in West Texas.*

Next, he passed me copies of a bank statement with my name on it. "As you can see, your biweekly payroll check from AMG is being deposited directly into your account."

I think it was only then that I first really appreciated how much of my life I had ceded to Schmidt. I distinctly recall a surge of righteous anger that faded as quickly as it arose, unable to persist in the face of my obvious complicity. I suspect that the sudden disclosure that I had both a reputation and a bank account would have helped to mitigate any outrage. I do not recall whether I felt then the other emotions that would become old friends, feelings to be called forth when an assignment went south – the fear, self-pity, or loneliness that were always so close to the surface.

Graduation

Magda was gone for two days. I think it was the only authorized absence for any of us in our time on the farm. When I commented on it to Riley, he said, "Her father died." After a few seconds, he added, "Somewhere in Ohio," as though the location justified her absence.

Would I go home for my father's funeral? I hadn't seen my parents since I had left for my freshman year in college. They were a pair of amiable drunks who hadn't wanted children and nothing that I ever did or said convinced them to change their minds. I felt no kinship, either with them or the small town where I spent my first eighteen years. My only curiosity was about whether my indifference signified some sort of emotional deficit on my part. So when Magda wandered in on Riley and me sitting in the kitchen on Sunday afternoon, I looked at her closely, wondering if she was changed by attending her father's funeral.

She was, but not in the way that I expected. Riley asked, "How was the funeral?" and she said, "Very satisfying, thank you." I looked at Riley, but he merely nodded as if her response made sense and sipped his coffee. So I said, "Why did you go?"

"I wanted to be sure." She looked at me, at first with some irritation and then a slowly emerging sympathy, as though I was the one whose parent had died. She said, "My father was ... special," in a way that made the word 'special' an obscenity.

Riley was watching the two of us closely and decided to intervene. "Spies are loners. Families are a handicap for spies. If they're bad ones, you can be blackmailed. If they're good ones, they foster notions like loyalty and caring relationships ... unhealthy conflicts of interest in our trade."

I asked him the obvious question. "Which kind do you have?"

"Me?" He smiled, but he was looking at Magda. "I was abandoned at birth, left on the steps of the local police station and raised by nuns ... or was it wolves?"

That kitchen conversation was as close as the three of us came to intimacy during that six month period. Much later, I would appreciate that Riley's and Magda's limited and highly personal disclosures in that brief kitchen conversation should have told me a great deal about the particular skills they brought. And, once I understood that, I should have gone on to wonder more about the dark corners of my own internal world.

Schmidt was gone much of the time. He would show up without warning and leave in the same manner. When he was on the premises, he spent most of his time talking with our instructors or cooped up in a small office in the farmhouse. A few times he sat in on our classes, always watching from the back of the space and always silent.

Alex was particularly bothered by him, referring to him as 'the brooding presence.' One morning late in the program, the six of us were sitting on a wooded hillside resting.   It was the turnaround-point for our once-a-week ten-mile run.   Suddenly Alex broke out. "He tells us nothing.   Expects us to meekly do what we're told.   No questions permitted.   All we know is that he directs 'special projects' for the CIA Director and that we're one of them."

Riley seemed amused by the complaint.   "How do we know that he works for the CIA?   Or that we do?" Because of his experience with the Office of Naval Intelligence, Riley had high credibility in our little group, and that always gave his questions extra weight.

"He told us that he ..." Alex began, but quickly realized the irrelevancy of that fact.   Still, the rest of us were intrigued by Riley's questions and I could see them mentally sorting through their memory banks for a piece of concrete evidence that would negate his cynical view of our status.

He pressed us.   "Have any of you met anyone other than him who claims to be CIA?   Or been on an official CIA property?   Do you have *any* document that has a CIA letterhead or a signature of an actual CIA official? A paycheck stub, maybe?"

We all looked at one another, but the silence was eloquent.   Finally, Roger tried another tack, "But Schmidt is in the 'covert operations' branch, and so are we.   We're *supposed* to be secret, even within the agency itself.   Spies don't announce that they work for the CIA."

Riley shook his head. "Have any of you signed a loyalty oath, been sworn in, taken a lie detector test or been given an actual ID card?   Gone through a rigorous physical exam? Received a security clearance? Those are all standard for CIA recruits whether they're analysts or prospective covert agents."

Magda was sitting next to Riley and something in their collective posture or the way that she was looking at him as he talked made me suddenly sure that they had become something more than classmates. It was a startling thought, not least because after almost six months of celibacy, I was intensely aware of Magda. I thought of it then as simple lust, but it turned out to be more complex than that. In the moment, it made me dislike Riley intensely and made it easy for me to go after him.

"So. Riley. With your vast experience in the Office of Naval Intelligence, what's your theory? Are we CIA or not?" The tone was sharp and Magda looked at me with real curiosity. I think she understood the source of my aggression.

He looked at me, at first with concern and finally, I think, with sympathy. He more than anyone else foresaw how each of us would be distorted by the moral ambivalence of Schmidt's world and he knew that there was nothing that he could change.

"I think we're one of Schmidt's special projects. That's good enough for me."

Arthur showed up with the van just then, and the question never came up again. "Get in. No more running. We have a new schedule." Halfway back to the farmhouse, Arthur turned south instead of north in the direction of the house, but it took an hour of driving before someone asked, "Where are we going?"

and Arthur responded, "To South Carolina. We need to work on jungle survival skills for a week or so."

Latin America (1985-90)

The guerrilla fighter is a social reformer, in that he takes up arms responding to the angry protest of the people against their oppressors, and that he fights in order to change the social system that keeps all his unarmed brothers in ignominy and misery.

Ernesto Che Guevara

Panama

Oficinas de la Empresa was a very old office building in a very old section of Panama City, a neighborhood known as Casco Viejo that – according to the Spanish-language guidebook that I'd picked up at the airport -- originated in the sixteenth century. The discreet brass nameplate at the front entrance looked of a similar age, but I had watched the workman screwing it onto the adobe wall as I arrived. The building consisted of a dozen or more offices of varying sizes, ringing a two-story atrium and interior courtyard with one very forlorn palm tree as a centerpiece. Entry into the courtyard was through an arched doorway with an oaken door that stood wide open, its hinges rusted and fused. The sad-looking palm tree and the unusable door hinted that here was a place for questionable endeavors.

I was the last one to arrive although I didn't know that until later. Schmidt had handed me a plane ticket two days ago, along with an index card with the building's address, saying, "I'll see you when you get there."

I noticed the motion detector mounted low on the frame of the wide-open entry door ... *All that tradecraft training apparently did some good. Carlee would be proud of me.* ... and so I was not surprised when Schmidt's voice boomed at me as I stood in the courtyard looking at the blank office doors, "To your left. The conference room."

Everybody was in the room, the entire ten-person menagerie from the Virginia farmhouse. The six rookies, our three instructors, and Schmidt. Three of them were reading the local newspaper and the others were standing around, clearly waiting for me to show up.

"Welcome to Panama, Mr. Mahoney," Schmidt said. "Now we can get started." He sat down at the head of the table and waited while the rest of us found seats in no particular order.

"Forget what you think you know about the Central Intelligence Agency or how it operates. Only the Director and I know of your existence, and we are the only ones who will tell you what to do or how to do it." He looked around the table, as if expecting a challenge. When none came, he shrugged and said, "OK, boys and girls, here's what you need to know right now. Havana and Mr. Castro are a thousand miles due north and a thoroughly left wing Sandanista government is in control of Nicaragua and eager to spread the communist gospel, most immediately in El Salvador. To our south, we are only a few miles from the drug capital of the world – Colombia and its Medellin cartel.

"The President of the United States – a Mr. Ronald Reagan – does not approve of any of this and has committed himself to bringing about appropriate changes. To that end, he has enlisted a very loose confederation of militias generally known as 'contras" who are dedicated to killing off the Sandinistas and restoring right-wing order. They mostly hang out in Honduras, the next country up from Nicaragua, and conduct cross-border terrorist raids. A mere mile from where we sit, an ex-General of the Panamanian

National Guard named Manuel Noriega but more commonly referred to as 'el Presidente' is eager to help us and Mr. Reagan, subject to his compensation requirements."

It was the longest uninterrupted speech I ever heard from Schmidt in the two decades that I knew him. And I also think that it was the best summary, certainly the most succinct, of the complex structure of the 1980's Central American geopolitical cauldron. I glanced around the table and noted that everybody except Riley looked slightly stunned by the flow of words.

I thought I knew where this was going and it was quickly confirmed. Peter asked, "And that's why we're here? To help Mr. Reagan make these changes?"

"Yes," Schmidt said. He was looking directly at me when he said it and then he waited, knowing that I would say the obvious. *He expects me ... wants me ... to say the things that he'd left out.* Which I did, wondering why he needed me as devil's advocate.

I was careful to look at the wall as I spoke. "But then there's this small nagging problem ... the Boland Amendment."

No one said anything. They all just looked at me. So I went on. "The U.S. government has been providing covert military and economic aid to the contras since the Sandanistas overthrew Somoza. But Congress is losing interest fast ... too many civilians killed ... nothing to show for it. So, approximately a year ago, they passed the third Boland Amendment. It *explicitly* forbids any such assistance by the Defense Department, the CIA or *any other U.S. government agency.*"

There was no reaction from the other nine people around the table. They sat watching me with an expression of patient amusement, like parents listening to their three-year-old explain why he shouldn't have to eat his vegetables. It was Arthur who asked, "Are you done?"

I should have stopped but didn't. It was a pattern to be repeated countless times in years to come. It was as if, by reciting all of the legal, moral and ethical reasons why we should all go home, I was clearing myself of the evil consequences that were sure to follow when we simply caved in and did what Schmidt told us to do.

I even raised my voice. "Manuel Noriega is a sadist, rapist, money launderer, drug trafficker and murderer. Not the kind of person you want as a partner."

Arthur said, "Means and ends, Thomas. Means and ends." Schmidt just looked out the window.

"That's bullshit, Arthur. We help Noriega run drugs from Colombia into the U.S., killing our own citizens in the process, so that he will help us funnel illegal arms to the contras so that they can terrorize civilians and restore a dictatorship that is friendly to American corporations."

"But –"

"And what about the Neutrality Treaty we signed with Panama as part of the handoff of the Canal Zone? It quite clearly prohibits precisely the kinds of activity that we're contemplating at this table."

I stopped, mostly because I'd exhausted the small stock of knowledge that I'd acquired in the short space of time after Schmidt had handed me the airline ticket to Panama City, but also because I feared I had gone too far.

"Anything else, Thomas?" Schmidt asked quite mildly, still looking out the window.

"No."

He turned in his chair and addressed the room. "Any questions about anything Mahoney said?"

Peter asked, "Is it true? What he said about Noriega, the Boland Amendment and the Neutrality Treaty?"

"Yes."

He sat and stared at us, his one-word answer hanging in the air, knowing that I would ask the important question, the one that we'd been putting off since that first meeting. So I did.

"So we're not employed by the CIA or any other branch of the U.S. government then?"

"Officially, each of you is an independent contractor. But you have only one client. Me. And I in turn have only one client – the Director of the Central Intelligence Agency."

All of us, including Schmidt, knew that he had not answered my question. But none of us said anything. I think each of us believed that we were as 'special' as he had promised and that that 'specialness' both exempted us from the ordinary rules and foreshadowed a limitless future. We were arrogant and ignorant in equal parts.

He looked at each of the six of us in turn, holding our eyes with his until we looked away. Then he said, "Congratulations on the completion of the training portion of your employment contract. As I promised six months ago, each of you now has the option of walking away from the program. All of the financial commitments I made to you will be honored. No questions will be asked and the last six months will be as if they never happened.

"This option expires in sixty seconds."

He waited through a profound silence for the required sixty seconds, which seemed to go on for an incredibly long time. There was an utter stillness in the room, an absence of both sound and motion. Finally, Schmidt stood up and said, "Welcome to the real world of intelligence. You are about to commit major felonies on behalf of an ungrateful American public. There is no backup except for each other, no 'get out of jail free' card if you are caught, and no assurance that you're actually doing any good."

Managua

"Reagan is an asshole. He sees communists under his bed."

It was easy for me to agree with Rafael. First, because it was part of my cover to be opposed to Reagan's strident anti-communist crusade, but, second, because I mostly agreed with the sentiment. All of the president's rhetoric about 'securing our southern border, regaining regional stability, and preventing the spread of ungodly communism' seemed to me to be more about paranoia than policy.

Rafael was the official Nicaraguan government liaison to our small group of international correspondents. His Spanish name was as long as his title, but we referred to him among ourselves as our niñera ... babysitter, in English. He was a fiery union organizer transformed into an ardent revolutionary, seeming almost regretful that the Frente Sandinista de Liberación Nacional, or FSLN, as it was commonly referred to, was now the official Nicaraugan government rather than still fighting for truth and justice in the streets. Perhaps that is why they had agreed to let four journalists spend a week in the northern provinces of Nicaragua, traveling with a Sandanista brigade in frequent and nasty contact with the contras.

Schmidt had set it all up. I didn't learn of the mission until three days ago when he handed me a copy of a newspaper article. "Here. You wrote this last week." I skimmed it quickly. It was more of an editorial than a news piece, clearly coming across as critical of U.S. Latin American policies. In the article, I -- actually my Abilene avatar -- disagreed strongly with our government's support for the contras.

I handed the article back to Schmidt, who shook his head. "You'll need it. Because of that article, you have been invited by the Nicaraguan government to be their official guest for two weeks, during which time you will have an opportunity to appreciate the tremendous benefits realized by the people of Nicaragua since the 1979 revolution."

I played straight man. "So I shall be writing puffy sychophantic stories about heroic revolutionaries fighting with and overcoming contra terrorists while …?"

"While you are paying particular and highly covert attention to the morale, readiness levels and real – or not real – military accomplishments of the Sandanista army."

It was my first day in Managua and I spent most of it walking around the old city. Much of it was still in ruins from the 1972 earthquake, as the corruption of Somoza's dictatorship and the violence of the subsequent revolution worked against any large-scale recovery effort. But Rafael had arranged for a welcoming cocktail party in the magnificent and undamaged National Palace of Culture in the Plaza de la Republica.

I was the lone American journalist. The three others were German, French and Brazilian, so English was our common language. Rafael asked each of us to introduce ourselves and provide some professional background and it quickly became apparent that I was a rookie working for a small-time regional newspaper and that the others were veterans of the trade with major readership. The Brazilian and Frenchman were international correspondents with major newspapers in their respective countries and the German woman was a freelancer with a lot of experience in Latin and South America. It was equally obvious that the other three shared Rafael's opinions of Reagan, and were willing to impute the same attributes to all Americans, including me.

And they're real journalists, not intelligence agents! I could not stop the thought from recurring and after a while, I no longer worried about whether it was the product of my fear of discovery or of my journalistic insecurities.

The Brazilian and the Frenchman left as soon as they could, claiming the need to meet deadlines, leaving me and the German – a thirtyish woman named Monica Holst – struggling for a way to interrupt Rafael's run-on revolutionary fervor. He reminded me of videos I had seen of Fidel Castro's speeches after the Bay of Pigs debacle ... more three-hour rants than speeches, really. *That was a major CIA screw-up, and certainly not at all the sort of historical parallel I should be thinking of in this particular moment.*

I was content to let him go on, figuring he might slip a few actual facts into his rambles, but Monica Holst was clearly tiring of it and finally broke in. "Fascinating, Rafael, but I have much to do. I will see you in the morning."

He wasn't done. "It's only nine o-clock, still early for Nicaraguans. Have dinner with me. There's a restaurant close by and I can tell you more about our struggle." He was speaking to both of us but from the intensity of his gaze and the proprietary way he reached out to touch Holst's forearm, it was pretty clear who he was inviting and what kind of struggles he had in mind.

She responded with a regretful half-smile, placing her hand over his where it rested on her forearm. "I'd like to, Rafael, but what you've said and your eloquence has made me visualize a five-thousand word piece in Der Spiegel about the role of the press in a post-revolutionary world. I want to write it while it's fresh." It seemed to me to be a textbook example of how to say 'not right now, but maybe later' to an amorous male, particularly one in a position of power.

He turned to me. "What about you, Mr. Mahoney?" I would have declined in any case, but over his shoulder, Monica Holst was looking at me and shaking her head. I had no idea why.

"Thanks for the invitation, Rafael. And the reception. But – like the others – I have much to do before we go north."

He seemed relieved by my rejection. "Very well. We leave early in the morning. You will see at first-hand the atrocities and where the loyalties of the countryside and villagers really lie. The contras are terrorists. They kill the mestizos and their leaders. And you will see that and will tell your readers so that they will understand our cause and what the revolution is doing for our people."

Holst and I walked out into the plaza together. There was a very enthusiastic band, heavy on trumpets, not far from us. "Mariachis?" I ventured, but she said, "They would be if we were in Mexico. Here they're called 'chicheros' and they'll expect us to tip them if we listen. They're trolling for tourists."

They must have identified us as such, because they headed straight for us. Their leader doffed an enormous sombrero and said, "Eres joven y enamorado, ¿sí? ¿Te gustaría que tocáramos una canción de amor para ti?" I had already established in my introduction two hours ago that my Spanish was primitive, so I looked at Holst for the translation. *I wonder how literal she'll be?*

She laughed. "He asks if we're young and in love, and whether we'd like them to play for us?" She replied to the young man in fluent Spanish, with a very faint German accent. "No somos ni jóvenes ni estamos enamorados y tu música no puede cambiar eso, lamentablemente."

We are neither young nor in love, and your music cannot change that, sadly. Just as with Rafael, she had turned away an overture with great diplomacy. But all I said to her was, "I think I heard you tell him that we were sad?"

"Approximately," she smiled, and handed the leader a hundred córdoba note. He bowed deeply, replaced his sombrero and led his troupe toward the cathedral where a thin stream of exiting worshipers was forming into a possible audience near the entrance. The half-dozen of them with trumpets began playing as they walked.

We stood in silence and watched them go. I was already starting to replay the evening's events in my mind, wondering if there was anything that would interest Schmidt. I thought not, but I asked Holst, "Are you expecting anything from this next week?"

"Rafael is un hijo de puta." She glanced at me. "That translates as son of a bitch, just in case your high-school Spanish didn't cover the common obscenities."

"I can handle street level insults, thank you. But I don't think that Rafael fully understands the nature of your feelings toward him."

She snorted, "This is Latin America, the land of machismo. We're going to be in the bush together for the next week. It will be a very long week if Rafael knows what I think of him … and there won't be any story to file at the end of it unless I want to write a polemic about unrequited sexism."

I think she's going to have a long week either way, but from what I've seen so far, I feel sorry for Rafael. "Good luck with that. But if there's anything I can do to help …"

She surprised me for the third time in the last ten minutes. "Actually, there is something you can do for me." I started to say, "Of course, what –" but she took my arm and pulled me along, heading for the taxi rank. "I would like you to fuck me."

Monica

I spent most of the fifteen-minute taxi ride asking myself, "What would Schmidt recommend that I do now?" *Can I argue that indiscriminate sex … promiscuity … is part of my journalistic cover? Am I opening myself up to blackmail?* That seemed unlikely, given that I had no reputation to speak of, nobody to be offended by my lack of morality. *Can I justify this as an attempt to gather information?* That hardly seems possible unless I want to expose the seamier side of the German free press. In the end, I stopped worrying about Schmidt and simply accepted the reality that I was looking forward to whatever it was that was supposed to happen during the rest of the evening.

I did make one brief stab at appeasing my conscience. Five minutes into the trip, I asked, "Are you sure this is something you want to do?"

She looked at me, hard, as if reconsidering. "How American of you to ask! But, yes, this is something I want to do. But you have the option to decline." After that, we said nothing to one another until we reached the hotel. Rafael had booked all of us into the Intercontinental and it turned out that she and I had rooms on the same floor. Hers was nearest the elevator, so we stopped there.

She walked straight to the bathroom, saying over her shoulder, "I'll only be a minute. Don't turn on the lights, please." I took off my jacket and tie and sat down on the chair to untie my shoes. I stopped when I realized I had no idea what the rules were. *Maybe this is supposed to be played like a seduction scene or* – But then she emerged from the bathroom and even in the very dim light filtering in from the outside lights, it was abundantly clear that she was naked.

She knelt and started to unbutton my shirt, her fingers fumbling in her haste. She swore in German, and said, "Help me. Next time, we'll do it your way, but right now, I'm in a hurry."

There was a next time, and – improbably – a next time after that. And then it was dawn and time to go. There was very little time or motivation for sleeping. We were to meet Rafael in the hotel's breakfast area in one hour.

"You have freckles," I said, tracing them across her bare shoulder. "And a serious scar." It ran for six inches, laterally across her left side. "A childhood memento," she said, "achieved by crawling through a broken basement window in an abandoned house in Munich. I was ten years old."

By then, I knew more about her through touch than the other senses. I studied her, really for the first time. Until she had said, "I want you to fuck me," she was a fairly distant and intimidating professional woman with a firm handshake. Between then and her hotel room, I was too busy worrying about Schmidt or consumed with lust to actually look at Monica Holst. And we never turned on the lights.

She was tall and angular with sharp bones in her shoulders, elbows and hips. There was no spare flesh although she was sinewy in the fashion of a rock climber or long distance runner. Her hair was dark, short and straight enough to comb into a rough order using just her fingers. I would not call her 'pretty' in any classical sense; her chin was too square, her nose long and slightly crooked. She looked like a poster from the Stalin era, one of the Heroines of the Soviet Union, the one who routinely exceeded her harvest quota. Her eyes were her best feature, brown and liquid, lending her an air of sadness.

"Are you done looking? Would you like to see my teeth, or the soles of my feet?"

"Uh, no. Sorry. It's just that everything happened so fast –"

"And so often!" She hopped off the bed and began gathering the clothing strewn around, tossing whatever belonged to me into the chair where I'd sat down to untie my shoes. She was totally un-self conscious about her nakedness and I wondered how she achieved that. In the end, I chose to assume that it was because she was a northern European. She headed for the bathroom. "I'll see you downstairs."

She stopped. "Thomas?"

I stopped buttoning my shirt and looked at her. She said, "I read the article you filed about the contras … the one in the Texas papers."

That surprised me. I had assumed that no one outside of the southwestern United States would see it. I said, "You must be hard up for reading material."

"I was doing research for this bit with the Sandanistas. I was impressed. It's quite professional for a relatively new reporter."

That's because it was written by an actual professional trying to pay for his wife's chemotherapy treatment. I wonder how much attention Schmidt paid to setting up my so-called cover? I hope she doesn't start quizzing me about any of the details!

"Thank you. I know my editor liked it ... and the Nicaraguan government. I'm sure they're not inviting journalists who are highly critical of their revolutionary government."

She stood looking at me while I worked hard on looking modest.   Then she changed the subject. "There's one more thing. It's important."

I waited, expecting a challenge of some sort. But she gestured at the thoroughly rumpled bed and said, "This was fun. But it's a one-time thing. It has no predictive value."

I said, "OK," but I didn't really believe her. But she was already behind the closed bathroom door.

Near Honduras

We spent a full day driving to the north, toward an ominous horizon of dark storm clouds that seemed to stay at a constant distance. Rafael and the four of us were in an SUV, escorted by a military personnel carrier with six uniformed soldiers. There had been isolated contra attacks throughout the country, but the serious stuff generally happened close to the Honduran border with Nicaragua. Rafael told us that President Daniel Ortega had personally instructed him to make sure we saw the raw side of the war, so we were headed for what Rafael referred to as a 'hot spot.'

It was never stated explicitly, but all of us were aware that we were viewed by the Nicaraguan government as a way to counter U.S. propaganda. The Reagan administration, frustrated by a Congress that did not believe in his covert war, and worse, was refusing to pay for it, was waging an aggressive and mostly false campaign in the world press, declaring the contras to be, in Reagan's words, 'freedom fighters, the moral equivalent of our founding fathers.'

On the next morning, in a town of a few thousand mestizos, we met Colonel Raul Gomez, the commandant of a five-hundred man Sandanistan army unit and a veteran of the vicious running war between the contras and the Sandanista government. He was an imposing figure, almost a caricature of the Latin military type – tall, ramrod straight, with an impressive mustache and tailored fatigues that lacked insignia of any sort.

He briefed us in heavily accented English with Rafael serving as occasional translator. "The contras are terrorists. Cowards and murderers. They are not soldiers who will fight us face to face. They hide in Honduras and come out when we're gone. They assassinate the leaders, the teachers, the priests, the doctors ... anyone that the villagers respect. They rape the women and steal what they can."

He paused and I had the feeling that he had been reciting the party line, probably drafted by Rafael for our benefit. When he began again, he seemed much more comfortable. "Yesterday, they ambushed a convoy of several vehicles here" – he used his pointer to tap on a large map taped to the wall – "and kidnapped a Canadian on a medical mission to local Indians. We've arranged an interview for you with a survivor of that encounter and will go from there to a small village that the terrorists have visited twice in the last month."

Monica asked, "This Canadian ... what will they do with him? Will you attempt to rescue him?"

"We will do what we can, which is very little. They will move him to a jungle camp in Honduras, maybe torture him a little to find out what they can, and then ransom him. If no one will pay, they will shoot him." He spoke in flat, expressionless tones and I couldn't tell if he was simply jaded by the never-ending war or perhaps felt that the do-gooder Canadian deserved whatever he got for being so dumb as to wander into an active conflict zone.

Schmidt told me, 'Your job is to find out whether the Sandanista military is fully committed to its mission and what its real capabilities are.' So I asked the Colonel, "You've been up here along the border for a long time. Do you think you can defeat the contras?"

He seemed to take my question as a personal insult. He stood straighter and his eyes flashed. He held his pointer with both hands and I could see it bend from the pressure. "You are an American, yes?" He did not wait for my response. "If your CIA" – he spelled the three letters out slowly and with great contempt – "would stop giving them cash and weapons, this dirty little war would end tomorrow. Write *that* in your newspaper!"

We left the village in the SUV, but this time we had a personnel carrier both ahead and behind, with some twenty soldiers. It was clear from the soldiers' body language and the rapid-fire Spanish between Gomez and his NCOs that they were taking the trip seriously.

The interview with the survivor of yesterday's ambush was a disappointment for everybody. For us journalists, because it was such an ordinary event. A Canadian doctor and a driver in a jeep were stopped by six ragged contras at an impromptu roadblock. They released the driver and disappeared into the jungle with the doctor. For Gomez and Rafael, the incident was disappointing because no atrocities were committed and it lacked the gory details that they thought our readers hungered for.

Then it got interesting. A jeep with four men pulled up and Gomez went to meet them. Two of the men were Sandanistas. They wore the uniform and saluted Gomez. The other two impressed me as military types, not just because they carried sidearms and looked fit, but also because of their apparent ease among Gomez's soldiers. One of them was a Latino in civilian clothes, barking orders at the two soldiers. The fourth man was a rough-looking Caucasian, wearing green fatigues from some army but with all insignia removed. Both of these two were in close conversation with Gomez and there was a lot of gesturing and pointing going on. Monica and I were close enough to hear them but it was tough to make out the words.

"A Cubano and a Russian," said Monica. "That's really very interesting."

"How do you know that?" I asked, although once she said that, it was easy for me to see that they fit the description.

"Accents. Very distinctive."

I remembered that she had been travelling throughout the Americas for some time now and recalled her reasonably intimate exchange with the chichero bandleader in the plaza. *She's got a good ear for languages.*

So. A Cuban and a Russian. Everybody knows that they're helping the Ortega government, but nobody's willing to talk about it except Reagan and the 'better dead than Red' crowd. And here we have a pair of real-life 'advisors.' I took the small point-and-shoot Nikon from my pocket and took a quick picture. Rafael saw me and it was easy to see his disapproval.

The impromptu conference had reached some kind of decision. Gomez shouted a flurry of commands that sent the soldiers scurrying for the vehicles. He, Rafael and the other two men then were clearly and heatedly talking about us, the journalists, and they were clearly not in agreement. There was a lot of finger pointing and argument. Finally, Rafael broke away and approached us.

"Good news," he said, but his expression said exactly the opposite. "You're going to be able to witness a live operation against the contras."

Interdiction

The jeep with the Cuban and Russian led the way, followed by the two military vehicles and then our SUV with the four of us and Rafael. He was holding a tactical radio and was in continuous contact with Gomez. He had also acquired an AK-47 automatic rifle and a martial air to go with it.

"We have an aviso ... a tip. From a very reliable informante. A plane from Mexico will land near here and exchange its load of weapons for a shipment of cocaine. There is very little time, but we have a chance to prevent the transaction."

The Brazilian asked, "Is the landing strip in Honduras or Nicaragua?" Rafael gestured at the dense foliage pressing in on both sides of our SUV and said, "Nobody knows where the border is in this kind of terrain." *And nobody really cares at this point.*

He would not answer any of our questions after that except one. When Monica asked, "Why are you bringing us along?" he said, "Colonel Gomez feels it is too dangerous to leave you alone on the road, and he cannot spare any soldiers to escort you back to the post."

We traveled for about forty minutes on a badly rutted road so narrow that the fronds of palm trees slapped against both sides of the vehicle. We stopped twice while Rafael consulted with Gomez via his radio link. When we stopped for the third time, our little caravan was pulled close alongside a long shed. From the strong odor, I guessed it was for curing tobacco.

The soldiers along with the Cuban and Russian started down a clearly marked path that ran toward and then through a series of small hills about half-a-mile away. They carried their rifles in a state of readiness.

Rafael said, "The landing strip is just beyond the hills. The plane is about thirty minutes away. The four of you are to stay here, no matter what. Is that understood?" He waited, and then repeated, "Is that understood?" Some of us nodded, but Monica asked, "You don't actually know how many contras are meeting that plane, do you?"

Rafael looked at her in a way that reminded me of the way they had parted two nights ago, with her sad eyes and 'maybe later' promises. I didn't think he was going to answer, but then he lifted the AK-47 from where it was leaning against the fender and said, "No, but however many, they are all cowards, so we shall be enough." He used the rifle to point at us. "Stay here, no matter what." And he started after the soldiers, walking fast.

The Brazilian and the Frenchman moved into the shade of the curing shed and started typing on portable typewriters. Monica stood with me, watching the loose column of Sandanistas as they approached the point where the path disappeared among the trees. When the last of the men was out of sight, she said, "Are you coming?" and started off, half running, half walking.

I followed her. I had guessed that she would be unable to stay in place. Ever since we'd met the Cuban and the Russian, she'd been tense, acutely aware of Rafael and his radio dialogue. She was talking as we went, half sentences more to herself than to me, as if narrating the events to a remote listener.

"Either the Cuban or the Russian is getting updates from a radar system.   Bringing in arms in exchange for drugs.   Short jungle runway.   Probably a small cargo plane, couple of crew.   Contras don't go places in large groups, but I think Gomez is going to be outnumbered. But he's got the surprise factor and better men."

She stopped so abruptly that I ran into her.   She'd heard it just before I did: the very faint sound of airplane engines coming from the north.   The dense tree canopy made it impossible to see it, but it clearly was getting closer.   She started running.

When we were about fifty yards from the crest of the hill, she made a ninety-degree turn, leaving the path and paralleling the crest.   It was difficult going, through waist high underbrush, and we were trying to be quiet, so it went slowly.   A hundred yards off the path, she turned uphill, moving as carefully as a point man in an infantry platoon, even when the engine noise abruptly shifted, telling us the plane was on the ground.   I imitated her every move, somehow knowing that she was quite competent at this new and dangerous world that had suddenly presented itself.

The trees ended abruptly at the crest of the hill.   We were at the head of a small valley perhaps two miles long.   A makeshift grass runway bisected the narrow valley and the airplane was just completing a three-hundred-sixty degree turn at the far end and beginning to taxi back toward our end.   The airstrip was a testimonial to simple jungle engineering.   They had clear-cut the trees from the northern slope of our hill to create an approach lane and then mown the 'runway' grass to a few inches. It was clear from the way that the plane swayed and bounced even at low speed that it was a very rough runway.

We stayed on the crest, crouching among piles of logs scattered about from the clear-cutting of the slope below us. There was nothing but stumps and piles of rotting logs between us and the runway.

The Sandanista soldiers had spread out between us and the airstrip and formed a line about halfway down the hillside, using whatever cover they could find among the clusters of felled trees. Gomez, Rafael and the two civilians were clearly visible in the middle of the line. Below them and at the head of the makeshift runway, there was a heavy duty military truck and a full-size pickup truck parked with a couple of dozen armed men sitting or standing in whatever shade they could find. The pickup had a large caliber machine gun mounted in the rear bed. Two men with automatic rifles were seated on overturned boxes next to the weapon and I guessed that they were the lookouts and the main security. But their attention was on the approaching plane. *They're incompetent as lookouts. The contras got halfway down the slope and into cover without them noticing.*

The plane reached our end of the runway, executed another three-sixty turn and throttled down the engines. I didn't recognize the aircraft type. It was a twin-engine prop plane, a stubby, boxy aircraft with an overhead wing and a twin tail. The propellers kept turning but as soon as the plane stopped, the pickup truck moved and positioned itself directly in front of the aircraft's nose. *So they don't trust one another all that much.*

Monica was taking pictures, still talking to herself. I finally realized that she had a voice recorder in her shirt pocket and that her fragmented monologue was being captured. "Medium sized cargo aircraft, twin engine, square fuselage, dual tail. I think it's what I saw in Venezuela. Called a Sherpa something. Pilot, copilot and cargo handler. Getting out now. Three men, white, middle aged, unarmed as far as I can tell from here." She was like a sports announcer, committed to conveying all the little details – what they referred to as 'color' – so as to make the action more vivid for the listeners.

As we watched, the plane's rear cargo door began to unfold. I touched Monica's arm and pointed toward the Sandanistas. The line of soldiers below us had begun to move forward, doing their best to stay hidden but moving rapidly toward the rendezvous point.

The status quo held for three more minutes. The three men from the plane used some kind of internal winch to pull one very large and obviously heavy pallet on skids out of the fuselage and leave it resting partly on the ground and partly on the loading ramp. The large truck had backed up to the ramp and the contras began taking burlap-wrapped bales from the truck and carrying them into the belly of the airplane. Another group was taking apart the contents of the pallet, breaking it down into individual crates and loading them onto the truck. There was a lot of activity, but everything seemed to be going with a practiced smoothness. It was obvious that they would be finished within a few minutes and the two pilots had already returned to the cockpit. The propellers had never stopped turning.

Monica and I had a ringside seat. Gomez would later describe it as a 'pitched battle,' but in fact it was over very quickly and with little drama. The contras were focusing on their quick turnaround and the loading and unloading process, their weapons laid aside for the moment. The two men in the bed of the pickup were the first to see the approaching government soldiers. They shouted and one of them raised his rifle while the other grabbed the handles of the machine gun and swung the muzzle around. But they died within seconds. It sounded like every one of the oncoming attackers fired on full automatic.

Two others who had been supervising the transfer of goods managed to fire a few quick bursts, but they drew concentrated fire from the attackers and survived only a few more seconds. Four of the others started a mad dash away from the line of soldiers, toward the protective darkness of the thick jungle that lined the far side of runway. Two of them made it, the other two were cut down while still in the bright sunlight. The rest of the contra party – about eighteen to twenty frightened men – were herded into a tight circle and forced to the ground. The three men who came with the plane walked down the ramp with the their hands held high and were made to sit in the dirt, guarded by a pair of soldiers. While I watched, the Cuban and the Russian went to them and sat down facing them.

Arthur?

I was a hundred yards away from the three white men sitting in the dirt and the man in coveralls was partly in shadow and hadn't shaved for a while, so I wasn't sure, but even from that distance he sure as hell looked like the man who I'd been locked up with for six months in Virginia and had last seen in a conference room in Panama City. *Part of an arms-for-drugs deal for the contras? Why not? Boland Amendment or not, Reagan – and Schmidt – haven't given up on the idea of supporting the guerrillas. And we know that CIA has a history of facilitating drug deals.*

Gomez was meeting with two of his NCOs and pointing back the way we had come from. Monica grabbed my shirttail, pulling me down behind our log pile. "Let's go, we've got to be back before they know we've been gone."

"Huh? Our story is out there!" I pointed back toward the plane and the soldiers.

She held out her camera. "I've got the story, and we're both eyewitnesses. But, believe me, it's not good for us if Gomez knows that we've been watching. C'mon." She scuttled backwards and once over the crest of the hill, broke into a half run, indifferent to the noise. I followed her, wondering why she was afraid of Gomez. And I was worried about Arthur.

The adrenaline propelled me along the path. When I had time to think about it, it was easy for me to see that I was experiencing the same kind of quasi-euphoria that any rookie feels 'the first time,' whether that rookie is a front-line infantryman, an astronaut trainee, a new medical intern in an ER, or an intelligence agent who's read too many novels by John LeCarré. *A real gun battle! Drugs and illicit arms deals at hidden airstrips in the jungle!*

The high lasted two hours, until I learned what real guerrilla warfare is like.

Guerrilla Warfare

Our two colleagues, the Brazilian and Frenchman, were both asleep in the back seat of the SUV, now shaded against the afternoon sun. The sight of them caused me to reassess my feeling of professional inferiority. *Real international correspondents wouldn't be sleeping while gun battles are taking place over the next hill.* Looking at them, Monica cautioned me once more, "Remember. We've been here the whole time. Heard some shooting. That's all."

Ten minutes later, three of Gomez's men returned, each of them a designated driver for one of our vehicles. Gomez's jeep stayed where it was. The drivers told us nothing except that the raid had been successful – *muy exitoso* -- and that we were going to drive to the site so that we could see for ourselves.

It took an hour to get there in the vehicles and I wondered why we didn't just walk back down the path. We stopped twice while the drivers conferred with much pointing and disgreement about which way to go. During our second stop, we heard the very faint sound of automatic weapons, but it was impossible to tell how close they were or in what direction. In any case, our driver didn't seem alarmed. By the end, we were using four-wheel drive and off-roading, simply following tire trucks made by a previous vehicle, probably the contra vehicles we'd seen at the airstrip.

The Sandanista soldiers were at ease, some of them eating rations, a few dozing and the rest in small groups talking among themselves, sitting in the shade of the large truck or the airplane. There was no sign of the captured contras or the plane crew. The pickup truck was gone and the crates of arms and bales of drugs were not visible. And the Cuban and Russian were also nowhere in sight.

Rafael and Gomez approached us as soon as the SUV parked alongside the airplane. I nudged Monica. "This is not the way we left it." She whispered back, fiercely. "Forget what you saw! It is what it is!"

"Our little operation was a total success," Gomez said. "We have confiscated a large shipment of automatic rifles and ammunition, seized a great deal of cocaine, and – most importantly – wiped out a major unit of the terrorist dogs."

The Brazilian had his notepad out and was writing. "Any casualties on your side?"

"No. My men are highly trained soldiers. Not like the cowardly terrorists. Come, I will show you." He walked around the back of the truck and pointed inside. There were three objects of interest. One was the pallet of arms. It had been reassembled more or less as it was when it was winched out of the plane's cargo area. Gomez pointed at it. "One hundred M-16 rifles and ten-thousand rounds of ammunition. The same equipment used by the U.S. Army." He was looking directly at me as he talked.

The second stack was composed of the burlap-wrapped bales. Gomez said, "It looks like cotton or marijuana, but each one of those little bales has one-hundred individually wrapped kilos of pure cocaine." Monica and I looked at one another. I guessed that the stack we were looking at was about a third of what we saw taken off of the truck a little over an hour ago.

The third display he had arranged for us in the back of the truck was a trio of contras, each of them no more than eighteen years old, scrawny and obviously scared to death.   Their little tableau reminded me of the grainy news photos of confused civilians who, through no fault of theirs, found themselves in a war zone.

"Where are the others?" I asked, causing Monica to show alarm and Gomez to look suspicious. "You said you had wiped out a major unit. Surely there were more than these three?"

He smiled, "Oh, there were more. They're over here," and he led our little party around to the other side of the truck. There were two neat rows of bodies lying in the short grass, aligned as carefully as if in a military formation. I counted nineteen of them. *Four were killed fighting back, two more shot in the back running away. Two reached the jungle. All the others were captured.*

I walked between the two rows of corpses. All of them were badly bloodied, with numerous wounds in the torso, and I remembered the sound of automatic weapons no more than thirty minutes ago. A number also had a single gunshot wound in the side of their head. Worst of all, most of them were young ... maybe eighteen or nineteen. To their credit, the Brazilian and Frenchman said nothing, but their disgust was clear. *I wonder how many times they have reviewed such staged 'battlefields' in squalid little wars?* I looked carefully at Monica, but she was stone-faced, taking pictures with her little camera.

She asked Gomez, "Where are the Cuban and the Russian. I'd like to get their impressions of the firefight."

He looked puzzled. "What Cuban and Russian? This was entirely a Nicaraguan operation."

I kept my voice as neutral as I could. "What about the aircraft crew? What happened to them?"

Gomez looked slightly embarrassed. "There was only a single pilot. A gringo. But he ran into the jungle. I have some of my men searching for him, but I am not hopeful. The border is very close. In any case, he will be a CIA contractor and they will have a way to retrieve him."

So we are missing one pickup truck, two thirds of the cocaine shipment, one Cuban, one Russian, and three aircraft crew, one of whom is Arthur.

Gomez had staged the scene very carefully and we obliged him by dutifully taking photos and quizzing him on details, being careful to write down the critical facts. We did not ask him why there were no wounded contras or how it was that there were no casualties on his side. We asked if we could interview the three prisoners, but he shook his head. "That is not permitted, lamentareblente."

The light was fading when we left. Rafael went with us in the SUV, still with his AK-47 but subdued. When we stopped and he got out, I checked the magazine. It was empty.

Twelve hours later, I was back at the Intercontinental Hotel in Managua and the next morning I handed Rafael the article I had composed for 'my' newspaper employer. It was the first I had actually written for them and I tried very hard to conform to the emerging style that my ghostwriter had already established. It was a straightforward account of my time in the jungle with Gomez, derived entirely from his 'official' version and leaving out what Monica and I actually saw from the crest of the hill. Basically, it was a puff-piece for the Sandanista cause. Rafael told me later that afternoon, "I showed it to President Ortega. He was very pleased." He sounded slightly surprised.

There were other and more personal surprises. Late on the night we returned to the hotel, I saw a man letting himself out of Monica's hotel room. I couldn't see his features but felt that I had seen him before. I saw him again the next afternoon. He was sitting in a booth with Monica in a grimy little café on a side street near our hotel. She had her notebook open and was writing while he talked. *So she found our missing Russian advisor and got an interview. I wonder if she said 'I want you to fuck me' to him?* I couldn't decide which of her 'betrayals' bothered me the most … her sexual inconstancy or her hoarding of journalistic sources. Surely, I was the most immature spy ever loosed on the intelligence world.

I called Schmidt, but we couldn't say much over public telephone lines. He told me, "Come back as soon as you can. There's a lot to be done, and I badly need your views on the Nicaraguan situation. Has it gone well there?"

"Mr. Ortega is pleased with my article, so I think it's gone well." I paused for a second and tried to make the question sound as casual as possible. "I thought I saw Arthur yesterday. Is he in Nicaragua?"

"No. He was just here ... left to get some coffee, I think. Do you want me to tell him something when he returns?"

"It's OK. Must have been somebody else."

"Magda will pick you up. Look for her at the curb."

Debriefing

She was behind the wheel of a very battered Jeep Cherokee. She looked different, but I wasn't sure if that was because she had changed or I had. The feeling apparently was mutual. *That idyllic farmhouse in Virginia seems like a long time ago.* She looked at me closely and asked, "Are you OK?" She didn't believe me when I said, "I'm fine" and tried again. "You look ... different." I wondered what adjectives she'd been considering to end the sentence.

I shrugged. "It's been ... interesting. Makes those six months in that Virginia farmhouse feel like preschool. What about you? What's he got you doing?"

She pulled out, dodging a multi-colored school bus. Then she looked at me with the same intensity and said, "Rule One, Thomas. Rule One."

'Rule One' was part of Schmidt's near-catechism. It was his single most frequent response to questions. I remember its first use, very early in our training. Riley had asked, "Why do I have to memorize Pushkin poems?" Schmidt said, "Rule One, Riley. I'll tell you what you need to know, when you need to know it. No more, no less."

We passed huge airbrushed photos of Manuel Noriega on the way into the city. They were on billboards, the walls of buildings and the sides of the buses. It reminded me of Moscow and Peking. I had joined a pair of international student tours for cultural exchange programs and seen the Stalin and Mao posters in the historical exhibits with their catchphrases for the worker's revolution. "Delusions of grandeur at their best," I said, pointing at Noriega's chin, which was all I could see of him because the bus was only six inches from my passenger side window.

"Neither he nor his retouched portraits are going to be around much longer." She said it like it was a fact, not just a wishful forecast or an opinion, causing me to wonder again about what she'd been doing while I was being a toady for the Sandanista regime. She would eventually tell me and her stories would make me wonder which of us had lost the most in those early days, me in the Honduran jungles or her in Noriega's presidential palace. But I know that, back then, I went to sleep and I woke up with the images of Monica naked in the dim light and those two rows of dead teenagers lying so neatly in the grass.

She dropped me at the office and left, saying, "I'll see you tonight." Schmidt was waiting in the conference room, alone with a laptop open in front of him. As soon as I sat down, I said, "Arthur was there."

He said only, "Later. Tell me about the state of the Sandanista military, particularly your Colonel Raul Gomez."

"Schmidt. I spent two days with him and his unit. He didn't tell me any state secrets."

"Rule Two, Thomas."

Another clause in the Schmidt catechism: 'Everything is important, especially what you don't think is important.' So I talked for forty minutes, describing my time in Nicaragua from start to finish. Except for the sex with Monica, thereby violating – and ultimately validating – the truth of Rule Two. He broke in only once, when I got to the part about the two men we met in the jungle.

"A Russian was part of your group?"

"Monica Holst labeled him as such, based on his accent. His Spanish was pretty ragged. And he looked the part. He and the Cuban were clearly important to Gomez."

"Describe him."

I did, in great detail. I felt very proud of how well I had mastered that part of Carlee's tradecraft, until Schmidt began to fire questions: "What was his name? Was it a Moscow accent? What was his relationship with the Cuban or Gomez – advisor, subordinate, peer? Did he smoke cigars? Was there any sign of a limp?" I couldn't answer any of them with any confidence.

Then I remembered that I had taken his picture when he and the Cuban first showed up. "I have a photograph of him." I dug the roll of film out of my bag and handed it to Schmidt.

After that single flurry of questions, he let me finish. Other than his curiosity about the Russian, he said nothing and he took no notes. When I finished talking, he sat back, thinking. And then he surprised me.

"You did well."

"I did?"

"We got an objective up-close look at a field operation and, thanks to Ms. Holst, neither side knows that you were there soaking up all that intelligence. So what's your personal takeaway on the military situation near the Honduran border?"

I thought about his question, for the first time setting aside the images of those two rows of bodies. "Three things, I think. All related to one another." I held up one finger. "First, Gomez is a professional soldier, but he can't engage the contras. They won't fight in any conventional way, and he can't pursue them in Honduras." Another finger. "Second, the contras are not a military force. They're either untrained kids with bad leadership or ex-Somoza thugs who want things the way they were." The last finger. "Third, both sides are terrorists. The only way this war will end is when enough people on both sides get killed, tortured or kidnapped and they just get too tired to keep on."

He stood up. I stayed where I was, staring at him until he sat back down and waited for me to ask the question that we both knew had to be asked.

"What about Arthur?"

Schmidt shrugged. "You were right. You did see him at that airstrip. He was the one overseeing the arms shipment."

Which means he was also the one overseeing the cocaine shipment!

I pictured the men walking down the cargo ramp with their hands held over their head. "There were three men on the plane."

Schmidt hesitated and finally said. "The other two were pilot and copilot. Not CIA. They came with the plane. A package deal."

"They weren't working for you?"

"No." When I waited, he added, "The plane and the pilots are part of the Colombian cartels, the Medellin bunch."

"So what happened to them?"

"We have some idea from satellite imagery and other sources. Two hours after you left that airstrip, your pickup truck came back with the bulk of your 'confiscated' cocaine shipment and the two pilots. They loaded the drugs back into the plane, got in and took off."

"To?"

"We tracked it all the way into the main airport in Managua."

I thought for a bit. "So it's not just the contras. The Sandanistas are trafficking in drugs, collaborating with the Colombian cartels. But they don't need arms; the Cubans and Russians are taking care of that."

Schmidt nodded, "But they need cash. And cocaine is easily converted into U.S. dollars. Lots of them."

"What happened to the two pilots?"

He looked at me with a trace of sympathy. "You won't like my answer."

When I just looked at him, he sighed and said, "I don't know, but I'd be willing to bet that both them and their plane are back in Colombia. Neither side wants to alienate the cartel."

I stood up, put my palms on the tabletop and leaned as far forward as I could, but the table was wide and there was still too much room between us. "Schmidt, where is Arthur?"

He looked out the window and spoke so softly that I barely heard him. "He's still there."

The three words stunned me, as was his intention. He went on before I could even begin to frame a coherent response. "The agency has maintained a back-channel with the Cuban Dirección General de Inteligencia – the DGI – to ...." He paused for a second ... "to facilitate matters of mutual interest. They approached our side yesterday. They said that the Sandanistas would return Arthur to us if the U.S. would publicly acknowledge arranging the arms-for-drugs deal that you saw three days ago. They included photos of Arthur, posed nicely alongside the cocaine and crates of M-16's."

I sat back down. He remained silent long enough that I knew – as surely as if I'd lived it – the rest of the story. So I took over the telling of it. "And we declined their offer, saying that 'we don't negotiate with terrorists.' Furthermore, we said that the U.S. was committed to total compliance with the Boland Amendment and all applicable international laws. And that we knew nothing about Arthur, but, whoever he might be, he absolutely was not representing any branch of a U.S. agency and most certainly *not* the Central Intelligence Agency."

Schmidt suddenly seemed enormously tired, like someone who had just lost all interest in the conversation. "Yeah. Not exactly those words, but pretty close. We tried a back-door cash offer, but they weren't interested."

"Was there a deadline?"

"It expired ten hours ago."

My next thought was so inappropriate that I almost laughed out loud. I was picturing Arthur, our self-defense guru, sitting in the dirt, surrounded by twenty men with automatic weapons. "You were right about one thing."

Schmidt looked at me with that raised eyebrow. I said, "You always said that all that hand-to-hand Kung-Fu shit that Arthur tried to teach us was wasted."

He didn't even smile, and I finally understood his response when I asked once more, 'Where is Arthur' and he answered, 'Dead, very dead.' I thought about Colonel Gomez and the intensity of his hatred for Americans in general and CIA agents in particular.

"We got this two hours ago." Schmidt turned the laptop computer around and pressed a button. It was a video. The quality was very poor, obviously taken with a handheld camera in low light. There was audio and I could hear the sound of birds and a man speaking an indistinct Spanish. All of the frame was taken up by Arthur. He was on his knees with his hands bound behind him, held upright by a man standing behind him, although the only visible aspects of his captor were the hands, one on each of Arthur's shoulders. Arthur's face was badly battered and he seemed disoriented, looking wildly from side-to-side.

It happened very quickly. An off-camera voice said, 'hazlo ahora' and the hand on Arthur's right shoulder went away and came back with a K-Bar knife and drew it from left to right across Arthur's throat. The blood was instantaneous and quite black. Arthur fell or was pushed to the side and the camera followed him. After he was irrevocably still, it panned back to expose the ground area around the body. Two pairs of legs entered the frame from either side and, using only their boots, pushed and kicked Arthur into a shallow grave next to where he had fallen. The camera moved to the foot of the grave and from then on focused only on Arthur's upper torso and face as dirt was shoveled in.

In the poor light, Arthur seemed to be smiling as the first clods of dirt began to obscure his face, but at the very end, I realized that it was not a smile; it was the gaping wound in his throat.

Negotiations

Schmidt closed the laptop and we sat in semi-darkness for another five or six minutes. Neither of us said anything. I have no idea what Schmidt was thinking – I never did – but I know that I was wondering why he had shared so much with me. It was a massive violation of his sacred Rule One.

I was first to break the silence. "The voice? The one that said 'Hazlo ahora?' That was Gomez."

"I thought it might be."

"Can we do anything about him?"

Schmidt looked at me like I had asked him to dance on the table. "*Do* something? You mean, like *'terminate with extreme prejudice?'* Isn't that how they say it in the James Bond movies?"

Just ten minutes ago, I would have withered away in the backwash of his sarcasm. But that video forever changed my relationship with Schmidt, as he knew it would. That was one of the reasons he shared it with me. I said nothing, but neither did I look away from him.

"Revenge is a luxury in this business. Forget about Gomez." After a few seconds, he added, very softly, "And forget about Arthur."

He looked away and I had the impression that he was not sure about what to say next. When he turned back, he said, "The one you need to worry about is Vasili."

"Vasili?"

"I'll develop the film you gave me ... the pictures of the Russian that was working with the Cuban and Gomez. But I'm almost sure that I know who it is. His name is Vasili and he's a major in the KGB. He's quite vicious."

The last three words trailed off, leaving Schmidt staring at the wall, apparently visualizing the exact ways in which Vasili was vicious. I said, "You have some history with this man?"

He shook himself. "In Afghanistan. The early days of the Russian occupation. And there was another time in East Berlin."

"What happened?"

"Nothing that you need to know." Then I learned the other reason he had let me watch the video. "I need you to go back to Nicaragua."

"OK. And what do I do when I get there?"

He paused, and I knew that however he answered my question, it would be a lie or incomplete in some important way. He said, "Negotiate a hostage release."

Incredibly, my first wild thought was, "Arthur's not dead!" But that lasted only a micro-second; that video was as real as it gets. Schmidt didn't notice; he was reaching down into his briefcase, from which he extracted a blue Post-It note. He handed it to me. "Here's the contact details."

I glanced down at it. There was a name and address. He said, "That's in a village near the border with Honduras. He'll find you there. That's all we know at the moment."

"Who's the hostage?"

"Remember your morning with Gomez? The incident with the Canadian doctor that got taken at a contra roadblock?"

Gomez said "They'll torture him a little and then try for a big ransom. If they don't get paid, they'll shoot him.' He didn't say anything about cutting his throat on camera; I suppose that's always implied.

Schmidt said something while I was envisioning Gomez, but it didn't make sense. "What did you say?"

"I said, 'Roger.' The hostage you're going to ransom is Roger."

"Our Roger?" He didn't bother to respond,

"Why was he even there? You already had me with Gomez and Arthur flying in with a planeload of M-16's. What the hell was Roger supposed to add?"

I knew he wasn't going to answer me, but I didn't wait, because something else was drastically wrong with the story. "The CIA is *helping* the contras! Why would they kidnap Roger?"

"They don't know he's CIA. They think he's a Canadian doctor there to run pop-up medical clinics for the mestizos. And they like to kill the doctors. Demonstrates that the government can't deliver basic services to the countryside. Right out of the 'How to be a Terrorist' playbook."

"Schmidt?" I waited until he was looking at me and then I spoke to him as one would to a dimwitted in-law. "Why doesn't Roger just tell them who he works for?   They can't ransom somebody who's on their side!"

"Exactly which side is that, Mahoney?"

That stopped me.   The so-called contras were a very fragile confederation of three distinct groups.   The strongest sub-group was composed of very right-wing ex-Somosan soldiers and supporters, a very thuggish lot. For them, the war was to regain their former status. Then there were the disaffected Sandanistas, those who fought because their revolution did not go far enough and they believed Ortega's policies to be a mockery of the revolution that carried him into office.   Finally, there were the peasant militias, made up of farmers and Indians, the kind of underclass that is swept up in any revolution.   Much of the CIA's past effort was spent on trying to unify the three disparate groups of fighters into an effective whole, but from what I knew of the contras, that strategy had a long way to go.

I asked the relevant question, "Who's got Roger?"

"A very small group – maybe thirty fighters – mostly mestizos with a few indigenous Indians thrown in. They're more like bandits than guerrilla fighters. They operate independently and have used the war as an excuse to loot, kill and terrorize."

"So, for them, Roger being CIA doesn't matter all that much."

"I doubt if they even care, and it's complicated because ..."

This was hard for Schmidt, sharing all the secrets, but after that video, I had little sympathy for him. I said, "Because ..." and that drew out the rest of the story.

"Because Roger was headed for a meeting with the ex-Somoza contingent ... with a suggested proposal for the contras' eventual participation in peace talks."

I thought about what he wasn't telling me, the 'between-the-lines' context. "And our small robber band, the ones holding Roger, would not approve? I don't imagine that either a left or a right wing Central American government would offer them much."

Schmidt nodded. "We think not. And even if they did, our kidnappers just might think they could get enough ransom money that they wouldn't care about making their partners unhappy. Remember, these are impoverished Indians and farmers with a grudge against most of the world."

"So why me? As a negotiator?"

"Because your Spanish is better than any of the rest of us. Because the Ortega government is already comfortable with you and won't think much about you running around the countryside. Because you're a journalist and the contras want to maintain good public relations with the gringos. Because Riley and Magda can't be taken off what they're doing at the moment."

I wasn't going to say it, but I was experiencing for the first time the inevitable shift in the balance of power between agent and handler, the delicate reciprocity that governs what is asked and what is answered.

Lies of omission, I thought. *Somebody said that it's what you don't know that you don't know that is the most dangerous. They must have known Schmidt.*

"And because I have seen your video, and so I know what happens if negotiations fail."

"Yes. That too."

A Special Envoy

I went directly from the Managua airport to drop in on Rafael at his office and I was pleased to see his flash of concern when he saw me. It made me wonder if he had been present for the Gomez video.

"You're back! So soon?"

"My editor wants a five-thousand word feature ... a 'day in the post-revolutionary life of an ordinary citizen' sort of piece. I thought I'd take three days to pull together a composite. Get out of Managua and meet some locals."

"Do you need an escort?"

"No thanks. I don't plan on being anywhere near your contested areas. I'm going to stay close to your famous beaches."

I turned to leave. When I got to the door, I turned and asked the question I had come for. "Anything new with Colonel Gomez?"

"Si. He has returned to his post near the border, but he and his unit received a Presidential Citation for their good work on the day you were with us in the jungle." He waved and turned back to his desk. "Enjoy the beaches." But before I got out the door, he stopped me, "You'll share with me what you write, yes? Once these cursed terrorists are defeated, tourism will be a major industry for Nicaragua."

"Por supuesto." *Of course.*

I went in the opposite direction from Nicaragua's beaches. For a crow, San Jose de Cusmapa was only eighty-four miles from Managua, but it took me five hours to make the drive. The address on the blue Post-It note was for one of the two restaurants in the village and when I asked for Ernesto, the proprietor said "No lo conozco,' and ignored me. But three minutes later, he called a small boy in from the street and whispered something to him before giving him a push back into the sunlight.

I almost fell asleep waiting. *Carlee would be disappointed. She was always saying, 'Be aware,' meaning much more than merely staying awake. It meant being able to identify anything or anyone out of place, and being able to describe every object or person within your visual range.* Thinking about Carlee, of course, brought back thoughts of Arthur, and that started me wondering about my career choice.

He sent three of us into the same zone. Arthur is dead, Roger is being held for ransom and I'm falling asleep in the Nicaraguan outback waiting for a Latin Robin Hood to show up. Nine months ago, I was considering writing about local zoning ordinances in Midland-Odessa. I wonder how long it will take to forget about Arthur in that grave?

Two men – Indians – came in and sat at one of the other four tables. They looked like field workers and each laid a machete on the table alongside the beer that the proprietor brought without being asked. Then they watched me and the three of us waited together.

Ten minutes later, a man who could have been their father came in, said, "Vamonos" and led all three of us to a waiting jeep. He drove and the two silent men with their gleaming machetes sat behind me.

Roger was in bad shape. He been beaten badly and from the way he moved, I guessed broken ribs at a minimum. *Gomez said 'They'll torture him,' so what did you expect? I wonder if he told them who he works for ...why he was here? Or who I am?* He gave no sign that he recognized me when they brought him into the space.

I thought we were in Honduras but I couldn't be sure. We'd driven another two hours from San Jose de Cusmapa, roughly due west through intermittent jungle and then cultivated fields. We were in a two-story storage unit with a dirt floor and a lot of musty bales stacked down both sides. The light came from the open doors at either end of the shed and a row of four windows on the second floor. They'd set up a small table in the center of the space. I was seated on one side, facing the driver of the jeep. They placed Roger alongside him and facing me, but he looked down at the table. The two others sat on a pair of three-legged stools at one side, their machetes sheathed.

The man opposite me said, "My name is Ernesto." He spoke English with a thick accent.

"I am Thomas." I said my name in the Spanish fashion, 'Tomas,' with the accent on the second syllable.

He inclined his head toward the shiny and very thin leather portfolio I carried. I'd bought it in the Panama City airport. "You do not carry a lot of cash with you."

"There is much street crime in Nicaragua these days. It would not be prudent to have much cash." He smiled politely and I went on, "Besides, I am here as a negotiator. If we reach an accord, I can get you the cash."

"So you propose to buy Dr. Weller from me *on credit?* I don't think –"

"I take Dr. Weller, you get cash. Both at the same time. First, we have to see if we have a deal." That made Roger look up at me and I think the very faint expression of alarm was real, not just good acting. *We never covered 'The Art of Negotiating Hostage Release' in Schmidt's six-month training program.* And I knew I was seriously handicapped by having seen that damned video ... and by having Roger sitting in front of me.

Ernesto asked, "Who is your sponsor? El Patron?" I answered, "An international humanitarian organization that does not want to be seen as paying ransom to kidnappers but also does want to see good people die."

"You are a journalist?"

"Yes."

"One who writes favorable things about the Sandanista bastards ..."

"Yes, and one who can also write favorable things – or unfavorable things – about the contra bastards."

He looked at me, for the first time seeming to be interested. "You are either very valiente or muy estupido."

I bowed my head as if complimented. "Does it matter which?" Then I said, "Caballo regalado no se le mira el diente." I probably should have stuck to the English version – 'Don't look a gift horse in the mouth' – but it seemed wrong to quote proverbs in a person's second language.

One of the watching men stood up, came close to Ernesto and said something that I didn't catch. While that was happening, Roger raised his head halfway and mimed two words. I thought they were "They know."

Know what? What the hell am I supposed to do with that?

I didn't have time to think about it. Ernesto sat up sharply and said, "Five hundred thousand dollars."

I blinked, but my voice was steady. "That is a great deal of money."

He leaned forward, smiling, and I realized that he came from a culture where negotiation was an everyday life skill, as natural as breathing. I was an American who was accustomed to paying list prices. He said, "Medical doctors are very expensive this year."

I wished Roger would look at me, but he maintained his head-down position. I wanted to reassure him, but didn't know how. It didn't help that I did not know the house limit on ransom payments.

"Can I have my phone, please?"

They'd taken it from me when we got in the jeep, removing the batteries as well. Ernesto nodded at one of the men and he handed the satellite phone and batteries to me. They watched as I inserted the batteries, waited through the warn-up and pushed the 'transmit' button. Schmidt answered promptly.

I said, "Dr. Weller is alive. He needs medical attention but his injuries are minor. They want half a million."

"The most we can do is half of that. We have no more money." His voice came through clearly, so there was no need for any translation by me.

So far, we were operating with a prearranged script. *They offer X, you counter with fifty percent of that number.* I was holding the phone so that Ernesto could easily hear the exchange, but I asked, "You heard?"

The Indian who had said something earlier stood up and whispered to Ernesto for about thirty seconds. Ernesto nodded and said to me, "How do we trade the CIA agent for the money?"

"The actual exchange is where people get killed," Schmidt told me as we were sitting in the Panama City transit lounge, "even if both sides *want* the trade to succeed. For a few seconds … sometimes a couple of minutes … both parties have physical possession of what they've negotiated for … either the cash or the hostage … and they can, if they're treacherous enough and skilled enough, take back what they just gave up."

I said, "We'll be on their turf. They'll dictate whatever terms they like for the exchange."

"Unfortunately, yes. But I have a couple of ideas. But you *have to* insist on one thing. You and the hostage – Roger – are allowed to leave, or at least get some physical separation from the kidnappers, before they can touch the cash."

I held up the radiophone. "This goes to a small plane flying in a circular pattern on the Honduran side of the border due west of San Jose de Cusmapa. Dr. Weller and I will take the jeep and move one-hundred yards along the road, but still within sight. I will tell the pilot our location, you will light a very smoky signal fire and the plane will drop a bag with two-hundred and fifty thousand U.S. dollars as close as possible. You get your money and I get the doctor and a slight head start. I'll leave your jeep in San Jose de Cusmapa."

The plan was riddled with flaws, but both sides to the exchange were equally at risk of betrayal. The important assumption was that if we paid them what they asked, they would honor the agreement, mostly because they needed to maintain their reputation as honorable kidnappers or their business model would stop working.

One advantage for our side was that the contras were a small band and apparently had no way to communicate with other units, so it would be difficult for them to adapt to last minute changes.

Ernesto looked at his companion and received some invisible signal. He leaned forward toward me. "Too much risk for us. Three hundred and fifty thousand."

I keyed the button. "He says three-fifty." We had no script for this part.

The response was instantaneous. "No. We don't have it. I have two-hundred and fifty thousand in the bag and am prepared to drop it where you tell me." The sound of the aircraft engine was quite prominent coming through the speaker,

The two Indians stood up. One moved behind me and the other behind Roger. Each of them unsheathed his machete and held it in his right hand while watching Ernesto closely. Across from me, Roger began trembling violently and hunched his shoulders. I think I stayed still, wondering if this was an extension of the negotiations or whether I was about to be hacked to death.

Collateral Damage

Ten minutes later, Roger and I sat in Ernesto's idling jeep at the far side of the clearing watching a small dot in the sky approaching from the north. Near the shed on the other side of the clearing, two of the contras were throwing still more green branches onto the small smoky fire. Ernesto was standing to one side cradling a rifle in his arms and watching us. About a dozen more dark men had joined him, also carrying rifles. *Not good. Even if they're terrible marksmen, we would be in range for far too long.* But the ones I was worried about were the ones I couldn't see. They could be just over the hill waiting for the jeep to appear.

"Are you OK?" I asked Roger. The trembling had lessened somewhat but was still perceptible. Beyond that, he seemed diminished, both physically and emotionally, as if the three days of captivity had drained him not only of physical substance but also of something essential. He sat hunched over in the seat, his arms wrapped around his ribs and his head down. He didn't respond to my question, so I tried, "What is it you were trying to tell me? What is it that they know?" The only answer was a worsening of his tremors.

The far-off dot was a helicopter, not a fixed-wing plane, and it came in very low and surprisingly fast, maybe a couple of hundred feet above us and moving at freeway speed. It passed close enough that Schmidt was readily identifiable. The front passenger door was missing and Schmidt was leaning out holding a black suitcase on his lap. With some effort, he maneuvered it into the doorway and when the copter was about midway between us and the group of contras, he pushed it out. The aircraft accelerated and began a sharp bank while the package was still in the air. It landed about twenty yards from the group, in a slight depression and with no bounce, the way you would expect a bag filled with two-hundred and fifty thousand dollars to impact on soft earth.

The contras raced to the bag. But not Ernesto, he kept his eyes on us. I heard him call out, "Jose ... contar el dinero ... rápidamente, por favor!" Our agreement with him was more than a little vague on the next moves, but I pushed the clutch in and shifted into first gear. I was watching Ernesto but behind him I could see the helicopter complete its turn and head directly for us, still at a tree-clipping altitude.

I still have difficulty remembering the exact sequence, but several things happened within the next few seconds. Roger screamed at me, "Go!" I pressed the accelerator to the floor. And the black suitcase exploded.

They tell me that the jeep was half imbedded in a drainage ditch with the engine racing and all four tires spinning. Schmidt tells me that I was standing waist deep in the water trying to lift the vehicle out of the trench and that I was screaming at Roger to come and help, but I don't remember any of that. However, I do remember the noise and vibration of the helicopter as it lifted off from the clearing, and the way that Roger kept staring at me accusingly until Schmidt reached over and closed his eyes.

It was a month before I got back to the office. Most of that time was in a U.S. military hospital and a series of clinics in Panama City. They talked about 'blunt force trauma' from the blast but the real problem turned out to be the shrapnel in my upper thigh. I was just leaving the recovery room when the surgeon handed me an L-shaped piece of black metal, "Most patients like to keep what we cut out of them. War souvenirs, I guess."

I looked at it. "Bomb casing?" He laughed. "No. Actually we think it's a hinge from a top-of-the-line Samsonite suitcase."

The post-surgery infection almost finished the job, keeping me either delirious with fever or severely drugged for the better part of two weeks. I vaguely remember Magda and Riley standing at the foot of the bed with looks of concern.

January 9th is a national holiday in Panama. It's a national day of mourning called Martyr's Day, commemorating the 1964 riots over the sovereignty of the Canal Zone. Schmidt was in his office in Oficinas de la Empresa but his desk was bare of everything except a telephone and his main occupation seemed to be staring out the window.

"Welcome back."

I placed the hinge precisely in the middle of his desk. Then I sat down and waited. He looked at the object once and then ignored it and me, resuming his staring routine.

"You never intended to go through with the hostage-for-money swap, did you?"

He swiveled his chair to face me and I had the impression that he was not quite sure of himself. More likely, it was that I simply saw the tells that had always been there but were invisible to his apprentices. He said, "Actually, there were two suitcases in the helicopter. The other one was filled with cash."

"Why didn't you toss that one out instead of the bomb?"

"Because they knew."

There it is again. Roger had mouthed those words at me – 'They know!'

"What is it that they knew?"

Schmidt sighed. "Ernesto ... the man you were negotiating with ... is ... was ... an emerging leader for the peasant faction of the contras. The other two factions wanted him out. When they picked Roger up, he was coming back from a meeting with them ... a meeting where we offered them our ... support."

I thought about what he was not saying. "You contracted to assassinate Ernesto ..."

He didn't answer directly. "It was just bad luck that Ernesto's bunch grabbed Roger on his way back."

I said, "But you didn't *know* that Roger told them anything!" even as I was picturing Roger sitting opposite me in that shed. *He'd been beaten badly. No signs of anything worse. But he was an emotional wreck.*

"No, I didn't know for sure. Until Ernesto asked you, 'How do we trade the CIA agent for the money?'"

If they knew Roger was CIA, he must have talked.

"So if you gave them the cash …?"

"I figured they'd assume you were CIA and that there was about a ninety percent probability that they'd shoot the two of you on the spot. Just to get even for the double cross."

"Did you calculate the probability that we'd be killed by your bomb?" I tried, but could not quite suppress the anger.

He shrugged. "I told you to put as much distance between you and them as you could. I thought it was enough. but the suitcase fell a little short."

For no apparent reason, I thought of Arthur and the images of the clods of dirt being shoveled onto his uncaring face. That vision made my next question to Schmidt come out in a strangled voice.

"Where's Roger?"

He looked at me strangely, but said, "We sent him home. I think he's in a graveyard near Liberty, Kansas."

Interlude

Schmidt's little band of spies, including me, stayed in Panama for another four years and it was during that time that I really learned how to be an effective agent. It was classic on-the-job training.   Given what was happening in Central and South America, there was much to learn.

Perhaps the Cubans' aggressive attempts to extend communism in the hemisphere was the catalyst, as Reagan feared, but it was inevitable that the abuses against the citizens of Venezuela, Peru, El Salvador, Guatemala, Nicaragua and others by their right-wing authoritarian regimes provided ample stimulus for revolution.   And during the latter 1980's, the U.S. government and the CIA were solidly committed to propping up those right-wing governments with military and economic aid, often via clandestine channels.

It seemed that the title on our building -- Oficinas de la Empresa, or Offices of the Enterprise, in English – was quite apt. Given the Congressional ambivalence about the morality of U.S. foreign policy in that time period, we operated as a private firm with private funding. We were called 'The Enterprise,' and Oficinas de la Empresa was our headquarters.   During those few years, it harbored a variety of colorful individuals, all of them except for Schmidt's little group under the approximate leadership of Colonel Oliver North until he and Reagan got fingered for the arms-for-hostages deal with Iran.

So I facilitated the smuggling of arms to the Shining Path guerrillas in Peru, made sure certain names were included on the 'to do' lists for the El Salvadoran death squads, bribed politicians in the Venezuelan legislature, and ran terrorist training programs for Guatemalan thugs. Schmidt kept me away from Nicaragua, figuring that my escapade as hostage negotiator and hobnobbing with contras might make me a person of interest to Ortega's secret police.

We lost Carlee somewhere during that time. Nothing dramatic or even in the line of duty. It was a recurrence of ovarian cancer. She was buried at a Catholic cemetery in Panama City and I think it was the only time that I ever saw Schmidt drunk.

He had Alex placed in the National Cultural Institute in Venezuela, supposedly as a resident fellow in antiquities. I know little about his portfolio, but I got the impression that he was running a trio of local double agents that were moving up in the still-formative communist cells that would shortly bring Hugo Chavez to power.

Right after Roger was killed, Schmidt sent Peter and Benjamin, our lone surviving instructor, somewhere in Europe. I wouldn't see them again for a long time. So it was the three of us once more – me, Riley and Magda.

I would see them intermittently. The two of them were The Enterprise's primary liaison to Manuel Noriega. They were spending every day in Noriega's offices and – in Magda's case – his private quarters. They did not talk about the content of their days, but the effects were both negative and visible. When we meet, it is apparent that all three of us are drinking more and sleeping less. It is also clear that the two of them are spending time in the same bed. There are no visible signs.   No steamy looks, lingering touches, endearments or verbal cues. But I think that the hyper-sensitivity that Carlee tried so hard to instill in us enabled us to easily detect the almost subliminal vibrations that radiate between and from lovers. Or perhaps it is just that I desire Magda and therefore watch for clues that she is receptive. Or not.

February 1989 was a bleak month. The United States and the Soviet Union were exploding nuclear bombs in Nevada and Siberia in the sort of 'tit-for-tat' belligerence that passed for diplomacy in much of the Cold War era. It snowed in Los Angeles and scientists were speculating that a serious 'ozone hole' was forming over the Arctic.   Ayatollah Khomeni, the Supreme Leader of Iran, issued a fatwah calling for the killing of Salman Rushdie for his authorship of the book *Satanic Verses.*

America's strategy in Central and South America, if judged by its own objectives, was an ongoing disaster. When Schmidt called, I was sitting in Mexico City reading the morning newspaper and the front-page article about Alfredo Stroessner.   He'd been President of Paraguay for thirty-five years and a right-wing favorite of the U.S., but he'd just been deposed by a military coup.   The domino theory was working against us.

"Is there anything you can't walk away from?" Schmidt sounded very far away. The telephone line had a tinny sound to it and there were lags between words. That and the phrasing itself elevated his question into something much more metaphysical than he probably intended. *Is he asking me if I'm committed to the mission? Am I? Is there anything or anybody that would notice if I disappeared? Have I become such a moral void that I feel no connection with what I'm doing?* But, of course, all he was asking was whether I was available.

"No. There's nothing."

"Good. I need you for ten days. For something special. Pack for high desert and meet me in the American Airlines first-class lounge at the Miami International Airport at nine AM on Friday. And brush up on your street-level Arabic."

I was there early and spent the time guessing at what Schmidt had in mind. Most of Florida is no more than a couple hundred feet above sea level, so Schmidt's 'high desert' assignment was clearly not in Florida. And everybody in the Miami International Airport seemed to be Venezuelan, Haitian or Brazilian, so Arabic language skills weren't much in demand there. But the truth was, I didn't care very much. Five years of ineffectual CIA meddling in the southern hemisphere had rubbed away all of the high-minded justifications and the motivation that went with them. I was thirty years old and as blasé about what I did as a toll collector on the New York Throughway.

Schmidt was an hour late. He was toting a carry-on bag and looked like he'd been on a plane for about forty hours.

"I haven't seen you for a while." *Five months, actually.*

He sat down heavily in the chair opposite me and spent twenty seconds looking for a file folder in his bag that he set on the table between us. "Been busy. And you're doing fine without me looking over your shoulder."

"Doing fine?   By losing most of Central and South America to left-wing regimes?"

"You're overrating your contribution to our collective failure."   He waved his hand.   "View it as a war of attrition.   The outcome was inevitable but you helped to make them pay for what they got."

He makes it sound like negotiating a divorce settlement. And it was Arthur and Roger – not me -- that did the paying. "So am I done there?"

"No.   But I have a side-job for you.   One that you'll like."

"Why?"

"Why the side-job?"

"No.   Why will I like it?"

He smiled at me in the way that reminded me that both of us were aware that he understood me, perhaps better than I did myself.   "Because, for once, you'll be squarely on the side of truth and justice.   None of that moral ambiguity that afflicts you these days."

I looked closely at him, but he was serious.   "Schmidt, I know that you believe in the CIA and what it does, and it may even *occasionally* be the case that it acts on the side of truth and justice, but – even then – it will use *means* that are reprehensible by most standards."

He waved away my comment. "An old debate, one for philosophers and rabbis." Then he leaned back and looked at me through steepled fingers and I knew that his so-called side-job was about to be revealed.

"Are you following what's happening in Afghanistan?"

"Of course. The last of the 40th Russian Army will be out by the end of next week. The press is calling it 'the Soviet Union's Vietnam War.' Nine years and fifteen thousand dead Russians."

He nodded. "And a million-plus dead, injured or displaced civilians. And what do you think will happen to Afghanistan once the Soviet Army is gone?"

The Soviet puppet government is still in place. The mujahedeen will continue their guerrilla war against it. They're being supported by the US, Pakistan, China and even some of the Arab monarchies, so they will eventually prevail. But then? "Vicious fighting for maybe a couple of years until the Najibullah government is overthrown. Then … chaos, I think. The mujahedeen are so factionalized that a really nasty civil war is the most likely scenario."

"I agree," Schmidt nodded. "And what the Agency wants is for the eventual winner of that civil war to be someone that we – the US -- can work with. A leader that will hold elections and resist corruption, among other things."

I said, "Sure." *Just like our partners in Central America … Noriega in Panama, Batista in Cuba, Somoza in Nicaragua …*

Schmidt knew from my expression what I was thinking, but he ignored the provocation. "Once the Russians are out, the American politicians won't care about Afghanistan. Unless they have a reason to."

"And you're going to give them that reason."

"Not me. You."

"How am I going to do that?"

"You're a journalist. You write."

He tapped his finger on the folder on the table. "There's a profile of an Afghan tribal leader in here. I want you to make him famous."

There were travel documents and a plane ticket in the folder as well, and two hours later I was at forty-thousand feet, headed for London and from there to Islamabad, Pakistan where I would meet some one named Mazoud who, Schmidt assured me, 'can connect you with the right mujahedeen.'

The profile was of an Afghan tribal leader named Asfand Ghazan. A portrait-quality picture of him was on the second page of the sheaf of papers, with both Pashto and English-language narratives alongside the photo. Small print in the corner identified the photographer as a Cambridge studio and the date as ten years earlier. The man was posed in relatively formal Afghan tribal costume against a mountainous backdrop. It was an impressive picture, the kind of visual image one would pick for a National Geographic cover or an anthology of Rudyard Kipling's work. I suspected it had little to do with the man I was supposed to meet. Ten years of fighting a bloody guerrilla war would change a person.

The rest of the dossier was interesting but lacked the level of detail that I needed. Ghazan was in his last year of studying history at Oxford when the Soviets occupied Afghanistan. His academic record was excellent and interviews with faculty and other students indicated that he was assimilating into English life quite nicely, a devout Muslim but open to Western culture and ideas. There was speculation that he would stay in England once his studies were concluded.

That speculation ended abruptly in 1979 when the Soviet-Afghan war began. His father was a leader of one of the larger tribes within the Pashtun population around Mazar-al-Sharif in northern Afghanistan and neighboring Pakistan and immediately committed himself, his son and his tribe to holy war. Asfand returned home.

The dossier was very sketchy after that, but it did chart Ghazan's progress as a guerrilla warrior, at first under his father's command and then on his own. The Russian command placed a high price on his head and attributed some of their worst losses to his band. One story, unverified but widely repeated, was that a team of twelve Spetsnaz airborne soldiers sent to assassinate him were returned to their base, an unholy heap of flesh in the bed of a dump truck, each of the twelve men having first been dismembered into six pieces – the arms, legs, head and torso.

"Mr. Mahoney, I am Mazoud. Welcome to Pakistan."

The serious looking small man in a perfectly tailored western suit was waiting for me at the foot of the airplane ramp, just a few feet from a black Mercedes with a pair of Pakistani flags on its front fenders.   *ISI. It figures.   The Pakistani Intelligence Service has been a major supporter of the mujahedeen.*

When we were seated in the limo, he asked, "How is Schmidt?"

"Uh, I'm not sure ..."   *Damn him! He could have briefed me on his relationship with the ISI. What am I permitted to talk about?*

Mazoud grinned at me, clearly seeing the discomfort. "It's OK. Schmidt and I have been collaborating for a long time. He's CIA, I'm ISI. We don't like or trust each other, but we both want the same thing in Afghanistan."

So far. But I suspect we'll disagree about what a post-Soviet Afghanistan should look like. The Pakis share a long and porous border with them.

"Schmidt is fine," I said. "A bit tired, the last time I saw him."

The smile broadened.   "He should be. He's been working very hard trying to get the mujahedeen to return his last delivery of Stinger missiles. He insists they don't need them now that the Russian Hind gunships are on their way back to Russia. He doesn't believe that, of course, but that's what his CIA Director wants him to say."

I didn't like the grin. "It's hard for boys to give up their new and shiny toys."

He shrugged. "Especially when those toys enable a lowly goat-herder to destroy a multi-million dollar jet warplane from a modern air force ... or a civilian airliner from a country they disapprove of."

I changed the subject. "When can I see Ghazan? And where?"

"When? At six this evening. And where? At your hotel in the center of Islamabad. I hope that is convenient?"

I hoped it didn't show, but I was disappointed. I was expecting – looking forward to -- a rough trek across the Indu Kush range into Afghanistan. I apparently harbored some shred of boyish desire for adventure, even after nearly getting killed in a Central American rain forest. "That's fine," I said. "Very convenient, indeed. Does he have some other reason to be in Islamabad?"

"No. Just you." He paused. "And what is it you want from him?"

So Schmidt didn't tell him. Nor shall I.

"What if I wanted to return to Afghanistan with Ghazan? Can that be arranged?" I had no plan, but I wondered how controlling the ISI was with respect to its Afghan partners.

Mazoud frowned. "We hadn't planned for that."

Classic dodge. Keeps all his options open.

I shrugged as though it was of little importance. "Let's see how the meeting goes."

The hotel was midway between the government complex and the diplomatic enclave, with a view of the U.S. Embassy. Mazoud left me at the entrance, saying, "Ghazan will come to your room at six. You'll have him to yourself for as long as you like. Or as long as he will tolerate, whichever comes first."

I did a quick sweep of the room and easily found a single microphone in the overhead light fixture. I left it alone, figuring that was the one I was meant to find.

The knock came at precisely six o'clock, just as the muezzin's echoing calls to prayer came to an end. The man who stood in my doorway was dressed like most of the other men on the street. *He is the essence of the man in the ten-year-old photograph, with so much added on. He still carries the confidence ... arrogance ... and the bearing of the handsome student in the Cambridge photo studio, but he seems twenty years older, mostly because of the eyes. Ten years ago, his eyes challenged the viewer to judge him. Today, they absorbed what was before them and accepted it for what it was. I think he is wiser.*

His thick, once-black hair was graying at the fringes, and he had a six-inch long scar down the left side of his neck. When he stepped forward into the room, he moved with a slight limp.

I had met and spent time with dozens ... hundreds ... of guerrilla fighters in the last five years in Central and South America, but this was my first mujahedeen and I think because of that I imputed a certain aura to

Ghazan, awarding him attributes and virtues that made him into the character I wanted him to be.

He said, "Mr. Thomas Mahoney. I am Asfand Ghazan, here because your person named Schmidt said that you could help me." He spoke quite good English, with an accent one would expect of an Afghani who had studied history at Oxford. However, both the tone of his voice and the calculating way he was watching me signaled that I was on probation, that the meeting could end at any time. *I wonder how committed he is to this idea of Schmidt's for a political campaign. Or if he even knows about it? It would be like Schmidt to put the two of us together and let us work out for ourselves what his intentions were for us.*

I started prattling. "Welcome ... thanks for coming ... heard a lot about you" kind of gibberish while I took his arm and pulled him to the center of the room and showed him the listening device in the light fixture. He smiled sadly, nodded. "Would you mind walking with me?" he asked. "I find the streets of Islamabad a pleasant change from caves and stone huts."

When we were outside, he said, "Mazoud and his Pakistani colleagues in the ISI have been invaluable to us, but they cannot help themselves. Especially when the CIA is involved." He stopped and considered me. "You are CIA, aren't you?"

"Mostly," I said. "More like what you might call an independent contractor."

"But you are also a journalist? A real one, not just a set of false identity papers."

"Yes. I write real articles, for real papers read by real people."

"Schmidt said you are very good at it ... that you like to observe ... to analyze. He said that you are more interested in *why* people act as they do, rather than *what* it is they do."

"I doubt that he meant it as a compliment. I think he would prefer me to be less ... equivocal." *And I am very surprised that he talks so freely about me to others outside of our little bubble.* I also realized that I was disproportionately pleased to hear of Schmidt's characterizations and knew that I would have to think more about what that meant.

Ghazan said, "I was like you. A long time ago. But that was a luxury that cannot be tolerated in a civil war." He touched the jagged scar on the side of his neck but I don't think he was aware of doing it. His unconscious gesture made me want to hear the story of that scar.

We were at the edge of a vast sports complex where a dozen soccer games seemed to be going on at once. It was a mild day and the players -- boys and young men – were mostly in shorts and T-shirts. We walked slowly around the perimeter of the complex, occasionally stopping to watch the play.

He asked, "Do you know Schmidt well?"

"Yes, I think so. Although he is careful to stay hidden." *In so many ways.*

"He is a collector." It was a strange comment and I must have frowned because Ghazan went on quickly. "He collects people, people that can be useful to him and his causes. People like you and me. And then he moves them around on this gigantic multidimensional chessboard that only he can see."

He smiled. "Do you know that he taught me to fire your Stinger missile? I will never forget how I felt when the Russian gunship fell out of the sky."

"And now the gunships are gone," I said, "along with the tanks and the airplanes and the Russian soldiers. Thanks to you and the other mujahedeen."

We walked in silence for a minute, then I asked, "So, what happens now?" Both of us knew that the question had multiple interpretations but that it was the real reason that Schmidt had put us together. Ghazan put off answering. "To me? To Afghanistan? To the Soviet Union?"

I said, "Any or all of those."

His answer was another question, completely out-of-the-blue. "Have you seen the movie, The Godfather?"

"Of course." *Is he envisioning himself as Marlon Brando?*

"Vito Corelone – the godfather – has an advisor –"

"His title was 'consigliere.' The actor who played him was Robert Duvall."

Ghazan nodded. "Consigliere. Yes. Well, Schmidt considers himself to be my consigliere. And he has definite ideas about the answer to your question about 'what happens now.'"

"What are those ideas?"

Ghazan spoke without any hesitation. "The Russians are gone, but their stooge Najibullah is still in Kabul, so the war will go on for a few months or years. The mujahedeen will eventually depose the puppet government. They have tanks and gunships, but we are more committed and, in Afghanistan, that is all that matters."

"And then, when Najibullah is gone?"

"There are two views. Schmidt – my consigliere – says that we shall hold elections and the people shall decide who will govern. The other view is more dismal. It holds that Afghans are not yet ready for democracy. We shall have another and even more vicious civil war to determine who shall rule Afghanistan."

"Which view do you subscribe to? You are an Afghan tribal leader. You surely understand your countrymen better than Schmidt?"

He smiled. "What you call 'the mujahedeen' is a collection of tribes – Tajiks, Pashtun, Uzbeks, Hazara, Turkmen – and each of them has internal factions unique to them. Particularly, we have Islamic fundamentalists who want to keep the old ways and we have the modernizers, those who believe we must change.

"Then we have our neighbors – Iran and Pakistan – who have strong views about what we should be ... and are doing their best to make it happen. And the so-called great powers, including America, who see us as a pawn to be played – and sacrificed to a greater purpose."

I waited, knowing that in a very real sense he was talking to himself, sorting through his own conflicts. Finally, he said, "We *must* stop fighting against each other. Elections are the only way. But to do that, we need western support, particularly from the Americans. But it must be a very different kind of support. We need schools instead of Stinger missiles, farm tractors rather than humvees, hospitals instead of mass graves, managers rather than mullahs, investment instead of destruction."

He sounds like a politician I could vote for. But I'm not Afghani.

"But we were a proxy war for the Americans and the Soviets. You were fighting to defeat the Russians, not to advance Afghanistan interests. Your politicians like the export of arms ... a trade that is both glamorous and profitable ... but will see little benefit in educating schoolgirls to read or in teaching new agricultural methods. Islam is mysterious and threatening to your Midwestern Christian congressmen, not something to squander American resources on."

Schmidt is right about this man. He is what Afghanistan needs. I wanted to argue with him, to defend Schmidt's view of the future. But that was not the mission. I finally understood what Schmidt wanted from me.

I said it for him. "So that's why I'm here. And you. On this multi-dimensional chessboatd."

"Yes. Schmidt says that I can be the first democratically elected president of the Republic of Afghanistan. He says that all I need is more visibility and what he calls 'the right optics.'"

His words evoked the very reaction that Schmidt had warned me against ... the irrepressible ambivalence and equivocation that somehow persisted despite the bribery, betrayal and killing. I asked him, "Ghazan, are you sure that *you* want to do this?"

He stooped to retrieve a stray soccer ball that rolled into his path and waited to hand it to the young boy chasing after it. Then he turned to me. "My name is Asfand Ghazan. Do you know the Pashto meaning?"

I shook my head and he recited: "Asfand signifies a hero or a king. Ghazan means 'a fighter of holy war.'"

He looked directly at me and I realized that that was his answer. To confirm it, he asked, "When shall we start the interview?"

"It started when you knocked on the door of my hotel room."

I spent the next two weeks with Asfand Ghazan, most of that in his tribal region near Mazar-al-Sharif and among his followers. The resulting article and photographs circulated worldwide, appearing in almost every significant newspaper or periodical in the Western world.

I had a voice message from Schmidt waiting for me when I returned to Panama City.

"Nice work."

Transition

A week later, I was in a bar in the Casco Viejo district of Panama City with Magda when the TV announced that a Miami grand jury had just indicted Manuel Noriega on charges of racketeering, drug smuggling and money laundering. Half the screen showed an arm-waving Noriega standing at a podium and shouting. I looked over at Magda, but she seemed uninterested in the TV.

"Looks like you might be out of work soon," I said, making it sound like a question. She shook her head. "Not soon enough. Somebody needs to shoot the bastard." She waved at the bartender and kept the bottle that he brought sitting in front of her on the table. An hour later, the bottle was almost empty and I was telling her about what I had come to think of as "Arthur's Video." I like to believe that I told her because I thought it would help if she knew that all of us had shitty jobs and that bad things happened. But the story as told by me became all about my own failures, how Arthur got his throat cut because I didn't do *something*.

Thirty minutes later, we were somehow in bed together in a motel room on the waterfront. It was her doing, an act of charity administered to a compliant but needy fellow human. It was more about consolation than any real commitment. It 'worked' in that there was pleasure and release, but there was little real passion involved that first time. We did not talk and she left me sleeping in the narrow bed sometime in the early morning. I think both of us knew that it would happen again and that it would mean nothing except to affirm that we were still human. What I really wanted to know, but never asked, was whether it was the same for Riley.

Schmidt's operation all came unwound, of course; just a small part of the CIA's massive failures at derailing the leftward drift of Latin America. The Noriega indictment, the surfacing of the 'arms-for-hostage' Iran-Contra scandal along with Colonel Oliver North's 'unofficial' involvement, the negotiated truce in Nicaragua, the popularity of Chavez in Venezuela ... It all coalesced into a perfect storm.

In December 1989, the U.S. Marine Corps invaded Panama. Schmidt was nowhere in sight, but Magda, Riley and I stayed in Oficinas de la Empresa and pretended to work at our cover jobs. On the day that Noriega was flown back to the states for trial and imprisonment, Schmidt appeared and announced that we were leaving in two days and each of the three of us had an indefinite leave.

"What next? After our *indefinite leave*"" Magda asked in a way that reminded me that she was the first one to ask a question of Schmidt on that very first day: "Who are you and who do you work for?" And he looked at her with the same bland expression as on that day.

"One month ago, the Berlin Wall was taken down. The Soviet Union is collapsing. Capitalism has won. Communism is, as they say, for the dustbin of history."

I played my usual role as straight man: "So the world doesn't need spies anymore? We can all go home?"

His expression changed from bland to amused. "We need spies more than ever. How else will we know who our real enemies are?"

Riley came into my office as I was packing. He watched me fit everything from my office into a single roll-on suitcase before he asked, "So, where are you going for your indefinite leave?"

I couldn't answer, because I didn't know. In the last four years, I had become something that I didn't recognize and Schmidt's directive to 'go home' did not provide any useable reference points.

"Magda and I are going to a very small fishing village on a Caribbean island," Riley said offhandedly. "A place where nobody fights about anything except food and sex."

"That's good," I said, but I didn't look at him. I don't know which of them I resented the most.

"Schmidt asked me to give this to you." He handed me a news clipping. A handwritten notation identified it as from the main Nicaraguan newspaper, two days ago. It described the shooting of a Colonel Raul Gomez, one of the more decorated members of the Sandanista Defense Force. He'd just left his hotel in Managua when an unidentified man approached and shot him twice in the back of his head. The police had no suspects in custody. The article closed by lamenting the reality that so many revenge murders were occurring now that the contras and Sandanistas were engaged in a democratic election.

He stood quietly, watching me read the article. I looked at him. "That was you? The shooter?"

He stood up and said, "Remember what Schmidt told us at that farmhouse in Virginia? That we'd all get to play god at some point?" He didn't wait for me to answer; he just walked out of the room.

Schmidt and I sat at the table and watched the video of Arthur's killing and I asked him, 'Are we going to do something about him? And Schmidt said, "Revenge is a luxury in this business. Forget about Gomez."

Russia (1990-1999)

"Look... we're getting to be old men, and we've spent our lives looking for the weaknesses in one another's systems. .... Don't you think it's time to recognize that there is as little worth on your side as there is on mine?"

John le Carre,

as George Smiley, in <u>Tinker, Tailor, Soldier, Spy</u>

Helsinki

Each morning, a brightly painted icebreaker traverses the Helsinki harbor several times, easily shattering the thin ice sheet that has formed overnight. The ferries that run from Helsinki to Tallinn must cope with the frozen Baltic Sea on their own. The daily struggle against the ice is an easy metaphor for the Baltic states of Estonia, Latvia and Lithuania, each of which has just declared itself to be independent of the rapidly imploding Soviet Union.

It seems that we are to be educated in all things Russian. We meet each morning at ten in a seaside resort about twenty kilometers outside of Helsinki. It is closed for the winter but Schmidt has arranged for the central part with its conference facilities to be heated during daylight hours. So the six of us sit at a massive circular table designed to seat twenty and listen to a parade of shadowy figures describe the disintegration of an empire. There is a long lunch break because Schmidt has also arranged for the sauna to be kept open, along with a path to the shore where the proprietor maintains a ten-foot circle of open water for the bathers.

"This is extraordinarily stupid." I say what I assume everyone else is thinking as we trudge through the few inches of new snow to the changing room.

Riley says, "I assume you're referring to the concept of daily sauna, rather than to the idea of learning about a world that no longer exists. Although perhaps it's one and the same. Benjamin says we'll never really understand the Finns unless we do the whole sauna bit, including total immersion in the Baltic. And that if we don't understand the Finns, we won't have a chance with the Russians."

He had a point. The Finns share an eight-hundred mile border with Russia. And, unlike almost all the other states that border Russia, they have maintained their independence. They must have learned something in the process that we can use.

"The sauna gets you superheated," Magda chimed in. "You won't even feel the freezing water. Trust me, I've seen it done."

She was right, and the sauna became a daily feature of our stay in Finland. However, I don't think I ever did achieve anything close to an understanding of the Finns. They were a people who easily harbored opposing views – fierce independence and passionate egalitarianism, national introversion and a dedication to tango! Our perfectly round conference table is a clue to the Finnish character: its circular design means that there is no 'head' of the table, although – for us – wherever Schmidt sits defines exactly that.

However, our group is vastly different than the one that assembled five years earlier in that Virginia farmhouse. No one mentions the three deceased members, but they are there, hanging about in the atmosphere. Magda and Riley are darker than when they left Panama City, and not just their skin tone. I have not seen Peter, Benjamin or Alex for a long time, so perhaps it is not surprising that they seem world-weary and much older. I wonder if they've seen what I think of as 'Arthur's Video,' or whether Schmidt has kept that to himself.

Schmidt was silent much of the time. It was mostly Benjamin's show. He was our Russian expert and Central America had been a form of exile for him. So with both Carlee and Arthur gone, he was the last of our original trio of instructors. But more than four years in Latin America had changed the five of us in ways made any further 'training' as irrelevant as snow to a Fijian. In Helsinki, his role was more like that of a talent scout, shepherding a series of self-described experts through our little seminar.

Magda started it off, thirty seconds after we had come into the room and confronted the circular table. Predictably, we chose seats such that each of us was equidistant from our neighbors and Magda was seated directly opposite Schmidt. As soon as he sat down, she asked him, "Why are we here?" She intended it to be a provocative question, a slightly less insulting way of saying that he was wasting our time. But, as always, Schmidt did not take the bait. He answered simply, "To learn to be spies."

Alex said, "I thought we were. Six months in Virginia and almost five years of practice in Central and South America fighting the spread of the red peril."

"You weren't spies. You weren't even 'intelligence agents.' You didn't recruit any doubles, steal any secrets, infiltrate any networks. You were a paramilitary force ... occasional propagandists ... but not spies."

"The Cold War is over," said Peter. "Or it soon will be. Our natural enemy is now China. So why aren't we holding this gathering in Hong Kong or Taipei?"

So. We have learned something in the last five years... to challenge Schmidt.

"The Cold War is *not* over," Schmidt said, "just suspended. Think of it like a rain delay in a baseball game.   And when it resumes, instead of a single monolithic enemy, we're going to have fifteen or twenty enemies, each with a different agenda.   And we'll need to know what each of them intends."

Benjamin took over and went on the offensive. "You've been in another hemisphere for five years. In that time, Mr. Reagan, with his 'evil empire' views, and Mr. Gorbachev with his programs of perestroika and glasnost have made the Soviet Union and Russia very different than what you knew.   You people are as obsolete as the crossbow!"

He pointed at Magda, "Who's going to wind up owning all those tactical nukes in Poland?" At Riley, "Will Russia allow its Muslim citizens to form their own countries?   And, if not, will there be internal revolutions?"   For Peter, "What will all those unemployed KGB agents do for a living?" And finally, his index finger pointed at me, "Will democracy even work in Russia? They've gone from the Peter the Great to Stalin to Gorbachev to ... what? The Russians have no experience with choosing their leaders and most definitely are not going to like their first exposure to capitalism. Will they revert? When? And to what?"

I pointed back at him. "I don't know the answer to any of your questions, and neither does anyone else! But I don't have to make those judgments. I'm a spy, or so you tell me. The answers to your questions? That's for our *leaders* ... the ones we elect."

Schmidt spoke very softly. "And where will they get the information they need to make those judgments?"

His question effectively ended the debate, leaving the floor to Benjamin.   He lifted a stack of five fat envelopes from the floor beside him and said, "OK, then. Here's tonight's homework. I've put together a selection of recent newspaper articles, analytical reports, and policy papers for you to read.   They are either in Russian or German, so you can work on your language skills as well."

Over the next three weeks, we listened to – and pushed back on – about twenty different presenters, a virtual who's who of self-proclaimed experts on the disintegrating Soviet Union.   History professors, kremlinologists, futurists, economists, generals, diplomats, journalists, retired intelligence agents from MI-6, the CIA and Mossad … and, for some reason, a Jewish dissident from Minsk.

Part of my time was spent on my cover job. I wrote two or three columns each week and faxed them back to Texas. My writing was mostly oriented to the rolling implosion of the Soviet Union.   It wasn't difficult because I borrowed liberally from the experiences and opinions of our guest presenters, without attribution. One day, I received a return fax from my editor – the presence in Texas that I never met. He enclosed several pages of reprints of 'Letters to the Editor' commenting on my columns. I seemed to be getting a bit of a reputation as a hawkish international relations commentator.

After Panama City, it was surreal. I felt like I was in a graduate school seminar, getting a doctorate in political science. We read, studied, and debated. We argued the merits of a planned economy over markets, the advantages of the parliamentary system of government, whether there should be some natural limits to free speech. But there was no mention of tradecraft or any of the other minutiae of espionage … no review of self-defense techniques, bomb-making, or debriefing as to the latest intelligence. Magda captured it nicely. "It's like Schmidt wants us to fit right in at a town council meeting in central Russia."

There was, however, ample evidence in the daily Finnish newspapers that both the Soviet Union and its seventy-year-long experiment with communism were ending fast and messily. There was a worldwide sense that the future was going to be quite different, but no one was quite sure in what way. It was a time for rethinking the premises of one's life, and not just for the citizens of the imploding Soviet Union.

Schmidt liked to take long hikes along the shore. He never admitted it, but I think he set himself the challenge of staying within ten feet of the water's edge. I once saw him wade knee-deep in icy water to avoid a fifty-yard detour away from the sea. I picked out a dry log in a sunny spot and waited for him to return. When he saw me, he said nothing, just came and sat alongside me.

I let him get settled and go through the ritual of lighting a cigarette before I asked, "Who are we, Schmidt?"

He halfway turned to look at me. "We? You mean, like you and me? That we?"

"You know which *we* I mean – our little band of spies. Are we the point-of-the-spear for capitalism? Comic-book super heroes who will save the western world? Are we being groomed as a shadow-cabinet for Gorbachev's final days?"

As usual, Schmidt understood my motives better than I did. He looked out at the gray sea and asked, "Are you thinking of quitting, Mahoney?"

I was, wasn't I? Why else all this angst? Panama had rubbed away any vestiges of optimism about who I was or what I was doing and my future seemed as bleak as the iron-gray Baltic seascape stretching in front of us.

He didn't wait for an answer. "About your 'who are we' question: We are what we have been from the start, an elite team of specialists available to the American intelligence community for important and clandestine projects."

"Projects? Like dismembering the Soviet Union?"

He smiled. "They're doing that for us. We're just spectators, like everyone else. That's Phase One. Our contribution will be in Phase Two."

"And Phase Two is ....?"

He seemed to think about it. "Reconstruction, featuring national humiliation for the Russians, a scramble for power and a massive redistribution of wealth. It will go on for a decade or more and none of us are quite sure what it will look like when it has run its course."

"And that's where we come in ... helping to determine what's at the end of Phase Two?"

He waved his hand, the cigarette creating a bright arc across the darkening sky. "We'll do what we can. But it's like trying to steer an oil tanker with a canoe paddle."

I thought about the metaphor and spent a few seconds visualizing the physics. "If you wait long enough and the tanker continues on, that canoe paddle can cause a significant course alteration."

"Whatever." Schmidt stood up, stepped on his cigarette and put the butt in his coat pocket. I said, "When do we start paddling?"

"Soon. When Phase One is over."

"Schmidt, you said we're a team of specialists. What is it we specialize in?"

"Don't you know, after those years in Central America?"

I don't. Everybody was always gone, each on their own little errands, doing whatever it was that Schmidt told us to do. And we didn't talk about what happened when we came back together.

He said, "Peter uses technology to discover the worst parts of people. Alex converts patriots into traitors. Riley kills people, and Magda fucks people."

It stunned me. I think it was the most demeaning assessment of human nature I ever heard, even though I would learn over and over that it was accurate.

"And me, Schmidt? What am I a specialist in?" *And suddenly I am afraid of what he will say.*

He looked directly at me, with sympathy, I think. "Moral ambivalence." And he walked away.

At the end of the following day, Schmidt handed each of us the customary fat manila envelope. "Your homework for tomorrow. It's mostly about physics and statistics. You need to pay special attention because this" – he placed his hand flat on the envelope in front of him – "and tomorrow's visitor are directly relevant to what happens next."

Our guest lecturer the next morning was a retired major general from the German army, a surprisingly cheerful character who affected red suspenders beneath his somber dark suit. His last assignment before retiring was at NATO headquarters in Brussels. He began with a question, "Do you know how many nuclear warheads are about to be available for sale to the highest bidder?" His cheeriness was so much at odds with his question that I didn't try to hide the sarcasm.

"That depends on the price, doesn't it? So how much would it set me back if I just had to have a hundred megaton ICBM of my own?"

He looked at me the way you would expect a German general to look at an impertinent civilian. "First, you can't afford it on a spy's salary. Second, the preferred metric is kilotons, not megatons. A Hiroshima-sized weapon would be equivalent to about ten-thousand kilotons of TNT. Today's basic hydrogen bomb would be ten times that. Third, technically, an ICBM is a delivery system; what you want is the warhead, the fissionable material. But you really don't want one of those big ones that sits on top of an ICBM. They're too complicated, aside from the reality that about all they're good for is destroying entire cities filled with civilians."

Riley said, "I know some folks that would like just that – North Korea, Syria maybe –"

He ignored him. "Those are the 'strategic' nukes. What you want if you're an everyday terrorist is some of the 'tactical' nuclear weapons, defined as something that's short range, low yield and reasonably portable. Think about mines, artillery shells, rockets and – for the melodramatic among you – the 'suitcase bomb.' They run anywhere from one to a few hundred kilotons of TNT. You wouldn't wipe out New York City, but you could make a very large bare spot in the middle of Manhattan."

Typically, Magda asked the important questions. "How many of those are there, and where are they, and who controls them?"

"Same answer for all three questions: Nobody is quite sure. The Soviet strategic nukes have gotten lots of attention, so the controls are pretty tight with Mother Russia as the custodian. But the tacticals are another matter. We know there are thousands of them in the ex-Soviet states other than Russia, many of them scattered among the Tank and Motor Rifle Divisions facing NATO – Poland, East Germany Czechoslovakia, Hungary, etc. Those are the ones that are likely to be on the market."

He flashed a lot of color-coded maps at us, talked through a series of tables where the columns were acronyms that stood for weapons – 'GB' was 'Gravity Bomb'-- and the rows were place names in Europe, and then, for two long hours, used a set of engineering diagrams with Russian script to instruct us on how a basic 155 mm nuclear artillery shell could be assembled and activated.

When he left, Schmidt said, "We leave in a few days. Somebody at Langley is pretty sure that another somebody is shopping for atomic warheads and may have found a source. We're supposed to get in the way of the transaction."

Riley played devil's advocate. "Without knowing exactly what's being sold by whom or to whom or where or when? We might as well stay in Helsinki and drink more aquavit until your 'somebody at Langley' gets more specific."

But Schmidt was unperturbed. "Rule One, Riley. Remember?" But then he went on. "Until three days ago, all we had was rumors and chatter, the kind of intelligence tea leaves that analysts love to muck around in. Augmented by paranoia, of course. But then we got a tip from a real live source."

Monica Redux

My Moscow hotel room had a view of the Kremlin, but the foreground was a bleak city park traversed by asphalt paths so worn that dirt patches occurred at irregular intervals. There were three bare trees, a massive statue of a figure with one arm raised, and two stone benches. The snow was crusted with gray soot but each morning, shortly after dawn, a trio of women with straw brooms swept the paths clean.

I spent three days at a succession of depressing government offices, dealing with a series of gray bureaucrats while trying to obtain 'press credentials.' No one knew what the new rules were and no one was willing to risk departing from the old rules. It was Catch-22, Soviet style. Late on the third day, I was sitting in the anteroom of one of those offices, on a long wooden bench that ran the length of the wall. I was alone in the office, apparently the only foreign correspondent in Moscow without the necessary endorsements. A woman entered, started to cross the room and then stopped to stare at me. It was Monica Holst. She came and sat down beside me.

"Buenas tardes, Mahoney." The Spanish phrase evoked an exquisitely vivid mental image of her naked in the half-light of that hotel room in Managua. I wondered if that was her intention.

"This is Moscow." And I said 'Good Afternoon' in Russian, trying to make it sound like something I'd learned from a tourist guidebook on the flight in. Then in English, "It's good to see you again, Monica. And a total surprise."

"Not so much of one, I think. Every foreign correspondent from the west is going to be somewhere in one of the Soviet Social Republics. That's where the stories are. They're calling it the 'end of history,' didn't you know?"

She was dressed like the average Muscovite housewife, a study in grays and blacks … fur hat, boots, leggings, black cloth coat and a gray scarf wound several times around her throat. Moscow in the winter of 1990 was the most monochromatic city I have ever experienced, as though the communist regime had banned colors as well as Xerox machines and western music. Even the buildings were gray, in their coatings of soot. But I was picturing Monica crossing the Managua hotel room, naked. *And she knows it, too.* She was looking at me with a slight and knowing smile. *She said that it was a one-time thing … that it had no predictive value.*

She asked, "Why are you sitting in this dreary office?"

"I need papers, it seems. Press credentials. Apparently the process requires me to be passed on to an interminable series of clerks, each of whom refers me to the next. They all look the same, so it may be that I'm cycling through some kind of Kafkaesque loop."

She laughed. "Kafka was Czech, not Russian. But he did capture the essence of communist bureaucracy." She looked more closely at me and said, "I gather this is your first time in Russia?"

"In any Eastern European country. Other than a one-week student tour."

She stood up and held her hand out to me. "Let me help you. Russians are used to authority figures, so you need to become an authoritarian. Watch and learn."

Twenty minutes later, we were on the street with my new credentials tucked into my pocket. I hadn't said a word, simply standing alongside Monica as she shouted in rapid Russian at a thoroughly cowed woman who used every one of the several large multi-colored rubber stamps on her desk to create a most impressive looking document.

She took my arm and started walking. I said, "Can I buy you dinner? For breaking me out of bureaucratic purgatory?"

To my total surprise, she said, "In one of Pushkin's poems, he says, 'I live alone with my sadness, and wait. When will come my end?' Like Kafka, Pushkin was also familiar with the communist system, even though it didn't emerge until eighty years after his death."

I remembered the early days in the Virginia farmhouse. *Benjamin required us to be able to recite Pushkin on demand. Did he foresee this conversation?* I said, "I was forced to read Pushkin's *Evgeny Onegin* in college. The only lines I remember are, 'We all have studied, if a little, some blurry thing in some vague ways.' It seemed appropriately subversive under the circumstances."

She held my arm more closely against her and said, "Russians are a sentimental people. If you recite poetry to them, they will forgive you for much."

"But you are German."

"I grew up in Germany. My mother was Russian."
With that, we walked in silence for half a minute, long
enough for me to become conscious of her breast
pressing against my left arm and to welcome what she
said next. "It is too early for dinner. Let's go to your
hotel room and play."

It was like Managua; at first frenzied and then
unhurried, a slow and reciprocal discovery of pleasure.
At some point, we ordered dinner from room service
and then slept. When I woke up, it was just past dawn
and Monica was standing naked at the window,
smoking a cigarette and looking out at the women
sweeping the sidewalk. With the dark red velvet
drapes and the gray light, it could have been an oil
painting by one of the Dutch masters. 'Mistress in
Window,' maybe?

I said, "Karl Marx said that religion is the opiate of the
masses. But he was wrong. It's sex."

"And vodka, I think. At least for the Russian male."
She sounded sad.

*Schmidt would be horrified. A western intelligence agent in
Moscow for three days falls into bed with unknown woman.
Worse, she isn't quite an unknown. She's half Russian and
the last time I saw her, she was drinking coffee with a
Russian providing military advice to a leftist government in
Nicaragua who Schimdt thinks is a high ranking Russian
intelligence office.. My only defense would be that I was
trying to recruit her.*

It was as if she was tuned to my thoughts. "Thomas, why are you here? In Moscow?"

"The same as you. To cover the end of history?" Before she could respond, I asked, "How did Nicaragua work out for you? Did you get what you wanted?"

She looked at me closely, as if to detect hidden intents. She shrugged. "I sold a series of six articles, including the last one featuring a two-hour interview with Daniel Ortega. So you could say it worked out. How about you?"

I watched one friend as his throat was slashed and then helped another die from friendly fire.   Oh, and I was wounded by a suitcase and facilitated the invasion of Panama.

"A lot of little things, mostly political but some cultural stuff. My editor kept telling me, 'Mahoney, remember who our readers are! Stop trying for the Pulitzer Prize!'"

She wasn't listening. Still not looking at me, she said, "Did you know that our Colonel Gomez was murdered? You remember him from our little trip along the Honduran border?"

"I remember Gomez, but I missed the news about his murder. I never got back to Nicaragua after our one excursion."

She found her bra and panties near the foot of the bed and began dressing. When she pulled her sweater on over her head, she asked, "So, what's first? Will you write about the breadlines, the proliferation of kiosks selling pirated consumer goods, the beautiful young women willing to sell themselves for exit visas, the bribing of civil servants --"

I cut her off. "Tactical nuclear weapons, I think."

She went still, her sweater half on so that I couldn't see her face and her voice was muffled.   "But your subscribers –"

"Are military junkies.   Veterans and their families, with a longstanding and serious distrust of the Russians.   They live in Texas, New Mexico and Oklahoma.   And Fort Sill, Oklahoma is the home of the U.S. Army's artillery and El Paso, Texas is the home of Fort Bliss, which in turn is where most of the training is done for the White Sands Proving Grounds and various rockets carrying the smaller nukes."

Her tousled head emerged from the sweater.   "So what's your angle? It's a big topic."

"It's pretty clear that the non-strategic nukes will be destroyed on both sides. I thought I would follow one particular Soviet batch from where they are deployed through to their final destruction. Part of Mr. Reagan's 'trust but verify' doctrine.'"

She came and sat beside me on the bed, clearly intrigued by the topic. She said, "You'll need access."

"I've got it. The operation will be monitored by a UN agency from start to finish, and I'll be an observer attached to it."

"Where are they deployed?   The warheads you'll be tracking?"

"Sorry. That's classified. They say they'll shoot me if I tell anyone. Especially a terrorist."

She smiled. "I wonder what a forty kiloton device would fetch in the Middle East? From say, Muammar Gaddafi in Libya or Saddam Hussein in Iraq?"

"Let's hope we don't find out." And I meant it. "What about you? What angle are you working on?"

She grimaced. "I'm stuck in Moscow for a while. I've signed up for a long feature on who's who in the emerging Russian government."

"Who are you betting on?"

"That's easy. There's only three types that will come out on top. The mostly likely are the old communist bosses. They'll declare themselves to be capitalists and the only ones who can make the trains run on time. Then there are the KGB officers that were smart enough to see this coming. They'll use their collection of dossiers and dirty tricks to stay relevant. The third bunch of possibles are the mafia kingpins. They already control a lot of the machinery of government, so it won't be hard for them to come out from under the rocks. I'm betting that by the time the dust settles, the New Russia won't look all that different from the old one."

"Monica, that's really depressing."

She looked at me with some sympathy. "For you, maybe, with your American sense of inevitable progress and the entitlement that goes with it. But remember ... they've still got vodka ... and sex."

Ukraine

Aeroflot, the Russian national airline, continued to pretend that it was a functioning airline, adopting a "See, we're still flying, so we must be OK" attitude common to zombie-like Soviet industries in those early days. So I wasn't sure whether I should be relieved or fearful when the Moscow to Kiev flight was half-filled with dubious passengers, including me, and ready to go, awaiting only the refueling truck.

The pilot was a rotund little man who waved his arms a lot and spoke fluent English. He stood at the head of the aisle, using a handheld microphone and began speaking in Russian, "Everything is in order, but ... " He was clearly searching for words, using phrases like "... difficult times ... unpaid bills ... inexperienced personnel ..." and sounding like the official apologist for all of the massive inefficiencies of the Soviet system, but then he threw up his hands and said, in one complete sentence: "The aviation fuel supplier will not refuel our aircraft unless he is paid ten-thousand Deutschemarks." He repeated this last sentence in English, but it was inaudible due to the shouting from the passengers.

It took another hour and much more shouting, but finally a distinguished looking gray-haired passenger with a German accent organized a campaign to collect cash from the passengers. He began with a short speech in English that emphasized the reality that – for those of us who really wanted to get to Kiev within the next three days -- we had little choice. He repeated the speech in Russian and then he used the pilot's hat to receive the money, making three trips up and down the central aisle before he had the ten-thousand marks. Several passengers threw in ruble notes, but he handed them back with a smile and a regretful phrase in formal Russian. He impressed me as either a diplomat or a banker.

I found him standing next to me at the luggage carousel in Kiev, in a cavernous room so dimly lit that I wished for a flashlight. It was a long time before the carousel started turning and, even then, no bags emerged. I said to him in English, "Perhaps we shall need to take up a collection for the luggage handlers as well?"

He looked at me very carefully. Jokes were always a risky business for westerners in Warsaw Pact countries. Apparently, I looked harmless. "Look on the bright side," he said. "It means that they are transitioning to a market-based economy quite quickly."

"I think that everything shall be for sale in the Ukraine," I ventured, and he responded instantly and with some noticeable anger, "Yes, but some things should not be."

I bowed slightly. "Thank you for facilitating our flight from Moscow. I wasn't sure we'd get off the ground."

He smiled a most rueful smile. "And I wasn't sure I wanted to. I could not help wondering about the sufficiency of the financial incentives for the maintenance crews. But thank you for the five hundred marks. I would have moved you to first class, but of course a communist society is classless."

So he paid attention to who gave how much. Maybe he is a banker, but one with a finely developed sense of irony.

"Are you a banker?" I asked.

He smiled. "No, but I am Swiss and many think that is the same thing."

I wanted to prolong our encounter but suitcases started spilling onto the carousel and I had no chance to respond. I found a driver holding up a placard with my name on it when I exited the border control line of booths and thirty minutes later I was in a soot-encrusted concrete building, standing outside an office door with a hand-printed sign with 'UNIDIR' in big block letters. The United Nations Institute for Disarmament Research – or UNIDIR for short—was an intergovernmental organization within the United Nations whose nominal task was to conduct research and monitoring around nuclear disarmament. Schmidt had arranged for me to shadow them for one particular assignment they were about to undertake.

Inside was a single harried clerk trying to install a phone that looked like something from the 1930's. He looked at me, said, "Wait. No one's here yet," and then ignored me. I spent the next thirty minutes reading various notices posted on the wall of the office advising me on the best ways to avoid or treat venereal disease. Apparently, the place had been a woman's clinic of some sort.

An inner office door opened and my Swiss traveling companion stepped out. We both were surprised, but he recovered quickly. "Hello again. You must be Thomas Mahoney, our designated journalist from the state of Texas. My name is Anton Weiss. I am the UNIDIR representative for this project. And the person who sent you the initial briefing materials." He held out his hand to direct me into the office.

Two men in uniform were already there, each standing looking out of separate windows into the street. There was a perceptible tension between them and they seemed relieved by our entrance. Weiss said, "Mr. Mahoney, this is Captain Yuri Vasnetsov from the Twelfth Main Directorate of the Russian Ministry of Defense and Vice Admiral Andrei Chayka of the Soviet Union's Black Sea Fleet."

Each of the men nodded stiffly at me. These were the early days and I suspect that the idea of fraternizing with an American journalist was so outlandish that it would take a long time to develop an easy relationship.

It probably won't help if Schmidt is right and one of them is brokering a deal with terriorists who want nuclear weapons!

One week ago, Schmidt and I were alone in his Helsinki hotel room, going over what little he saw fit to tell me.

"Ukraine has more non-strategic nukes than any of the other SSR's, so it's a logical place for a terrorist with big ideas to go shopping. Our intel is that the seller will acquire his inventory from a shipment of nukes coming from the Black Sea Fleet in Sevastapol."

"Naval weaponry. So they could be torpedoes, artillery, mines —"

"All of those are possible, but missile warheads are the most likely candidates. The Fleet's flagship is a Slava-class guided-missile cruiser ... they call them 'carrier killers.' It and several other ships have a variety of cruise missiles, anti-aircraft and anti-ship missiles ranging in size from five tons to shoulder-fired."

"OK, so we know where –"

"No we don't *know* anything, but we can guess. Russia has excellent physical controls over the weapons, both when they're deployed and when they're stored. The 12th Directorate in their Ministry of Defense is a thoroughly professional bunch. So, our people in Langley are *guessing* that the theft will almost certainly take place when they're being transported during the Ukrainian leg."

"Where are they going?"

"If the disarmament agreements hold, all the tactical nukes from the fleet will be taken to Engels Airbase in Russia for storage and eventual destruction. That's a distance of several hundred miles and the trip will require temporary storage and multiple stopping points."

"Schmidt, why don't we just tell the Russians what we know? They'll beef up security. Problem solved."

"No. Problem *diverted*. The buyer and seller will just look for another venue. And there are plenty of them. And even worse, the Russians may be the ones who are setting up the deal."

"What am I supposed to do? I have no authority and know next to nothing about the logistics of transporting nuclear materials."

"You watch. The weak spot in the system is the people. The insiders. What's making this deal possible is somebody with both power and grievances ... maybe a KGB officer, a local unit commander, maybe even a politician. The whole system is coming down around their ears and they're looking for a way out for them and their families."

"So they sell state assets." I thought about it. "The high value portable ones that can be carried off."

"It's happening all over the place already. Two weeks ago, a Soviet submarine captain sold his boat to an unknown buyer, probably a South American drug cartel. Last week, a Yugoslav pilot flew his MIG-29 with state-of-the-art avionics to Italy and demanded a million dollars."

I said the obvious. "It would be much easier to steal a few pounds of plutonium."

"Congratulations. You're thinking like a terrorist. What we want you to do is to identify the sellers ... before the transaction takes place."

"How do I do that?"

"Same as Central America. You're a journalist, so I've arranged for you to be an observer for one of the first batches of tactical nuclear weapons to be decommissioned. You'll do in-depth interviews with the key parties and write about the transit."

Neither of us said what I was thinking. *And we know how well that Central American project worked out, don't we?* But I think Schmidt knew because he said, "Riley, Peter and Magda are working on the same assignment from different angles. You won't be alone."

Peter had performed some electronic tricks and hacked into some of the lower-level Soviet networks. From what he had learned, it was clear that the two officers in the room with me were—at least on paper -- candidates for treason. They were definitely insiders. Vasnetsov was from the 12th Directorate, the Russian agency that designed, installed and managed the elaborate controls over nuclear weapons. He would be responsible for the shipment of Black Sea Fleet weapons once in Russian territory. Chayka was responsible while they were either in the fleet or in transit within Ukraine.

They both had a lot to lose in the emerging new order. *Vasnetsov's a zealot. A relatively young officer with great patrons in the vast military hierachy. Ordinarily, he'd be the last person to commit treason, but his world's gone upside down with the Soviet collapse. He could well be one of those already yearning for a return to Soviet great power status.*

Chayka's even more interesting. A very high-ranking officer in the Soviet Navy. But he's Ukrainian and Ukraine and Russia are at serious odds with one another. They're fighting about who gets the Crimean Peninsula, who retains control of the Black Sea Fleet and the bases at Sevastopol, and who shall control the gas pipelines that run through Ukraine.

And they're both poor. The Soviet military has been starved for funds for a long time now and that has translated into lousy pay and benefits for officers and their families.

Vasnetsov was staring at me in a way that I had experienced frequently during my short stay in Moscow ... as if I was personally responsible for the destruction of his way of life. He made no effort to disguise his antagonism. "So, you shall write about how miserable life is in the Soviet republics?"

"No. I shall write about the destruction of nuclear weapons, a good thing for both of our countries." *Maybe it would help if I recited some Pushkin at him.*

He gestured at Weiss. "Are there UN officials watching and journalists from Izvestia writing about the Americans destroying the contents of the Los Alamos storage vaults?"

"I hope so," I said as mildly as I could. "But I don't know."

My answer seemed to irritate him even more. He snapped, "The Soviet Union –"

"Does not exist any longer. Mr. Gorbachev dissolved it." Admiral Chaya broke in loudly. "Your so-called Union is now a collection of fifteen independent countries. One of them is Ukraine. Another is Russia."

The interruption clearly startled Vasnetsov. The flash of anger was brief but clearly visible before his face settled into the stony mask of a man suppressing his emotions. *He's an army captain and a Russian, Chaya a vice admiral in the navy and a Ukrainian. This could be an interesting pairing.*

Logistics

Weiss and I were the only two patrons in the restaurant in the center of Kiev. He told me that, not so long ago, it had been a popular place for the party members, mafia bosses and foreign visitors, but the present political hard times had readily translated into deep recession. There were shortages of most consumer goods, including particularly food and fuel, and rolling power outages throughout the city.

Peter also compiled a dossier for me about Weiss. No hacking required, so it was more complete. Swiss from birth, from Basel, Jewish, ex-professor of humanities, now head of a foundation whose mission is a united Europe. On loan to the UN for a two-year sabbatical as an observer of nuclear disarmament.

I said, "I looked at the materials from your foundation. You have an impressive history."

"I have been fortunate to live during interesting times. Since 1950, European countries have been inexorably moving toward a united whole. We now have the European Economic Community, and – very soon, I hope – we will have the United States of Europe. Germany will move quite quickly toward reunification and NATO is talking of taking in ex-Soviet states. Communism is on its last legs. I am privileged to have been a part of all that."

"It's not over though, is it? All these things you mention … they will require decades to complete."

My question made him somber. "Not so long as that, I hope. But after this project, I am done. I have a family – a wife and daughter – that I want to spend some time with. My daughter, she is a journalist, like you."

"In Basel?"

"Geneva, but she is actually in Bulgaria right now. She is helping to put on a workshop for young journalists from Warsaw Pact countries."

He waved his hand. "Enough about me. A dull subject, indeed. Tell me, what did you think of our two military partners in our venture?"

"I don't think they like each other."

He sighed deeply. "It's a legacy of their system. Trust, let alone friendship, with colleagues was ... is ... dangerous. Both personally and professionally. And there's a natural antagonism because of the weapons, of course."

"In what way?"

"Our naval officer, Chayka, has physical control of the warheads and is responsible for using them if conditions warrant, but he must ask permission of our Army captain, Vasnetsov."

"The mistrust and personal dislikes would seem to facilitate control. It means that they will watch one another more intensely, doesn't it?"

"Yes, but control and effectiveness are different outcomes."

He is Swiss, from a place where nothing is ever out of place and everything works. I ventured, "I'm not sure that I would want nuclear weapons to be used *effectively.*"

He smiled at me. "Of course not." Then he asked, "Did you know that there are more than seven thousand nuclear warheads in Ukraine?"

Actually I did, courtesy of Peter's hacking skills. But what I said was, "No, I didn't. They don't share that kind of information with journalists."

"Tomorrow, we begin the process of dismantling them. A car will pick us up at five AM. We'll be in Sevastopol by noon to watch the transfer from ship to shore."

"Are we traveling with the admiral and captain?"

"No. They're already there, starting the paperwork."

"What happens once they're offloaded?"

He hesitated, but finally said, "A military convoy to Engels Airbase in Russia. The exact schedule and routes are known only to Chayka and Vasnetsov. Once there, they'll be dismantled and the fissile material converted to a non-weapons grade level."

"How many warheads are we taking?"

"One-hundred and twelve. They say that is the entire nuclear inventory of the Soviet Black Sea Fleet."

A drop in the proverbial bucket, if there are truly seven thousand such devices scattered around. Weiss was watching me closely and shook his head. "I know. But it is a start. And there are other projects like ours that are already at work."

"How big an escort –"

It was a question too many. He looked at his watch and stood up abruptly. "I have to go." I'd appreciate it if you would take care of the check. And please leave a big tip. The waiters are being paid with the leftover food. I'll meet you in the lobby at five. Good night."

Apparently, mistrust is not limited to the Soviets.

The naval base at Sevastopol was sprawling but strangely quiet. When I commented, Weiss said, "The Soviets have curtailed almost all training and everyday operations. They've simply run out of money. Chayka told me that some of his officers have not been paid for more than three months."

The pier that was our destination was under tight security. Our car was searched thoroughly and our papers were scrutinized by three different officers. Once cleared, we followed a lead jeep and were trailed by a second one, finally stopping near a large truck, an unmarked sixteen-wheeled van that was surrounded by a semi-circle of naval marines with automatic weapons at the ready. The truck cab was extended in such a way that several passengers could be accommodated. There was no ship docked at the pier. Chayka and Vasnetsov stood at the rear of the van at the foot of the loading ramp, apparently waiting for us.

Weiss exploded. "Damn it! We were supposed to observe the ship-to-shore transfer! This is not a good start."

But he said nothing to the two waiting men except, "The procedure calls for me to be on hand at all transfer points and to observe.   I'm supposed to *personally* observe one-hundred and twelve warheads being transferred."

Vasnetsov was uninterested. "Well, you are here at the transfer point, so *observe!*"   He walked up the ramp, clearly uncaring as to whether we followed or not.

The interior was lit by a row of caged lights down the center of the van.   A single aisle ran from end to end, flanked on either side by a steel grid made up of fifteen columns and four rows of compartments.   *Sixty compartments on each side.   One-twenty total, each about the size of a three-foot cube.* We walked slowly down the aisle. Each of the compartments contained an identical metal box that fit into the space with less than an inch of clearance.   Each box had the atomic symbol emblazoned on it and in the lower left corner, a jumble of Cyrillic letters and numbers on a metal plate that looked like it was welded to the box.

Chayka handed Weiss a very fat envelope stamped 'Top Secret' with an elaborate wax seal across its middle.   "Here's the manifest and details, not to be opened until we arrive at Engels.   One hundred and twelve boxes, each containing a spherical plutonium core and cladding material … the entire nuclear inventory of the Black Sea Fleet.   All detonating explosives and electronic triggers have been removed. Each box has a unique identifier on the nameplate, along with the weight of the plutonium and its kiloton equivalence. Both Captain Vasnetsov and myself have personally observed and verified the contents of each container."

I looked at Weiss, but he was apparently satisfied. So, feeling a fool, I said, "But there are one-hundred and twenty boxes ..."

Vasnetsov said with some obvious reluctance, "The eight boxes in the columns nearest the doors are empty. The theory is that those would be the ones to be taken if there is a theft enroute."

As soon as we were down the ramp, it retracted beneath the truck and the pair of heavy metal doors closed, activated by a remote control that Chayka held. There was a distinct sound of metal bars sliding into place once the doors met. He held up the controller. "There are two of these. Captain Vasnetsov has one; I have the other. Each has a unique password and, once turned on, a second code is required to open the doors. Neither of us knows both of the other's codes. Both controllers must be used sequentially or the doors will not open.

"We will be traveling for two days, stopping only for fuel. Captain Vasnetsov and I will ride with the driver in the cab of the truck. We have arranged for you to accompany us in one of the military escort vehicles."

The two days passed quickly and without drama of any sort. The transport van was either in motion or parked in full view of Weiss and myself as it was being fueled. I used the time to do a series of interviews with Chayka and Vasnetsov, but they were both at their

'Hero of the Soviet Union' best and cited 'security reasons' for not talking about details of the shipment.

I left the convoy when it reached the outer gates of Engels Airbase. The truck would be unloaded under strict security arrangements and the boxes put into storage until the base disarmament facilities could handle them. Weiss said that he would stay with the shipment until it was offloaded into the special-purpose storage vault. Given that Vasnetsov estimated that it would another week before the actual degrading of the plutonium, there was little for me to do at Engels. But the real reason I left was that I'd received a message from Schmidt: *Get back to Moscow ASAP.*

I told Vasnetsov I had to leave, but he didn't like it. "Your readers will say that the Russians didn't finish the job, that we still have the weapons hidden and that we'll redeploy them."

You never wanted me along on this trip. Now you don't want me to go? "From everything I've seen in the last two days, your security arrangements are quite good. And Anton Weiss is still here. I'll be sure to get a quote from him that he personally observed the storage and destruction of the weapons."

Weiss made it easy for me. "I'll watch the off-loading and then I'm off to Sofia to see my daughter. All that's necessary is that I sign off on the documents attesting to the delivery of one-hundred and twelve cores. A UN colleague will monitor the integrity of the storage process. The final processing will be next week and I'll be here for that." He held out his hand. "Go write your article," he urged. "That will do far more good than watching me watch them watch each other."

He was right.   And he also saved my life.

Unexpected Losses

The imperative 'ASAP' immediately ran into the realities of the Russian transportation infrastructure. It took me a full day to get from Saratov to Moscow. Schmidt met me in what passed for a living room of a two-room apartment not far from Domodedovo Airport. He had Magda with him.

Carlee would be upset with us. One of her cardinal rules for operating on foreign turf was to 'never, but never' meet with each other. 'If one of you is blown, you'd all be blown.'

When I walked in and saw them, I said, "Kind of violates Carlee's tradecraft principles, doesn't it? Meeting like this."

Schmidt clearly wasn't worried about first principles. "Most of the KGB counter-intelligence directorate is looking for a new line of work these days. Besides, principles are flexible in this business."

"OK. I'm here. What's up?"

"Anton Weiss is dead." Magda watched me carefully as she said the words.

Weiss? Dead? "I saw him less than twenty-four hours ago. We were basically done. He was going to see his daughter in Sofia ... What the hell happened?"

Schmidt and Magda looked at one another. He nodded at her and she said, "It was within an hour of when you left him. Apparently he opened a package of top secret documents that were protected by some kind of explosive device."

We were at the foot of the ramp into the truck. Chayka handed Weiss an envelope ...'Here's the manifest and details ...' Nothing was said about explosive devices being included.

She went on. "The UN's got a team on site. They say that the Russian in charge – your Captain Vasnetsov – told Weiss that the packaged was armed and how to disarm it before he broke the seal."

I shook my head, "No. He didn't. First, it was Chayka, not Vasnetsov, who gave it to him. And he just handed him the envelope. There was no caution of any sort."

Schmidt leaned forward, into my line of vision. "Mahoney, why would they kill Weiss? What was it that made him dangerous to them? You saw everything he saw, didn't you?"

I thought back. "Yes, from the time we left the hotel in Kiev until the front gates at Engels. And there was nothing. The whole operation ran like clockwork."

Magda said, "Everybody agrees with you. The UN has interviewed every man from the truck driver through the lowliest private in the escort team and has gone through all the paperwork. They moved fissile material from one-hundred and nine nuclear warheads from the Black Sea to –"

"What?" I exploded.

They both looked at me. Magda began, "The UN said –"

"No. You said one-hundred and nine. But there were one-hundred and *twelve* boxes of plutonium on that truck, plus eight dummies."

Schmidt walked over to a grimy window that looked out at a blank concrete wall of another apartment building. "Who was told that there were one-hundred and twelve plutonium cores on that truck?"

"I don't know. But I do know that Weiss expected to see that number and that Vasnetsov was standing there when Chayka told Weiss and me that there were one-hundred and twelve. And he didn't blink when he said it."

"So they did it together ... Chayka and Vasnetsov," I breathed. "We thought that there was enough mistrust to prevent collusion."

"Mahoney? Care to share with us?" Schmidt asked.

I stood up and started pacing. The room was small enough that it was only four paces in any direction. "The Twelfth Directorate records would show one-hundred and twelve warheads in the Fleet, so that's how many had to be taken off the ships, and that's what Weiss needed to see ... " I stopped pacing. "But the discrepancy would be apparent when the truck arrived..."

Magda was ahead of me. "The records could have been altered when the convoy was on the way. Vasnetsov almost certainly had access to the data base. There's enough chaos in Russia right now that a lot of the controls are slipping."

I wasn't listening, thinking of an even simpler explanation. "Maybe they don't even care if the phony count is discovered. As long as it happens after they're unloaded and they've gone to wherever it is they're going."

That would explain why Weiss was killed. He would have exposed them as soon as he heard the number 'one hundred and nine.' And I would have been included if I hadn't left unexpectedly.

They both looked at me. Then Schmidt said, "Magda, get to our UN contact at Engels. Find out where Vasnetsov and Chayka are now. And for god's sake, don't mention anything about missing nukes!"

Magda went into the next room and started telephoning. Schmidt and I just sat looking at one another until he said, "You missed it."

I did. We assumed that we could rely on Chayka and Vasnetsov to watch one another, that their mutual dislike would be more than enough to ensure that neither could cheat without the other blowing the whistle.

"Three warheads never got on the truck. They colluded from the very beginning."

"So it seems," Schmidt said.

"For money, I suppose?"

"Or patriotism, just maybe. Chayka is a Ukrainian and Ukraine is now independent but seriously threatened by Russia. Keeping a few nukes could be handy for future negotiatios. And Vasnetsov is unhappy about Mother Russia being humiliated and the type to dream about military coups."

"Hard to divide three nukes in half ... They can't both get what they want."

"Yes. I don't think it's going to be a long-lasting partnership."

Magda came back into the room. "Three things. First, nobody at Engels – including the 12th Directorate and the UN observers – is aware of any missing fissile material. They expected one-hundred and nine plutonium spheres and that's what they got.

"Second, Weiss's death is being treated as an unfortunate accident. Apparently, it's pretty common for the Russians to implant an explosive device in top-secret files when they are being physically transported by couriers."

I said, "So Chayka and Vasnetsov can rest easy. Their scam worked to perfection."

Schmidt said, "Except for one thing."

Yes, there's that. "Except for me. I know there are three missing weapons."

*I think," said Schmidt with a thoughtful expression, "that it's a good thing you left when you did."

"Why did you pull me out early?" *The message was clear: Leave now.*

He ignored me and looked at Magda. "You said three things. What's the third?"

She said, "Both Chayka and Vasnetsov left Engels three hours ago. Each of them had arranged a week's leave, beginning when they handed off the warheads at Engels."

St. Petersburg

"Mikhail!"

That's me! But it was the irritation in her voice and her persistent pulling on my arm rather than my pretend name that finally penetrated my vodka-soaked brain. *You're supposed to recognize your own name. You're Michael Popov – Mikhail to a Russian.*

Schmidt told me, "Popov is like Jones for an American, so common that people won't bother to ask you if you're related to so-and-so."

For the first time since Schmidt had walked into my life, I felt like a real spy, operating behind the lines with an assumed name and identity and all of the forged papers to support the story. Anybody looking through the official records would find that I was born in Seattle, but of Russian parents. I had an undergrad degree from the University of Washington, an MBA from Wharton and had spent the last five years on Wall Street, working for Merrill Lynch and helping medium-sized companies raise money. I had returned to the homeland when the wall came down, mostly because I thought I could get filthy rich faster in Russia than I could in New York.

I even wore a disguise. Schmidt thought it prudent, given that I had spent some time in Russia and therefore incurred the risk that I would meet someone who had met me. So I grew a beard and wore some clear eyeglasses. It wasn't much but at least when I looked in the mirror during the first week or so I was startled by my reflection.

Schmidt, as usual, had an ulterior motive. "If either Chayka or Vasnetsov want to resume their ordinary life again, you're a danger to them. You're safer with a new identity and a new address." So I was Mikhail Popov, a bright-eyed American capitalist off to Russia to advise ex-Communists on the finer points of market-based economies.

"Your immediate target is a lawyer named Arkady Mikulin. He is a primary legal advisor to a thug named Oleg Petrykin who is of interest to us."

He handed me a thick envelope. "Here's your passport, visa and some supporting material that shows your deep roots in the Russian community in Seattle. You've got reservations for a week at the Kempinski Hotel in the middle of St. Petersburg."

"And what's my rationale for approaching Mikulin?"

He grimaced very slightly. "Don't worry. You'll get a personal introduction. It's all arranged."

Arranged was a bit of an overstatement. The day after I arrived, I was sitting in the lobby bar reading the Herald Tribune when a hand rested on my shoulder and a familiar voice said, "Michael, is that really you?" even as her fingernails dug painfully into my skin.

I turned around to see Magda smiling uncertainly. The hand that was not digging into my shoulder was entwined with that of a slender dark-haired man dressed like he had just stepped off the cover of GQ magazine. "It is you!" she exclaimed brightly and threw herself at me. In close, she whispered, "Be careful with him. I'm Magda. We met briefly at a party in Seattle."

When she stepped back, her smile was now confident and she switched to Russian. "You remember, surely? Seattle … two years ago. We wound up in that overpriced bar after some forgettable concert … You were with my friend Melanie …"

It was easy for me to look surprised. I was. "It's Magda, isn't it? And yes, I do remember. But –"

"Isn't the world such a small place!" She turned to the man with her who was standing slightly to the side with an uncertain smile of his own and she tugged his hand to pull him closer. "This is Arkady Mikulin. He's been showing me this wonderful city. Arkady, this is someone from my past life … Michael … or Mikhail since we're in Russia …."

Mikulin extended his right hand to me while at the same time putting his left arm around Magda and pulling her close in against him. It clearly established that, old friend or not, Magda belonged to him, not me, in every sense of the word. And she reaffirmed his rights by smiling up at him with an expression of pride in her very own alpha male.

She is really good at this. This was the first time I had seen Magda in action and I was impressed and jealous all in the same moment. Somewhere in my back brain, I also recognized that, by watching this, I was forfeiting yet another piece of my already tenuous claim on her.

Mikulin's smile was warm and genuine. "I'm pleased to meet you, Mikhail. Please, won't you join us for a drink?"

'A drink' became dinner, and then we were back in the bar, although this time in a very secluded corner and with a very attentive, young and scantily-clad waitress hovering nearby. Over the course of the evening, it became quite clear that Arkady was a well-known and valued customer at the Kempinski Hotel.

He was quiet at first, saying "You two need to catch up with one another. Don't mind me." But he kept Magda close to him and he seemed to pay close attention to what she and I said to one another. She rattled on at first, all about herself and what she'd been doing. Beneath it all, she was telling me that she was operating within her longstanding cover as an advisor to NGO's and that all we had in common as far as our little charade with Mikulin was that one brief meeting in Seattle.

That was a relief, but I couldn't help resenting Schmidt. *He could have told me Magda would be the link to Mikulin so that I didn't have to worry about how to back up her story.*

"So that's why I'm here … trying to set up a cultural exchange arrangement between Russian arts agencies and their counterparts in the U.S. And that's how I met Arkady. He's some kind of civic VIP in St. Petersburg and offered to help."

Mikulin shrugged, "All I've done is set up a few meetings. And I'm not a VIP, but I know people who are." He made a slight motion of his hand and the waitress appeared with an elegant crystal decanter and topped off our slender glasses of vodka. I think it was the fourth refill, but I was no longer quite sure.

"What about you, Mikhail?   Why are you in St. Petersburg?" It was a perfectly natural question.

"Actually, I'm here as a tourist.   From Moscow. I've never been to Russia and everyone – no matter where they're from – tells me that I have to see St. Petersburg while I'm in the country. So I came up from Moscow for a week."

"And those people you talked to are right about St Petersburg. It is one of the world's truly great cities. But what are you doing in Moscow?" He slurred his words very slightly. It was the first sign that the wine and vodka might have had some effect and it made me wonder about my own condition. *Not a good idea to try to match Russians drink for drink.*

I gave him the minimalist version, the kind of response that one would use for a casual, one-time encounter late at night in a bar. "I thought that my investment-banking experience might be put to better use in Russia than in New York City. So I wangled a three-month posting with the European Bank for Reconstruction and Development in their Moscow office. I start next week."

Magda asked, "Will you stay? In Russia?"

Before I could answer, Mikulin said, "A western-trained investment banker who speaks fluent Russian and may have some of his ancestors buried in the tundra? I think you will have many opportunities. Tell me, who are you working for at the EBRD?"

Another perfectly natural question. No reason to think he's testing my story. "An EVP named Neil Grossman. He's the —"

"Managing Director for Eastern Europe. I know him. He's ex-Goldman Sachs, isn't he? I hear that he plays in a jazz band every weekend."

Magda was looking at me and shaking her head very slightly. And I knew why. "Actually, his last position was at Lehman Brothers, and his music gig is country western." I made it sound apologetic, the way one would sound if slightly embarrassed about correcting his host in a foreign city. He waved it off, saying, "Country western! Even worse. Musically speaking."

An hour later, we were in yet another bar, this one apparently a private club. It was very dark and the tables were separated by high moveable partitions covered in tapestry-like materials. There were five or six parties in the room, each occupied by a pair or quartet consisting of well-dressed middle-aged men and younger, quite attractive women. As before, we were attended by a very attentive and beautiful hostess.

The alcohol was definitely showing now, for all three of us. Magda had a lopsided smile and had mostly dropped out of the conversation. Arkady was doing most of the talking, and he made no attempt to disguise his contempt for the ordinary Russian people.

"They are sheep!" He said loudly. "They wait for somebody with a brain to tell them what to do. Then they do it. Badly!"

I ventured, "But times are changing. You'll have free markets instead of five year plans, multiple political parties, more choices ..."

He wagged his finger at me, almost tipping over the candlestick in the center of our table. "Mikhail, Mikhail! You have Russian blood, but you are an American. You think that you have 'defeated' communism ... like winning the World Cup in football or the most gold medals in the Olympic games!" He poked the same finger into Magda's bare shoulder, including her in his complaint. "You Americans come here with your bankers and your consultants to teach us how to be like you. Like Napoleon and Hitler with their armies ..."

He leaned forward over the small table and I thought he was going to lay his head down on the table. I said, "Arkady, it isn't just your Soviet economic system that suffered a cataclysmic failure. Your *political* system also failed. The communist ideals of Marx and Engels got turned into a totalitarian state. It ran for seventy years, but it didn't work! Russia is seriously fucked up."

That made him sit up straight. "And you think ... what? That *democracy* will take its place? That *the people* will decide the big questions?" He paused, as though to let the thick sarcasm dissipate. "Joseph Stalin said, 'Those who vote decide nothing. Those who count the vote decide everything.' Right now, there is a void. Yeltsin is a drunk and a buffoon, the Politburo is a collection of provincial clowns, and the Central Committee is paralyzed."

Magda waved her arm in a grand gesture, "So we shall have chaos for a while."

It's been more than twelve years since the three of us were in that dark room arguing about the future of Russia, but what Arkady said next proved him to be a better predictor of what would happen than all of the learned professors and pundits stacked end-to-end.

He leaned forward again and put one hand on Magda's arm and the other on mine. We looked like a classic trio of conspirators and he even spoke in hushed tones. "To outsiders, it will look like chaos, yes. But all that matters for the next year is who gains control of the state-owned assets, particularly the natural resources. The winners will run the country for the next fifty years. And there are only two groups in Russia capable of exercising any rational form of power: the intelligence service and the mafia. They are the ones who will run the new Russia."

I don't remember much after that. Until the repeated "Mikhail! Wake up!" got through to me. It was Magda and she was pulling on my arm. "Wake up and get dressed. Arkady wants you to meet Oleg Petrykin."

Oligarch

It was only a few minutes walk from the Kempinski to the Hermitage Museum and the adjacent Winter Palace Gardens. We strolled, indistinguishable from the many other couples enjoying the warm air and the greenery, and I had a sudden intense sadness come over me. *This is what it's like for normal people.*

The thought lasted only a few seconds, until Magda gripped my arm and spoke softly. "Arkady Mikulin is … was … KGB, part of the counter-intelligence group assigned to East Germany and the rest of Western Europe. He was high enough up that he was forcibly retired when the KGB's coup attempt against Gorbachev failed. But he's been posted outside of Russia for the last few years, so he wasn't directly implicated."

"I'm surprised he talked so freely."

"A toxic combination of bitterness, booze and disillusionment. And I think he liked you." After a few more steps, she added, "And he trusts me." She sounded sad and I wondered again about the price she had paid for that degree of trust. After a bit, she went on. "It's like the whole country is suffering from a massive post-traumatic stress disorder. Some – like Arkady – are angry and bitter, but most of them are just plain scared. None of the old rules apply anymore."

"So what about Arkady? What's he do now?"

"It's like he said. He knows people that know people. It's a far more valuable form of currency these days than the miserable ruble.   And one of the people he knows is Oleg Petrykin."

"Tell me about Oleg."

"The two most important things you need to know about him are that he's a gangster and that he wants to control the port of St. Petersburg."

There's also a third factor. Schmidt wants him for his own pet oligarch!

"The port? That's a bit ambitious, isn't it? It's by far the largest seaport in Russia and a huge part of their economy. Will it be privatized?"

"Not a chance. Even in capitalist companies, the ports – the real estate and waterways -- are owned by the government, either local or federal.   But everything else will be up for grabs ... stevedoring, warehousing, servicing ships, tugboat operations ... And that's a lot of stuff."

"You said 'gangster.' What kind?"

Magda smiled at me.   "Think Jimmy Hoffa, only meaner and with fewer lawyers."

Hoffa ran the Teamster's union like his private piggy bank until he got crosswise of the wrong prople.   Rumor has it that he's buried in twenty tons of concrete somewhere in a Detroit construction project. "So, our Oleg, he's a labor kind of guy."

"Nobody works on the docks and no cargo gets loaded or unloaded without Oleg's approval. He's lived quite well off of the bribes."

"And the communist bosses tolerated that?"

"They share in the bribes. Corruption is a way of life in the Soviet Union. It was that way under communism and it's not going to suddenly go away. It's as much a part of their culture as vodka and borscht."

"So when do we meet him?"

"In about thirty seconds." She pointed to a large black car that was just then stopping on the Admiraleyskiy Prospekt, about a hundred feet from where we were sitting on our stone bench. It was a Chaika, one of the large executive-type cars favored for parades and ferrying communist bigwigs from home to office. I stood up and waited for her to join me, but she said, "You're on your own. Arkady doesn't include me in his business meetings."

I started for the car, but she stopped me. "Be careful with Petrykin. He's easy to underestimate and the so-called rule of law gets applied very selectively in this part of the world."

Arkady got out and opened the rear door for me. He nodded to me and then at the man in the rear seat. "This is Oleg Petrykin." The car started moving as soon as Arkady and I were in.

The man was short, perhaps five-and-a-half feet tall and quite stocky. I realized Magda hadn't been kidding; he even looked like Jimmy Hoffa ... broad features, dark hair combed straight back, and an aura of belligerence that seemed to fill the space around him. He was wearing dark slacks, a white shirt and a black seaman's coat.

We shook hands and he squeezed hard enough that it was painful. His skin was rough, the hand of someone who was familiar with manual labor.

"Arkady tells me that you are a finance person."

His Russian has the cadence and tones of rural Russia. Maybe he won't quote Pushkin to me. He and Arkady make a strange pair.

"Yes, an investment banker."

"And an American."

It was not a question and something about the way he said the words made it clear that it was important to him.

"Yes, but my parents were Russian. From somewhere in the east."

He looked at me very closely, perhaps to check for Slavic features that would confirm my ancestry. "Arkady tells me that there are many western companies that want to make investments in the new Russia. Do you know of them?"

I looked at Arkady, but he just smiled blandly at me. I said, "Yes, there is a lot of interest, but –"

"Good. We shall talk about that."

We drove in silence for the next twenty minutes, staying on the southern bank of the Neva River and finally stopping at a restaurant that overlooked a stretch of the riverbank where five or six very rusty barges were lined up against the concrete seawall. All of the tables were empty except one, where an unhappy-looking man sat drinking coffee. Petrykin led the way to a back room where a table had been set for four. A bottle of vodka and a large platter with a variety of breads, cheeses and sandwich meats was in the center of the table.

As soon as we were seated, Petrykin poured vodka for the three of us, immediately drank his in the Russian style and refilled his glass. Then he started making himself a sandwich. He did not take off his coat.

"I have formed a joint-stock company. There are one-hundred thousand shares and I am the only shareholder. Arkady says that this will be a 'holding company,' to be used for buying more companies." He took a very large bite out of his sandwich.

A corporation. Very capitalistic. "That sounds like a good idea. It is a common structure for making investments. What will you do next?"

He seemed puzzled by the question. Arkady came to his aid. "Mr. Petrykin – Oleg – does not own any tangible assets. Up until now, his business has been strictly services ... as a broker or agent for others. In the Soviet system, there were many such small enterprises and I have advised him to consolidate – you would say, 'roll up' -- some of these within his new joint-stock company, particularly those enterprises engaged in operations within the Port of St. Petersburg."

It was my turn to be puzzled. "And he wants me to advise him on how to do that?"

Petrykin laughed out loud and Arkady looked at him, annoyed. "No, he knows how to do that. And I also have some expertise in that area.   But he thought you should see how the process works, so that you can properly advise him on subsequent transactions with western companies."

At that, Petrykin called out, 'Boris!' and a fourth man entered the room. He was the one who'd been drinking coffee in the outer room, looking both then and now like a man who would much rather be somewhere else. He was perhaps fifty years old, dressed like a laborer and weathered, like someone who spent most of his life outdoors. He looked even unhappier than when he'd been sitting by himself in the outer room, but he sat down and promptly drank the vodka that was poured for him.

Petrykin said to me, "This is Boris. Perhaps you saw the barges moored at the levee across the road? Boris operates and apparently is about to own a dozen such vessels for the Port. They transport goods along the Neva, using tugboats for propulsion. I say he 'apparently' owns them because he has operated them for many years and the state committee that manages the Port of St. Petersburg has awarded him the rights to bid on the contract for barge operations in the Port ...." He looked at Arkady. "They call it ...."

"The right of first refusal," Arkady said.

"Such an elegant phrase," said Petrykin, "and so un-Russian, the idea that one has the right to refuse."

He poured the vodka once more and then turned to Boris, who looked progressively unhappier as he sat listening to Petrykin's liitle speech. "So, Boris, I would like to buy your right of first refusal. I will give you five hundred shares in my new company. You will be a wealthy capitalist."

As he spoke, Arkady slid a single sheet of paper into place in front of Boris and placed a pen on top of the paper.

Boris had not lifted his eyes from the tabletop since he came in, but now he raised his head and looked directly at Petrykin with a mixture of fear, defiance and uncertainty. I felt sorry for him. Petrykin's offer of five hundred shares was an insult and everybody in the room knew it.

Petrykin raised his glass. "Shall we drink to that, Boris?"

Boris swallowed and looked at his vodka glass as if it could tell him a safe response. But he did not reach out for the glass. "Thank you for your offer, Mr. Petrykin, but the authorities have set the price of the barges very low and will allow me to pay them out of the proceeds from the contract. So I shall buy their barges and do what I have always done for the last thirty years – transport goods from the ships to the towns along the Neva."

It was a long and obviously rehearsed answer to a question he had clearly anticipated. He stood up and turned to leave, but Petrykin said, "Sit down, Boris. Perhaps I can make my offer more appealing to you." Boris did sit back down, but his reluctance was like a flashing red light.

"Here's the rest of my offer, Boris." Petrykin reached behind him and under his coat, pulled out a large black revolver and placed it gently on the table between the two of them. "For your right of first refusal, I offer you five hundred shares and my promise that I will not kill you."

Boris was gone and the signed piece of paper was back in Arkady's briefcase. Petrykin had also left. He was in a very good mood, partly because of the vodka, I think, but also because this one small venture into the world of capitalism had gone so well.

His parting words were, "Next, I think, Vadim's three ocean-going tugboats. I have heard that he has obtained the same kind of offer from the authorities. I shall leave you two to the working out of details."

Arkady and I sat in silence until I finally asked, "Would he shoot Boris? If he had not signed?" *And why did he want me there to watch his little psychodrama?*

I was relieved when Arkady said, "No. Oleg doesn't shoot people anymore." But he went on, "He has other people that do that for him, and I think they prefer knives, not guns."

"And Boris, or Vadim with his tugboats ... they have no recourse?"

"You mean, like the police?" His sarcasm was so thick that it was a complete answer to his own question.

"Arkady, this was very ... instructive. But you don't need me ... or any kind of financial expertise ... for this kind of ... consolidation."

He shrugged. "As you Americans say, Boris and Vadim are 'little potatoes.' Oleg can play this same game fifty times in the next two weeks and the outcome will be the same. But he is smart enough to know that there are two areas where he does need help."

I waited. "The first is money.   Yeltsin and his economists are moving very fast to privatize state industries, but they will try to get a good price because the Federal government needs the cash.   They have what they call the "Loans for Shares" program. Certain bidders – like Boris -- will be favored but they will need to have some cash in hand, even if they're only buying a few barges or tugboats."

"So," I said, "Oleg needs to use his new joint-stock company to raise some capital.   Probably from European or American institutions ... from people that won't be impressed by a revolver on the table. What's the other area where he needs help?"

"It's related to the money.   Russian companies – especially the state-owned ones – need western expertise. Many of them, perhaps most, will collapse if left to market forces. Privatization is not enough; they need modernization."

I know where this is going. And so did Schmidt when he concocted my cover. He is not content with turning a few mid-level bureaucrats into doubles; he wants his own oligarch! A person with deep roots in the Kremlin hierarchy.

My role in this conversation was as clear as if I was reading from a script. I said, "There are a lot of western firms that would love to get a foothold in the Russian market ... Oleg could probably find somebody who has both the money and the expertise."

He nodded. "And they'll need a readymade Russian partner."

Magda warned me to be careful. Arkady is smart and ex-KGB. Maybe not so 'ex' as he lets on. And they put on this little drama with Boris to make a point. What would he expect a naïve American banker with a 'get rich quick' mentality to say at this point?

"Uh, Arkady …"

He looked at me expectantly. I continued, trying to sound like a slightly fearful advisor. "Your western investors looking for Russian partners? They'll expect to pay a premium but Oleg will have to give up something … a lot more than a few hundred shares. And those first investors will expect to have a major role in the direction of the company." I did not say what we both knew: that a revolver on the table would not work as a negotiating tactic.

Arkady's response was perfectly bland. "Of course. He knows that."

Magda had described him as 'forcibly retired' from the KGB, but Arkady demonstrated that his claim that 'he knew people who knew people' was quite genuine. He slid a manila envelope across the table. It was about an inch thick. "Here are two lists. The first is a list of all of the operations in the Port of St. Petersburg that the Port Authority deems to be eligible for privatization, along with those individuals they deem to be 'preferred' bidders, who shall be given this 'right of first refusal.' The second list is from a source within Yeltsin's council of economists. It has the names of two-hundred and twelve western firms who have already expressed 'a strong interest' in making equity investments in the new Russia. I've highlighted the ones that have a maritime emphasis."

I looked at him, impressed. And I didn't have to fake it. I held up the envelope. "This puts you – and Oleg – way ahead of the competition. It's a road map for his new company ... sort of a 'this way to a billion dollars' kind of document. What do you want me to do with it?"

He shrugged, but was watching me closely. "Tell us which firms to approach and what we need to offer them."

I paused just long enough to establish that I was weighing options. Then I said, "I can do that" in my best investment banker voice.

He said, "Good. But there is one important limitation: No American-owned companies will be considered."

I frowned. "You'll exclude some really good candidates. Why such a restriction?"

"For a reason that has nothing to do with high finance. Oleg had two sons. They were both killed in Afghanistan in 1985, by the mujahedeen. They were on a Russian Mi-24 gunship that was brought down by a stinger missile supplied by the American CIA."

I stood up. With the envelope. "OK, let me look at this, and then we'll talk."

"The driver's outside and will take you back to your hotel. I'll pick you up at ten on Tuesday."

I was almost outside the door when he called out, "And Mikhail?" When I stopped and looked back, he pointed at the now-empty tabletop and said, "Remember the revolver."

Reunion

"We lost Benjamin."

Immediately, wild thoughts and visions of Arthur in his shallow grave and Roger staring at me with his dead eyes ran around in my head. I sat bolt upright and said, "No!" very loudly.

Riley held up his hand and said, "Not in that way, Mahoney. Schmidt told me that Benjamin's taken a job with the Reconstruction Fund. He'll be evaluating and managing projects on the eastern side of the Urals."

Peter expressed the skepticism that all of us were feeling. "Is it a real job, not just a new cover story for his intelligence role?"

Riley shook his head. "Schmidt says no, that Benjamin is tired of the game and wants out."

Magda said, "I believe him for once. Benjamin got what he wanted. In more ways than one. No reason to stay." When the three of us turned to look at her, she said, "He hated the Soviet system. Not like us. For him it truly was an evil empire. When it collapsed, he was like the dog who finally caught the car ... he didn't know what to do with it."

"And he's probably getting salary and options close to a million bucks a year," I added. One of the things I'd learned in the last few months was the compensation structures of the so-called 'country funds' that had sprouted to invest money in the ex-Soviet states. The Reconstruction Fund was one of the more aggressive ones in the market and I knew that Benjamin, with his vast knowledge of Russia, would be invaluable to them.

My million-dollar comment clearly startled my four companions. I don't think that any of the five of us had ever thought about money very much. We spent what we needed to and sent expense reports to Schmidt, who always deposited the money in our accounts without asking questions. We were like perpetual teenagers with unlimited access to their parent's credit card.

It was the first time since Helsinki that Riley, Magda, Peter. Alex and I were all in the same room at the same time. Schmidt was there when we arrived but left after ten minutes.

He told us, "You're all working in St. Petersburg. I think each of you needs to be aware of what the others are doing. Broad outlines only, just in case you cross paths. Mahoney – new name Mikhail – is the only one of you operating outside of your normal cover story."

He left the room, leaving the five of us to look at one another and figure out what he had in mind. Riley, however, started with his "we lost Benjamin" comment and I wondered if Schmidt had delegated him to pass on the news.

As always, Magda took the lead. "OK, Schmidt wants us to play 'Show and Tell,' so I'll start. I've formed a close relationship with Arkady Mikulin, an ex-KGB officer who is close to several potential future bosses who may emerge once the political dust settles."

She looked at me, obviously expecting that I would mention Petrygin. But before I could say anything,

Riley said, half under his breath, "You're very good at forming *close relationships.*"

The atmosphere in the room changed instantaneously. Not because we were surprised; everyone knew what Magda did and how she did it. But Riley's *disapproval* of what she did was new. And surprising. I wondered if the others knew of their on-again, off-again affair.

I spoke next, louder than was required. "Magda's introduced me to Mikulin, who in turn got me involved with a mafia type named Oleg Petrykin. I'm advising him on how to form an alliance with a deep-pockets western company."

Peter was sitting to my right, so he went next. "These so-called potential future bosses that Magda mentioned? They're going to need a safe place to stash all the money they're about to steal. It's called capital flight. I'm trying to follow the money. From St. Petersburg to Switzerland, London, Dubai, Panama or wherever it winds up."

Alex's turn. "OK, I'm an arts contractor working on cataloging the Hermitage art collection in St. Petersburg. It's one of the largest in the entire world, but they're not even sure of what they've got because the communists did not disclose that they looted Nazi Germany in 1945 and brought to St. Petersburg a lot of major works from German private collections. Degas, Van Gogh, Renoir, Monet ...."

Magda said, "What you're doing ... it sounds almost legitimate."

"It could be, but Schmidt thinks – and I agree – that some of the really good stuff will disappear into private collections in the new Russia. My assignment is to identify the new owners."

"But not to blow the whistle on them," she said.

"Nope. They can loot all they want, and they will. Schmidt just wants to know who they are and what they've got."

I said, "Peter's following the money; you're following the art."

Riley said what we were all thinking. "It's not just tracing the stuff. You're in a position to *facilitate* such disappearances ... to those particular oligarchs that Schmidt finds to be deserving, aren't you?"

Peter said nothing. After thirty seconds of uncomfortable silence, Alex asked, "Why are you in St. Petersburg, Riley?"

All eyes turned to Riley. He said nothing, just sat on the sofa with his legs crossed and a smile on his face that slowly changed from amused to irritated. "I wish I knew. He's got me sitting in an office, writing 'position papers' on 'market-based strategies for state enterprises.' I seem to be waiting for a higher purpose to reveal itself ... perhaps for a *close relationship* with an important source perhaps." He looked directly at Magda.

She came back to my hotel room with me. She didn't talk and 'making love' was not what we did that night. It was savage rutting, as primeval as consensual rape. I was a male who was not Riley and that's all that she needed from me. She left before dawn. Her note, propped against the bathroom mirror, said simply, "I'm sorry."

Strategic Alliance

Six months later, Oleg Petrykin's new joint-stock company was thriving. He'd titled it OPCo Ltd, the 'OP' based on his initials. When I suggested that he should change it because western companies used "OpCo" as a shorthand placeholder for "operating company" in their valuation models for mergers and acquisitions, he liked it even better. "All those bright young analysts with their spreadsheets filled with equations ... my company's name will be already preloaded!"

I put together a PowerPoint presentation in English and Russian that made OPCo Ltd. look like the Russian equivalent of a Silicon Valley startup. A leading western law firm with a brand-new office in St. Petersburg endorsed it and we sprinkled half-a-dozen endorsements from city and port officials attesting to its outstanding service levels.

By now, the organization chart listed a dozen subsidiaries. They included the Neva Barge Co. and Baltic Marine Tow Services and I thought of Boris and Vadim every time I looked at the chart. I had advised them to revise the ownership structure to be more appealing to western investors and Oleg Petrykin's name no longer appeared on any document related to the company. The 'official' owner was Arkady Mikulin, with several Russian shell companies as minority partners.

I was meeting with Dutch, British, Swedish, German and French companies and investment firms. Each of them owned companies engaged in some aspect of shipping or port operations and were eager for a foothold in Russia. I was meeting weekly with Arkady and Oleg to review the candidates. They did not know, of course, that I was also reviewing the list with Schmidt. He didn't tell me whom *he* was consulting with. We'd been through a dozen plausible candidates before he said, "This one. Put this one in front of Oleg."

So I called Arkady. "It's time to talk to a potential partner." Three days later, five of us met in a conference room at the Kempinski.

Hans Yunger was the Chief Executive Officer of Northern Maritime Services, a private Dutch corporation that was the single largest port operator in Scandinavia and the North Atlantic. He had worked his way up from a stevedore to CEO and claimed to know every shipping executive in the Northern hemisphere. He brought along Alexei Petrov, a partner in a Moscow law firm that represented their interests in Russia.

The two men were a contrast in almost every dimension. Yunger still looked like a stevedore. He was bulky and his suit didn't fit very well, a reality that did not seem to concern him very much. Petrov, however, could have passed as a successful financier in London or New York.

Arkady had brought Oleg to the meeting. I had advised him not to do that, but he said, "I don't tell Oleg what he can or cannot do. No one does." He introduced Oleg as "one of our minority investors and a businessman who knows every aspect of the St. Petersburg port."

Petrykin and Yunger are alike. They both started on the docks and made it all the way to the top of the heap. I wonder if that's a good thing?

Yunger did not speak Russian, so we agreed on English, with Arkady translating for Oleg as required. I went through the PowerPoint slides quickly, knowing that Petrov and Yunger would have done their own research. I also knew that there was very little for them to discover. OPCo was too new and the dozen acquisitions of the last six months had all been quiet 'agreements' between Petrykin and hapless sellers like Boris. In any case, the quality of economic data in Russia was laughable; there was no history, no market data, no audited financials. It was the Wild West of international finance.

The other thing I knew was that Yunger had a serious reputation as a risk-taker. He had built Northern Maritime Services into a billion dollar company by making deals that his peers called 'crazy,' but – with hindsight – turned out brilliantly. He was like a Texas wildcatter on a roll, and Russia was his next big play.

When I finished the presentation, Yunger spoke up immediately. "Very smooth, Mr. Popov. You make Mr. Mikulin's company look very attractive for an outside investor. But I'm Dutch, so your slides remind me of a joke." He paused and then asked, "Why do girls put on makeup and perfume?" He paused and waited for Arkady to translate. "Because they're ugly and they stink."

It was a startlingly offensive line and both Mikulin and Petrykin frowned and sat up a little straighter. Petrov reacted even more strongly, like a man receiving an electric shock. But Yunger went on. "The truth is that *nobody* sitting in this room knows what your company is worth or even if Russia will allow private enterprise to exist once the honeymoon is over.   But what I do know is that you need capital and I need access to your port."

Arkady began, "Mr. Yunger, I respectfully –"

He was cut off by Yunger. "I have a formal offer." He nodded to Petrov, who referred to a single sheet of paper in front of him and began speaking in Russian. He spoke directly to Petrykin, with only an occasional glance at Arkady. *They know who the real decision maker is!*

"Our offer has six key parts.   Mr. Yunger has instructed me that the terms are non-negotiable and that his offer expires in twenty-four hours, which is how long he expects to be in your city."

"Northern Marine Services will invest fifty million dollars in return for forty-nine percent of the voting shares of OPCo and two of the five board seats.

"All board decisions shall require the approval of at least two thirds of the directors.

"The fifty million dollars will be spent to acquire either physical assets or long term service contracts from the Port of St. Petersburg. There shall be no distributions to existing shareholders.

"An executive from Northern Marine Services will be appointed as an Executive Vice President of OPCo and will direct port operations.

"Additional staff from Northern Marine Services will be provided as required for advice and modernization of port facilities.

"This offer is contingent on OPCo obtaining the right to buy the First Container Terminal, currently owned by the Port of St. Petersburg, or the exclusive rights to operate the Terminal for at least a ten year period."

Both Arkady and I were writing notes, but Petrykin sat quietly, looking at Yunger the entire time. When Petrov stopped his recitation, Arkady said, "Let's break so that the three of us representing OPCo can discuss your offer."

Yunger shrugged and stood up. "I have a room in the hotel. Call when – or if -- you would like to reconvene."

When the two men left, Arkady and I looked at Petrykin, trying to get a reading on where he wanted to go with this. He finally said, "I like him. He's like me."

I said, "Yes, he is. But he doesn't have a revolver to put on the table." As soon as the words were uttered, I thought, *That's provocative!* But Oleg surprised me. He said, "A man with fifty million dollars doesn't need a revolver."

Petrykin turned to me. "So Mikhail. We need your advice now. Is this a good offer?"

This is whom Schmidt wants, so I should be positive. But I can't squander my credibility with Petrykin ...

"I think it's a *genuine* offer. But we have nothing to compare it to –"

"The fifty million. For forty-nine percent. Is that a good price?"

That's easy to answer. "It surprised me. As he said, nobody really knows what OPCo is worth, but I don't think you'll get another offer anywhere close to that amount. Yunger clearly views this as a preemptive bid and I believe he is serious about his twenty-four hour deadline."

"This forty-nine percent share ... that means that they will have the largest single share, but that they can be overruled by the fifty-one percent group?"

"Yes, and by the other three board members since they are a majority of the board. This is standard business practice in the capitalist world. So you" – here, I spoke to Arkady, but was looking at Oleg – "will still have final control."

Arkady said, "Yunger is very clever. With three board seats, we have the majority. But remember the other clause: it requires a *two-third's* majority vote for major decisions. We have sixty percent, not two-thirds. That means that one of the two other board members would have to vote with us."

Petrykin looked slightly puzzled and I thought I knew why. "Oleg, in their world, it is the law that all shareholders must be treated equally. It is illegal to discriminate. For example, if you pay a dividend to one shareholder, you must pay the same amount to all shareholders."

He waved his hand as though to dismiss the idea that he would behave otherwise. "But of course!"

"The contingency?" I asked. "The contract for container operations in the port? Will that be a problem?"

He looked at Arkady, who nodded at him in response. Oleg said, "Yunger knows his business. Five years from now, most of the real value will be from container ships. And no, Arkady assures me that's not a problem."

Arkady said, "I can get us a ten year non-cancellable operating agreement with an option to buy at the end of the ten years."

The First Container Terminal is on the list of state assets to be privatized. Arkady must already have the right of first refusal in his pocket, and for a sweetheart price as well.

"OK," I said. "Shall I call Yunger?"

Once we were all back at the conference table, Petrov presented a single sheet of paper for Arkady and Yunger to sign. He and I witnessed the signatures. Oleg took five glasses and the decanter from the credenza, poured the vodka and said, "A toast to OPCo, and to Mother Russia!"

We drank, but an awkward silence set in, exacerbated by the way that Petrov was staring at Petrykin, not in a friendly way. "I know you, Oleg Petrykin. You are an important man in St. Petersburg."

Petrykin bowed slightly. "That was then. A time when the communist party was important ... a time for bosses. Now we shall have the rule of law."

"The rule of law. I wonder." Petrov continued to stare. "Just how big is your minority share in OPCo?"

"Not worth mentioning. I think I own ten percent of a company that owns ten percent of OPCo. That's –"

"One percent," Arkady said, "in return for his management advice ... and connections. Mr. Popov here " – he pointed at me – "has the same percentage."

I kept my expression bland, but that was the first time I'd been told that I was part of the byzantine financial structure that Arkady had cobbled together.

Petrov turned to Arkady. "Mr. Yunger has notified me that I shall be one of the two board members he shall appoint for OPCo. I am looking forward to that opportunity, but ..."

When the hesitation continued, Arkady prompted, "But ...

"But ... I am concerned that the Port of St. Petersburg in its present form may be under the control of ... criminal elements. We must be sure that such undesirables are not involved in your operations. They do not fit with the society and economic system that is emerging."

Arkady started to speak, but Petrykin put a hand on his forearm to stop him. "You, Petrov, are from the city ... a place with traffic lights and many rules. I come from out there" -- he waved his arm in a vague arc – "where there are fewer and different rules. Out there, we have a proverb -- 'If you fear the wolves, do not go into the forest.'"

Petrov moved a step closer to Petrykin so that the two men were inches apart. "Proverbs are cheap. Cautionary tales for superstitious babushkas. But since you seem to like them, I shall tell you my favorite: 'There is no law for fools.'"

He did not wait for a response.

Briefing

"Will it work, do you think?"

There was a very slight note of pleading in Schmidt's voice, or maybe it was the way he looked at me, as if he genuinely needed me to reassure him. It was unlike him.

We were in Moscow's Zaryadye Park, standing looking at the onion-shaped domes of St. Basil's Cathedral in the middle distance. It was gray and drizzling, so there were few strollers in sight and the multi-hued domes of St. Basil were muted.

"Will what work?" I asked in response. "The joint venture between Yunger and a new private sector company in Russia? Or your wacky scheme to acquire your own pet billionaire in the new market-oriented Russian economy?"

His look shifted to one of irritation. "Both. Either. I don't think there's any difference between the two initiatives."

"OK. The joint venture deal makes a lot of business sense, *assuming* that all of the players behave honorably. And that includes the entire spectrum of Russian politicians, from Yeltsin on down to the Governor and Mayor of St. Petersburg down to the Port Authority. Not to mention Yunger and Petrykin."

"What do you think the odds are that such ... honorable behavior ... will happen?"

"Close to zero. There's too much money on the table and not enough time or incentives to eradicate the bad old habits."

"So you think it will fail?"

"No, just the opposite. I think the new company will in fact become a dominant business in St. Petersburg, but the manner in which it does that will not be anything like what the liberal reformers envision. And I don't think Yunger will be pleased."

It's a microcosm of the entire Soviet Union. How do you transform a totalitarian, centrally planned state into a democratic and market-driven economy? Yeltsin and his advisors are emphasizing speed and are willing to put up with the inefficiencies that go with it.

Schmidt was silent for a few seconds. Then he asked, "What about Petrykin? Does this help us with him?"

"It will probably make him ungodly rich. How rich depends upon the relationship between him and Arkady. It's an interesting combination – a crime boss and an ex-KGB officer – and I don't think it's very stable."

"What about Petrov?"

"He's an idealist from Moscow, one of those enlightened but naïve Russians who genuinely seeks reform. But neither Petrykin nor Mikulin like him. His only advantage is that Yunger trusts him. He'll be untouchable until OPCo gets firmly established."

"Back to Petrykin. Do we have any leverage after all this high finance stuff?"

I thought about it. "Not much, I think. He seemed to like my advice enough to give me one percent of the shares. But I don't think Mikulin really trusts me and Petrykin will listen to him."

"Magda may be able to influence Mikulin." Schmidt watched me closely as he said it. "And her relationship with him gives her access to Petrykin."

I turned away to hide my sudden anger. It was gone as quickly as it came, leaving me to marvel at my stubbornly simplistic views of the world I had chosen to join. *He told me: "Magda fucks people."*

I said, "There's another problem. He doesn't like Americans." When I told him about Petrykin's sons dying in Russia's occupation of Afghanistan, Schmidt mused, "I didn't know that." And after a short pause, "It could have been me that gave that Stinger missile to the mujahedeen … I was there in the eighties."

It was raining harder now and St. Basil was just an odd-shaped shadow in the gray mists. Schmidt turned to go. "I'm working on another way to get closer to Petrykin. Meet me tomorrow. I've got something else for you to do."

"I want you to go to Vladivostok."

"Why?" Even as I said the word, I was struck by the fact that I had *not* asked, 'what do you want me to do?' *Our relationship has changed.*

He answered with his own question. "What do you know about Vladivostok?"

I started reciting. "Gateway to Russia's Far East. Major port. Closed city until very recently because it was the home of Russia's Pacific Fleet. More Asian than European. Vast natural resources – minerals, timber, fishing. Eastern terminus of Trans-Siberian Railroad. Very far away from Moscow, in a lot of ways."

I stopped, realizing that I didn't really know all that much.

"I have been asked for an assessment of two factors: How receptive is the area to American investment and what is the state of readiness of Russia's Pacific Fleet."

"Those are big questions. It will take some time to develop answers."

He merely nodded.

"Do I go as Mahoney, the journalist, or as Popov, the investment banker?"

"Mahoney, I think. But you will probably need to be Popov every now and then."

The Economist had an article on the Russian Far East. It described Vladivostok as "one of the ugliest cities imaginable, consisting mainly of windswept concrete tower blocks in varying states of decay.   It sprawls across hills overlooking a great sheltered port. It has the Pacific at its feet and the vast natural resources of Russia's Far East at its back. It ought to be humming with trade and investment.   Instead, Vladivostok's reputation for lawlessness and misery makes even hardy Russians wince."

Vlad was in fact six thousand miles and seven time zones distant from Moscow, and major differences arose from that physical separation. I would spend a lot of time there, punctuated by frequent trips to the U.S. and elsewhere to keep my cover as foreign correspondent intact and for other one-off projects that Schmidt came up with.

For the first time in my intelligence career, I developed 'sources' … double agents, traitors, well-placed Russians who would divulge secrets. There were four of them, and I came to know each of them intimately, as though we were identical twins born into an Amish family.

They were easy prey.   America was no longer their archenemy, but their model and benefactor. The KGB with its army of informers was momentarily irrelevant, as unthreatening as the local dogcatcher. The collapse of the Soviet Union and the widespread and simultaneous failures of the defense-based regional economy tipped them into instant poverty, and the social safety net was non-existent. They needed money for the basics of existence.

Ivan Egoshin was sixty and the oldest.   He was a banker for Sberbank, the sprawling government-owned savings bank that – when I met him – was transitioning from federal to state control. He had lost his housing subsidy and his salary had been slashed in the transition. But he had retained his authority to access the banking balances of almost every citizen in the Oblast.

Stepan Fedorin was his social opposite. He was a thirty year-old recent graduate of the Far Eastern University in Vladivostok and had a position with a law firm that was the local representative for Japanese and South Korean companies that were eager to establish a market position in the Russian Far East. He had expensive habits, including cocaine, so that an additional income stream was welcome.

Igor Vankin was the most unlikely traitor. He was a Captain - Third Rank in the Russian Navy, assigned to a Sovremenny-class destroyer sitting idled and rusting in the port. Ordinary sailors on his ship were literally starving to death and Vankin needed funds to keep them from deserting. He was the ultimate true believer. He told me, "We Russians crave authoritarian leaders. We will grow tired of democracy and all of its requirements very quickly and a Stalin lookalike will emerge."

I asked him once, "When will you go to sea again?" His response was, "When Yeltsin is gone, and whoever comes after Yeltsin. By then Russia will have a leader that will respect our greatness and the Red Fleet will be restored." I think that he shared naval secrets with me not just for the money, but in the hope that his acts of calculated treason would accelerate the conflict that he saw both as inevitable and necessary for the rebirth of Russian nationalism.

Svetlana Morozov was a forty-year old woman who lived with her father, a retired naval officer. She worked as an event planner on the staff of Yevgeny Nazdratenko, the newly elected governor of Primorsky Krai. Part of her job was to provide him with sex on demand. She said that my promise of an exit visa to the United States was sufficient motivation for treason, but she also hated Nazdratenko passionately. For me, she was a triple winner. She would repeat the stories that her father told her; mostly complaints about the decline of the Russian military, but also gossip about movements of senior officers and unrest among others. The second and most material benefit was from her association with Nazdratenko. He used her to organize meetings and she passed on to me the contents of those meetings within a few hours.

The third benefit was that she would knock on my hotel room door two or three times a month and crawl into bed with me. I think she mistrusted my promise to get her a visa and viewed the occasional sex as a more binding form of insurance. The sexual encounters were intense but as transactional as if I had left a hundred-dollar bill on her bedside table.

Nobody knew of their status as informants except me, and I told only Schmidt. They provided me with a steady stream of invaluable intelligence on Schmidt's questions about the investment climate and military readiness.

So when the South Korean company Hyundai got tired of the new taxes and bribes being piled on and decided to withdraw from its fifty million dollar business center project, I knew a week before the public announcement. When Weyerhauser was in early-stage discussions about the three-hundred billion cubic feet of timber in the Russian Far East, I knew the problems before they did. When the desertion rate among sailors reached twenty percent, or the reactor on a nuclear submarine was down, I knew

It was Fedorin who said, "Who cares? If there is no state, how can there be any state secrets? If the KGB itself has plotted a failed coup against Yeltsin, they are the traitors, not me. If we are now a market economy, then everything is for sale, including information!"

Svetlana was even clearer: "Nazdratenko is a thug, a corrupt man with an iron fist. He calls Moscow's economics minister a 'blind Bolshevik' and arrests his political opponents. He is a pig, and pigs deserve no loyalty."

The ongoing social dissolution and chaos around me made intelligence gathering seem dull and safe, a crime akin to throwing rocks at windows in a house about to be demolished. It would turn out to be a false sense of security but for a while I felt more like a bartender listening to a patron's woes late at night than I did a lonely defender of U.S. interests in a far off place.

But that was about to change.

Financial Restructuring

I was in Vladivostok when Magda called, standing at the reception desk of the most expensive hotel in the city and experiencing one of those 'only in Russia' kind of encounters that marked their rocky transition to a consumer-oriented society.

I said in English, "My name is Mahoney. I have a reservation for three nights."

The woman on the other side of the counter clicked on her keyboard and said, "Yes, I see that. But we have no rooms." She waved at the person next in line, standing behind me.

I pushed my passport closer. "I have a reservation. I'd like my room now, please."

"We have no rooms."

"But I have a reservation. It's prepaid."

"Yes? I see that you do." She seemed as puzzled as me by the impasse.

"So you need to find me a room. Because I have a reservation."

Predictably, she shifted to a time-honored defensive tactic. "I'm sorry. I don't speak English."

I said in fluent Russian, "It is not necessary that you speak English, only that you find me a room."

"But we have no rooms." Her expression of puzzlement was now one of exasperation.

"May I speak to your manager, please?"

"Of course. Please wait and I'll try to find him." So I sat in a lobby chair, directly in her line of vision. I watched her give room keys to the next two guests to check in. To my surprise, it was only a minute or two after them that she called my name and I returned to the desk.

I said, "That was quick. May I have my key –"

"Oh, we have no rooms. But you have a message." She handed me a note-sized envelope with the hotel slogan on it – 'Customer Satisfaction Guaranteed.' It also had a time stamp from thirty minutes ago.

It was from Magda, saying only "Return to Moscow ASAP. Call me on arrival."

Several new privately owned airlines had come into existence since privatization had begun, so Aeroflot was no longer the only choice for the eight-hour flight to the capital. And the new companies used new Airbus and Boeing aircraft, improving the survivability odds even more.

I was in the Vlad airport waiting for my flight to board. The lounge attendant handed me a glass of champagne and the daily newspaper. The photograph on the front page was grainy and a few years old, but still easily recognized. Alexei Petrov looked out at me with a mournful expression that seemed appropriate given that the accompanying article described his assassination as he was leaving a St. Petersburg nightclub. The writer described him as a 'western-trained lawyer' who 'rumored' to be involved with the mafia.

There was a second photograph of a chalked outline on a sidewalk outside the nightclub. The stick figure reminded me of a prehistoric petroglyph of a running man that I had once seen on the rock wall of a cave.

When I landed at Sheremetyevo Airport in Moscow, there was another message from Magda with a flight number that left two hours later for St. Petersburg. She was already on the plane, in coach, but we ignored one another until she got in my limousine just before it pulled away from the airport in St. Petersburg. She gave the driver an address that I did not recognize.

"We have a meeting with Petrykin."

"I thought I was done with that. Has something gone wrong?"

She didn't answer me right away. "You saw the newspaper? About Petrov?"

"His murder? Yes. There have been quite a number of similar events in the last couple of years. What do you know about it?"

"A Russian form of negotiation."

No surprise. I said, "In America, we'd have a proxy fight. Attack ads in the Wall Street Journal. Lawsuits claiming breach of contract … maybe even a CEO gets fired. But we don't shoot the middlemen."

Magda said, "You were there when the Yunger deal was put together. You know the players. Would Petrykin put out a contract on Petrov?"

OPCo was doing well. The investment by Northern Maritime Services was relatively glitch-free and had worked out well enough that OPCo was the dominant private sector company in the Port. I had seen speculation in the financial press that it was a good candidate for an early offering on the stock exchange. But then there was that parting bit of hostility between Petrov and Petrykin -- that exchange of personal insults disguised as Russian proverbs.

Magda prompted, "Mikhail?"

"If I were betting on who had killed Petrov, my money would be on Petrykin." Then it sunk in. "You called me Mikhail. That's who I was for Mikulin and Petrykin. I can't show up as a reporter named Thomas Mahoney."

She handed me an envelope. "Here are your papers. You get to be Mikhail Popov again for a day. You'll note that you've been at the EBRD in Moscow and then back in Seattle for the last six months." She took a pair of eyeglasses from her purse. "You'll need these. Just say you got tired of the beard and decided to shave."

We drove for another thirty minutes in silence, slowly leaving suburbs behind. "Where are we going?" I asked. "I've never been out of the city proper."

"We're meeting at Petrykin's new estate. He's upgraded his quarters quite a bit since you last saw him."

Ten minutes later, we stopped at a steel gate flanked by a serious stone wall that ran for at least half a mile in both directions. It was opened by some unseen agent and, once through, a cobblestone drive took us several hundred yards to the front of a gigantic house that reminded me of the Winter Palace.

As the car glided to a stop, Magda said, "By the way, Riley will be in the meeting. And you don't know him."

Riley? What the hell is going on?

A young woman was waiting at the foot of the stairs and led Magda and me through a long gallery-like hall lined with oil paintings. One of them was brightly lit and placed at the end of the hall, so that one became more aware of it as he walked. I stopped six feet short of it and stared. "That's a Renoir," I said, but Magda kept walking, turning right and into a parlor that looked like a movie set for the Great Gatsby. Three men were waiting, sitting in large wing chairs so deep that they were mostly in shadow. They were holding brandy snifters and watching us approach – Riley, Arkady Mikulin and Oleg Petrykin. Two identical chairs were vacant, awaiting us.

None of the three stood, so Magda and I simply sat down and waited. Arkady was the first to speak. "Hello Mikhail. I saw you admiring the painting. And yes, it is a Renoir. And you look younger without the beard."

Arkady had gained weight but still wore an elegant perfectly tailored suit. Petrykin looked exactly the same except he'd acquired a different aura. I could not think of a better word to describe the change. Before, he exuded a need to intimidate those around him, a need driven by his own insecurities. Now, he had a *stillness* about him, a man with no need to prove himself to others. I wondered if he still carried a revolver under his coat and thought not.

Riley was himself, ever watchful, with that expression that hinted at some inner sadness.

Arkady inclined his head toward Riley. "This is Riley, a countryman of yours. He's been working with Oleg and myself for the past few weeks. We needed some ... specialized services ... and Magda introduced him to us. Just like you. She's been a very good talent scout for us."

Schmidt said he wanted to get close to Petrykin. Now's he's got three of our group as ... what? ... trusted advisors.

I looked at Magda, wondering what she was feeling. *She's been Riley's occasional lover for almost a decade now, played a part-time role as Arkady's mistress, and climbed into bed with me half-a-dozen times in as many years. Yet xhe looks the same. How can that be?*

All four of them were looking at me and I realized that I was the only one who didn't know the purpose of the meeting. "It's good to see you again, Arkady. And you too, Oleg. I'm following the St. Petersburg news as much as I can, and it looks like your OPCo is doing very well. There are rumors of a public offering in the near future."

Petrykin stood and poured two glasses of brandy from a side table, handing one to Magda and the other to me. When he sat down again, he said, "Yes. Our plans have gone well. OPCo is a proper company and our Dutch partner -- Mr. Yunger -- thinks that he has made a brilliant investment."

That's an interesting phrasing. I think maybe Mr. Yunger should be worried. "Excellent, and my congratulations. But what can I do? Why am I here?"

Petrykin waved his glass at Arkady Mikulin. "We are contemplating some changes in the ownership structure in anticipation of the public offering and would like to get your opinion. Arkady will explain the details."

Arkady leaned forward. "I will give you a quick outline … what you Americans call 'the forty-thousand foot view.' You are an investment banker, so you will appreciate all of the implications."

I sat back in the deep chair and sipped the brandy, still wondering why they needed me for this.

Arkady began, speaking quickly and in recitation tones. "First, OPCo's container division is very different from the other business units, so, for reasons of operational efficiency, we shall spin that off into a separate company. It shall –"

I shall play my assigned role. "Who is the buyer, the new owner of that separate company?"

Arkady smiled. "Officially, a corporation in Malta. But effectively, Oleg Petrykin."

"And what price will the Maltese corporation pay to acquire the spun-off container division?"

The smile intensified. "A fair price, of course. But there is a great deal of uncertainty as to what that is. The real value of the division is our contract with the Port of St. Petersburg, which has only a few years to run."

A classic scam, with a Russian twist. . asset-stripping. OPCo transfers a major asset to Petrykin in return for a token price ... a direct redistribution of wealth from Yunger, the foreign investor, to Petrykin, the silent owner.

"What else?"

"The continuing rationalization of the ownership structure. In its original form, a majority of the shares – fifty-one percent – was held by a number of individuals. For example, I own twenty percent, you and Oleg own one percent each, and another half-dozen Russian corporations own five to six percent each.   It always was a cumbersome arrangement, necessary for starting up, but it needs to change now that OPCo is entirely modernized."

"What do you propose?" I asked, even though I was pretty sure that I knew the broad outlines of what was about to happen.

"Mr. Petrykin has quietly acquired the shares of the other Russian investors, excluding me.   In private transactions." Once more, he smiled, just for me. "At *fair* prices, of course. He now has effective control of thirty-percent of the shares.

"Our plan is to award newly issued shares to five different individuals such that each will own two-percent of OPCo. These individuals are Russians who offer great value to the company in the form of advice and connections."   He paused, expecting me to ask 'who?' but I already knew.

Right out of the corruption playbook. Arkady told me himself: the intelligence agents and the mafia would run the country.   And get wealthy in the process. Petrykin couldn't help himself. He said, "Our advisors and new shareholders are all well-placed politicians.   It is reciprocal. I am on a business council that advises Yeltsin himself."

I thought I now knew why I was invited to this meeting. "So you want to buy my one percent now?" I was picturing the revolver on the tabletop and the way Boris stared at it. "At a *fair* price, of course."

Arkady was clearly amused. "No. In fact, you are one of the individuals we want to have as a two-percent owner. And we want to appoint you as a board member to replace Andrei Petrov."

Later, I would come to despise myself because my first reaction was "I am rich!" followed immediately by an image of the chalk outline on the sidewalk. Greed, and then fear. Only later, did I suffer from the realization that I would be contributing to a gigantic fraud.

I think that Arkady and Oleg took my startled reaction at face value, a natural outcome for the little surprise they had planned for me, but I was acutely aware that both Magda and Riley were watching me closely, but for different reasons. All three of us had made intentionally unethical and immoral choices for the sake of the job, but those choices were made alone and in the figurative dark. This was the first time where the moral failure was unambiguous and observable. I did not know it at the moment, but Riley would soon face the same glaring spotlight.

"But Petrov is … was … one of the 'outside' seats … Yunger's appointment."

Arkady leaned back in the chair, so that his face was deep in the shadows. "Yes, he had a hard time acting in the best interests of *all* of the shareholders. His death is sad for his wife and children, but fortunate for us."

I said nothing and he went on. "I talked with the head of the St. Petersburg police this morning." He turned in his chair to face Riley. "He said that the killer was a tall man, well-dressed, and that he stopped Petrov when he came out of the club, talked with him for a few seconds, and then shot him twice in the head. That's all that they know. He says that they suspect a mob connection."

His deliberateness and focus on Riley was curious, but then he asked Riley, "Tell me. What did you say to him?" and I knew with an instant and pervasive sense of horror that this was the more important reason that I was in the meeting.   It was Oleg's twisted way of reminding me of that revolver that he had placed on the table that day with Boris.

Riley did not answer immediately. First, he looked at me and then at Magda, not in search of absolution or even understanding, but as if to say 'I'm sorry you have to hear this.'

He turned back to Arkady. "I quoted a few lines from Pushkin ...

> Each day, and every hour
> I habitually follow in my thoughts,
> Trying to guess from their number
> The year which brings my death.

"Then I told him that I was sorry."

A deep silence settled over the room, until Petrykin said in a wondering tone, "Pushkin!" and looked at Riley as if seeing him for the first time. He stood to pour more brandy into his own and Arkady's glass. When he sat down again, Arkady said, "So we are well-positioned for the public offering. I shall –"

Petrykin broke in. "Just a minute, Arkady. I am thinking that we should wait on the offering. The market will be nervous about the deaths of board members so close to the offering date. The price would be adversely affected."

Arkady's first and quite obvious reaction was surprise. *This is not part of the script that he thought he knew. Petrykin has his own agenda.* But he responded quickly. "I disagree. Petrov's murder will not be connected to his board position." Arkady's tone was dismissive. "He was on other boards and had a number of clients with violent histories –"

Petrykin shook his head. "It's not Petrov's death that I'm talking about."

Arkady looked perplexed, only slowly becoming aware that he was missing something important. All that Riley, Magda and I could do was watch what was playing out between the two men. Oleg went on, speaking gently. "Our agreement … two years ago … was that your twenty percent was really mine. I think it's time that the arrangement is formalized."

"But, Oleg, I have been –"

"And the other shareholders, the Russian ones, they agree."

"I am … you can't –"

"I can. Your colleagues in the KGB … from the old days … they have moved on. Your alliances are obsolete. You no longer have patrons. And, yet, you continue to take payoffs from our ... my ... companies."

The first faint note of alarm was evident in Arkady's voice. "Oleg, please. We have been –"

"No. We haven't." Petrykin nodded to Riley, whose right hand emerged from the shadows of the chair holding a pistol. *A Russian Makharov. Not the Beretta that he always preferred.*

He fired twice into the left side of Arkady's chest. The large caliber slugs slammed him back into his chair and the shadows. His two hands, palms up and very white against the dark fabric were the only visible parts.

The silence in the room was profound until Petrykin murmured, "No Pushkin for Arkady?" but Riley got up, placed his weapon on the table, next to the brandy decanter, and walked out of the room.

Progress Report

We met at the *Memorial to the Fighters for the Soviet Power in the Far East* in the main square of Vladivostok. The memorial was as ugly as the title was absurd, and the square itself was bare concrete. The entire area should have been swaddled in shrink-wrap plastic and preserved as a memorial to the Soviet era. I was standing at the base looking up at it when Schmidt said from behind me, "Even the pigeons don't like it."

I didn't turn around. The image of Arkady slumped in the chair with the large splotch of blood on his shirtfront was still with me. "Maybe they should commission a new memorial … call it 'In Memory of Lawyers Who Briefly and Mistakenly Believed in the Rule of Law.'"

He ignored me, as usual. "Do you know that there are no monuments for spies?"

"You're wrong," I said. "Nathan Hale is the official state hero for the State of Connecticut and there is a fifty-foot statue of him somewhere in the state." I felt a surge of satisfaction go through me at being able to contradict him, and the sensation made me realize how much pent-up hostility was lurking so close to the surface. *But should it be directed at him? Or me? I sat there and watched Riley kill Arkady. Said nothing. Did nothing.*

"I stand corrected. I never really studied the Revolutionary War. Let's walk for a bit." He didn't wait for an answer, just headed for the harbor. Ten minutes later, we were on the broad promenade walking past the rank of warships from the Soviet Pacific Fleet. Long reddish streaks of rust striped the hulls.

He started, "Magda told me what happened with Petrykin."

"Not Riley?"

"He's back in the States. Phoned me from Kennedy Airport. Asked for – told me he was taking -- an indefinite leave of absence." It was easy for me to recall the long look of regret that Riley shared with Magda and me before he quoted his epitaph for Petrov.

Might as well get it all out on the table. "There was a Renoir in the hallway at Petrykin's estate. Was that from the Hermitage?"

He didn't answer, just stared at me. I went on, "Perhaps from the inventory that the Red Army 'liberated' from the Nazis and kept hidden? From the collection that Alex was 'helping to catalog?'"

No response. "Schmidt, before I left for Vlad, you said 'I'm working on another way to get closer to Petrykin.' So you aimed Magda at him, offered Riley to him to assassinate Petrov and Mikulin ... had Alex divert a Renoir or two...."

His continuing silence was an eloquent non-denial of my list of indictments. Finally he said, "How are you doing here? In Vlad?"

"You asked me two questions, and I have the answers. First, as to receptiveness to American investment: They are very receptive, but the investors should view it as a charitable contribution rather than as an investment.

What Oleg did to Yunger is a model for how Russians will view foreign investors. They'll either cheat them or shoot them, probably both. Second, as to the readiness of the Pacific Fleet: The ships are not seaworthy and they do not have the officers or sailors to man them. The Red Fleet is a Potemkin Village on the water."

He didn't seem to be paying much attention. I think it was the first time that I sensed the layer of depression that he always carried around with him.

"Schmidt, what are we doing here?"

He turned and stared out into the harbor. It was a minute or two before he spoke. "You understand the Russians better than any of us ... seen more dimensions of them ... the military, the politicians, the criminals. Where do you think the country is going to be in ten years?"

I flashed back to Helsinki, to Benjamin's finger pointing at me, with his drumbeat of questions I couldn't answer. The memory made me realize that Schmidt was right, that I had learned a lot and that I had definite opinions. I thought about Chayka, Vasnetsov, Petrov, Petrykin and Mikulin. I ran through images of my own quartet of double agents, especially Svetlana. I thought about the babushkas who swept the park's sidewalks every morning with their brooms made of twigs.

"Russia will be back," I said. "Right now, the country's a mess in almost every way. But the people are resilient, there is huge and untapped economic potential, and a patriotic streak that will be even deeper because of their humiliation. They will rebuild their military and the nukes aren't going to go away."

Schmidt nodded. "They – and China -- will be our primary rivals. And it's not that far in the future."

I wasn't listening. "And this Pollyanna belief of ours that a quick dash of capitalism will change the fundamentals is crazy. Russians crave authoritarian leaders. Democracy will take too long and require too much change. Elected dictators will emerge, but the elections will be a farce."

And whatever they turn out to be, we've helped them do it.

We started walking again. Schmidt said, "Russia has eighty-nine provinces. They all hold elections, but look who they elect." He pointed straight ahead to where the Administrative Offices for Primorsky Krai towered over the street. "One of the worst is in there."

Vladivostok was the capital of the Russian Far East – the Primorsky Krai, a huge land area – and the building Schmidt pointed to was the central office for Yevgeny Nazdratenko, an ex-welder appointed as Governor by Yeltsin and then re-elected with the support of local factory owners. He jailed his political opponents, closed the newspaper that spoke out against him and ran a totally corrupt government.

"Svetlana thinks he has a heart condition."

He stopped and looked at me. "That's very interesting." We walked in silence for another two or three minutes and then Schmidt said, as though the conversation had continued in his mind, "She's not going to last much longer."

Svetlana? Does he know something I don't? "Schmidt. Are you keeping something from me?"

"The others – your three doubles – are helping us because we pay them. But what Svetlana wants is to get out of Russia. The paradox is that the more she does for you, the more valuable she becomes as an informant. She's worthless to us in the U.S. And, since she's smart, she'll work this out for herself and – one day soon – she'll issue an ultimatum ..."

"Which we will honor ..." I looked at him closely as I said it and could not detect any reaction. But neither did he agree. Instead he said, "Our friends in the KGB are starting to get their act together. It's taken them a while to recover from the attempted coup against Yeltsin, but he – Yeltsin – needs them. He's just appointed one of the younger crowd to head the new agency – they've renamed it; it's now the 'Federal Security Service' -- and the man is making real changes."

"Who is it?"

"He's an ex-KGB Colonel. Worked with the East German Stasi during his formative years, then switched into politics ... vice-mayor in St. Petersburg briefly ... and then to Moscow with Yeltsin."

It is not like Schmidt to engage in sweeping generalities. He is trying to tell me something that is both specific and important. I said, "Schmidt, what –"

"This guy owns a piece of OPCo, courtesy of our boy Oleg Petrykin. It was him who told Petrykin that Mikulin and Petrov had to be done away with. He made it a condition for his support."

"So he's greedy, murderous and corrupt. What's new about that?"

Schmidt's impatience was showing. "He's also smart and very much a believer in Russian greatness. He's putting a lot of time and attention into counter-intelligence. So be careful … and tell your informants to be careful."

"Who is this arch-villain?"

"His name is Vladimir Putin."

Saturday Morning Run

Monica Holst was waiting for me in the lobby when I came down for my regular Saturday morning run. She stood when I approached. She'd cut her hair shorter and it made her look younger than I remembered until I noticed the small lines around her eyes and the corners of her mouth. Like me, she was wearing running clothes and sneakers.

"Monica. What a nice surprise. It's been a long time." *Eight years ago, in Moscow. She found me waiting in that Izvestia office.*

"I hope you don't mind. I saw the piece you wrote that got picked up in the Herald Tribune about the opening up of Vladivostok. I called your editor and he said you were staying at this hotel."

I reached out to pluck at the sleeve of the sweatshirt she was wearing. "And you just happened to be dressed for a run along the waterfront …"

"Your editor also told me about your Saturday habit."

"I'm flattered that you came. Vladivostok is at the end of the world for most people."

"Not for me. I've been in Khabarovsk, four hundred miles north of you. I'm chasing a story about some Sino-Soviet military frictions along the Amur River. I came to Vlad for a meeting with Nazdratenko, but he stiffed me and I wondered if you were as bored as I was in the great Russian Far East. Can I run with you?"

It's more than just a run. Igor Vankin, my naval captain turned informant, is meeting me at the midpoint, near the seawall. He says that he has new information 'that will be of great interest to the American navy.' No way I can reach him before the meeting time. I'll have to wave him off.

I hesitated long enough that she said, "I promise that I will keep up with you. And I'll buy our breakfast when we're back."

I took Monica's arm and headed for the revolving door. "OK, I have about a six mile route - 10K – down the hill to the waterfront, left along the seawall and then uphill back here. Quite a bit of elevation change, mostly pavement and some of the worst scenery imaginable."

"Good by me. Give me ninety seconds and I'll meet you out front."

It was three minutes rather than ninety seconds. She walked up behind me, said, "I don't talk when I'm running," and just started off. I fell in behind, content to let her set the pace. *She runs like Magda, silent and hard, as if to establish that she can do what men can do, better than they can. And they're both aggressive in bed too.* The thought bothered me and I spent some time wondering if it was my fault, whether I catalyzed that sort of behavior in women and, if so, was it because I was too assertive or too meek?

The sky was a uniform leaden gray, a perfect monochromatic backdrop for the drab buildings and the choppy bay that was just coming into view. It was still early, so there were few pedestrians and traffic was light. After several years in ex-Soviet cities, I had come to think of running as a decadent western habit, a symptom of capitalistic excess. One did not see joggers in Vladivostok, Moscow or St. Petersburg. There were environmental as well as cultural factors at work. Soviet infrastructure had been crumbling for decades, so the sidewalks were uneven, strewn with obstacles, and occasionally dead-ended into a brick wall. Drivers paid no attention to pedestrians of any form and seemed to view a runner as an affront, an uppity challenger that had neither the means nor the authority to compete for the scarce space.

Since there was no traffic on the narrow street, more like a country lane, that the hotel fronted on, we were running in the road and, as if to confirm my views of Russian drivers, a battered reddish Toyota suddenly pulled out into the road just as we approached, almost hitting Monica. I heard her yell a Russian curse and she stopped and raised her arm with the middle finger fully extended.

I ran past her. "Right hand drive," I said loudly. "He can't see what's passing him." She came alongside me and said, "They're worse in Khabarovsk, but he's still an asshole," before she sprinted ahead again.

Most of the cars in the Russian Far East were used cars from Japan, imported illegally. A lot of them came in on fishing boats, bypassing customs and import duties. They were much cheaper and a far better quality than the Ladas and Zghuli's that Russian factories produced, and Japan was a lot closer than Moscow, so the citizens of the Primorsky Krai put up with the steering wheel placed on the wrong side of the car.

There were better routes for running, but this was the one that Vankin preferred for our meetings. His rusting destroyer was moored stern-first at the seawall and it was easy for him to meet in one of the many waterfront bars or near one of the monuments that lined the half-mile long stretch of the wide promenade near his ship.

We sped up to cross the single railroad track just ahead of a rumbling freight train and onto the broad promenade.   It allowed us to run side-by-side and made it easy for me to see Vankin standing at the edge of the seawall. He was in civilian clothes, smoking a cigarette and watching the passersby. I slowed to let Monica get ahead and altered my course slightly to pass Vankin a little closer. We had arranged a crude 'abort' signal – the right hand brushing at the forehead, one of Carlee's first bits of instruction – and I used it when I thought he was looking directly at me.   It worked; or at least he turned away from us and looked out into the harbor.

The success of our little maneuver made me think about Carlee and those months in that Virginia farmhouse, but what I should have been doing was concentrating on something else she had taught us. She called it 'situational awareness' and it was a phrase that she built into every lesson, part of what she called her 'Catechism for Survival.' But I'd gotten sloppy, as complacent as Aesop's hare racing the tortoise.   The Russian government couldn't even feed its own citizens or pay its bills; so stealing an occasional state secret didn't feel like a high-risk venture any longer.

Was I at fault? Was there anything I could have done that would have changed the outcome? I don't think so, but I can't stop replaying what happened in those next ten seconds.

I *did* notice the reddish Toyota, the same one that had almost hit Monica. It had pulled over, its engine idling, in a bus zone about ten yards ahead of us and directly opposite Vankin. The driver was sitting in the car, at curbside because of the right-hand drive, with his window open and his right arm resting on the doorframe. I could see his face in the driver's side mirror. He was watching us approach and I thought, 'He didn't like Monica's cursing at him, nor the obscene gesture. He wants to get even.'

I was seriously wrong about what he wanted. Monica was about ten yards in front of me and she ran by the car without incident. As soon as she passed, he extended his arm fully out from the car, an arm that seemed incredibly *long*. But that was because he was holding a pistol with a sound suppressor screwed onto the muzzle. There was no hesitation; he fired within a second of the gun coming level. The sound of the single shot was swallowed up by the sounds of the freight train running parallel to the seawall.

He shot Monica! But she was still running, apparently untouched and unaware. The arm retracted and the Toyota began moving just as I pulled even with it. The driver looked at me and seeing him stopped me as surely as if he'd fired that shot into the middle of my chest. I watched him drive away, noting that the rear license plate still had its original Japanese characters and the rusted trunk lid was tied shut with a piece of rope.

"Why did you stop?" Monica was standing in front of me, running in place and looking annoyed.

"I thought he shot you," I said, feeling stupid and pointing at the Toyota just now making a left turn about a hundred yards further on. I turned in a complete circle, seeing another half-dozen people near us on the promenade, none of them looking concerned.

But Monica was nodding. "I did hear the shot. Barely. I thought I was imagining it."

"He was using a silencer."

She did a slow pirouette, noting the same lack of excitement that I had. "No bodies. Nobody screaming, 'I've been shot!'"

She was right, but the scene had changed. *Vankin's gone!*

"There was a man standing by the seawall." I pointed at the spot where I'd last seen Vankin, standing there smoking his cigarette and looking out into the harbor. *A naval captain who was my informant and here to meet me.*

We walked to the spot. There was no railing or barrier of any kind, just a ten-foot drop to the incredibly polluted seawater lapping at the base of the concrete seawall. Igor Vankin was floating face down, swaying in concert with the plastic bottles, beer cans and human waste that formed the surface of the famous Golden Horn Bay.

Belated Regrets

You knew.

I wasn't sure.

That's bullshit! You're not in the kind of business where you're entitled to be sure about anything. Not even about who you are, let alone an attractive woman that wanders into your life every few years and people around you end up dead.

It doesn't matter. I gave her nothing.

That's what you say. But why does she keep coming back?

Maybe it's just a coincidence ... Vankin being shot while she's with me ...

Sure. Just like the man in the Toyota was a random assassin.

We stood looking down at what had once been Igor Vankin. The wake from a ferry passing a hundred yards out in the harbor was roiling the water beneath us, pushing his corpse back and forth and submerging it beneath all of the other garbage. Monica tugged at my sleeve and said, "We should go. You know that there is no such thing as an innocent bystander when the police show up at a Russian crime scene."

"But he's ..."

She waited and when I didn't go on, she said, "He's what? An innocent bystander? Someone that deserves 'justice?' That's for another place, another time. Not here, not now. What he is is someone that made an important person angry enough that he sent a professional assassin armed with a silenced pistol to kill him."

She was right, of course. Nothing good could possibly come from either of us playing the public-spirited citizen role, even if we were guiltless. Which we weren't, neither of us. We turned away and resumed our run. Not a panicky flight from a murder scene, just a couple of obsessive fitness types out for a regular Saturday morning jog. We were back at the hotel half-an-hour later and went directly to the rooftop garden of the hotel.

By then, I had tried out several different scripts in my head, testing each for the threats it might elicit and the weaknesses it might expose. This was new territory for me. I couldn't decide whether to confront her or to continue with this intricate dance, one where each partner is unfaithful to the other and unsure of whether he or she has been found out. But Monica decided it for me when she asked the question that I knew was coming.

"Did you see the shooter? Well enough to identify him?"

"No. The door frame blocked a view of his face." *An outright lie. I could pick him out of a hundred-man lineup, with absolute certainty. I even know his name – Vasili.*

"But you did see the person he shot? You told me 'There was a man standing by the seawall.'"

"Yes. He was smoking a cigarette." *The exact truth. And a major lie by omission. I knew him because I recruited him to spy against his own country. He was waiting there to meet with me.*

"What are you going to do ... about what we saw?"

I hesitated, a natural pause for a person confronting a serious ethical dilemma. Then I shrugged and said, "Nothing. Maybe prepare a plausible story just in case there's a witness that reports us or maybe there's a video camera that covers the promenade area." *Another significant lie. I intended to do quite a lot, but I had no intention of telling her any part of it.*

I asked her, "What about you?"

"Back to Khabarovsk as fast as I can. Watch the local news and see if there's any mention of the murder."

She pushed back her chair. "Would you like to go to your room for a while? I have some time and we could ... distract ourselves for an hour or so." She was leaning forward, intent on me.

"No. I can't." *A compound lie. I would like that, and I could do it. What does that say about me?*

I went on the offensive, completely unsure of what I was doing. "Maybe I'll come up to Khabarovsk for a few days. How long are you there?"

The question seemed to trigger an internal switch. Before I spoke, I think she viewed me as a real prospect, an active CIA agent that she could turn. After, I was a lost cause, a nuisance to be disposed of. Her expression flipped from 'concerned' to 'indifferent' and she stood up abruptly, saying, "I don't think that's a very good idea," even as she turned for the door.

She stopped halfway there and what happened next would be the counter-intelligence equivalent of a 'Hail Mary pass' in American football. Looking over her shoulder at me, she said, "Your CIA will be disappointed with what you've done. Sleeping with a member of the Russian secret service ... getting Vankin killed ... losing those tactical nukes. You should change sides ... work with us."

At least she didn't include my contributions to the long list of Latin American failures in her recruiting pitch.

I realized that I was relieved to have it out in the open. "So what happened this morning ... Vankin's assassination ... that was staged for my benefit?"

"It was either him or you. And there are fewer ... complications ... if he's the one." She turned to face me, but stayed standing halfway to the door. "We know there are others that you have recruited, and we will find them, just like we found Vankin."

I didn't think she could surprise me any more than she already had, but then she said, "You know ... there are some very senior people in my organization that think that you – the CIA – are the ones that caused those three warheads to go astray. They want them back ... badly."

I rolled my eyes and said, "The thieves are named Chayka and Vasnetsov. You need to talk to them."

"We did. But they didn't have them."

"If I agreed to work for you, what would you expect me to do ... other than expose my informants?"

She smiled. "Our game is over, Thomas. No more pretending." When I said nothing, she said, "You need to leave Russia."

"Is that an official recommendation or a personal one?"

She said, "Just go before you become like Vankin," and turned for the door.

I said, "Say hello to Vasili," but she kept walking.

"If you're blown, get out. As fast as you can."

The policy was unequivocal and the spy's natural instinct for self-preservation reinforced it nicely. I was out of Russia four hours later. I used the time to leave 'Immediate Cease and Desist' messages for my three-person band of surviving traitors – Ivan, Stepan and Svetlana – and send a coded message to Schmidt via the American Embassy. Seoul was only a one-hour flight from Vladivostok, but until the Korean Air flight lifted off the runway at Vladivostok, I experienced for the first time the intensity of loneliness that Schmidt warned us about in that first screening session.

Once in Seoul, I checked into the Intercontinental Hotel and waited for Schmidt. It took him eighteen hours to get there.

He took one look at me and read the anxiety clearly. His first words were, "I sent Magda to Vlad. She'll make sure things get shut down properly."

He looked closely at me. "So, what happened?"

Where to start? "The FSB killed Vankin. In front of me. Then they tried to recruit me. When I said no, they said 'Get out of Russia.'"

"Who?"

I must have looked blank because he quickly added, "You said 'the FSB,' but who exactly?"

"Do you remember the pair from Managua? The German journalist and the Russian advisor to the late Colonel Gomez?" *Not likely. Fifteen years past and another continent.* But, once again, I had underestimated Schmidt.

"Monica and Vasili. So Putin's brought them back to the motherland. He's calling in the pros." He sat back in his chair and stared at the opposite wall, clearly bothered by what I had told him. I didn't pay any attention; I was busy processing what I had just learned. *What did you expect from him? You're not the only one who can lie by omission!*

He said, "It's time for all of us to get out," and reached into his briefcase and brought out what looked like a phone. At least, it had a tiny screen and a keypad. He typed in a dozen characters, pushed a 'send' command, and then waited, clearly anxious. Thirty seconds later, the device emitted a series of 'beeps." "That's Riley." He repeated the steps and when the beeps came again, he said, "That's Magda." He did it a third time but there was no response.

"Alex?" I asked. He said, "Yes. He's in St. Petersburg. He's supposed to respond immediately."

"How about Peter?"

"He's in San Francisco. Claims he needs to be where the computer geeks are."

He looked worried, but I didn't give him a break. I had my own grudges to be worked through. "You *knew* that Monica Holst was Russian intelligence? And you didn't bother to tell me?"

Schmidt was amused by my anger. "I didn't know, but I suspected that she was, mostly because she was hanging out with Vasili, who is a known counter-intelligence agent. She was with him in Central America, now in Vladivostok. And she popped up again in Moscow as soon as you showed up there. That's a whole lot of coincidence."

I knew I sounded like a petulant child, but I said it anyway. "I should have let her recruit me."

His amusement increased. "Mahoney, you are the least likely person to go to the dark side that I have ever met. The sex is one thing, but treason? Not a chance."

I didn't know whether I should be offended or pleased. Schmidt inhabited a world with moral standards that I could only speculate about. So I gave a very histrionic deep sigh and asked, "What next?"

"Stay put here. I'll send word as soon as Alex reports in."

He stopped in the doorway. "You've done good work. More than you know."

"I still need a visa for Svetlana."

"Yes, I know. I'm working on it."

Exit Strategy

Schmidt's text message was brief, nothing but nouns. "Rodos, Aegean Boutique Hotel, March 15."

The Greek island of Rhodes was a long trip from Seoul and I spent most of the travel time trying out alternative speeches that I would use on Schmidt. They ranged from angry – "You're using me!" – to utilitarian – "We're not accomplishing anything!" – to confessional – "I can't do this anymore!" I gave up the speechwriting when I was sitting in the Athens airport waiting for the connection to Rhodes because I recognized that I had tried them all at one time or another during the last dozen years and, in the end, had simply gone back to doing what Schmidt told me to do. The realization did not help me to feel good about myself.

The streets were quiet. The cruise ships, vacationing Northern Europeans and the honeymooners wouldn't start showing up in force until mid-June. The hotel was within the ancient stone walls of the medieval city, one of the UNESCO World Heritage sites. Its cobblestone streets and views of the harbor made me wish that I was still innocent enough to look forward to a honeymoon.

Magda and Riley were already there when I checked in, drinking coffee in a small cobblestone courtyard ringed by olive trees that the reception clerk assured me were two thousand years old. They were at a table set for four, sitting with their backs to me and I watched them for a few minutes, thinking that I might pick up a clue as to the state of their relationship. I gave up the vigil after five minutes, when it became crystal clear that they were as insulated from one another as two introverted strangers at a bus stop.

Riley ordered me a tiny cup of Greek coffee as soon as I sat down. The liquid looked and poured like mud, a perfect antidote for both jet lag and sleep in any form.

"Alex?" I asked. Magda and Riley looked at one another and he said, "Still unaccounted for. Schmidt's working it."

I looked at Magda. "He said that you would shut down my operations in Vladivostok?"

She sat up straighter. "All OK, I think. The shooting of Igor Vankin got almost no public mention. We – Schmidt and me – think that the FSB is enforcing a coverup. I've told your other three informants to stand down and given them a bundle of extra cash. I'm pretty sure there's no surveillance on any of them. There's no indication that Vasili is onto them."

"Svetlana was not in it for money. All she wants is a visa to the U.S." *I wonder if Magda knows about the occasional nocturnal visits?* The follow-on thought was jarring: *Is there any difference between what she does with her targets and what I did with Svetlana?*

She said, "Schmidt is the one who has to manage the visa. He said he's working on it." She didn't look at me while she was talking, however.

The awkwardness afflicted each of us and the silence dragged on until I asked, "How's our pet oligarch doing? The last time I saw the two of you was in his living room." *That would be the night that Riley killed Arkady while we watched.*

"Petrykin is her department," Riley said, inclining his head toward Magda without disguising the look of disapproval. She gave Riley a blank look and said, "Oleg Petrykin is still there, but his wealth is seriously diminished. The ruble devaluation and austerity has really hurt. I'd say he's one of the lesser oligarchs these days." After a pause, she added, "But he's still in good standing with the Kremlin, so I would guess that Schmidt is pleased."

Riley asked, "Did you know that the word 'oligarch' is derived from classic Greek? It means rule of the few. Oh, and OPCo has been renamed; it's now called Northern Cargo Services and is ninety-percent Russian owned."

"How ... but what about the Dutch? They had forty-nine percent."

Both of them looked at me as if I had asserted that the earth was flat and I remembered Petrykin sitting in his new mansion, waving his brandy snifter and saying, 'We are contemplating some changes in the ownership structure in anticipation of the public offering.'

"So he wanted still more."

"Of course," Riley said. "More shares, more art, more control, more everything." He smiled at me in a way that told me he was enjoying this. "And Mikhail Popov lost out as well."

I actually had a micro-second with the question, 'Who's Mikhail Popov?' but Riley kept talking. " ... did the calculation. Your two percent has been diluted down to 0.0017 percent." He enunciated each digit carefully, in keeping with the mathematical precision of the calculation.

So I'm no longer rich. "Easy come, easy go," I said. "I'm right in there with the investors in the pre-1917 Tsarist bonds."

We sat in silence for a minute or so while I worked through some of the implications. I started to ask, "What about –" but Magda had run out of patience or, more likely, wanted to get away from Riley's steady stare. She interrupted. "Ask Schmidt. He's the one pulling all the strings." Then she stood up and left.

She came to my room that night. When I opened the door to her faint knock, she walked past me and sat in one of the two facing chairs near the window that looked out over the old city. I was on the top floor, so we could see most of the original wall and some of the port. When I joined her, she pointed to the northern tip of the island. "They say that the Colossus of Rhodes stood there, one of the Seven Wonders of the Ancient World. I went to see it, but there's nothing there."

"It's been gone for over two thousand years. They're talking about constructing some sort of look-alike for the tourists."

She wasn't listening. "That was my goal. Before I met Schmidt. I was going to see each of the Seven Wonders of the Ancient World."

"And did you?"

Her brow furrowed. "I spent a year after college ... a classic 'backpacking in Europe' cliché ..." She raised her right hand from her lap and began counting, using her fingers to keep track. After a bit, she said, "Five. I saw five of them. Nobody really knows whether the hanging gardens of Babylon even existed, and I never made it to Rhodes until yesterday. The Great Pyramid at Giza is the only one where there's much left to look at. But I saw other things ... places that should have been on the list. That's what got Schmidt's attention – the places I'd been."

Her dark mood was contagious and I felt myself receding into that part of myself that held all of the pent-up insecurities. "It's funny. I have no idea why he chose me. It's the question I've always wanted to ask him, but I never have for some reason."

She said, "The orphan's second question."

"Huh?"

"'Why did you pick me?' The question that the orphan can't ... won't ... ask the parents that adopted him."

"What's the orphan's first question?" *But you already know the answer to that.*

"Why didn't you want me?" *For the parents that put him up for adoption ... another question never to be posed.*

Knowing that it was irrelevant, I said, "But we're not orphans." She just smiled at me in a way that made me feel incredibly naïve. Then she asked, "Can I stay?"

"Sure." I held out my hand.

She borrowed a T-shirt to sleep in and we slept spoon-like and chaste in the exact middle of the bed, like a pair of ten-year-old orphans in a stone-cold red-brick institution who knew they would never be chosen.

Schmidt didn't show up until the morning of our third day in Rodos. I spent most of the time in my room, rereading LeCarré 's *Tinker, Tailor, Soldier, Spy* and marveling at George Smiley's hard-won wisdom. I memorized the line, '*.... he wondered whether there was any love between human beings that did not rest upon some sort of self-delusion,*' and then worried because it made me feel better about myself.

Schmidt was waiting for us at breakfast. There were enough people and waiters coming and going that we kept the conversation innocuous, the strain visible only to us. After that, we moved to a small conference room with a square table. There were four chairs and four water glasses, all very symmetric.

The first question was obvious. I said, "Alex?"

"Detained in St. Petersburg." His expression was completely blank, as though to negate the import of his words.

"Detained?" It was a word that could mean anything.

"It seems that several valuable paintings are missing from the Hermitage collection. There's an investigation by an 'Antiquities' task force and they say that they've found paintings by Monet and Degas in Alex's apartment."

"That's bullshit." Riley asked, "What are you doing about it?"

"I've arranged for a Russian lawyer with a large budget for an investigator."

Magda said what we all knew. "That won't work."

"No. It won't."

There were four of us sitting around the table, but I was thinking of our first days in Virginia and the ones who were there. *Arthur in a shallow grave in the Nicaraguan jungle. Roger dead from my failed hostage negotiation tactics. Carlee in a cemetery in Panama City. Benjamin and Peter – our dropouts -- getting rich in the civilian world. Now Alex in a Russian jail, probably for a long time.*

Schmidt's next words made my reminiscing seem well-timed.

"I'm closing down. You can all go home."

Each of the three of us stared at him, but he sat quietly, his hands on the table in front of him, his eyes focused on something in the middle distance.

"Schmidt," Magna said. A one-word equivalent of a lawyer's brief; at once an accusation, a question and a denial.

We waited. Schmidt seemed unaware of the three pairs of eyes fixed on him. Finally, he began, "I've been at Langley the last two days. They want satellites and cryptographers, not live agents on the ground. Even more than that, they *don't* – I repeat, *don't* – want independent contractors. *Rogues* is their preferred term for people like us. They're cutting off funding. We're done."

I suppose there are certain categorical phrases – 'You're fired.' 'I want a divorce.' 'You have inoperable cancer.' -- that, the instant after you hear them, are incomprehensible, so unexpected and context-free that it takes seconds for the words to even register, for denial to set in. So it was when Schmidt said, 'I'm closing down.'

"They'll be sorry." It came from Riley, the classic playground retort of a spoiled child that didn't get his way. But in this case, we all agreed with it.

I heard myself say, "They think the Cold War is over ..." and incredulously, "and that we *won*." Magda was even more scornful, "They think Russia is no longer a threat, that it's all about China." Riley was as sardonic as ever, "Who needs spies, those sneaky amoral creeps whose next-best alternative would be as a shoe salesman in a WalMart?"

A silence set in until I said what each of of us was thinking, "What the hell are we supposed to do now?"

Schmidt roused himself and for the first time seemed to be aware that there were other people in the room. "Go home. You've all got real jobs with real companies. They'll be glad to have you. And don't worry about money: I've used our remaining funds to make a major tax-free deposit in each of your bank accounts."

He stood up and, without a hint of irony, said, "Thank you for your service to your country," and walked out of the room.

That's not good enough. We're not done yet. I caught him halfway across the courtyard. "Schmidt, what about Svetlana? The visa –"

He wouldn't look at me. "I tried, Mahoney. I really did. But the State Department said no." He tried to walk away, but I held his forearm. Very tightly. "Schmidt! We owe ... I *promised* her –"

He pried my fingers loose from his arm. "She shot herself. In Nazdratenko's bedroom. Two nights ago." Then he walked away.

It was a long night. I drank quite a lot and it took me a long time to find the quote that I halfway remembered in *Tinker, Tailor, Soldier, Spy.*

'After a lifetime of living by his wits and his considerable memory, he had given himself full time to the profession of forgetting.'

The next day, I went home and began forgetting.

Interlude (1999-2001)

I am from there. I am from here.
I am not there and I am not here.
I have two names, which meet and part,
and I have two languages.
I forget which of them I dream in.

Mahmoud Darwish

Fresh Start

Sitting there in Rhodes, Schmidt had said, "Go home," a blithe and well-intentioned instruction, but one that was meaningless. I had no 'home' to go to. There was a set of estranged parents somewhere on the east coast that I had not seen since high school graduation.   I had lived in four states and nine physical residences between high school and when Schmidt found me. After that, I became a virtual nomad, lacking address or a feeling of belonging to any particular person or place.

So, on the morning after told to go home, I stood with my suitcase outside the front entrance of the Aegean Boutique Hotel, as rudderless as a parolee released from a life sentence after serving forty years, as susceptible to suggestion as a toddler in a candy store. From where I was standing, I could see one of the inter-island ferries leaving the harbor. It was a bright white object on a shiny blue sea, as good a sign as any, so I went to the port and bought a ticket to Athens. When the boat docked in Piraeus eighteen hours later, I took a taxi to the airport and bought a plane ticket to Chicago because I pictured it as more or less in the center of the U.S. and therefore a good place to start a search.   I even got that wrong; Chicago is seven hundred miles from the geographic center of the continental U.S.

I made two phone calls from Chicago's O'Hare Airport. The first was to my editor at the Armstrong Media Group in Texas. It was a strange conversation.

"I'm resigning as your international columnist."

"You can't resign." He actually began to whisper. "You need the job to ... you know ... for cover." And then louder, more confidently, "Besides, the readers like your stuff."

"But I'm no longer international. I'm moving back to the states."

"So write domestic stuff. Or keep on with the international. These days, the feature writers and columnist types keep up with what's going on without even getting on a plane."

"I'm not sure I want to write anything about anything. Can't I just quit?"

He repeated what he had just said. He was clearly nervous, enough so that I began to wonder what kind of leverage Schmidt had used on him. He concluded with, "Let's just call it a leave of absence. As far as I'm concerned, you're still on the payroll."

His use of the word 'payroll' was the stimulus for my second call. Pamela was another person I'd been dependent on for the last fifteen years but never met. She was a Certified Financial Planner in Los Angeles that I talked to about once or twice a year. She had a great voice that – for me at least -- hinted at the possibility of sultry late-afternoon dalliances. I wondered what Schmidt had on her and hoped that I would never meet her and suffer disillusionment about the dalliance.

"Pamela, it's Thomas Mahoney. I'm making some changes in my life style and I need an update on the state of my finances."

I heard computer keys start to click even as she was responding. "Thomas, how nice to hear from you! And I do hope those changes mean that you'll get to LA so that we can actually meet one another." Her voice rose on the last few words, making it an almost-question, one that I chose to ignore.

"How was your flight?"

"Flight?"   My paranoia – what Schmidt called 'a constructive distrust of those around you' – immediately kicked in. *How can she know* –

"I'm looking at your American Express account. I see you've booked from Athens to Chicago. Your card balance, by the way, is about twelve-thousand dollars. I presume you want me to pay it as soon as it's billed. Our usual arrangement?"

"Yes. Assuming there are adequate funds."

She laughed, evoking images of a dimly lit bedroom in my imagination. *She could make a fortune running phone sex operations.* "You're kidding, right? At the moment, you have over seven-hundred thousand dollars in your *checking* account."

Schmidt said, 'And I've used our remaining funds to make a major tax-free deposit in each of your bank accounts.'

"OK. Please transfer as much of that as you deem appropriate into my investment fund."

More keys clicked and she said, "Done. No reason to let Bank of America have all that interest-free cash. Did you want to go over the performance stats on the investments? You've done quite well in the internet stocks and –"

"That's OK, I trust you."

"Oops! Here's something odd." I waited, fantasizing that all my accounts were slowly disappearing from her screen as some computer geek in the CIA erased digital traces of rogue agents.

"This is a first." She sounded like a scientist coming across a new and deadly virus. "You received a paper dividend check from a Russian company ... OPCo, I think ... through Sberbank in St. Petersburg ... but it either bounced or they canceled it. I can't tell which."

The always conditional two percent! My very brief career as a beginning oligarch! "That's OK, Pamela. I know about that."

She lowered her voice, shifting to sales mode. "You're better off without it. Foreign accounts like that get lots of IRS attention. And Thomas, while we're on the subject, you're paying much more tax than you should. There are better ways to display your patriotism and there are lots of avenues to give the government less."

But that's what I'm doing. I'm not going to do their dirty work any longer! "Maybe I'll buy a house. Isn't that a good tax deduction?"

"One of the best. Where would you buy?"

"I have no idea. I've been out of the country too long to have a preference."

"So, are you done with all the offshore work? Time to come home?"

This is the kind of conversation that ordinary people have ... everyday stuff ... the kids, weather, the neighbors, local sports ... Or maybe Schmidt has asked her to probe into questions of loyalty and patriotism ... to test if Svetlana's suicide has altered my allegiances ...

I wonder how long it will be before the paranoia stops kicking in?

"Thomas?"

"Oh, sorry. Come home? Yeah, at least for a while. Thanks Pamela. I'll try to get to LA. Goodbye for now."

It was mid-morning in Chicago and I had no idea where I was going next. But on the way to find a restaurant in the sprawling terminal, I passed a newsstand and bought a copy of USA Today because one of the headlines was "The Ten Best Small Cities in America." I read the article while having breakfast and then booked a flight to Santa Fe, New Mexico. I think it was because the article described it as being in the 'high desert' and I had once gone to Afghanistan and liked the mountains and valleys,

I became a resident of Santa Fe as soon as I got off the plane, as randomly as I chose the ferry to Athens and the flight to Chicago. I could just as easily have wound up in Modesto or West Palm Beach or Lebanon, Kansas – the true geographic center of the U.S. I became a civilian, an ordinary person in every way except for the memories I harbored. I played golf, taught a journalism course at a local community college, collected some Navajo artifacts and – yes – I bought a house, a small and very old adobe affair near the central plaza. I wrote a few columns on purely local stuff for my editor, mostly because the paychecks continued and it was easy for me to do. And for the first time, I had what I thought of as a meaningful relationship with a woman.

Rachel was like me in many ways. The most important one was that she too had committed fifteen years to a cause that, in the end, rejected her and told her, figuratively, to 'go home.' We gravitated toward one another as inevitably as a pair of shipwreck survivors on a desert island.

Her cause was social justice; in this case, the sorry treatment of Native Americans in a New Mexican culture that resented their claims to the land, their 'sovereign' rights and their casino-generated wealth, while failing to notice their poverty, addiction and the eradication of their heritage. Rachel was Jewish, the daughter of an ancient pair of Russian immigrants, ex-communist organizers from New York who worked in the garment center. According to Rachel, they had known Julius and Ethel Rosenberg, who were executed in 1953 for passing atomic secrets to the Russians.

She was a civil rights lawyer who worked for a small foundation dedicated to preserving Navajo language and culture in New Mexico. She brought considerable passion, leadership and legal skills to the task, but, one day, she was summoned to a convocation of tribal elders who expressed profound regret, but said that she was 'too white' and that she should 'go home to her own people.'

We met after I had written a column for the Albuquerque newspaper arguing that a real change in culture – such as is required in the transitioning

Russian economy – should be done quickly, even if massive inequalities emerge in the short run. Rachel was waiting on my doorstep with a copy of the newspaper. Her first words to me were, "This is bullshit," a theme that continued in the kitchen and finally, although muted, in the bedroom. I learned that day that her passion was a fungible commodity, that she applied it to everything that she did, whether it involved writing letters to the editor or making love in a sun-dappled bedroom.

She moved in and, for the first time, I realized how deprived I had been for so long, in ways that hadn't registered until now. My legacy with Magda, Svetlana and Monica was a sorry basis for forming a relationship that, if not lasting, was real and uncalculated. Rachel used the word 'stunted,' saying things like, "You need to learn to trust, to be vulnerable, to compromise." And, "Love, whatever it is or isn't, has a cost and you must be willing to bear it." And, a quote from somebody who must have read LeCarre, "Love requires you to run the risk of betrayal."

She was therapy. I still do not know what form of reciprocity I offered to her, although she once said, "I like the way you treat me … like an undeserved gift … a thing that is accepted and valued but does need to be *understood* or *protected* … a thing that can be lost if you are not careful." I took what she said as a literal threat and tried not to analyze why she stayed.

Despite the florid language, we never said 'I love you' to the other, nor did we talk of marriage. I think we both knew that we would go back to our own particular causes, the ones that transcended individual needs. It was that same realization, I think, that kept her from probing very deeply into my history. I did not have to pretend because she did not ask.

If one wants to drop out but keep most of the amenities, Santa Fe is a good place, a kind of bubble in time and space, a carefully maintained human ecosphere where social classes and cultures can mix comfortably. It has art galleries, an opera and a quality of light that makes artists, nuclear physicists, new age hippies and retired spies feel comfortable with one another and at home while enabling them to ignore the larger world around them.

In my case, I went cold turkey. I had no television, did not sign up for the early smart phones, and did not enroll in any of the on-line services. I paid my bills by check and used my land-line telephone for the occasional contact with Pamela and my editor. I was as off-the-grid as any of the Bahai Buddhist monks that prowled Santa Fe's central plaza. The only exceptions to my hermit-like life style were Rachel and the New York Times.

I read the Times cover-to-cover every day. So I knew about Yeltsin appointing Putin as his successor, about the Gore vs. Bush election debacle, about the resurgence of Russia as rising oil prices enabled the oligarchs and the military to prosper, about the continuing shift of our southern hemisphere to leftist values, about the seemingly endless embarrassments of the Central Intelligence Agency.   At first, the stories affected me as personal accusations of failure on my part, but after a while they became just stories; things happening to other people in far off places that had nothing to do with me or my past.

The bubble lasted eighteen months.   In the first few of those months, I deluded myself that I was well and truly done. Not only permanently out of the game, but that the past fifteen years were somehow sufficient and, even if they weren't, I was better off in my new world with all of its openness and conventional morality.

Today, I think of those times as an extended vacation, a time-out; the kind of sabbatical leave they offer to professors to regenerate themselves. It ended on the same day that many other phases ended, the day that everybody in the U.S. experienced a similar transition from the way the world was to the way it would be.

Inflection Point

For Rachel and I, the world changed in small increments on that eleventh morning of September, like watching a very blurry slow motion video of a train wreck. We were driving back from Taos, dependent on a car radio with intermittent reception and stunned newscasters struggling to make sense of the impossible, so the one-hundred and four minutes between Flight 11 intersecting with the North Tower and its ending as a pile of smoking rubble could be absorbed bit by bit. I feel tremendous sympathy for those who turned on the TV and were confronted with endlessly repeating images of passenger planes flying arrow-like into skyscrapers filled with people and those same skyscrapers collapsing onto themselves like improbably high houses of cards.

Rachel's parents lived in Manhattan, not far from the World Trade Center, and after two hours of trying to reach them, she gave up and started driving. It was the last time I saw her and I still wonder how she reconciled her belief in ultimate goodness and her passion for social justice with the cold-bloodedness of the 911 hijackers.

I experienced an intense need-to-know. Who did it? Who were the state sponsors? What kinds of capabilities have they kept in reserve? How can we find them and kill them? The questions had to be answered, but I had no one to call, no deep inside source that would know someone that knew someone. I tried my editor and Pamela, the two cutouts that Schmidt had empowered to maintain the fiction that I was an ordinary, harmless American citizen, but both of them insisted that they knew no one named Schmidt and that I was just another high-value business relationship.

More than just getting answers to my questions, I wanted back 'in,' but I was as clueless as to how to accomplish that as an Iowa farm girl who wanted to be a Hollywood star. I played fantasies in my head, things like calling the CIA switchboard and saying, "I once worked for you. How can I rejoin?"

I bought a TV set so that I could follow all the real-time news and speculation that was swirling around in those early days. Along with everybody else, I learned of Osama bin Laden, al Qaeda and Mohammed Atta. I watched grainy satellite images of Afghan training camps unroll on screen and thought of my two weeks around Mazar-al-Sharif with Asfand Ghazan.

Bush was being respectably presidential, focusing on Afghanistan for the moment, but anybody reading between the lines could see that Iraq was going to be in the crosshairs sooner or later.

Magda showed up on my doorstep on the fifth day. She had gained a few pounds but seemed otherwise unchanged.

"How did you find me?" I asked.

"Google," she said. When I just looked at her blankly, she shook her head. "You're not just off-the-grid, you're living on another planet! In any case, how I found you is irrelevant. I got a call from Schmidt: we're back in business."

"Why didn't he come instead of you?"

"All flights are still grounded. He's coming, but he sent me to brief you."

So he assumes I'll consent to this restart. He's so confident that he sends her to 'brief me,' so that his time won't be wasted on the mundane stuff ...

"What about Riley?"

The question startled her. She looked at me closely with a slightly disbelieving stare. "You really don't know anything that's happened in the last eighteen months, do you? Since we left Rhodes?"

"Not unless it's been printed in the New York Times."

She looked away from me and spoke so softly that I barely heard the words. "Riley was in the World Trade Center ... the South Tower ... he was working as a country risk analyst for one of the big hedge funds that officed there."

I felt like I'd been punched in the gut. "He was there ... he didn't ... "

"He's listed as 'missing,' along with a couple of thousand others who went to work there that morning." Her speech was precise, the undertones of anger and something else barely concealed. "It's one gigantic tomb."

It's been five days. There are no more survivors to be found under one-hundred and ten stories of concrete and steel.

Rachel told me once that the wrong thing to say to someone whose husband or wife has just died is, "I know how you must feel." Sitting there with Magda, I almost said those words. Because I felt that I was entitled to the same level and quality of grief that she was; that she had no right to feel worse than I did about losing him. But grief, like politics, is always local and I would learn that lesson the hard way.

In the end, I said nothing. But we both knew that we would come back to the topic of 'Riley.'

I asked, "Will you stay here?" and was surprised by the uneasiness that the question caused her so I quickly added, "There's a spare room." When she didn't respond to that, I left her alone and went for a run around the capitol grounds. She was gone when I returned, leaving a note that said, "I'm at the Inn of the Anasazi. Breakfast tomorrow?"

She was waiting for me in the lobby when I arrived. I gestured at the setting. "Very upscale, especially for an unemployed spy."

She looked at me as if I had no right to such familiarity and I began to see that this was not the same Magda that I had last seen in Rhodes. So my next question was not just an idle one.

"Where have you been since Rhodes?"

"Everywhere and nowhere," she said. And then she turned and walked into the restaurant. I followed and when we were seated and the coffee had been poured, she went on. "Riley and I jumped around the Greek islands for a month but one morning I woke up and he wasn't there. No surprise. We had nothing to talk about … except all those things we couldn't talk about. So I went to Turkey for a while, then Egypt. Lived on a canal boat in France for a summer, did some trekking in Nepal …"

"Sounds pretty aimless."

"It was. What would you expect of a person that always did what she was told to do, even when she didn't like it, and then was left on her own?" She made no attempt this time to hide the bitterness. Her question, and the manner in which she said it, as if it was a genuine question, not a sarcastic comeback to a critic, made me afraid for her. *She has become fragile.*

She changed the subject, realizing that she had exposed more than she intended. She smiled in the old way and waved her hand at our surroundings. "So I've decided to spend Schmidt's money. I've become a decadent consumer of luxury goods."

I objected, "It's not Schmidt's money. It's yours. You earned it." But, listening to myself, I realized that I was trying to reassure me as much as her.

"Sure," she said.

What would I have done without Schmidt's final deposit into my account? Probably gotten a real job, maybe gotten hooked on an actual career ... Instead I – her too-- entered into the equivalent of suspended animation ... or maybe we knew in some part of our subconscious that the interlude was just that, a time-out from a game that would be restarted as soon as the weather shifted .

"So you see the money as golden handcuffs? His way of keeping us in reserve?"

She didn't answer, other than to gesture at the newspaper on the table and say, "They've lifted the flight ban. He'll be here tomorrow."

Reentry

We met in a conference room at one of the Indian casinos near I-25 north of Albuquerque. Schmidt was wearing a suit, looking like a banker. But he didn't stand up to greet us nor did he acknowledge the twenty-month gap.

"Hello, Thomas. You look well." He said nothing to Magda.

He's late-fifties now. Added some wrinkles but otherwise the same as the man who sat across from me in the Student Union sixteen years ago. And I still know nothing about him except that he will do what he thinks is right no matter what the consequences.

"Hello Schmidt. I don't think I've ever seen you in a suit. You look like a banker." *Or an undertaker.*

He frowned and I wondered if I'd insulted him. "They don't trust consultants that don't wear suits. Tenant says, 'Wear a suit if you want them to listen. Red ties are good.'"

I noticed that he had on a dark red tie. *OK. George J. Tenet is the CIA Director. So Schmidt is connected again ... and has an audience.* Twenty months ago, I would have waited, but that was a long time ago, so I simply asked him, "What is it that you want, Schmidt?" I tried to make myself sound like a skeptical prospect in front of an insurance salesman, but all three of us knew that to be a sham.

"They need us. They always have, of course, but they float in and out of denial."

When he paused, I wondered if he thought that was sufficient explanation, as though the vague pronouns *they* and *us* were placeholders for proper nouns we all knew. But he went on. "The Agency is the only group that saw this coming. Not the 911 attacks specifically, but people like al-Qaeda and bin Laden. And we're the only ones that Bush can call on to do what he's promised – to end the Taliban rule in Afghanistan, to find and kill the terrorists, to prevent another 911."

"Schmidt," I said, and when he looked at me, I asked, "*Specifically*, what does that have to do with me?"

"I'm putting together a team of intelligence agents for Afghanistan operations. The same as we did in Panama and Russia."

"A team." *There were ten of u when we started.* "So you're bringing back Benjamin, Alex and Peter?"

The question caused him to look sharply at Magda and say, "You haven't told him?" She looked at me and said, "Only about Riley."

Schmidt sighed deeply and addressed the opposite wall. "Alex is in a Russian prison in the northern Urals … a twenty year sentence at hard labor. His chances of survival are not good."

I think he expected a stream of protests or accusations from me. When I stayed silent, he continued. "And Benjamin was shot dead in his office last year, almost certainly by mobsters hired by his Russian partner. He's one of six high-level foreign executives murdered in Russia since we left."

"What about Peter," I asked. He shook his head. "He's out, permanently. Has been for a long time.

Turned himself into a technology guru with a wife and a child.   Living the American dream near San Francisco."

And Riley's gone. So his so-called 'team' consists of him, Magda and me.

He knew what I was thinking, as usual. "It's more than just the three of us. I can call on Agency resources as I need them. Both at Langley and in the field. And they've told me that money is no object."

"So we'll be working in Afghanistan?"

He paused slightly. "There and other places."

"Tell me about these 'other places.'"

He seemed to relax slightly and I realized that this is where he wanted the conversation to go, that his real sales pitch -- the hook -- was based on whatever he said next.

"Do you remember Yuri Vasnetsov?"

It was a startling question, as he intended it to be, and it sent me off in my head, to the year 1990 and the Ukraine. My first intelligence assignment in Russia and a complete failure, even though no one except Schmidt and me knew of the failure. *And whoever it was that had taken possession of three tactical nuclear warheads.*

I recited, "Captain Yuri Vasnetsov of the Twelfth Directorate of the Russian Ministry of Defense.   He and Admiral Andrei Chayka of the Black Sea Fleet were joint custodians of the shipment of –"

Schmidt finished for me. " ... of one-hundred and nine nuclear warheads, where there were once one-hundred and twelve."

"Did the plutonium ever turn up?" *It sure as hell has not been used!   That would make our 911 look like a playground tantrum.*

"No, but Vasnetsov has. And he has a bearing on what we're going to be doing in Afghanistan. I want you to follow up on that end of things."

"OK. Where do I start?" It was not until that instant that I realized how badly I wanted to know what had happened to those three missing warheads and how much I hated Vasnetsov and Chayka for killing Anton Weiss.

"You and I will meet at the InterContinental Hotel in Islamabad, Pakistan one week from today. You need to spend a couple of days in Geneva on the way. Stay at the Sofitel on the Rue du Cendrier. My source on Vasnetsov will contact you there."

Elena

The Hotel Rotary Geneve Sofitel was a two-block walk from Lake Geneva and the Quai du Mont Blanc. It was a great place to be in mid-September and I spent most of my first two mornings there walking for great distances along the lakeside. On the second morning, a woman stood up from a bench as I approached and stepped in front of me in a blocking position. When I tried to divert around her, she sidestepped to prevent my passing. I made another try, but she countered again, never breaking eye contact. Finally she said "What's the password?"

When she saw the look on my face, she smiled and said, "In the movies, there's always a password." When I just looked at her, she said, "I'm sorry. It's just that this whole thing seems so melodramatic. Schmidt sent me. I'm the contact you'e supposed to meet."

Despite her attempt at humor, she seemed quite nervous, standing with both hands clutching a large handbag in front of her and unable to keep her eyes still. She was about my age, with shoulder-length dark hair, green eyes and sharp cheekbones. She was wearing dark slacks and a pullover sweater. *Schmidt said the contact knows all about Vasnetsov, but I was expecting some weaselly Slavic type in a trenchcoat, not an almost-pretty schoolteacher who likes to play games!*

I mustered the most sinister look I could, looked all around in a very obvious manner, and muttered "Trotsky." She brightened as she caught on, matched my look, leaned close and whispered "Vasnetsov."

We both laughed and I said, "We've both seen too many spy movies. Let's walk and you tell me what I need to know about Captain Yuri Vasnetsov."

It turned out that she knew a great deal. Within our first ten steps, she said, "First, he's much more than a captain now. *Euromoney* just listed him as the newest Russian billionaire. He's officially qualified as an oligarch. One of Putin's favorites, they say."

That can't be. I would have heard of him. I've been in and out of Russia for almost ten years and have watched for any sign of Vasnetsov every day.

"Second, his name is no longer Vasnetsov. He's reincarnated himself as a man named Boris Volkov. He's manufactured an entire new history for himself. Officially, he's an ex-military officer with an advanced degree in engineering from a defunct Siberian university."

"How did he get to be a billionaire this late in the game? Most of the state industries have been privatized by now. Khodorkovsky got the oil and gas, others got chemicals, metals, banking ..." *Oleg Petrykin got the Port of St. Petersburg ...*

"Russia never really privatized their defense industry ... what you Americans call the 'military-industrial complex.' It was too big and inefficient and its only customer – the Russian military – didn't have any money to buy their goods. So the industry became dependent on arms exports. Vasnetsov – Volkov – used his Kremlin connections to set up a complex of vertically integrated export firms – assembly, transport, training, financing -- to service the industry. He connected with some prominent mob folks and turned his business into the front office for the Russian arms business."

The Times just ran an article on this. Russia's the number-two arms exporter in the world. If there's a war, or even a rumor of a war, they're there with all the toys. Sometimes on both sides. The unbidden thought came naturally: *Just like the United States, the number one in the world of arms exports.*

But would he sell nuclear warheads to terrorists? I didn't want to even think about the question, probably because I knew the answer.

I wonder if she even knows about the theft? "Do you know why I'm interested in this Volkov person?"

She looked at me with a curious expression. "I think so. Because he stole three nuclear warheads from under your nose? Because he would have killed you if you hadn't left Engels when you did?   Because you probably work for the CIA?"

Who is this woman? "Uh, do you know of a man named Andrei Chayka?"

"Of course. In 1990, he was aVice-admiral in the Soviet Black Sea Fleet. A Ukrainian who was assigned to partner with Vasnetsov on the transportation and demolition of the warheads."

She was looking at me with a definite mixture of curiosity and sympathy. She said, "Schmidt didn't tell you, did he?"

Schmidt doesn't tell me much of anything. His stupid Rule One! "What didn't he tell me?"

She held out her hand. "I should have introduced myself. My name is Elena Weiss. I am the daughter of Anton Weiss, the man that travelled with you from Kiev to Sevastapol to Engels. The one who was murdered when you left."

We sat at one of the waterfront tables in a café near the ferry terminal. I told her of my time with her father, beginning with the impromptu cash collection on the Aeroflot flight and then through all of our interactions, until the final one where he urged me to leave, saying, "Go. I'll watch the unloading." He lived only another hour after sending me off.

She was silent throughout, and she kept her head averted. When I stopped talking, she said, "He called me from Kiev on the day you both arrived there. He told me, 'They've sent along a young American reporter. He's quite nice, but I suspect he works for the CIA. But he listens to my stories, so I like him.'"

I remembered what he told me that last day. "He was going to meet you in Bulgaria. As soon as the weapons were safely in storage."

"I waited two days in Sofia. The Russians didn't notify the UN of his death until the next day, and then they had to track me down. I tried to go to Engels but they wouldn't let me in. And Chayka and Vasnetsov were gone by then."

"Your father was a good man. I liked him."

She smiled sadly. "That's not such a bad epitaph. Even coming from a spy."

Enough about dead people and ancient history. Ten years is forever these days. "He said that you're a reporter, like me."

She shook her head. "I was. Five years ago, I switched to my father's foundation."

I thought back. "In furtherance of a United Europe ...?"

"Yes. It has a significant research capability. And I've used that to chase after the men who murdered my father."

"So you're a crusader." *An avenger.*

"I don't think you mean that as a compliment." She seemed to think about it. "Probably I was ... at first. But the more I learned about Vasnetsov, the less I cared about grand ideas like a united Europe or the inherent goodness of man. I just wanted to find him and kill him."

I pulled back and looked at her the way one considers a dinner party guest who announces that she belongs to a coven of witches. She nodded. "Yes, I know. It sounds ... impractical, maybe even silly. Anyway, after a while, I realized that if I could make the world aware of what he's doing, one of his clients would do it for me."

One of his clients. Like the CIA. "So you told Schmidt what you were finding out."

"He found me. Rather, Peter did, whoever that is."

"He's a hacker. If there's a digital trace, he can find it."

She shrugged, indifferent to Peter's capabilities. "Schmidt knew that I was tracking Volkov and asked me three questions about him."

It struck me. "You keep using the singular noun, but Chayka and Vasnetsov were in it together."

She gave me that same 'Schmidt didn't tell you, did he' look as before. "Chayka turned up three months after the warheads went missing. They found what was left of him stuffed into one of the empty containers they used for transporting the warheads, in an abandoned warehouse at Engels."

I thought back to that first year in the collapsing Soviet Union. "It wouldn't be hard to get away with murder. And the Ukrainians and Russians were fast becoming enemies." *But they fooled me. I thought they disliked each other enough that they couldn't possibly collaborate well enough to steal nuclear devices. But they did. I'll bet Chayka intended to kill Vasnetsov, but he was too late.*

"I guess. Anyway, Vasnetsov went to Chechnya with a Spetznaz combat unit for three years and returned as a different man ... literally. The official records have Captain Yuri Vasnetsov doing heroic deeds against Chechen rebels and then dying a tragic death, burned beyond recognition in a helicopter crash. The pilot of the helicopter survived. His name was Boris Volkov and he bears a striking resemblance to Vasnetsov."

"Neat," I said. "You said Schmidt asked you three questions about Volkov. What were they?"

"Whether he was really Yuri Vasnetsov, whether he was selling high-tech arms to the Taliban in

Afghanistan, and if I thought he still had the plutonium warheads?"

I waited.

"The answers were the same. Yes, to all three. Then he said that a man named Thomas Mahoney would come to see me and that I should share my information with him ... that he would want the same things I did and could help me get them."

She stood up from the table and looked out at the lake. Then she held out her hand to me and said, "And look ... here you are."

"Some would say that you have an obsessive-compulsive disorder."

Elena Weiss looked at the chaotic tangle of multi-colored lines spread across the blank white wall of her office, projected there from a small black box hooked up to her laptop computer. She seemed to consider the merits of the accusation, but finally simply shrugged and said, "He killed my father."

"And stole three nuclear devices."

"That's incidental. At least to me."

I pointed at the wall. "So that's a picture of Volkov's arms deals for the last five years?"

"Almost six years, and it's only those that I could trace. There are bound to be others, lots of them."

"It looks like a Jackson Pollock painting." I moved close to the wall to study the lines. There were thirty or forty lines drawn in a half-dozen vivid colors and superimposed on a map of Europe and the Middle East. Each line had a tiny number at its midpoint. She moved alongside me and when I looked at her, the beam superimposed a colorful grid on her face. She said, "The numbers connect to a data base that has the specifics of that particular trip – date, origin, destination, mode of travel, etc."

"And the colors?"

"The colors are my coding – very subjective – as to the types of armaments being shipped."

"What does 'red' signify?"   It was by far the most frequent color on the wall.

"Unknown."   After a short bit, she added, "Sorry," as though it was a personal failure. "The data is built up from UN data, flight records, arms export licenses, end user certificates and field investigations from actual conflict zones.   But the arms trade is riddled with secrecy and outright corruption."

I waved at the wall. "So how does all of this help you get even with Volkov?"

"He's indiscriminate. He uses mob money to buy arms from Russian and ex-Soviet manufacturers and resells them to both sides in every vicious bloody war in Africa and the Middle East, including the Taliban." She gestured at the wall. "With this, I and a couple of others like me in Belgium and Sweden have convinced the EU and Interpol to issue an arrest warrant for Volkov."

"But he's loose … and still dealing."

"Yes. He stays in Russia, or other ex-Soviet republics that will not extradite him."

She walked back to her laptop and pushed a button on the keyboard. Most of the colored lines disappeared, leaving four bright blue lines that began in the middle of Russia and ended in Iran, Saudi Arabia, Yemen and Iraq. "These four deals were major ones, involving high-tech, high value goods – missile components, night vision goggles, … I think that Volkov accompanied the merchandise to the end buyer."

"So he does occasionally expose himself."

"Yes, but only in the Middle East and we don't learn about it until after the fact."

Standing in the beam of the projector, she had two bright blue lines running diagonally across her face. *She's an avenger, in war-paint.*

"Elena … the arms industry is forever. There will always be Volkov's."

"Not if I can help it."

We went to dinner together that night and continued talking about the arms industry, Boris Volkov and her quest. For my part, I dredged up every memory I had of my brief time with her father and tried to arrange each of the vignettes into a story that might restore him to her in some way. The dinner lasted a long time and since it was a beautiful late evening, we walked from the restaurant to her apartment building. At the entrance, she held out her hand and said, "Thank you.

This has been very good for me." She quickly added, "Goodnight," and went inside. I think she was crying.

I headed downhill toward the lake, infected by her sadness and loneliness. It depressed me that an intelligent, attractive and extremely capable woman living in one of the most advanced civilizations in the world would spend all of her time and emotional energy battling against forces that were as indifferent to her as the fictional windmills were to Don Quixote. It bothered me that she was so unaware of the corrosive power of loneliness when coupled with fanaticism.

It never occurred to me that I might be suffering from the same maladies.

Afghanistan (2001-2002)

Does he feint or strike in force?
Will he charge or ambuscade?
What is it checks his course?
Is he beaten or only delayed?
How long will the lull endure?
Is he retreating? Why?

Crawl to his camp and make sure --
That is the work for a spy!
(Drums) -- Fetch us our answer, spy!

The Spy's March

Rudyard Kipling

Islamabad

Schmid, Magda and I landed in Islamabad fourteen days after the 911 attacks and twelve years after my first and only visit to Pakistan. It was the same day that George Tenet presented a proposal to President Bush for what became known as the *War on Terror*. It proposed to send CIA teams into Afghanistan to mount covert operations against al-Qaeda and the Taliban, acting in concert with Special Forces units.

"We're a little ahead of the curve, aren't we?" I asked Schmidt when he told me about the still classified report. "I mean, given that we're in Pakistan and already well underway."

Sarcasm never worked with Schmidt. He said, "Relax, Mahoney. 911 has changed all the rules. Asking permission is no longer required." After a bit, he added, "That's good news, bad news. The good is that we get some backup from the Agency."

He didn't go on, so I asked, "What's the bad news?"

"That we get some backup from the Agency."

"Why are we going to Pakistan?" Magda asked. "They're at least halfway in bed with the Taliban."

There was a long pause before Schmidt replied. "Because our esteemed Director Tenet thinks – wrongly, in my opinion – that, if we cooperate with them, they'll deny Osama bin Laden and his friends sanctuary in the Northern Territories."

"So we pretend to cooperate?"

"Absolutely. That's what spies do. They pretend."

The same ISI officer as twelve years ago – Mazoud – was waiting with a black Mercedes at the foot of the ramp, looking the same except for the graying at the temples. But this time he was accompanied by two men I didn't know, clearly Americans. They didn't introduce themselves until we were in an office building next to the American Embassy.

The older man said, "I'm Robert. Your CIA liaison." He didn't see Schmidt roll his eyes. The other man was obviously a military type, so much so that he didn't even look comfortable in civilian clothes. "Philip Nolan," he said as he extended his hand. He watched me struggle with the name and finally said, "The Man Without a Country ... the short story by Edward Everett Hale. Philip Nolan was the army lieutenant who was sentenced to never set foot in the United States for the rest of his life."

"CIA?"

"No way. Captain in the Special Operations group that you're paired with. You get me and – once you're in-country – access to my best troops. For use as you see fit."

Schmidt took over the meeting, "Let's review the mission specs." Magda and I looked at each other, startled by his uncharacteristic descent into buzzwords. When the five of us were seated, Schmidt said, "Mazoud, why are we here?"

The little man looked uncomfortable but he started talking. "There's going to be an unusually large contingent of the Taliban at one of their major training camps. We don't know exactly why they're gathering, but we've got the time and GPS coordinates. I gave the intel to Robert here and he's received a go-ahead to hit them."

Robert picked up the cue. "That's why you're here. This will be one of our first on-the-ground operations and the Director wants this to be handled by you for some reason." He did not sound as though he approved of the Director's decision or the secondary role he'd been assigned. He said, almost inaudibly, "He said to give you all the support you ask for."

They don't have any other options at the moment. The CIA has zero assets on the ground in that region, whereas Schmidt knows the terrain and the locals. He probably told them he has his 'team' already lined up and ready to go.

Schmidt looked serious, like a man who actually valued his colleague's opinions, a man who was weighing options, calculating odds, anticipating the unforeseen. It was all show, of course. He was probably thinking about what to order for dinner. But he rubbed his chin and asked, "What about the size of the force? Any numbers or names of the Taliban leading the party?"

Both Mazoud and Robert shook their heads. But Nolan spoke, "That's why there will be a hundred Special Operations people in place, with air support if called for. Enough for any possible enemy force."

It sounded a little too canned. I also happened to know, because Schmidt had told me, that it would take another couple of weeks to get the first sizeable contingent of rangers mobilized and into Afghanistan.

We left Magda with Mazoud and Robert sitting in the conference room.   The two men looked very uncomfortable with one another.   When we were out on the street, I said, "That was a fun little charade."

Schmidt said, "On our part, maybe.   But it was deadly serious for Mazoud."

"So the intelligence is real?"

Schmidt looked at Nolan before responding.   The man saw the look and stopped, suddenly becoming very much a military officer.   "Look, Schmidt.   It's a brave new world.   I need what you've got, and vice versa.   Either you trust me or you don't.   Your choice.   But I've got ten good men that may get killed if we can't work together."

Ten men?   I wonder what happened to the hundred that he had five minutes ago?

Schmidt said what I was thinking.   "I thought you had a force of a hundred."

"That was for Mazoud's benefit.   That oily little ISI bastard is not our friend."

 Schmidt started walking again and Nolan and I fell in alongside.   Schmidt said, "No, he isn't our friend.   But to answer Mahoney's question, his intelligence is genuine.   There is a Taliban camp and there will be personnel there when he says.   And it's our job to kill them.   Mazoud's dirty little secret is that he wants us to kill these particular Taliban, but not others."

Nolan said, "Grudges?"

"Get used to it.   Somebody doesn't like somebody, so they tell us 'That guy?   He's Taliban.   You should kill him. That other guy over there? He loves Americans, and he's my uncle.'"

Schmidt walked faster. "The Pakis know that the Taliban can't stand up to the U.S. and that it's inevitable that they are going to wind up with a passel of them in their Northern Territories. So the ISI wants to make sure they get only the Taliban that they want."

Schmidt looked at Nolan. "You OK with that kind of war?"

"You mean the kind where I get to kill Taliban?" The question spoke for itself but he went on. "My sister worked in the North Tower of the World Trade Center. This seems exactly my kind of war."

That afternoon, the three of us helicoptered to Peshawar and from there to a mountaintop somewhere on the Pakistan-Afghanistan border. It was dark when we landed. Waiting for us were ten heavily armed men in traditional Pashtun dress who greeted Nolan with an assortment of profane insults. "These are your soldiers?" I asked, and he responded in mock horror, "Absolutely not. The U.S. Army is not yet authorized to engage in combat operations in Afghanistan. These people" – he gestured at the group standing in a ragged line in front of us – "are highly-trained, Arabic-speaking American tourists who just happened to be in the vicinity and volunteered for temporary combat duty."

A strange looking aircraft sat beneath a canopy of camouflage nets. As soon as we were on the ground, the men began loading the last cargo aboard and we followed. Once we were strapped in on the bare metal benches on either side of the cargo area, the two engines started and the vibrations made me experience what I imagined a tuning fork would feel like. Schmidt, sitting next to me, shouted into my ear, "V-22 Osprey. Tilt-rotor aircraft built for the marines. Fly like a plane, land and take off like a helicopter. Ideal for missions like this one."

I said, "I've heard of these but never seen one."

"It's a Bell Helicopter and Boeing Aircraft joint development program. So far, they've only built four prototypes for testing. This is the fourth one."

"What happened to the others?"

"They crashed. The program's on hold."

Nolan and I looked at each other and then at Schmidt. He smiled benignly and said, "My kind of war."

Balkh Province

Once in the air, the noise and vibration made both conversation and sleep impossible. I spent the time scanning the ten men seated opposite me. They were older then I expected, late twenties and thirties, and they emitted a calmness that was surprising to me. Some of them fiddled with their weapons; a couple of others were trying to read with the light from pen-sized flashlights.

We landed uneventfully two hours later. Because of the way we were seated, I was the first one out the door. The props were still turning and the dust was thick. A group of men was standing fifty feet away so I headed for them. As I approached, a man stepped out from among them. "Welcome back to Afghanistan, Mr. Thomas Mahoney, journalist." It was Asfand Ghazan.

I saw his eyes change. He was looking behind me, at Schmidt. "So you came back."

"I try to go where my enemies are," Schmidt said. It was unclear if 'enemies' referred to Ghazan or the Taliban. But then he asked outright, "Am I your enemy, Asfand?"

The two men stood facing each other as Nolan and his troops filed past. Asfand seemed to consider the question. "You promised much. And delivered little. You said you would be back. And never came. You saved my life. And killed my son. And then you ask, 'Am I your enemy?'" He looked off into the darkness and said, "Not today. Today there are others ahead of you. Tomorrow? We shall see."

We had landed on a hilltop about a hundred yards from a collection of a dozen or more stone houses. An assortment of battered military vehicles stood close by. Once the aircraft was unloaded, it took off and flew toward the first rays of sunlight just appearing among the jagged peaks that formed the horizon.   Schmidt and I watched it go.

"So it's OK to fly in daylight?" I said.

"The U.S Air Force owns the airspace. It's more at risk here on the ground with us than it is flying over Taliban territory."

Two hours of flying. Maybe a few hundred miles from the border. I knew it was a dumb question, but I asked it anyway. "So how do we get back?"

"Who said anything about going back?"

Asfand said, 'You promised you would come back, but never did.' "What was that bit between you and Ghazan … about saving his life and killing his son?"

He looked at me for a long ten seconds, but finally he began. "It was 1987. The Russians were making a last ditch attempt to pacify the countryside, mostly by sending helicopter gunships and T-62 medium tanks to level villages, whether or not there were any mujahedeen fighters in the village. It was mindless killing for the sake of killing.

"I was with Asfand."   He looked around at our surroundings. "In a village about the same as this one. A dozen families, some cows and goats. We thought it was safe as a meeting place; it was nowhere near any of the fighting and had no value to either side.   I brought along a pair of M72's for a demo -- a shoulder-fired antitank weapon.   Use it once and throw it away. We planned on giving the mujahedeen a dozen of them and I wanted to get Asfand's opinion. He brought his son along. He was eight years old. His name was Rahim.

"I had just fired a test round with the M72. We were using a pile of discarded oil drums for a target and Asfand and Rahim were checking out the damage. So we were out in the open when the gunship came. It was one of the MI-24 Hind machines. The mujahedeen called them Shaitan-Arba – Satan's chariots – and were frightened to death of them until the Stingers came along. The pilot hovered, maybe twenty feet off the ground and head-on to them. Asfand had an AK47 with him – he always carried it – and fired on full auto. I could see the sparks from the rounds deflecting from the armor."

Schmidt paused in his story, looking at me but unseeing, and I wondered if he was rethinking his options on that day in 1987. When he came back to the present, he said, "They were dead. Or would have been in the next few seconds if I hadn't been standing there with an anti-tank weapon in my hands. For me, it was an easy shot. I put the rocket right into the cockpit. The machine went nose down, exploded in a fireball."

He paused again, and I knew that this was the part of the story that he didn't want to tell.

"The rotor blades hit the ground and snapped off. One of the flying pieces cut Rahim in half."

Except for Schmidt and me in our western civilian clothes, it could be a scene from an ancient tribal war council ... a quartet of grim-looking men in tribal costume hunched over a small fire, drawing diagrams in the dirt with the point of a serious knife.

Asfand, the man with the knife, said, "Mazoud's intelligence is correct, but incomplete. The Taliban training camp is six miles from here, in a small valley. It is near the border with Turkmenistan and accessible by a dirt track that accommodates heavy trucks. But the camp has been shut down for a week. The Taliban knows that all such camps will be early targets."

Nolan was angry. "So Mazoud sent us on a wild goose chase!"

"No. There's a party of Taliban meeting an incoming shipment of weapons at the camp. Tonight."

"How many?"

"Forty to fifty." He looked at Nolan closely before he said, "Too many for you, I think."

Nolan merely smiled. "What kind of shipment is arriving? Small arms? Ammunition? Explosives?"

Asfand shook his head. "My source only knows about the Taliban receiving party. But they will have three trucks with them, so they are expecting a sizable shipment."

"Your source? Will he be with them?"

"No."

"So there won't be any friendlies in that camp tonight?"

"No. It's –"

Nolan stood up. " … a free-fire zone."

Four hours later, Nolan and his ten men were belly-down and strung out along a ridgeline overlooking a barren valley distinguished only by a few ramshackle buildings along the far side and a cyclone-style fence that enclosed about two square miles of the valley floor. Schmidt, Nolan and I were in the approximate middle of the line. Two machine guns had been set up to command the sole entry and exit point into the camp. Another pair of men were fiddling with a laser type of setup with a projecting antenna.

It was a moonlit night and it was easy to follow the small convoy that came through the notch in the low hills on the other side of the valley and snaked around to the entrance. They drove in a tight bunch, three trucks with canvas covers and another pair of open troop carriers filled with men. Once into the encampment, they jumped off the trucks but stayed clustered together. A couple of small fires were started.

"Lousy security," Nolan muttered. "They deserve what they're gonna get."

An hour later, another three trucks appeared. They were heavily loaded and stayed in the lower gears even on the slight grade. They stopped alongside the other party.

Schmidt said, "Now, I think, Captain Nolan."

Nolan raised the handheld radio he was carrying and keyed the talk switch. "Tango here. You have the coordinates from the laser?"

"Clear as a bell."

"The mission is go."

"Confirm. Enjoy the show."

Nothing happened for two minutes. Then a low droning sound began and became the sound of airplane engines. High above the valley floor, long vertical streams of light appeared, moving from left to right across our front, accompanied by a sound like tearing cloth. At the same time, the physical space below us that the Taliban occupied erupted – that's the only word that fits – into a cauldron of explosions, both large and small, that went on and on until they were invisible in the dust cloud that rose around them. The tearing sound and the fiery streams made a slow circle over our heads as if it was just another spectator to the butchery beneath it rather than its cause.

Incredibly, two figures emerged from the dust cloud, staggering and screaming, silhouletted against the flames from burning trucks. Nolan said, 'Gonzo,' and the man next to him sighted his rifle carefully and fired two spaced shots. The only sound after that was the crackling of the flames from the burning trucks.

Nolan's radio squawked. "This is Tango. Need a follow up?"

"Negative. A picture-perfect run, right out of the textbook."

"Roger that. Stay safe."

Schmidt stood up with Nolan and, after them, all of the men except for the two-man teams on the machine guns. I looked at Schmidt, "What *was* that?"

"An AC130 gunship, a converted Hercules transport plane with multiple rapid fire guns mounted along its port side." He pointed at the device with the antenna. "That locks onto the target coordinates with a beacon picked up in the plane. The pilot flies a tight elliptical course to keep a stream of continuous fire focused on the same small area. They say it's like a hailstorm of metal."

Nolan led six men into the camp. They fanned out with their rifles at the ready, but there was no need. Schmidt and I came when Nolan waved us in.

"Nice of them to stay in a tight little grouping." We stood on the edge of the killing ground. It looked like a trunk full of dolls – and parts of dolls -- had been dumped from a tenth floor window. The wounds were massive. It looked like each of the men had been killed three or four times over.

One of the trucks was not on fire and Schmidt was standing in the bed manhandling crates, breaking them open with the butt of a rifle. "Handguns, rifles, night vision goggles, communications gear ... Looks like our arms dealer is running a one-stop shopping service."

I looked around, at the scattered bodies lit by the flames of the burning trucks. It was a hellish scene. *This is the real world part of Elena Weiss's color-coded charts and data bases. I wonder if Boris Volkov was on the other end of this particular transaction?*

Nolan had his men collect a single sample from each of the crates and then they torched the truck and its cargo. Schmidt searched the bodies for papers but found nothing.

Once more, we arrived at Asfand's village at dawn and when we got there, he was waiting, as before. He was inscrutable as we filed in, but I wondered if he was disappointed that we showed zero signs of having been at war.

He said to us, "BBC says that your President Bush has announced a name for his war against the Taliban. It shall be called 'Operation Enduring Freedom.' He also said that the first air strikes were being launched even as he was speaking."

I think that we saw it happen. The clichéd phrase 'the front line of history' popped into my mind, reminding me that I had once been a journalist and a spy. I wondered what I was now.

Nation Building

I posed that question to Schmidt the following morning. "Am I a journalist again? If so, I need to get back to the part of the world where they have telephones and internet service."

"You can be whatever you want to be, but I want you to stay here."

"Here?"

"More precisely, I want you to stay with Asfand Ghazan."

"Why?"

"Because I can't, and you're the next best thing." Both of us knew that was non-responsive and he quickly went on. "You were here in 1989. You met Asfand ... wrote his story that got picked up on all the wires ... made him the face of the emerging Afghanistan."

"Your idea, Schmidt. You were positioning him for the democratic process that was sure to follow the Soviet departure. He was going to be your boy. But democracy never arrived."

"Because all the goddam politicians in Washington cared about was Russia! Afghanistan was interesting to them only because it embarrassed the Russians. And then the whole Soviet empire collapsed of its own weight and goddam Saddam invaded Kuwait so it was all about Iraq!"

He's angry! He had his own personal long term 'Afghan Strategy' and his superiors didn't do their part!

"So instead of an election, they get another three years of bloody civil war and at the end of that, the goddam Taliban with their seventh century mentality!"

"Schmidt, I –"

"We deserted them, Mahoney. We conned them ... and Asfand knows it."

He told us ... Schmidt ... 'You promised much. And delivered little. You said you would be back. And never came.' Asfand's indictment of Schmidt.

"So you think we've been given a second chance? To make amends"'"

"More than that. Much more. 911 changed the rules. It's not just about Afghanistan, it's the whole bloody Middle East! The US government has overtly committed to depose the Taliban government and, with it, Islamic fundamentalism. The State Department and the Defense Department are talking openly about 'nation building'--

"Schmidt –"

" ... even though they know nothing about what it will take. Afghanistan will need leaders – Afghans, not Americans or Russians or Brits."

"So you're dusting off your 1989 strategy? Get your man in power?"

He didn't bother to answer. Instead he asked, "How long do you think it will take to chase the Taliban out?"

I visualized last night's one-sided engagement with the Taliban force in that moonlit valley, the thirty seconds of rain-like bullets. "With our support, no more than three months to overthrow the government. But the remnants will move into the countryside and we've got a replay of the Afghan-Soviet war." I thought but did not say, *And with the same miserable outcome!*

"I agree. So it is vital that the new Afghan government has the support of the provincial governors, the tribal chiefs …. the opinion leaders."

"Like Asfand." I thought back to my time with him twelve years ago. "You want me to be his consigliere."

Schmidt looked at me with a curious expression. *Maybe he didn't see the Godfather series.* "Whatever. But take good notes. Once the fighting stops, we're going to be his public relations office."

"Tell me what you want me to do." *The same line I use at the end of every conversation with Schmidt.*

"There's going to be a very short but intense war. It will be fought by a combination of Afghan militias, American Special Forces and the CIA. You're in that third category. Some CIA people who have been here before, including me, are pulling together a coalition of ex-Mujahedeen fighters, mostly tribal groups who've already been fighting the Taliban in this part of the country for a long time. We'll offer them air support, weapons and money to take on the Taliban and help us find Osama bin Laden. Asfand has already agreed, as you saw last night."

"U.S. troops?"

"Limited to a very small number of Special Forces types. Like Nolan and his people."

Like most of Schmidt's so-called briefings, this one left out a lot, but we both knew that any 'plan' was irrelevant, that realities on the ground would be chaotic and fleeting. Asfand, Nolan and I would have to work it out on the fly. But both Schmidt and I also knew that there was one more question that needed to be asked.

"Schmidt?" I waited until he raised his eyes and looked directly at me. "When we've done what we came to do – overthrown the Taliban and killed Osama – we'll stay, right? This time, it's no con job?"

He looked suddenly tired. "Mahoney, I can't control Bush or Cheney or Rumsfeld or the pointy-headed neo-cons that inhabit our capitol and hold press conferences. I can tell you that Langley -- the people that you and I work for – understands that Afghanistan is important in its own right and that we need to be here for the long term."

It was not a guarantee, not even a promise; nor could it be. As it turned out, we were there for the long term, but not for the reasons we announced in those early days. Afghanistan had its own time-honored ways of entangling the great powers.

A Wedding Party

Afghans had been fighting for a long time and for a variety of reasons. It was a tribal society with a code of conduct based on the Koran and – for the Pashtun, like Asfand -- 'Pashtunwali,' a complex set of societal mandates that regulated behavior and, among other things, kept ancient grudges alive and well. So when the Americans came with their twenty-first century weapons and their simple-minded belief in military solutions, Asfand and his countrymen took vengeance to a new level.

Asfand summarized it nicely. "You want us to fight for you? We shall, so long as we agree on who needs to be killed. And you will pay us!"

The United Front was an uneasy coalition of militias held together by CIA agents bearing suitcases filled with cash and vague promises of an expanded role in the post-Taliban Afghanistan. Asfand was one of the half-dozen commanders operating around Mazar al Sharif. The war-fighting strategy was basic: find and defeat the Taliban. But they could be hard to find. They looked like everybody else; they did not wear a uniform and had no conventional military forces. So-called 'military intelligence' consisted mostly of a stream of local villagers identifying Taliban members.

In early December, three months after 911, Nolan, Asfand and I crouched in a jumble of rocks above a small village. It was a typical rural village, about twenty miles from Mazar al Sharif, straddling a road that ran among rolling hills, surrounded by fields of wheat, rice, and vegetables. It hadn't changed much from the days when the single dirt road through its center accommodated the invading armies of Alexander the Great and Genghis Khan. It still did not have electricity or running water and there were few vehicles.

It was a farming community. We could see women and girls tending the crops and carrying water, dressed in brightly colored Afghan dresses worn over baggy pants. But the civil war in the 1990's had touched even this outback. There were half-destroyed houses and craters throughout the village.

Asfand said, "They are Taliban. The whole village. Their leader is Asif. He is the fat man with the black cap, near the blue pickup truck."

"It looks like they're setting up for a picnic in the square," Nolan scanned the square with his binoculars. "There are a lot of men standing around but women and kids too. No weapons in sight."

Asfand said, "Asif's daughter is marrying her second cousin. The groom is the son of Naji, who is the tax collector for the Taliban government in Mazar al Sharif and one of its leaders. More guests will be arriving tonight and the wedding ceremony will be held tomorrow. Naji and many other Taliban will be there for your planes and helicopter gunships."

Nolan lowered his binoculars and looked at me with a very clear, 'this is your department' kind of look. I plunged in, knowing that Asfand was well versed in close air support and its capabilities. He'd learned about it the hard way from the Russians. "No air support, no gunships" I said. "Too many non-combatants mixed in."

Asfand's expression did not change, but he asked, "Suppose I told you that Osama bin Laden will be one of the guests?" Nolan wheeled around and stared at him, but all I said was, "Will bin Laden be one of the guests?"

"No." But he'd made his point. The definition of a 'non-combatant' was flexible, the morality of war-fighting a relative thing, to be loosened or tightened depending on the target values.

We spent the rest of the afternoon setting up the operation, starting with a session with Asfand's three lieutenants. Between them, they would number about two hundred fighters and be our main force. Nolan and his men would observe, advise if called upon and – their major role – call in air support if justified. I left them to it and spent my time trying to verify the little bit that Asfand had told us about Asif and Naji. Using one of the new radios that Schmidt had provided, I also arranged through an NSA post somewhere in the United Arab Emirates for a satellite to provide us with a thermal imaging pass over Asif's village early the next morning.

Sometime during the night, the absurdity of what we were doing struck me. *We've got satellites, advanced warplanes, sophisticated weapons and the most highly trained soldiers in the world … all about to be unleashed because an Afghan tribesman with questionable motives has identified what he says is a target.*

Near dawn I received a radio call from Robert, the CIA's man in Islamabad that we had met. "Mazoud and his ISI team say that Naji is in fact a tax collector and is *probably* one of the top four or five Taliban in Mazar al Sharif. Your village chief – Asif – was a major mujahedeen fighter against the Soviets and the subsequent puppet regime they left behind.   They *think* he's been relatively neutral since 1999. He's not one of the fanatics, but he hasn't signed up for the United Front either."

I thought about sharing the intel with Schmidt, but I knew what he would say about Azif's ambiguous loyalties: *If you are not my friend, you are my enemy.*

Nolan and I were back in the rocks above the village at noon. He had two-man teams on the pair of machine guns, flanking each side of the dirt track into and out of the village.   Another two men were ten yards away, ready to light up targets for an A-10 Thunderbolt aircraft lurking over the horizon.   The plane was affectionately referred to as a 'Warthog' by the US military, and it was a masterpiece of lethality for close air support operations.   Nolan was in direct radio contact with the pilot and would act as forward air controller if needed.

Nolan's remaining four soldiers would go in with Asfand. The senior member of the quartet was called simply 'Woody,' and Nolan told him, "Stick close to Ghazan and tell me what you're seeing in that village. He's gonna do whatever he's gonna do, but there's no way I'm calling in an air strike on a wedding celebration, so watch your ass."

Asfand had divided his fighters into three groups that would come at the village from three sides, leaving the open end to be covered by Nolan's machine guns. My thermal imaging download from the NSA satellite indicated that there were slightly more than two hundred and fifty warm bodies either in the cluster of buildings or the central square. Given the number of women and children we saw yesterday, we figured there would be about seventy or eighty adult males.

Nolan had direct radio contact with his ten soldiers and the A-10 pilot. He had tried to talk Asfand into joining the radio net, but he refused, saying, "I do not like committee meetings while I am fighting." Nolan's restatement was, "He wants to kill people without me interfering."

From our elevated vantage point, we could see two of Asfand's three groups. On two sides of the village, the ground was uneven and there was sufficient cover that they could get within a couple of hundred yards undetected. To the north, it was all flat farmland, so that contingent would approach in a convoy of pickup trucks packed with riflemen. It was a good plan, mostly because of its simplicity. What it lacked, as usual, was good intelligence. We didn't know if we were attacking a bucolic country wedding party or a hornet's nest of Taliban crazies.

Naji, the father of the groom and – according to Asfand and Mazoud - an important Taliban official, had just arrived in a convoy of three identical black SUV's. They had horns blaring and as soon as they stopped, they were surrounded by the celebrants already in the square, waving and yelling. Naji was driving the first

SUV, with one other man as a passenger. Four women, and five children were in the second vehicle, and six black-clad men in the third. The man riding with Naji was clearly special, in that Naji was introducing him to others and clearly paying extra attention.

Nolan said, "Reminds me of the time I brought the general home to dinner. I wonder who the dude is and what he's doing here?"

"We'll know in about twenty minutes if Asfand doesn't waste everybody in sight." *I told him: "We want Naji alive, not dead." He just smiled at me.*

"Mahoney, the man's brought some soldiers along." Nolan handed me the binoculars and pointed to the center of the square. The six black-clad men from that third SUV had pulled Kalashnikovs from the vehicle and formed a crescent around Naji and his mystery guest. Nolan said, "Bingo" and keyed his mike. "Woody, we've got six probable Taliban with AK-47's. Middle of the square."

"Roger that. Ghazan says they're the man's personal bodyguard. They go where Naji goes."

Two other features bothered me. There were more than twenty vehicles on the edge of the square, mostly medium-sized pickup trucks, other than the SUV's. That would be consistent with a farming community and a wedding celebration, which this clearly was. But they were parked with military precision, side-by-side and facing out, as if positioned for a fast escape. The second disturbing sign was a single man armed with a rifle, standing on the narrow roof of the only two-story structure in the village ... a classic lookout.

Nolan looked at me. I shrugged. He spoke into the mike. "Woody. All the players are here. Tell Asfand to go." He changed the channel and said, "This is Groundhog to Bird Dog: Attack underway. Move to close-in support pattern and hold. I repeat: Hold."

Thirty seconds later, the sound of multiple fast-approaching vehicle engines was easily heard. The rooftop lookout picked them up instantly and fired a long burst at them even though they were still out of his range. All of his attention was on the oncoming motorized assault and he failed to see the two groups on foot, each in a ragged line, but moving rapidly toward the low wall that surrounded the cluster of stone houses.

Nolan and I each had our binoculars fixed on the throng of people in the central square and it was easy to see the abrupt change brought about by the sharp stuttering sound of the lookout's AK-47. The village square became instant pandemonium, with people of all ages and sizes running in every direction. But even in the grand melee, one group moved with discipline and purpose. Naji's little force formed a tight cluster around him and the other man and moved through the running bodies toward the black SUVs, the muzzles of their rifles pointing outward.

The other sign of order was harder to detect at first, but far more ominous. Weapons started to appear, fetched from houses, the cabs of pickup trucks or the deep shadows of the primitive mosque on one side of the square. Shouted orders were sending men with rifles to defensive positions, mostly to defend against the vehicles racing in from the north. Apparently, Asfand's foot soldiers were still undetected.

We had a bird's-eye view of the brief and very one-sided battle below us. The motorized assault group stalled when it encountered concentrated head-on fire and the narrow road prevented maneuvering. The lead vehicle was in flames, but the men in the others fanned out to both sides and began to advance among the houses straddling the road. Asfand's two flanking teams swarmed over the rock wall and quickly overwhelmed the few dozen Taliban fighters that were highly exposed to the attack from their rear. The sound of gunfire went from continuous to isolated single shots within a couple of minutes and we could see men tossing weapons aside and holding their arms in the air. There were bodies strewn in the square, and some of them were women and children.

"Shit!" Nolan muttered. "It doesn't help much to be a non-combatant, does it?"

I had Woody in my binoculars and was hearing his voice on my headset. His voice was calm and matter-of-fact. "The square is secure. Asfand's people are setting up for house-to-house search. Could be nasty."

"What about Naji and mystery man?"

"No sign." Then, "Oops! SUV's on the move!" I could see him raise his rifle and fire a sustained burst. "No good. It's got some serious armor. He's coming your way."

Nolan switched the channel. "Bird Dog: We may need you. Stand by." The reply was instantaneous. "This is Bird Dog. I've got visual. Locked and loaded. I'll wait for your OK." One more channel switch for Nolan: "Fire teams. Black SUV exiting village. Fire to disable vehicle. We want occupants alive."

The SUV accelerated once out of the village. I heard the machine guns open up and could see the impact of the rounds on the hood and sides, but it kept moving.

"Shit! Bird Dog: One black SUV on the road moving south out of the village. He's yours. Engage."

As he spoke, the SUV moved past our position at a high rate of speed. Five seconds after it passed, I heard and then saw the Warthog. It was no more than a hundred feet off the ground and tracking the centerline of the road. I heard the rattling sound and watched as a stream of explosions chewed up the dirt, starting about fifty yards behind the racing vehicle and ending about fifty yards ahead of it.

The plane banked sharply and continued the turn to pass over the now motionless vehicle. I heard the pilot's voice in my ear. "This is Bird Dog. Anything else, groundhog? Something with a higher difficulty rating, maybe?"

"Not today, Bird Dog. Thanks for the help." We both stood up and looked at the SUV slewed sideways on the road with smoke spiraling from the engine compartment. Nobody was climbing out.

"I need to see what's left of the occupants," I said, and started down the hill.

"There may not be a whole lot to look at," Nolan said. He gestured at the sky. "That thing uses a Gatling cannon. It fires 30 mm armor piercing shells ... three thousand per minute." He came with me, leaving one machine gun in place while he took the other four men on the ridge with us to check the smoking vehicle.

Aftermath

Except for the bodies, it could have been just another morning after an out-of-control frat party. The village square was littered with overturned tables and party detritus. Colorful paper plates and cups were blowing around in the slight breeze and a twenty-foot-long banner with Arabic writing was dangling from a window in the two-story building. Woody and the other three men of Nolan's team were sitting in the shade of a food shop fronting on the square, watching Asfand in the center, directing his followers.

I asked Woody, "Did we get Naji?"

"He was wounded, I think. The SUV took off without him. Asfand and a couple of his people carried him into the mosque."

The main activity going on was that of dragging the bodies of the adult males to the center of the square, where they were aligned in three neat rows with ten or more occupants in each row. Other twenty-five or so Taliban, some of them with wounds, were herded into another corner of the square, watched over by a dozen men with rifles. There were no women or children in sight, either dead or alive, but there was a piercing ululating wailing sound that seemed to come from everywhere and nowhere.

Asfand came over to Nolan and me, and Nolan said, "Naji?"

Asfand raised his arm, still holding the AK-47 rifle and used it to point at the neat rows of dead men. "There.

Second from the left in the third row. Asif is next to him." He held Nolan's gaze for a long time before finally looking away

Nolan looked somewhere into the distance. "What about his daughter? The bride-to-be? Or Naji's son? The groom?"

There was no response. Asfand looked like a man who was bored by a conversation that had gone on far too long. *I wonder if the Oxford education and all that time in England made any real difference? Or if twenty years of guerrilla warfare have made compassion an irrelevant, even dysfunctional, emotional response?*

Nolan gathered his men and told them, "Pair up. See if you can find any useful intelligence. And while you're at it, look for any women or kids with damage. Help if you can, but be careful. As far as these people are concerned, we're on the wrong side."

While he was organizing that, I went over to Asfand. "The man who came with Naji, do you know anything about him?"

"He's not Pashtun, maybe not even Afghan. I've never seen him before." He was silent, clearly picturing the two men together. "He was clearly important to Naji … somebody that he wanted to please."

Naji's mystery guest was one of the two men still alive in the SUV, although it was clear from the massive hole in his side that he had little time left. He was deep in shock and chanting a string of phrases that sounded like a prayer. I found some identity and travel papers in his pocket and kept them and took a quick head-shot photo. He died two minutes later.

The other takeaway from the SUV was a laptop computer, probably Naji's. Unlike the passengers, the computer came through the A-10 strafing run unscathed. The bodyguards were dead except for a lone survivor with a serious leg wound. Nolan put a compress bandage on it while I bombarded the man with questions. None of the answers told me anything useful.

Schmidt was waiting for us when we got back to the village. He watched silently as the Taliban prisoners were herded into a single stone shed. He stopped Asfand and said, "A good day's work."

Asfand looked at him as if to identify other motives. "Yes. There's a lot to do, but this was a good start." He looked at me and then at Schmidt as though deciding whether we could be trusted. Then he said, "We need to talk. Now." to Schmidt, and walked away.

I gave Schmidt a quick recap of what I found in the SUV but he didn't pay much attention until I told him about Naji's mystery guest. "Naji is – was – a high value target for the Agency," he said. "We think he's the financial brains for most of the northern provinces – taxes, oil, opium … the whole schmear. I wish we could have had a chance to talk with him. And if he was acting like this guy was somebody even higher up --"

"I don't think Asfand ever intended that Naji would survive the raid." I didn't comment on what Woody had told me – that Naji was alive when Asfand took him into the building. I paused. "But I've got this ..." I showed him the laptop. "Naji's, I think. I tried it, but it's password protected."

He took the computer from me. "I'll have the whiz kids at Langley take a look at it. We've gotten some real breakthroughs from recovered computer files."

He turned to leave, but I stopped him. "Schmidt, this other guy with Naji?   The VIP?   He was Persian, speaking Farsi."

He turned to look at me. "Are you sure? Iranians are not big fans of the Taliban.   As a general rule, they don't like anybody that Pakistan likes."

"I know. I've also got some papers he had with him and I took a photo of him. Maybe that will help identify him."   I gave Schmidt the bloodstained identity papers and the camera with a single photo on it. "His name is Habib something. The papers are hard to read because of the blood, but he's important. I don't know how, but he is."

"You know Farsi?"

I shrugged.

"What was he saying?"

"Prayers, I think. I heard a few words – 'Allah,' 'implore,' 'grant mercy'... stuff like that. But he also said something that didn't fit."

"Like?"

"He said it three times. Sounded like 'Fuck off.'"

He thought about it and then waved it off. "Sounds to me like he meant that bit for you rather than Allah."

Asfand yelled something at Schmidt. He was standing alongside a truck with a dozen heavily armed men on the open bed. Schmidt held up two fingers to Asfand and turned to me. "I have to go with Asfand. You see what you can find out from the prisoners they've got. And never mind the mystery guest; ask them about where we can find more of their Taliban comrades."

He turned to leave, but stopped and smiled back at me. "It's going to be a lovely little war."

Iran Gambit

It was September 2002, one full year after 911, and my predictions were coming true with alarming precision. The mujahedeen United Front, supported by the CIA and Special Forces, had driven the Taliban out of Kabul in three months and made way for a process that would lead to a democratically elected and representative government. Also as I predicted, the Taliban did not go away; they osmosed into the villages and mountains and continued to terrorize the populace in pursuit of a return to Sharia law and their seventh-century caliphate. We were still chasing Osama bin Laden and, true to Schmidt's commitment to Asfand Ghazan, we were still in Afghanistan.

But that commitment suddenly looked a lot less sure. I had just finished watching a very grainy video of Bush's speech to Congress, outlining all of the reasons we needed to invade Iraq. To spread democracy and stabilize the Middle East, of course, but also because Saddam Hussein was stockpiling weapons of mass destruction – making WMD a worldwide acronym – and posing a threat to the entire world. He didn't say so directly, but the clear implication was that Afghanistan was a lot less important. I wondered if Asfand had heard the speech.

Schmidt had been missing for the last two months except for two phone calls where he needed specific information about the now-deceased Naji. As for me, I spent most of my time in an ex-Taliban office in Kabul.

I didn't like it, but Schmidt gave me no choice. He said, "The real action is going to be in Kabul. We have to set up a brand new government and I need you in the middle of that."

An interim government was hastily constructed with a mandate to hold free elections within two years. They called it 'a maximalist model of post-conflict reconstruction,' as though the sheer weight of such a title would be sufficient to overcome the massive amounts of corruption, incompetency and inter-tribal rivalries that were baked into the Afghan culture.

So I skulked around NATO briefings, prowled through Sunni and Shia neighborhoods, drank with State Department eggheads carrying white papers on the rebuilding of infrastructure or the redesign of judicial systems and spent one sex-crazed weekend with a twenty-two year old congressional aide who wanted to set up a program to adopt 'all those unfortunate Afghan orphans injured by mines.'

I wrote feature articles for my U.S newspaper while I recruited a pair of Afghan informants in the Afghan Interim Authority who had close connections to Hamid Karzai, the American choice for the new President of the Republic of Afghanistan. I passed on all of the intelligence to Schmidt, but as far as I could tell, it had no effect.

That morning, on the one-year anniversary of 911, there was a three-second message on voicemail. "Are you still longing for Magda? Call me." A phone number with a Bay Area prefix was included. The caller did not leave a name, but there was only one person left alive who would know about my tortured relationship with Magda.

One of the civilized advantages of my new office was that I had a secure phone line. Peter answered on the second ring. "Hello Mahoney. How's Magda?"

"I wouldn't know. Why did you call me, Peter? I thought that you were filthy rich and out of the game?"

"I am and I wish, respectively. But it's hard to get rid of Schmidt. And that's why I'm calling. I need to find him."

"Have you tried calling the Central Intelligence Agency?"

"Very funny. Do you know how to reach him?"

"Nope. Have you tried Magda?"

"She hasn't seen him in two months."

So he's got something going on that is just him. "Neither have I, Peter. I can't help you other than to send a message to Schmidt that you're looking for him."

"Do that, and when he turns up, tell him I need to talk to him about the Taliban PC he sent me."

He said he was going to give it to the whiz kids at Langley.

"Is it something from Naji's laptop?"

There was a long silence and I wondered if Peter was thinking about Schmidt's 'need to know' fanaticism. Maybe he wasn't, because he answered my question. Or maybe it was just that he was truly out of the game and felt he could flaunt his indifference to its rules.

He hedged slightly. "You know about the laptop?"

"I was the one who found it. Gave it to Schmidt." *Maybe a small lie would help tip him over the edge.* "He's got me working another angle on Naji."

"OK, then. I finally got through the encryption series. I could have done it a lot faster if Schmidt would have let me talk to the geeks at Langley. Your guy Naji was a major money guy for the Taliban in the northern provinces. The laptop is basically his record of the cash coming in and going out, sort of a QuickBooks for Dummies version."

So Schmidt did not want Langley in on this? "Is there anything that indicates any transactions with Iran?"

"Iran? Why would there be? The Taliban and Iran are not on good terms. And they weren't then either."

"Peter …."

"OK, OK. And no, there's nothing."

"Is there any mention of a character named Habib?"

There was a long pause and more shuffling. "He kept his personal calendar on the laptop, more or less unprotected. He had three meetings with somebody named Habib in 2001 – July, August and October … on the day he died … the day his son was getting married, it looks like. Nothing about the agenda or place of the meeting. Just the name."

The accounting – QuickBooks stuff – would be interesting, but it's mostly history. What would it tell me about something that hasn't happened yet?

"Are there any unusual transactions? Extra large numbers, one-off kinds of outflows, code names –"

I heard papers being shuffled. "The biggest outlays were for weapons, and for that he had a special file with extra layers of security. He liked cute code names for locations and types of arms. For example, 'hot straws for camels' means rocket launchers coming in near Herat."

"Anything in those first days around 911? Late 2001?"

"Yeah. His largest single outlay since he started keeping records was in August 2001 … a twenty-five million dollar deposit for a future arms shipment."

"Twenty-five million dollars?" *A month before 911. The U.S. and NATO weren't threatening to erase them at that point. The Taliban government wasn't at war with anyone except a few local warlords.*

"Yeah. He ran it through a friendly bank in the United Arab Emirates. And that was only an upfront deposit according to his records. Must have been a lot of expensive toys."

"Any clue as to the type of weapons?" I asked.

"Nope."

"Delivery date or place?"

"Nope."

Peter was getting suspicious. I could hear it in his voice when he said, "Look. I told all this stuff to Schmidt a year ago. All I want to know is what he wants me to do with the PC and what I took off of it. He's left me hanging."

I ignored the suspicion. "Anything about the seller?"

Peter sighed. "I'm guessing here, but I think it was Naji's usual vendor. He used the same guy for almost all of the weapons. His name was Volkov."

Volkov! It's like a gigantic jigsaw puzzle where you find the first single point of linkage between two major subsets that you have painstakingly assembled.

"Mahoney? You there?"

"I'm here. One more favor, Peter? Pretend you're a street vendor in Teheran. Tell me to fuck off. In English but with a Persian accent."

"I never got to Farsi school. I'll have be an Arabic-speaking vendor in Cairo, with an Egyptian accent. You sure about this?"

"Yep."

"Fuck off!"

Sounds a lot like 'Volkov,' I thought, picturing Habib dying and muttering prayers in the bullet-ridden SUV. "Thanks. I'll tell Schmidt to call you as soon as he shows up." I ended the call and sat thinking. Then I consulted the small black book that served as my list of contacts, looked up a number and dialed.

"This is Elena Weiss."

"This is Mahoney. Remember me?"

"Let's see … Are you the international espionage agent who accused me of being an obsessive-compulsive fanatic who paints fake Jackson Pollock pictures. A crotchety old man with thinning hair who hates women, as I recall. Is that you?"

She's consistent, I thought, remembering her irreverence at our first meeting when she stepped in front of me and demanded a password. It was surprisingly easy for me to recall what she was wearing. And the smile.

"I don't hate women. Otherwise spot on."

"Have you killed Volkov for me yet?"

It was a serious question. "No but I'm working on it. That's why I'm calling. How big were the deals he was doing in the last couple of years?"

"All over the proverbial map. The 'official' out-in-the-open ones for missiles, tanks, airplanes and the like were pretty big. Tens of millions of dollars, but he was only the broker for those, working on commission. You might not like the arms trade or his customers' morals, but the deals were legal, done by the book."

"What about the unofficial and illegal ones, where Volkov was a turnkey provider – sourcing, quality control, transport, financing?"

"The ones I know about – which is most of them – were usually a few hundred thousand bucks or less. The occasional one or two million. Always done for cash."

"And he dealt with the Taliban?"

"One of his best customers at that time."

"What if I told you that he received a covert twenty-five million dollar *deposit* from them – through international banking channels -- for a future clandestine shipment?"

There was a protracted silence and I waited through the silence by picturing her on that promenade along the shore of Lake Geneva. When she finally answered, her voice was different.

"I'd say he's found a buyer for his three nuclear warheads." And then quickly, as though trying to argue against her own case, "But why would the Taliban want nuclear ..." Her voice trailed off and I knew she was engaged in the same internal monologue that I had gone through with increasing disbelief. Sure enough, her next question was, "When was the deposit made?"

"August 2001. Almost six weeks before the planes flew into the World Trade Center and the Pentagon."

She said nothing, so I filled in the gap. "And that – the planes – was a totally hare-brained scheme based on box cutters and the questionable fanaticism of spoiled Saudis, with a barely finite chance of success. At best, a very inferior Plan B."

"So you think Plan A was –"

"Three nuclear explosions ... Maybe New York City, Washington D.C. and ... take your pick. Personally, I'd do Las Vegas ... all that ungodly Sodom and Gomorrah behavior."

"Thomas, that's ..."

"Fanciful? Unimaginable? Far-fetched? All those and more. Good fodder for a paperback thriller. Speculative fiction ... except for that very real twenty-five million dollars paid to an amoral Russian who happens to have nuclear warheads on hand."

"But it never happened."

"Not the explosions. But I wonder if the nukes got delivered?"

She said, "I don't think so. To everybody's surprise, Plan B worked beautifully, so there was no need for expensive plutonium. And after 911, the Taliban were scrambling for their existence ... no time or incentive to complete the deal."

We were making it up as we went along, playing off of each other, but the string of hypotheticals seemed to make sense. She kept going. "So the buyer is out his twenty-five million, and Volkov doesn't like counterparties who welsh on deals ..." I could hear the excitement growing as she built her story. "Volkov's usual terms were half up front and half on delivery, so that makes it a fifty million dollar deal."

One more intuitive leap to make. "It's a major problem for both parties. But there's an easy solution in cases where a buyer is forced to default on the purchase contract."

"Find a replacement buyer?"

"Yes. And I have an ideal candidate. A country that badly wants weapons-grade plutonium but is not allowed to produce it and has a cadre of atomic inspectors on hand to make sure they don't. They're perfectly willing to do business with the Taliban and happy to let the Afghans manage the deal just as it was drawn up. The seller won't even know the final destination."

I could hear the smile in her voice when she said, "Volkov wouldn't care who the end user was. It's like when I was fifteen. I would send my older brother into the store to buy my cigarettes."

It was an apt metaphor, but I knew she was running through the candidates in her mind. She confirmed it. "It has to be a Middle Eastern country. Pakistan and Israel have already gone nuclear ...There's Libya ... Egypt ... Syria ... Turkey ... Jordan ..."

It was a long list of plausibles and I began to doubt my theory, so convoluted and riddled with assumptions, but then she said, "It's Iran, of course."

But the buyer's agent – Naji -- was dead, laid out in that unholy matrix of corpses in the village square, along with his Iranian partner.

I said, "I think Volkov still has the nukes."

Barroom Conversation

Sharia law bans the production or consumption of alcohol by Afghans, but the substantial number of military, diplomatic and aid workers in Kabul had a number of bars available to them after the ouster of the Taliban. One popular spot was called the Tora Bora Bar and I made it a point to stop in every now and then. I found that the combination of alcohol and the pervasive dislocation that foreigners felt in Kabul made them talkative ... and talkative people yield nuggets of intelligence.

I was listening to a pair of British SAS types complaining about their units being pulled out of Kandahar and shipped to Baghdad. Apparently, they were being tasked to search for and deactivate the supposed weapons of mass destruction that Hussein had hidden away. They didn't like it and shared their opinions quite loudly with most of the other patrons.

"Bloody WMD, my ass! Bush wants to invade Iraq because Goddam Saddam threatened his daddy and he invented WMD to scare the goddam congress into letting him do it." I should have been listening harder but what I had heard just made me think of Schmidt's promises to Asfand and it depressed me. Then I heard a familiar voice shouting for a beer and turned to see Woody, Nolan's second-in-command. He saw me at the same time and waved me to a table in the far corner.

"Hello again, Mr. CIA man." He was more than slightly drunk.

"Woody. Are you still humping around the countryside chasing bad guys? Haven't you heard that we won the war?"

"Yeah, I did hear that. But they forgot to tell al Qaeda."

We clinked the beer bottles together, an unspoken cynical toast to rear echelons everywhere. "How's Nolan?" I asked.

"Shot up," he said. "I just left him with the medics at Bagram. That's why I'm in Kabul."

Shit! Not Nolan! The sudden surge of concern surprised me. I had thought I was immune to those kinds of feelings by now. "How serious is it?"

"He caught an AK-47 burst square in the back. The vest stopped most of them but not all. We stabilized him and put him on a medevac. The docs at Bagram are working on him."

"What happened?"

"Schmidt got a tip from your man Ghazan about an incoming arms shipment ... a planeload of HE coming in to an abandoned Soviet airstrip just over the line from Uzbekistan... 155 mm artillery shells ..."

He tipped the beer bottle up but it was empty. He shook it, looked at it with a puzzled expression and then placed it very carefully in the long row of identical others. He stood up to wave at the bartender.

The 155's were perfect for roadside bombs, suicide missions ... good against armored vehicles ... the kind of improvised weapons favored by guerrillas in an occupied country. Intercepting a shipment like that would be high priority.

Woody sat back down and I asked, "Why not send an F15 to intercept the incoming plane? Or let it land and have one of those AC130 gunships make a pass? Like that first operation we ran in September 2001."

"Schmidt said no. The intel was that the dealer was personally delivering the goods and he wanted him alive and talking. So the plan got cute. Never a good idea. We split up. Our Special Ops team ambushed the Taliban party on their way to the pickup while Ghazan and Schmidt took six of Ghazan's people to meet the plane. The idea was that they would pretend to be the Taliban buyers."

"But the ambush went bad and Nolan went down?"

He turned away to deal with the bartender bringing his beer, but I caught a flash of something ... anger or maybe just scorn at the idea of screwing up an assignment. "No. Our part of the gig was textbook. Eight hadjis in a heavy truck. Stopped the vehicle right where we wanted it with some fifty-caliber rounds in the engine block. They piled out shooting every which way. We had night vision gear and they were in a wadi with no cover. More like a shooting gallery than what the papers like to call a 'firefight.'"

He took a long pull at his beer and I wondered what he was seeing in his head. I said, "So what happened? How did Nolan –"

"He found something in the cab of the truck ... a small box ... and it bothered him. He told me to mop up at the ambush site and then bring the others and join him at the airstrip. That was it. He took off and took the box with him.

"We heard the plane go overhead when we were still ten minutes out from the strip. We stopped on a ridge overlooking the strip and about a thousand meters from where the plane was parked next to a truck. There were a lot of people milling around, but they were unloading the plane so I figured Schmidt's little game was working and he didn't need a bunch of uniformed Special Ops types barging in right then."

"Was Nolan there? Could you tell?"

"I didn't see him but there were a lot of places where he could have been. Anyway, everything went to hell. First, some shouting, then gunfire – AK-47s. And in the middle of it, the truck took off and the damn plane started taxiing. We went in fast, but Schmidt stopped us. He said that Ghazan's people were chasing maybe ten Taliban."

"Where was Nolan?"

"I asked Schmidt. All he did was point toward a stack of ammo boxes and say, 'Over there. I think he's had it.' Nolan looked bad. His flak jacket was shredded and there was a lot of blood. But he was alive. We did what we could, called a medevac and waited. You know the rest."

The hospital at Bagram Air Base was small, only fifty or sixty beds, but they had world-class surgeons with lots of experience treating bullet wounds. I found Nolan sitting propped up in bed and arguing with one of them. I waited in the doorway and listened. It wasn't much of a conversation. Nolan wanted out *now* but the doc wasn't even pretending to listen. He finally walked out, saying, "You'd look funny walking around trailing all those tubes behind you." I noticed three different plastic tubes plugged into his forearm or upper left back and chest.

He looked markedly older, not so surprising given that it had been the better part of a year since I'd seen him and he'd spent that time fighting a very dirty little war, and been shot in the back very recently. I said, "Hello, Nolan," and walked to the foot of his bed. He clearly was not pleased to see me. His first words were, "Where's Schmidt?" and then in rapid succession, "Did he send you?" and "Is my team OK?"

"Your people are fine. Worried about you. And no, Schmidt did not send me. I haven't even seen him for months. I met Woody in the Tora Bora Bar. He told me the story, at least the little bit he knew. How are you?"

"Alive. But I don't think I'm supposed to be." The way he said it made it sound like an accusation.

What the hell? "Nolan, what happened out there?"

He replied, but with his head turned away from me and speaking softly. "Ask Schmidt. I was just an innocent bystander caught in the crossfire."

"Woody said you found a box –"

His head snapped around and one of the plastic tubes lost all of its slack. "There was no – Oh, yeah, a box. It had a bunch of papers. I thought Schmidt might need them for his little charade at the airstrip."

Then he asked me a question. "The delivery. Did we get it?"

Woody had checked the stack of unloaded crates. "Forty new and shiny 155 artillery rounds. Russian markings."

"That's it? What about the plane or the delivery man ... and the truck?"

"All of them got away in the middle of the firefight."

He cranked his bed back to semi-recline and turned away from me, looking out a window facing a solid wall of sandbags.

I asked him again, "Nolan, what happened out there?"

"I don't know. Ask Schmidt."

"Nolan, I –"

His voice was harsh, accusative. "It's called psychogenic amnesia, a common after-effect of a traumatic event – like taking six 7.62 mm rounds in the back. They say it may go away someday and I may remember then what happened. I'll give you a call when it does."

I stood for a full minute, saying nothing. But he did not look at me again. Finally, I said, "I'm glad you're OK," and headed for the door. Halfway there, he said, "Mahoney?" and I stopped.

"The CIA likes to play games, the kind where they get to say what the rules are."

I waited, knowing there was more.

"They generate a lot of road kill along the way."

Iraq (2003-2004)

"...in the hands of politicians grand designs achieve nothing but new forms of the old misery..."

John LeCarre

Tinker, Tailor, Soldier, Spy

A New War

Schmidt resurfaced a few weeks later. By then, I had a TV set in my closet-sized office in Kabul and I was watching a BBC news video of the runup to Operation Iraqi Freedom, George Bush's invasion of Iraq, designed, as he put it, "... to disarm Iraq, to free its people and to defend the world from grave danger." Secretary of State Colin Powell had just made his UN speech backed up by satellite photos to make the case that Saddam Hussein possessed weapons of mass destruction and needed to be stopped. I watched the video of his presentation to the General Assembly and tried to be objective, but it came across as flimsy and I felt sorry for Powell. He was a good man caught in a game that had different rules than he was accustomed to.

He and Magda just walked into my office in Kabul. They looked like a typical Pashtun couple in the big city for a day. Magda even wore a veil and walked respectfully behind the man. It took a couple of seconds for me to register who they were.

Magda said, "Hello, Mahoney," in a way that made me acutely aware of how much I missed her. As usual, Schmidt picked up as though we had talked a few hours ago rather than a few months. "What are you working on at the moment?"

"Spying on Karzai. Running informants. Writing reports. Aren't you reading them?"

He ignored the sarcasm. He pointed at the TV. It was running a video of armored bulldozers filling in trenches that Saddam's Republican Guards had abandoned before the fighting started, showing excellent sense on their part. "Are you following that?"

"Bush's war? Yeah, I am. Another sure victory for the American military ... and another disaster for the Iraqis, I think."

"What? You don't believe Saddam has those WMDs?" He asked in a sharp tone.

"What I believe is that we'll capture Baghdad in a week, declare a great victory and leave the Iraqi's with nothing except dead civilians, non-functioning institutions, and a civil war that will run for decades!"

"Bullshit!"

The exchange left us with raised voices, glares and a very real sense of surprise that we had escalated so quickly to confrontation. It was not at all like Schmidt to let that happen.

Magda played mediator. "Whoa! Leave all that crap for the politicians. That's not what we do."

She's right. Empathy is not part of our job description. But it's interesting that Schmidt cares.

I took Magda's message to heart and changed the subject. "Did you get the message that I passed on from Peter?"

He looked blank for a moment and then glanced quickly at Magda. Some message was shared that I was not in on. But he shrugged and said, "The laptop stuff? Yeah, I got that."

"I saw Nolan. A couple months back. He told --"

"I want you in Iraq."

That was abrupt. "Why?"

"Because you've seen how regime change works in this part of the world, or doesn't work, up close. Like it or not, Afghanistan is secondary. We may not like Karzai, but he's in place and not leaving for a while. Baghdad is the same old game, but the stakes are a lot bigger. I want you to develop channels that we can use."

"Sunni or Shia? I can't do both."

"Shia. Hussein and his Sunni cronies have run things for a long time, so our simpleminded masters will deem them to be the problem, erase them from public life and leave a void for the Shia – that means Iran – to fill."

Not very much later, I would remember that prediction and marvel at the way Schmidt's cynicism came to seem a form of clairvoyance.

He went on. "And there's one more thing ... some homework you can do before you get there. The CIA and British intelligence are getting hammered about the bad intelligence they've provided their masters around Saddam's WMD capabilities. I told them we could help."

"Schmidt, they've had thousands of people on this, ever since the invasion of Kuwait in 1991. I can't –"

He waved me off. "Not since 1998 when the UN inspectors pulled out. And Saddam stonewalled the so-called inspectors the entire time they were there."

I sighed. "I'll do some research, but –"

"Start out by assuming that he has WMD. Where would he hide them? And forget about the usual suspects ... the chemical plants, military bases, research labs. Assume he's imported the nasty stuff rather than developed it himself. And I need you to brief me on this before we meet in Baghdad."

"Should I focus on chemical, biological or nuclear?"

"Yes." He stood up to leave.

I said "Schmidt" and waited until he met my eyes. "What happened to Nolan? That operation you ran on that old Soviet airstrip close to Uzbekistan?"

The alarm in his eyes lasted only a millisecond, but it was there. "Mahoney! I ran dozens –"

"The planeload of 155 rounds ... the night Nolan got hit."

He glared at me, but we both knew that I would keep asking until he answered my question ... or pretended to. He sat back down. "It was a screwed up operation from the start ... too many moving parts and Asfand's intelligence was shaky. Nolan's team intercepted the Taliban who were the buyers, the ones that the arms dealer was expecting to meet. But there was another batch that we didn't know about. They showed up when we started to unload the cargo. Everything went to hell after that. Nolan went down, the damn plane got off the ground with half the cargo still on it and Asfand spent the rest of the night chasing and not catching Taliban." He shook his head. "It was not one of my prouder moments."

"Who was the dealer?"

His response was instantaneous. "No idea. All Asfand knew was time and location of the shipment. We never saw any dealer … he may not have even been there. No markings on the plane, an old Ilyushin-76 transport."

He waited for my next question. When I was silent, he asked, "Are you done now?" making it perfectly clear to both of us that I was in pursuit of a goal that had nothing to do with the tasks I was assigned. And that he would humor me until I realized either the irrelevance or the futility of whatever mistaken quest I was on.

He stood up once more. "Magda's been hanging around Kuwait during the buildup. She can brief you on what she knows about the coalition forces. I'll see you again in Baghdad."

"When?"

"When Bush declares victory. Like you, I predict that will happen no later than two weeks from now. But I need those WMD locations before then." He left as abruptly as he came, leaving Magda and I looking at each other. *She's different.* But I could not identify the source of that perception.

"Well," I said. A single word with multiple interpretations.

"I haven't seen you since –"

"Islamabad. Right after 911. I went to Afghanistan and you went …" I left it as a question mark, but was still surprised when she answered.

"At first, I stayed in Pakistan. Schmidt was sure that Osama bin Laden would turn up there eventually, so I cultivated an ISI connection. The last six months, I've been in Kuwait and the Emirates."

"And what have you –"

"Peter's dead."

The two words hung there between us, irrevocable and as freighted as any two-word sentence could contrive to be. She looked relieved, as if the saying of it somehow made it less serious.

She was talking. " ... two months ago. In San Francisco. He got in a stupid argument with some psycho vagrant in the Tenderloin. Stabbed to death."

"Why was he in the Tenderloin? What was he fighting with some homeless guy about? Did they catch –"

She stopped me cold. "Do you really care?" And I realized that I didn't, that the fact of Peter being dead in a far-off place that I could no longer relate to made all my questions irrelevant.

We sat in silence. She tugged at the cowl of her robe, exposing the rest of her face. Again, I had the sense that she was different from that last time in Santa Fe. Part of it was her nervousness, like she had other disclosures to make. And she did.

"There's something else." When I looked at her, she said, "Riley's not dead."

Riley alive? There were too many emotions, all at the same time, and all I could blurt out was, "But I thought –"

"That he was in the World Trade Center on 911. He was, but on a lower floor. Below where the plane hit. He got out. Both Schmidt and Riley thought it would be useful if the world continued to believe that he was dead, so he's officially one of the two-thousand, six-hundred and six victims."

That's why she seems different. Last time I saw her, we both thought Riley was dead. I wonder ...

"Have you seen him?"

She was staring at me but not seeing. I suspect that she was somewhere in her head with Riley. After a few seconds, her eyes refocused and she said, "Yes. Several times. He's different."

"Maybe being dead changes a person?"

She wasn't listening. "Nine-eleven affected him ... it made him ... patriotic."

It was a curious choice of words. She made it sound almost an epithet. I said, "Magda," and when she looked at me, I said, "Why we do what we do ... you, me, probably even Schmidt ... it's all about patriotism at some level. We're probably more infected with it than your average flag-waving, right-wing NRA member who's chanting 'USA, USA' at the fourth-of-July parade."

She shook her head. "He's joined the 'my country, right or wrong' crowd."

He was our resident cynic; the first one to point out the hypocrisy that was always there.

Magda knew the argument I was building in my mind. She said, "He told me that it was the jumpers that did it to him."

The jumpers. The ones who were on the floors above where the planes struck. They went up. To the roof. And prayed for helicopters. Until the flames came and made them choose.

She went on, knowing the kinds of images that she had evoked. "He was out of the tower on the street. He watched a dozen of them hit the pavement twenty feet in front of him. He said, 'they weren't screaming' and that he couldn't stop hearing the sound of the impact. He kept trying to describe it for me."

"He's with Schmidt again."

She nodded. "Yes. Doing ugly things. Targeted assassinations of tribal leaders, politicians, reporters, bankers ... take your pick ... anybody that some analyst at Langley flags as important to the Islamic terrorists."

It's what Riley is good at. Killing people. Schmidt told me that a long time ago.

"I'd like to see him again."

"Schmidt doesn't even want you to know that Riley's alive. He wants to keep him deep undercover."

"Does he have a new name?"

"For the moment, it's James Kent."

"Are you and him ..." I paused, trying to find the word or phrase, but she solved the problem for me with her typical directness.

"Still fucking? Consoling one another? Fooling ourselves about what's possible 'some day'?'" It came out as equal parts sadness, anger and disgust. "I would, oh so gladly! Any or all of those! But he just sits and stares at me ... like I'm another piece of the furniture."

She stood up, adjusting the cowl and the veil again so that all I could see of her face was her eyes. Even then, she exuded a deep sadness.

"Magda –"

"I'll see you in Baghdad. Then I'm quitting. If Schmidt will let me."

Homework

Schmidt was impatient. He called me in less than a week. "OK, I need to know where Saddam would hide his WMD supply."

The homework assignment. Actually, it's a fascinating little mystery. As tantalizing as the searches for the Loch Ness Monster, Bigfoot or the Yeti of Nepal. And with about the same chance for success.

We met at dusk in a café during one of the frequent power outages that plagued Kabul, sitting at a table with a checkerboard surface and stacks of irregular small black and white tiles that served as checkers. The proprietor gave us a single candle for illumination. I started out where I had left off at our last meeting. "I don't think there are any weapons of mass destruction." *That's not quite an answer to the question he asked, but it could shorten the conversation and save a lot of time.*

It was hard to read expressions in the candlelight, but Schmidt didn't seem to react to either my non-answer or to the sweeping nature of what I said. He nodded and said, "But we know he had them at one time."

"Yes, he used chemical agents in the Iran-Iraq War and against the Kurds more recently. And the reason we know that is because those weapons came from the U.S. Reagan didn't like Iran. "

"And we know that he *wanted* them."

"Yes. He definitely had aspirations ... plans even. For producing his own chemical agents, starting a nuclear program, maybe even for developing some really nasty germs. But they never got off the ground. Iraq's been on everybody's watch list for the last ten years."

Schmidt always was a good devil's advocate. He would have made a great college professor with his dedication to the Socratic method. He continued in eminently reasonable tones to argue with me. "He had them, he wants them, and both American and British Intelligence – good people – think that he has serious stocks of WMD stashed somewhere now."

"Yes. But they're wrong."

"How can you be sure?"

"Three reasons, maybe more if I think harder."

He leaned back and spread his hands in the classic "tell me more" fashion.

I took one of the white checkers and pushed it midway between us on the table. "First, it was lousy intelligence work. Our people got played – both the Brits and the Americans. They sat in their paneled offices and interviewed exiles and defectors; Iraqis who needed to seem important or were already starting to work us for their own purposes. Or they looked at their satellite photos and saw centrifuges instead of storage bins. There were no agents on the ground, the kind who actually *see* what's happening."

I placed another tile – this one black -- on top of the first one. "Second, they heard what they wanted to hear. More precisely, they heard what the politicians needed them to hear. Bush and Blair needed public support for their war and *needed* Saddam to have stocks of WMD, the more the better. So the spooks tweaked their satellite photos, edited out the interviews with the dissenters, and talked about what was possible rather than plausible."

Still no reaction from Schmidt. I added one more checker to the stack between us. "Third, a lot of people have been looking very hard for WMD and they haven't found any."

"But –"

I cut him off and placed another tile on top of my stack. "UNSCOM – that's the UN Special Commission – had inspectors on site from 1992 to 1998." Another tile: "UNMOVIC – that's the UN Monitoring, Verification and Inspection Commission – was here right after 911." I added another checker and the vertical stack began to show a slight instability. "IAEA – that's the International Atomic Energy Agency – were on site with them."

I looked at him but his face was in deep shadow. He said nothing, so I stacked yet another checker, placing it as carefully as a two-year-old playing with colored blocks. "Now we have Bush's ISG – that's the Iraq Survey Group – with fifteen hundred searchers dedicated to finding these elusive WMD."

I leaned forward and said very distinctly, "And not a single one of these highly motivated groups with their fancy acronyms has discovered a weapon of mass destruction. Some of them have even publicly declared that there are none."

Schmidt held up a cautionary finger. "But until we invaded, Saddam pretty much determined when and where they could search."

"I grant you he did his best, but –"

Schmidt finally went on the offensive. "The CIA – that's the Central Intelligence Agency in case you are unfamiliar with the acronym – discovered that Saddam had acquired high-strength aluminum tubing used in centrifuges and was trying to buy uranium in Niger."

I raised my voice for the first time. I was beginning to view our debate as personal. Somewhere in the last few minutes, it had become important to me to win the argument, regardless of whether I was right or wrong. "More bad intelligence. The tubing has multiple non-nuclear purposes and – so far – the uranium story is just that ... a story."

There was only one checker left on my side of the table other than those in my carefully constructed column. It was larger and heavier than the ones I'd used, which is why I'd saved it for last. I placed it very carefully on top.

"Sorry, I don't know the correct acronym. Bush called it 'the Coalition of the Willing,' but it consists of approximately two-hundred thousand individuals with unlimited access – the invasion force – and every one of them is looking with great diligence for two things – Saddam Hussein and WMD. They have found neither."

I sat back, feeling like a prosecuting attorney who'd just made a world-class summation to a jury.

"You've done your homework," Schmidt said.

"Journalism 101. Everything's in the public domain. No spying, bribing or coercion required."

"And do you believe that you're right about the WMD? Or have you just gotten caught up in constructing a story that will sell newspapers?"

Trust Schmidt to ask the painful questions. As always in our relationship, he found the edge, the ambivalence that exists in every cause, the need for 'balance' that reasonable people harbor. It's the ability that made him the supreme intelligence officer.

And, as always, I tried to answer honestly. "I don't think we'll find any weapons of mass destruction. I could be wrong."

"You know what will happen if no WMD are found?"

"Yes. Bush will be blamed for leading us into a war based on false pretenses. It will be a political disaster. He'll blame 'bad intelligence' and the CIA Director will probably fall on his sword."

Our lone candle fluttered brieflly and went out. At the same time, my column of checkers toppled over. Premonitions were easy to come by for the next few seconds.

Schmidt finally got to the point that I knew he would, the one that made all my reasoning just so much academic theorizing. "If Saddam had WMD, where would he hide them?"

"Schmidt, Iraq is a hundred and seventy thousand square miles of hiding places –"

"You're stalling, Mahoney."

I shrugged, knowing this is where we would wind up. "OK, I can narrow it down quite a lot. First, start with the reality that the main problem with secrets is that people talk. So he'd pick a sparsely populated place, among people he can trust."

"That helps a lot. Saddam and his regime are Sunni Arabs, so we can eliminate those parts of the country inhabited by Shia, Kurds or Turkomen."

"That's most of the eastern half of the country. Then, second, I would rule out most of the western half. It's mostly empty country and any kind of activity would be easily detected, especially by satellite. Third, it won't be in a city – too many eyes; or on a military base or near any plausible construction facility – fertilizer factory, power plant, that sort of thing – because those will be the obvious places to look. And, obviously, you can rule out those places that have already been inspected … if you knew where they were."

Schmidt was following closely. He said, "So what we're left with is an ordinary building, maybe a warehouse or a farm, in a relatively rural area inhabited mostly by Sunni Arabs."

I nodded. "I'd check the little villages and towns along the Tigris and Euphrates river valleys. And I'd start in the area around Tikrit. That's Saddam's home town."

Schmidt took a sheaf of folded papers from his jacket pocket, took a small flashlight from his jacket and spent a minute sorting through the several papers. He picked one and handed it to me. "Here's a map of Northern Iraq, mostly Sunni territory and including your river valleys. It's marked to show any sites that inspectors or search teams have looked at and cleared as of two days ago. I want you to identify, say, three high probability areas that you would look at next."

"All that will do is to demonstrate that I have a sense of humor. What you're asking?   It's a waste of time. There aren't any WMD and if there were, you and I can't find them."

"Humor me."

I took his flashlight and looked at the map. There was a surprisingly large number of tiny 'x's inked on its surface. The searchers had been busy. I took a pen from my pocket, studied the map for thirty or forty seconds and then drew an irregular perimeter that encompassed an approximate forty square mile area northwest of Tikrit, a space that was drawn so as to avoid the x's and larger villages.   To me, the shape resembled a mushroom.

I handed him the map. "Here. Somewhere within that perimeter.   But it's no more than a case study of the ignorant in pursuit of the unfindable."

Schmidt didn't look at the map, just folded it and put it back into his pocket. "Ah, Mahoney. You have just described the entire world of inteiligence. But cheer up. If nothing else, we can rely on serendipity."

When I just stared at him, he said, "Who knows? Maybe we'll find Saddam Hussein."

Istanbul

Elena Weiss called two days later. "I have news."

"About?"

"We should meet."

She was worried. I could hear it in her voice. And this was the first time she was wary of a telephone conversation. At the same time, I felt a small surge of anticipation at the idea of seeing her again.

"Where and when?"

"Can you be in Istanbul on Saturday?"

"Yes."

"Good. I'll see you on the terrace of the Ciragan Palace Hotel at two PM. It's on the European side of the Bosphorus."

"I know it. Very decadent." But she had already ended the call.

Schmidt had said he wanted me in Iraq, so I spent the next two days in Kabul doing the sort of things that are required to manage an ongoing intelligence network without being there. Most of that consisted of setting up new communication arrangements and reassuring my very nervous informants I had recruited that nothing had changed, that I would look out for them. I thought of Svetlana quite a lot during those conversations: a woman who blew who her brains out when my promises went unfulfilled.

One of my recruits, a secretary for one of Hamid Karzai's advisors, told me, "I quit." He spoke in quiet reasonable tones. "You are leaving. The Americans are spending all their time and attention on Iraq. Why should I risk my life for people that don't care about me or my country?" I had no rebuttal ... or at least none that I believed in.

I am a spy. I lie for a living. What does it mean when I can no longer do that? Is that why Magda wants out?

I arrived in Istanbul a few hours before my meeting time with Elena, so I walked around in Taksim Square, visited the spice market and sat for a long time in a sidewalk café drinking coffee and watching a pair of side-by-side television screens. One of them was tuned to BBC's coverage of the Iraq war and featured an embedded journalist following a British armored unit that he kept calling 'the point of the spear.' They slipped in some grainy videos of cruise missiles being fired from ships and brightly colored maps with dramatic neon arrows arcing toward Baghdad, all of which seemed to be confirming Schmidt's forecast of a two-week-long war. The other TV set was tuned to a local station and even though my Turkish language skills were poor, I could tell that it was focused on the likely impact of the Iraq invasion on what the Turks called 'the Kurdish problem.'

The net effect was that a pervasive depression had set in before I ever got to the Ciragan Palace. I was early, so I picked a table on the veranda, off by itself and situated between two massive marble columns. I ordered coffee and watched the continuous and varied traffic on the Bosphorus. As always, it ranged from oil tankers to small skiffs. There was even a submarine flying a Turkish flag.

The view was absorbing and I didn't notice Elena until she sat down opposite me and said, "There are no oil tankers on Lake Geneva. I like that."

She was dressed simply; black slacks and a blue silken blouse with earrings and a gold chain. She was carrying a matching headscarf in her hand and I wondered if she wore it when out on the street in Istanbul in deference to the Muslim culture. She had cut her hair short and there were traces of gray at the temples and a hint of wrinkles at the corners of her eyes. *She's older. But it's been almost three years since we met and a year since we last talked. She seems even more intense.*

Part of the intensity was physical. She sat very still, leaning forward slightly as though ready to spring ... or flee. She gave the impression of *studying* whatever she was looking at, as though assessing its – or his – less visible qualities. It was disconcerting.

"How are you, Elena?"

She smiled. A very fleeting smile. "Can I have some coffee please?" I waved at a waiter nearby and went through the process of ordering, aware that she was studying me the entire time. *Fair enough. I wonder what she sees?*

"You've changed, Mahoney."

I tried a quick deflection. "Comes from my dissipated life style. I haven't –"

She paid no attention, her eyes still fixed on mine. "You're sad, like a man who's been disappointed one too many times by something or someone."

"You're confusing sadness with cynicism. And it's an occupational hazard, not a temporary condition. Comes and goes, like malaria."

She shook her head, undeterred by my attempts to deflect. "There's a difference. Sadness is curable, cynicism is forever. Sadness is how one feels, cynicism is how one acts. Sadness is honorable, cynicism is self-serving."

She's been sitting there for ten seconds and we're already deep into stuff that I really don't think I want to talk about. Those damn eyes!

"Uh, Elena. Can we change the subject?"

"Sure, for now." She sat back, crossed her legs and turned to look at an improbably large gleaming white yacht passing the Besiktas ferry, becoming nothing more than an attractive cosmopolitan woman sipping coffee at the point where Europe and Asia meet. It was as if she had an internal on-off switch for intensity.

We chatted for thirty minutes, like two ordinary casual acquaintances that happened to encounter one another in a foreign city. She had been in Istanbul several times and it was one of her favorite cities. She was here for three days, her main purpose being to participate in a conference having to do with Turkey's bid for membership in the European Union. Her other reason was to meet with a UN team that was attempting to gather data on the scope of Turkish involvement in the shipment of armaments into conflict zones. Somewhere in there, we switched from coffee to wine and ordered a cheese plate.

"So you're still chasing arms dealers?"

Her eyes flashed. "Just one. Boris Volkov. That's why I wanted to meet you."

"Don't take this the wrong way, but couldn't we have done this on the phone?"

She looked at me closely. "Is this a bad time? Have I taken you away from something important?"

"Not at all." *You might say that I'm in transition. Not just from Afghanistan to Iraq, but also from one failed operation to another one with about the same miserable prospects for success as the last.* "I'm in the process of moving from Afghanistan to Iraq, so this is a good time for a break. Besides, I wanted to see you again. It's been a long time."

"I'm glad you came. And, yes, we could have done this on the phone, but I'm getting slightly paranoid. I'm starting to hear imaginary clicks on the phone line and feel like I'm being followed."

"Paranoia can be constructive if you have enemies. And I'm sure you do. The international arms trade is worth hundreds of billions of dollars and you – and others like you – are a threat to the players."

She smiled again. "So Boeing will hire a hit man?"

I didn't smile. "Not Boeing, but maybe somebody like Volkov. Seriously Elena, you need to be careful."

She shivered slightly, perhaps from the light breeze off of the water. "I've learned more about him. That's what I wanted to share."

"OK."

"He's developed a pattern. He's got a residence in Baku and is spending a lot of time there."

Baku is in Azerbaijan. No extradition to the US from there. On the Caspian Sea with direct sea route access to Iran, Uzbekistan.

I said, "Makes sense in his kind of business. Perfectly safe and close to some of his really good customers."

"It also makes it easier to monitor what he's up to. We've got watchers there who can tell us what he's doing."

"And?"

"He's got a warehouse on the waterfront. Very high security. We think he keeps his inventory there, particularly of the high-value stuff that he wants to keep out of sight ... the kind of military hardware that would require a lot of hard-to-get approvals and paperwork. He's also moved a bunch of his transport assets to Baku. Some aircraft, a couple of small freighters, trucks ..."

"Your watchers? Do they have eyes on him personally?"

"Not all the time. Maybe sixty-seventy percent coverage. They'll usually know when he's leaving, coming back, and – sometimes but not always – where he's been. If he flies, there are records ..."

"You're getting real close, Elena. He's bound to make a mistake ... the kind where Interpol can pick him up. Or the CIA if we need to cut some legal corners."

She looked at me with a trace of pity. "The CIA won't help us. We've tried. They need Volkov for their own purposes."

I suppose I should have been shocked, but after almost twenty years of more-or-less continuous disillusion, I could not muster any surprise. But there was a puzzle in what she said. "Elena, I am CIA." *Maybe not officially, but close enough.*

"That's why I didn't trust your phones." She stared intently at me and asked, "But I can trust *you*, can't I?"

I didn't answer immediately and both of us recognized that the very hesitation, my failure to blurt out an instant and emphatic, 'Of course you can trust me,' signaled that it was a real question, one with more than one possible answer, and it deserved a serious response. After a few seconds, I said, "I want the same things you do. Especially where Volkov is involved."

Does this make me a traitor? Withholding information from my employer? Working against their interests? Some kind of a covert conscientious objector in wartime? On the other hand, didn't Schmidt say that he valued me for what he called my 'moral ambivalence?'

Elena broke in on my purely internal monologue. "There's more. The other twenty-five million dollars has been deposited in Volkov's account. Last month. It came through the same Emirates bank as the first payment."

"But that means —"

"Yes. That the tactical nuclear warheads have been delivered to the buyer. The fifty-million dollar deal has been completed."

"But who's the buyer? Iran? But Naji and Habib were dead, the Taliban fragmented and running. Doesn't seem likely that the deal could be salvaged at that point."

"Maybe it was already agreed upon, with a delivery date set for last month? Or maybe somebody else, either Taliban or Iranian, impersonated Naji and made the final arrangements. As far as we know, Volkov didn't know the specific individuals he was dealing with."

Too many scenarios. "OK. Let's assume he had the nukes stashed in this highly secure warehouse in Baku. Do you have data on shipments out of Baku at about the same time the final payment was made?"

"I know there were some. I'll see if I can pin down the dates." She leaned against the marble column beside her and reached down for the large handbag at her feet. The instant she sat erect again, there was a sound like a hammer hitting a rock and a very fine plume of marble dust spouted from the column about twelve inches from her head.

"What was that? Did somebody throw something?" She was watching the dust settling on the tablecloth, barely visible against the grayish pattern. I stood up and moved between her and the waterfront. "Why don't you ask the concierge for a phone line? See if you can get those dates? I'll join you in a minute."

When she was gone, I left enough cash on the table for the bill and a substantial tip. Then I looked at the column, the side facing the waterfront. There was a cone-shaped depression in its surface, about four inches in diameter at the impact point and narrowing to a one-inch funnel after about three inches of penetration. I'd seen similar shapes in the sides of buildings and monuments in Managua, Kabul and Moscow. At the center of the depression, in that one-inch funnel, was a misshapen piece of metal.

We've been sitting in that spot for about ninety minutes. Plenty of time for a watcher to hire a boat for a short tourist trip on the Bosphorus.

The column was about thirty yards from the water's edge and I walked out to the low wall separating the land from the water and looked at the waterborne traffic. *Lots of small craft possibilities. A stable platform within a few hundred yards. Plenty of diesel engine noise to mask the noise. Surefire escape route even if detected. A very professional setup. Except that he missed.*

I found Elena in a small room off of the lobby designed precisely for guests making international phone calls. I tapped on the window and she held up five fingers, so I used the time to make another circuit around the veranda. The marred column remained unnoticed. *I wonder if they'll call the police when they finally recognize what caused the damage.*

As soon as she was done, I hustled her out of the hotel and into a cab. Once we were underway, she asked, "What's the hurry?   I have –"

"Somebody just tried to kill you."

Her eyes widened and she put her hand on my forearm with a grip tight enough to be uncomfortable. "That sound … the dust from the column…."

"A high-powered rifle. From a small boat on the Bosphorus. A first-rate setup."

She looked at me. "Except that he missed."

"Yes. I'm glad he did." I put my hand over hers, feeling the tendons gradually relax and wishing that I had not brought her into the game.

Convergence

Istanbul's Grand Bazaar is perhaps the world's oldest still-functioning covered shopping mecca. It also was an obvious destination for someone who does not want to be followed. It has four-thousand shops, dozens of entrances, miles of twisting lanes and a hundred thousand daily visitors. No watcher would be able to follow us in that setting.

We went from there to the Swiss Hotel near Taksim and I checked in using a passport and credit card for one George McKinnon, a Canadian who had died at age two.

Elena said nothing and asked no questions during the two hours of dodging around the Bazaar or in taxis. I think she was still processing the idea that some one wanted her dead and had almost succeeded in achieving that goal. Her first words since leaving the Ciragan Palace did not come until the door closed behind us in the Swiss Hotel.

"I have no luggage."

"We're only here for a few hours. You have your passport, visa, air tickets?"

"Yes." She held up the large handbag.

"Good. Call your hotel that you're booked into. Tell them you've had to leave for an emergency. Ask them to pack up your bag and ship it to your home address in Geneva."

She made the call. When she put the receiver down, she said, "This is what you do, isn't it? Cover up your tracks."

"Every now and then. Mostly, I go in and out the front door just like ordinary people."

"Can we get some dinner? I'm starving. That cheese plate was a long time ago."

"Sure. This hotel has a rooftop restaurant with a great view of the Bosphorus. And good food."

She looked uncertain, and that was an aspect of Elena that I had never experienced, so I added, "And you're invisible from the street level and out-of-range for any passing boats."

It was just the two of us in the elevator. She stood in the far corner and said, "I'm sorry. I know you're trying to help, but this is hard for me ... the idea that I'm a target."

I'm glad she didn't see that cone-like hole in the marble column. It's too easy to extrapolate to what her head would look like. But all I said was, "Three things. First, you are perfectly entitled to whatever you're feeling. Emily Post did not have any suggestions for correct behavior in this situation. Second, you *are* safe here, with me, in this place. And third, --"

I never got to finish my reassurances. The door opened and we had to force our way out through a crowd of very loud Turks in soccer jerseys, all trying to get in at the same time. I paid the maître de a fistful of Turkish lira to get us an isolated corner table near the parapet closest to the Bosphorus. It was still early evening and a gigantic moon was rising behind the distant walls and minarets of the old city. A lone violinist was playing on the other side of the terraced roof from where we were sitting.

I felt strange, disoriented. I was in a place where no one knew who I was, running away from an unknown threat, in a time where I had no responsibilities for anything except self-preservation, and with a woman unlike any other I had been with – Magda, Monica, Svetlana … Except for Rachel. Elena was like Rachel squared except she existed in my real world, not the artificial Santa Fe world that I had mistakenly assumed I could inhabit, as though history had no bearing on the present, something to be put on and taken off to suit the situation.

I ordered a bottle of wine and upset the sommelier by waving off the tasting. I don't know why, but ritual in any of its forms seemed inappropriate. After the first sip, Elena gave a deep sigh, gestured at the moon and said, "I'm glad I'm alive. I would regret missing this. Thank you."

Her few phrases struck me, setting off a spontaneous torrent of words that surprised both of us. "I am forty-four years old. I have traveled all over the world, had many experiences, done things that others will never do. But this is the first time in my life that I have seen a moon like that in a place like this with a woman as beautiful as you." I raised my wineglass to hers. "Here's to being alive."

Where in the world did that come from? It was completely instinctive and unforeseen. I felt like a Pentecostal worshiper suddenly finding himself speaking in tongues.

She reached for her wineglass but then stopped and looked at the moon for a long time. Then she stood up and held out her hand to me. Her eyes were shiny and incredibly bright. I was slow and trying to think of something to say, but she stopped me. "Mahoney, just shut up and come with me. Dinner can wait."

An hour later, the moon was an ordinary-sized orange sphere obscured by a smoky haze from the coal-fueled cooking fires of Istanbul, but it was still visible through the window across the room from the bed. That and the light from a lamp in the alcove were sufficient to create deep shadowy patches on Elena's naked body. The interplay of light and dark reminded me of Pushkin, but no rhymes came to mind. *That's progress, I think. But it's probably only because I did such ugly things in Afghanistan, things that did not fit with poetry.*

"That was nice, Thomas."

Such an incredible understatement!

"Do you have other women?"

Such an artless and complicated question. I can't even begin to answer it. But I tried. "I did, but not now. *Not since that day in September.* I don't seem to be very good at it … being with a woman." She propped herself up on a pair of pillows and said, "The sadness, maybe?"

"Before I met you, there was a woman in Santa Fe. She told me, 'Love requires you to run the risk of betrayal.' I don't know which of us she was trying to discourage."

"Did she leave you … betray you?"

"No. One day, we just realized that we were unimportant to each other … No, that we were not sufficiently important … that there would always be something else that was bigger, more important. It was depressing, and mutual."

I put two fingers on her lips to stop the questions, and I asked her, "Do you have other men?"

"Oh yes! But not in the way you mean. One that I cannot stop thinking about. And you know him."

Volkov.

My question and her answer changed the atmosphere in the room as surely and quickly as if a battery of floodlights had been switched on. She pivoted off the bed, stalked around the room picking up her few pieces of clothing and went into the bathroom, closing the door behind her. I was still buttoning my shirt when she came out fully dressed.

"I'm sorry, Thomas. But I meant what I said: I really enjoyed the last hour. I wish it could last."

"I can see you again?" I gestured at the disheveled bed. "Like this, I mean?"

"Of course." She ran her long fingers down the side of my face. "I would like that."

We went back to the restaurant, had a three-hour dinner and talked about the kinds of things that a man and woman would want to know about a person that they had quite spontaneously and surprisingly taken into their bed. We talked about Russian novels ... too long with too many characters ... American movies ... overly committed to happy endings ... favorite cities, our childhood, hobbies ... neither of us seemed to have any ... and whether sadness was a temporary malady or a fact of life for any thinking person. Then we went back to the room for four hours of sleep before she had to leave for the airport.

During our last few minutes in the lobby, she asked, "What was the third thing?" When I looked blank, she said, "On the elevator, you were trying to tell me why I shouldn't really worry about someone wanting to kill me. You said there were three things. The first two were about Emily Post and that I was safe for the moment. We never got to the third reason."

"Oh. I wanted to say that you would be fine in Geneva. Volkov can't go where he's at risk of arrest, certainly not to a country like Switzerland."

That was a lie, but a well-intentioned one. I didn't want to tell her the real omission: that the rifle shot was aimed so as to deliberately miss her. A warning, not an errant shot. And I *really* did not want to tell what else I suspected: that it may not have been Volkov or one of his subordinates using the rifle, but someone else even more deadly.

But I wasn't the only one keeping important secrets. When the doorman signaled that the cab was waiting, she reached into her handbag and handed me a postcard-sized piece of paper embossed with the Swiss Hotel logo. "Here are the dates you asked for. Volkov's shipments out of Baku within a few days of the twenty-five million dollar final payment. Volkov went along on one of the trips. I've circled that one."

Then she was gone.

Baghdad

I spent most of the time during the return to Afghanistan thinking about my rapidly growing list of misgivings, many of them dating from my first meeting with Schmidt and others from as recently as yesterday. But what started as a simple undifferentiated list of curiosities slowly morphed into something more sinister, like Elena's multicolored map of arms deals. It was like filling in a crossword puzzle: some of the clues made no sense until enough blanks had been filled in and then became obvious.

It's time to fill in more of the blanks.

Nolan wasn't in the Bagram hospital and no one that I talked to knew where he had gone. One doc who remembered him thought that given the severity of his wounds he would have been rotated either to Germany or the US mainland. Another said he'd seen him leaving the hospital escorted by two soldiers in fatigues.

I couldn't reach either Schmidt or Magda and wasn't sure that I wanted to find them at the moment. I hung out at the Tora Bora Bar where I'd last seen Woody, but none of Nolan's people came in.

That left one other possibility. I found Asfand Ghazan in Kabul, attending one of Hamid Karzai's grand councils with all of the tribal leaders that he could convince to attend. I had to sit for two hours on a stone bench waiting for the forty or so men to break up their session for the day. When I stood up in his path, Ghazan seemed startled, but a broad grin quickly appeared. He took my arm and pulled me along with him.

"Mahoney. I'm glad to see you. It has been a long time and I wonder how you are doing in that tiny office in our capital city where they fight their wars with car bombs and twelve-year-olds wearing suicide vests. You need to be out in the country."

"Salaam, Asfand. And I 'm glad to see you too. I too wonder about you and your people. But why are you here? Are you going to become a government minister?" *That's what Schmidt wanted – for Asfand to become an important part of the official Afghan power structure.*

He laughed outright. "Me? No. I am an advisor to Karzai. Not the most important one, but not the least either. I have convinced him to invest in infrastructure in my tribal region. Water systems, highways, schools …"

What I said was, "Excellent!" But I had been long enough in Kabul to know how funds are disbursed and I wondered what kinds of side-deals had been necessary to win those concessions. But that wasn't why I was there, so I said. "Do you have ten minutes? For a cup of tea?"

"Of course." So we sat in a small garden with several tables and a single waiter missing one leg and a hand. He was surprisingly adept at serving tea. Once the tea was poured, I asked Asfand whether he had seen Nolan recently. His face changed in a way that telegraphed a sudden irritation that he quickly covered up.

"Not for a while. Not since ... last month. We're no longer operating jointly."

No mention of Soviet airstrips or running fights with the Taliban after Nolan is down.

I couldn't let that pass. "Not since that night you and Schmidt intercepted that plane with its cargo of 155's?"

Quite suddenly, the friendly and open man sitting opposite me became suspicious and calculating, as though I had accused him of cheating at cards. "Schmidt told you about that?"

"No. I ran into one of Nolan's people, the man named Woody. And he didn't know much about what happened at the airstrip."

Asfand fussed with pouring tea for both of us, taking more time than he needed. Then he surprised me. "Is Nolan OK? I assumed he was dead."

I told him about my meeting with Nolan in the hospital, leaving out my impressions of Nolan's sudden distrust of me or his comments on the CIA. "That was several days ago. I went back this morning to see how he's recovering, but I can't find him. The Special Ops people are a secretive lot."

He laughed at me. "And the CIA is not?"

I smiled politely. "He couldn't remember what happened to him that night ... between the time he left the ambush party and woke up in the hospital."

Asfand was watching me closely, as though mistrusting what I was telling him. Finally, he shrugged and said, "We were unloading the shipment when he showed up. I think that's what triggered the attack on us ... the sight of a uniformed American soldier kind of undercut our cover story. The dealer had half-a-dozen gunmen on the plane with him and Nolan was the first one to get hit."

That's an interesting variation on Schmidt's version. "Did Schmidt —"

Asfand stood up suddenly. "I have to go. Come and see me when you're tired of city life." And he left without looking back.

Baghdad is about fifteen-hundred miles west of Kabul, but the country of Iran sits squarely between them, so we flew south from Kabul to Qatar and then north again to Baghdad. I was the lone passenger on a C130 loaded with supplies being transferred from Afghanistan to Iraq, given the shift in warfighting priorities. It was mostly boxes of leaflets. Each box had a sample of its contents taped to the top. One of them was a primer on Islam, another was titled 'You are an Ambassador' and listed ten rules for interacting with Iraqis. My favorite was apparently intended for Iraqi school children. It featured a photo of a very friendly looking soldier surrounded by a crowd of children and was titled 'What are Americans like?' Unfortunately, the children were obviously Afghans, not Iraqis, and the text was in Pashto, not Arabic.

The rest of the cargo seemed to consist of MREs – freeze dried military cuisine or "meals ready to eat" in military jargon – crates of desert boots, and a large consignment of body bags, although the discreet labels on those particular crates listed the contents as 'Human

Remains Pouch" and assured me that the bags were of the highest quality vinyl.

Donald Rumsfeld said he was going to streamline war-fighting ... make every dollar count. So we're shifting inventory from Afghanistan to Iraq. Very efficient.

We were on the ground in Qatar for four hours and I watched an Armed Forces Television channel along with a squad of marines. The program was live, featuring President Bush declaring 'Mission Accomplished' from the flight deck of the carrier Abraham Lincoln. A very young Marine corporal yelled, 'Damn! I missed the war!' and there was a lot of high-fiving going on. The testosterone was almost visible in the air and I felt as ancient as dirt.

Once on the ground in Iraq, the transport was directed to a far corner of the airfield, where there was a boy about fifteen-years old waiting for me. "Mr. Thomas, yes? Schmidt waiting." Outside the fence, he pointed to a motorbike and got on in the driving position. My triumphant entry into Baghdad was on the back of that bike, clinging to the bony shoulders of a boy who shouted 'Goddam Saddam!' at every soul we passed.

He dropped me beneath the portico of a very large and expensive-looking residence, seemingly untouched by war except for a single cluster of pockmarks next to the front entrance. They reminded me of that brand new flaw in the marble column at the Ciragan Palace and I wondered whether Elena's paranoia had abated. Another boy showed me to a bedroom on the second floor and yet another popped in five minutes later to tell me that Schmidt would be here tomorrow. I began to wonder if Schmidt had recruited a gang of teenaged orphans for logistical support.

There was no electricity working and I had no means of communication. When I wandered downstairs, I found a pair of American civilians sorting through packages of MREs strewn across a dining table that must have been twenty feet long and had about a dozen candles dripping wax onto its glossy surface. They ignored me until I said, "Where am I, other than somewhere in Baghdad?"

The taller and younger man made a mocking bow and said, "Welcome to the city residence of the honorable Tariq Aziz, until recently the Foreign Minister for the Republic of Iraq. Unfortunately, he is detained elsewhere." He waved a hand and said, "I'm Ian McKell. This other fellow here is John Brady. Would you like some fine military cuisine? Who are you, by the way, and why are you here?"

"Thomas Mahoney. I'm a journalist. What about you?"

"I think I've read some of your stuff. Us? We're State Department, supposedly here to help the new government modernize the judiciary."

The three of us stood looking at one another. It was hard to read expressions in the meager candlelight, but I suspect we all came to the same conclusion. *Spooks.*

"I'm meeting a man named Schmidt. Have you seen him?"

"Never heard of the fellow, but I can tell you that he hasn't been here since we arrived two days ago."

"How can I get from here to … *where do I want to go* … to wherever they're holding press conferences or briefings?"

The man calling himself Brady spoke up. "Transport's very iffy, more Abrams tanks than taxis, and there's still a lot of gunfire. I'd wait for daylight if I were you."

There was a sharp sound from the next room, something metallic. I noticed that both men reached inside the loose jackets they were wearing and stepped away from the candlelight. A dark shape came into the far door and stopped. Then a voice said, "Mahoney? It's me … Schmidt."

The Misgivings of Spies

The man calling himself McKell gave us a small box filled with brick-sized candles and we moved to one of the several small conference rooms surrounding the internal courtyard. My last meal had been some bread and hummus in the Qatar airport, so I also scooped up some of the MREs from the table. Schmidt set about arranging and lighting a cluster of candles in the center of the table, while I sorted through the little brown packages.

"Would you prefer beef teriyaki or vegetarian?" I asked Schmidt. He didn't answer but reached out and took one of the MREs from the pile at random. He tore it open and starting chewing on it, apparently some kind of energy bar.

"I saw Asfand two days ago," I said.

His head jerked up. "Did you go looking for him? That's a long way from Kabul."

"He was in Kabul. Advising Karzai as to how to best spend the reconstruction funds. Apparently he convinced him that his needs should be at the head of the queue."

He picked up on the sarcasm without much effort. "It's an old, old dance, Mahoney. Wars are not about borders, or religion, or trade. They're about money. Asfand's been fighting other people's wars for twenty years. He deserves some compensation."

"He thought Nolan was dead." *Why do you have this need to go back to that night? There are some puzzles that don't need to be solved.*

Schmidt apparently agreed with me, because he didn't respond other than to stare at me like a high school principal looking at a kid sent to his office for tardiness. Finally, he asked, "Any more thoughts about where Saddam would hide his weapons of mass destruction."

He was quieter than usual, probably because he knew that the old rules no longer applied, that I was experiencing a level of doubt that had to be addressed. He had seen the phenomenon too many times in his informants not to recognize the characteristic symptoms among his own team.

In thinking back on that conversation and the way he gave unfiltered answers to all of my questions, I realized that his ironclad 'Rule One' was no longer in force and that this new transparency was the clearest possible signal that our relationship had changed. And that the change was mutual, irreversible and ominous.

"Schmidt. Am I in the Central Intelligence Agency?"

He looked at me for a long time before he answered. "No."

"Was I ever?"

"No." And then, in a tone of genuine curiosity, "Do you care?"

It was a startling question and even as I opened my mouth to reply, I thought, *No, I don't. It makes no difference whatsoever.*

Instead of replying, I asked, "Are *you* in the CIA?"

Another long pause. "Not now. I was at one time. And many senior officers at Langley think I still am. It's handy to let them think that."

Time for a changeup. "You've arranged for lots of under-the-table arms shipments over the years, haven't you?"

He looked at me sharply. "Of course, you were in on some of them."

"So you've used Boris Volkov as a source?"

"Once or twice, but nothing recent. He's not high up on the agency's list of preferred providers. Being Russian and all that." He smiled slightly and said, "Ms. Elena Weiss has enlisted you in her vendetta, I think. She wants us to kill Volkov for her."

Keep Elena out of this "Are there others that work for you? Besides Riley, Magda and me?"

"Not regularly. There are … specialists … that I use from time to time. But what I … we … do is best kept to a very small circle."

"Who pays us? Who is it that tells you what to do?"

He paused for several seconds, looking at me as if expecting me to recall the question. "Those two questions have different answers. We have only one customer – the Director of the CIA. We do things that they cannot … are not permitted … to do. Things that are illegal, unauthorized and/or risky enough that the agency can't undertake them without threatening its very existence, but that still need to be done for the good of the country. As for who pays us, some of the money comes from dark corners of the agency, but most of it is provided by a group of individuals who still believe in American exceptionalism."

"Right wing wackos with too much money."

He was unbothered. "I'd call them patriots, but the word no longer has meaning. You'd be surprised at the diversity. All that they have in common is an appreciation for what is necessary as opposed to *permitted*. They are realists."

"And you, Schmidt? Do you always do what the realists tell you to do? Even if you have personal doubts?"

He was thinking hard about how to answer, but I had no idea if it was to construct a plausible lie, to justify his compliance with the realists, or to give me a sales pitch on the importance of 'the mission, right or wrong.'

He shrugged and looked away from me. "What I will do is *always* consistent with the *spirit* of the mission, although not always with the letter of my instructions."

"That's a convenient sophistry, isn't it?"

"Yes, I suppose it is. But moral philosophy is your specialty, not mine."

I asked my last question.

"Can I quit?"

His reply was instantaneous. "Of course. The only condition is absolute silence about our arrangement and what you've been doing for the past couple of decades."

"You mean the lying, cheating, stealing, killing ... that sort of thing?"

"Yes, that. And the betrayals. Those most of all." He hesitated and then said something very strange. "Especially those yet to come."

He got up. Slowly and in stages, like a life-sized inflatable doll being filled with air. *He is old before his time. But, then again, his time is past, or about to be.* He walked away, saying, "I'll see you in the morning. There's something we have to do."

Puzzles

The power was restored somewhere during the night and every light in the residence was on when I came downstairs just after dawn. There was no sign of Schmidt or the two other men, but an Arab man in blue jeans and a UNESCO T-shirt met me at the foot of the stairs and asked me in perfect English if I wanted some breakfast. It was an easy question to answer, given my diet of MRE's from last night.

The candles were gone from the dining room table, but there was an impressive formation of multi-colored candle wax caked on the gleaming tabletop, resembling mini-stalagmites erupting from the floor of an underground cave. The man brought me some toast and oatmeal and then came back with a camera and proceeded to take pictures of the impromptu sculptures of wax.

"You like art where you find it?" I said. He smiled at me and said, "Yes, but I'm taking the pictures because the Americans have promised to pay for damage to private residences that they occupy. I need documentation."

"Do you live here?"

"Yes. My name is Abdul. I was a personal assistant to Mr. Aziz." He hesitated and then asked, "What do you think will happen to him?"

An Iraqi Christian who was close to Saddam Hussein and his primary defender and mouthpiece to the international community during three bloody wars and the killing of tens of thousands of Kurds and other Iraqi citizens. I doubt if he'll do well.

"I think he will be tried for war crimes. In an Iraqi court."

The man nodded. "A Shia court. And found to be guilty."

"Yes."

I tried to think of something less coldblooded to say, but I didn't know whether he was grieving or celebrating Aziz's almost certain hanging. His expression gave me no clue. But just at that moment, Captain Philip Nolan came into the room and sat down opposite me. He looked exhausted.

"I hear you're looking for me."

"I was, but I'd given up."

"Why?"

"I wondered how you were. I went to Bagram but no one there would tell me anything other than that you left. I tried Asfand but he didn't know where you were. In fact, he thought you were dead."

"The docs wanted to send me to Ramstein in Germany for rehab, but that didn't seem right to me. So I left."

"Forgive me for saying so, but you don't look very combat-ready. I think you should have gone to Germany."

He smiled for the first time, a very rueful smile. "I agree with you, but I never was very smart. I convinced one of the lesser generals to take me on as staff officer. Commanding a desk."

"How did you get here? Baghdad?"

"Special Forces troops made an amphibious landing at Basra on the Persian Gulf to secure the oil fields. Me and my general were part of that."

"And now?"

"Here to catch a ride to the states. I'm going home and checking myself into an army hospital. These muscles" – he reached across and rubbed the spot near where the tubes had been trailing out of his chest – "are pretty screwed up. Fighting's pretty well over for the moment, so I won't feel like I'm deserting."

Aziz's man came back into the room and fussed around with setting food and coffee in place. Nolan and I were content with the silence for a bit, each with his own thoughts. I don't know what his were, but I was wondering if I could – or would – do what he had done ... sign up for yet another fight instead of choosing a quiet place to heal. And then take even more time in a war zone to track down a person he didn't like or trust very much. *Which leads to an obvious question.*

"Nolan, why are you here? We didn't part on very friendly terms."

He didn't answer, just sat there absently rubbing his shoulder and staring at the impromptu wax artwork. When he started talking, I think it was more for him than for me. "Special Ops is all about the mission, getting it done. Keeping your people safe. What you see or do in the process is whatever it takes to do the job. Our usual mission debrief starts out with, 'This mission never happened.' It's nasty stuff –

assassinations, 'enhanced interrogation,' better known as torture. You see it, you do it, but then you forget it … or don't."

And you're one of those who don't really forget it, aren't you, Nolan? It's always there, as indelible as an inkblot on a white dress shirt. Memories of what you saw or did. I wonder if any of it helped you deal with the stone-cold reality of your sister dying in the World Trade Center.

He was still talking. " … wasn't right. Asfand and Schmidt were using a playbook all their own. But in those first days after 911, we all looked the other way. Then we got used to it. We told ourselves, 'It's the mission,' but the truth is, we envied the CIA people … the way they just did what was *right* when other people want to kill you, even when it meant you couldn't tell the difference between you and them any longer."

His voice was fading, almost inaudible. I repeated my question "Nolan, why are you here?" and he snapped upright. "When you came to see me in the hospital, I thought you were probably in on it with Schmidt. I didn't figure it would do much good to bitch to you."

In on what? "So what's changed?"

"Two days ago. We were in Basra, trying not to breathe because of the burning oil wells. A kid walked up and shot Woody in the face from three feet away. I emptied my clip into him. He was no more than thirteen years old."

There was another long pause, neither of us having words that would fit. "So I'm taking Woody home to his wife and daughter, so they can bury him properly.

Then I'm checking into Walter Reed and – as soon as they'll let me -- checking out of the U.S. Army. I'm done."

"So why are you here to see me? What can I do?" *You need to talk to a priest, not someone like me, with the same doubts.*

"*Do?* I have no idea, but somebody needs to know what happened that night. I picked you."

"So, no more … what was it you called it at Bagram …. psychogenic amnesia?"

He shrugged. "Be careful what you ask for. I'm not doing you any favors." He inhaled deeply and drank half of his coffee. Then he sat back and started telling me about that night.

"Woody told you most of it. The grand plan, the ambush, the bit about me going off solo with the mystery box? Then finding me bleeding out at the strip?"

I nodded. "All of that. But what I don't know is what made you go lone wolf, or what happened from the time the plane landed until Woody came on the scene and found you almost dead."

For the first time, Nolan looked uncomfortable. "Didn't Schmidt tell you?"

"Sort of, but not very much. And I got a little bit from Asfand. Neither of them wants to talk about it." *And their stories conflict with one another.* The answer seemed to bother him, so I added, "As you know, Schmidt has a need-to-know rule, and he doesn't make exceptions for my curiosity."

He leaned back and took a deep breath. "I got there just as the plane was lowering its ramp. It was a turboprop Antonov AN-12, probably one of the leftovers from the Soviet war in Afghanistan. It kept its engines going and was pointed straight down the runway for a quick getaway. I watched Schmidt and Asfand walk up the ramp and into the interior. They met and talked with a guy in civilian clothes at the head of the ramp. The two of them came back out and Asfand's men began unloading boxes, along with three or four others who came with the plane."

"Are you sure it was an AN-12? Not an Ilyushin?"

He just looked at me and said, "Mahoney." I went on quickly. "Sorry. And there were no Taliban in sight? No shooting going on?"

"Other than the engine noise from the plane, it was quiet. As far as I could tell everybody except Schmidt, Asfand and the civilian who came with the plane was involved in moving boxes. I got within five feet of them before they even noticed me. And they weren't happy when they did. Schmidt said, 'You're not supposed to be here.'

"I told him I needed to see the cargo and I walked up the ramp. And that's the last thing I remember until I got to Bagram."

I sat thinking, trying to visualize the scene. "The man on the plane, the one in civilian clothes ..."

"I was too far away for an ID, but they all shook hands before he went back toward the front of the cargo area and the unloading started. They sure looked and acted like they knew each other."

He stopped to drink the rest of his coffee and looked at me with the expression that asked, 'Any more questions?'   But we both knew the story was incomplete.

I asked, "What was in the mystery box, the one that you found in the Taliban truck?"

He told me, and I sat stunned as all the whirling seemingly disconnected bits and pieces aligned and fell into place, like iron filings reacting to a magnet. Nolan said, "Now you have to decide what to do with the information." Then he stood up and walked out.

I sat staring at the wall, regretting the last eighteen years of my life and wondering what I was going to do.

Loose Ends

I found the scrap of notepaper from the Swiss Hotel in Istanbul that Elena had given me, listing the dates of Volkov's arms shipments around the time of that final twenty-five million dollar payment.   I was not surprised to find that one of those dates was the day that Nolan got shot.   The date was also circled on Elena's list, her code that indicated Volkov had gone along on that particular trip.

I called Elena.   When she answered, I said, "This is Mahoney.   I have a question for you."   Listening to myself, I realized again how inept I was in so many ways.   *What happened to all that eloquence about moonlight and toasts to living?   You sound like a cold-caller selling timeshares in a condo development!*   Elena made it even clearer.   "Hello Mahoney.   I've been thinking about you quite a lot since Istanbul."

"A high point of my life, Elena.   Thanks to you."   *That's better, I think.   Maybe I can learn to do this after all.*   "Any more assassination attempts?"

She laughed.   "I'm in Geneva.   Murder is against the law in Switzerland."

"I hope to get there soon.   But I'm still chasing that missing shipment that we talked about."

"Is that why you're calling?"

"That's what I thought, but I'm beginning to think there may be other, more sub-conscious forces at work."

"Those will eventually have to be dealt with, but it's best done in person rather than on phone lines. So what's your question?"

"More than one, now that you've reminded me. First, any activity on Mr. V's part?"

"No. He's staying in Baku as far as we can tell. And there haven't been any other shipments since we last met. Maybe fifty million dollars is sufficient for him."

"I seriously doubt it. My other question: You said that he maintains his own little vertically integrated freight business. What brand of airplane does he own?"

"He has two Antonov cargo planes. The AN-12 models. Very old, but very reliable. He keeps them at Baku."

"Would he traffic in artillery shells? Conventional ones?"

"Oh my, yes. Both on and off the books. It's a high volume item with a great profit margin. They can't be used but one time … no after market to compete with."

Should I tell her that we almost had him? But maybe that wasn't him standing at the top of the ramp that night. Or maybe the men greeting him had no intention of detaining him. Too many unknowns.

A silence set in and dragged on longer than it should have. I was trying to think of some way to tell her about all of my doubts, both professional and personal, without revealing too much. But there were too many of them and I hadn't worked out all the possible consequences myself. In any case, I lost the chance. Riley, the ghost from the World Trade Center, walked into my office and sat down in the single chair opposite me.

"Elena, I have to go. I'm sorry." I replaced the receiver before she could respond.

It had been almost four years since I last saw him in Rhodes and it was easy to pick out the differences, although they had nothing to do with his outward appearance. He was still the same older-than-his-years, seen-it-all version of 'cool' that other men in their mid-forties aspire to; the kind of person you would cast in the lead role for a movie about spies. But something had been added, or perhaps taken away.

Magda said, 'The jumpers got to him. He's different.'

We sat staring at one another. He was openly appraising me and I wonder what he saw. Finally, I said, "I saw Magda, she told me of your resurrection. It's --"

"James Kent now." He grimaced. "Schmidt picked the name. Very bland. Makes me feel like a Chartered Accountant."

He gestured at the phone. "Elena Weiss, of Geneva?"

How does he know about her? Does Schmidt tell everybody what I'm doing while sharing nothing with me? I didn't answer. Instead, I asked, "Where have you been? Since 911?" I didn't expect him to tell me, but he did. At least, he told me the version of it that he wanted me to hear.

"A little time in Canada to establish my new identity. Then back to Russia. I tried to see Alex, but I couldn't get close to him."

So Schmidt didn't just walk away from Alex. I said, "The expensive Russian lawyer didn't do him any good. But I would think we could get the State Department to work on his case. His cover was solid and the work he was doing at the Hermitage was UN-sanctioned. They could show that the theft charges were trumped-up –"

"Mahoney."

The single word stopped me and told me that I was missing something. He said, "Alex had three jobs. The official one was, as you say, UN-sanctioned and he was doing a lot of good. His second job, his work for us, was deep underground, helping 'our' oligarchs acquire world-class, black-market artworks by the French impressionists at rock-bottom prices. He was good at that too. Remember Petrykin's Renoir? Then there was his third job, the one that we didn't know about, the one on his own account."

I finished it for him. "So the paintings in his apartment weren't planted there. Alex really was stealing the Monet and Degas paintings for himself."

"Greed and stupidity are usually a deadly combination." Riley nodded. "But in that case," I said, "why were you trying to see him?"

"We wanted to know if he had told Russian intelligence about our connection to Oleg Petrykin."

He said 'we.' Him and Schmidt? Were you there to visit Alex just to ask him that question? Or were you there to prevent him from talking. To keep Petrykin safe in the same way that you did that night when you shot Arkady.

"And how is Petrykin? I see he's still moving up among the crowd around Putin."

He smiled, a very thin smile. "He's well. I'll tell him you send best wishes ... the next time I see him."

"Have you seen Magda?"

"Occasionally."   The one-word answer to such a loaded question seemed to bother him, and after a short inward-looking pause, he added, "She's become like me. There's nothing either of us can do for the other anymore. We've become *colleagues.*" The word oozed with contempt.

Then he said something very curious. "Do you remember our first day in that Virginia farmhouse? The nine of us with Schmidt and his trio of trainers?"

He didn't wait for a reply. "Now it's just the three of us – you, me and Magda. And Schmidt, of course. And you're the only one of us with a shred of humanity still operational."

Is that a compliment or a criticism? But he stood up to leave before I could pursue it. Instead, I asked, "Riley, why are you here?"

"To see you, of course. We're going to be working together for a bit, so I thought we should catch up."

A Quiet Talk

I had no idea where Schmidt was, but he had left a message to meet in Tikrit at the Presidential Palace complex. When I showed up at the entrance gate, the MP looked at my press credentials and said, "All the spooks are in the servants quarters," and pointed at a two story building in the distance.

I said, "I'm a journalist," but without any real outrage. He said, "Right," as though I had claimed to be the Pope. "There's a temporary press office set up inside the main entrance to the Palace. They can find you a place."

The encounter bothered me. There was a floor length mirror in one of the many ornate rooms inside the palace and I stood considering my reflection. *Mid-forties white male civilian, unshaven with unruly dark hair and deep tan. Carrying a very frayed red backpack and dressed like every other non-combatant, non-Iraqi in sight. What made him think I was a spook? Do I give off an aura of some sort?*

Schmidt found me two hours later and we sat on a wide veranda watching the sun set in the western desert. He seemed both tired and excited.

"I saw Riley," I said.

He nodded, not really paying attention. "Yes. The three of us will be working together on the next little project."

"I'm serious about quitting."

"Yes, I know you are. Magda too." Then he seemed to come back to the present. He turned to look at me closely, perhaps to look for something that he had missed over all these years. "You lasted much longer than I thought you would." He paused for a long time. "The Arthur video ... Svetlana ... Mikulin ... I thought you'd have lost the stomach for this after each of those."

Only a sliver of the sun was visible on the horizon and I wondered if the rumored 'green flash' occurred in this part of the world. It was getting dark very fast.

"I should have. Something made them ... the losses, the waste ... tolerable."

"Yes. The pursuit of the greater good."

"A myth."

"Of course. But myths have the power to change ... events, people ..."

"Have they changed you, Schmidt? Are you different because of the things you've done for the greater good? All those losses – Arthur, Alex, Peter, Benjamin, Carlee, Roger. For what?"

The sun had sunk below the horizon and we were in near darkness. Perhaps that is why it was permissible for us to be talking on such a metaphysical level. The darkness made the audience invisible, perhaps not even there, and the words had no permanence and were therefore safe to utter.

"Have I changed?" Schmidt repeated. "Yes, but from what to what? I don't know, but I know I didn't like the original version and and I don't like the current one any better. I also know that I long ago stopped trying to calculate the net effects of what I do, unlike you."

For me, Schmidt's words evoked an image of him standing in the middle of the killing field in those first days in Afghanistan, among the shredded bodies of the Taliban after the AC-130 gunship had done its bloody work I remembered him standing there with a wolfish smile and saying, "It's going to be a lovely little war."

I stood up, suddenly tired of his sophistries, particularly because I knew that he intended to kill me tomorrow.

An Unsurprising Discovery

He was waiting for me in the courtyard in the predawn darkness, standing alongside a large black SUV and holding an M-16 rifle loosely in one hand. Riley was with him, also with a rifle.

"Nice wheels," I said. He got in on the driver's side, saying, "Confiscated from the garage of Mr. Tariq Aziz. I was surprised to find it still there." He handed me the rifle, "You're riding shotgun, as they say in the western movies. This is still enemy territory."

The sun emerged from below the horizon as we drove out onto the street, turning north to parallel the Tigris River. "Where are we going?" I asked, just to see how he would answer.

"About two hours to the northwest. A visit to a farm."

We drove in silence. We passed through two checkpoints manned by American soldiers and saw several tanks and low-flying helicopters. There was plenty of visual evidence that a major battle had been fought here not too long ago and, judging by the dark looks of the Iraqis we passed, it was clear that they didn't agree with the outcome and that the fighting would start up again.

"Hussein country," I said. "This is where the Sunni Baath Party was strongest."

"Yes. And this will be a major flash point for a resistance movement. We'll need to maintain a significant force here for a long time."

The road ran arrow-like to the north along a canal. To our left, toward the river, the fields were lush green rectangles of irrigated crops that I could not identify through the heavily tinted windows. To our right, the land was desert-like and the farms were small and vegetation of any sort was scarce.

We made a series of turns, always onto less traveled and narrower roads running away from the river and through ever more sparsely inhabited farmland. The last few miles were on a one-lane dirt track that transected barren weed-filled cornfields populated only by goats.

Riley spoke for the first time. "Even the goats look hostile."

The track dead-ended in a cul-de-sac formed by a crescent of low rocky cliffs that framed a compound with half-a-dozen stone buildings. The roofs on the two larger structures had fallen in and the walls were half standing. The body of a small truck -- solidly rusted, weed-infested and without engine or tires – sat in the center of the open space like a sculptural tribute to some past or future apocalypse. Other than the skeletal remains of the truck, the scene could have been lifted from the middle ages.

Schmidt stopped the car and turned off the engine. "Welcome to the ancestral home of Omar al-Dulami, recently of the Republican Guard and one of Saddam's personal bodyguards," he said. We got out of the SUV. Both Riley and I kept our M-16's. Schmidt made a sweeping gesture with his arm. "All of this has been in the al-Dulami family for hundreds of years, but the last person to live on this farm was Omar's grandfather. It's been abandoned for the last forty years."

"OK," Riley said. "But why are we here?" He was clearly nervous and for good reason; we were three unaccompanied Americans in a highly conspicuous vehicle deep into Saddam Hussein's home province. "What is it we're supposed to see other than the decline of the family farm in Iraqi agriculture?"

Schmidt and I looked at one another long enough that the refrain 'I know that you know that I know ...' began to repeat itself in my head. He finally simply nodded at me, so I said, "What Schmidt is going to show us is the rationale for the invasion of Iraq."

Riley looked at me with a quizzical expression. I repeated for his benefit, "That's what he wants us to see. Saddam's weapons of mass destruction."

"They're in there," I said, and pointed to the largest stone structure, the one without a roof.

It was a good hiding place, one that was unlikely to be discovered unless an informant pointed the way. The building had once served as a barn and the boxes were against the back wall and behind mounds of rubble, covered with piles of rotted burlap material. The shiny metal containers were now encased in battered wooden crates with Arabic lettering identifying the contents as agricultural implements.

Riley said, "That's it? Three boxes! What is it? Nasty bugs? Anthrax? Sarin?"

"No," I said. "Three tactical nuclear weapons. Stolen from the ex-Soviet fleet at Sevastapol. Weapons-grade plutonium. Enough for several hundred kilotons of explosions once they're armed."

Revelations

There was a stone slab table and benches alongside a wall of the main building that provided some shade and the three of us sat there. The silence that pervaded the compound was impressive, as though the insects and birds had abandoned the place as well as the people. There was only the very faint sound of a large helicopter, moving north on a course parallel to the Tigris.

"How did you know they were there?" Schmidt asked. I chose to deliberately misunderstand his question. "In that building? Because of the tire tracks."

He smiled at my game. "How long have you known?"

"I haven't *known* anything for sure since that day you walked into the Student Union and offered me a job. But all the little things began to add up. It probably started with Peter and that laptop. He gave you – and then me – the connection between twenty-five million dollars, Volkov and the Iranian. Knowing that Volkov was really my old friend Vasnetsov made it easy to get from there to the missing nukes."

Schmidt nodded. "I didn't need the laptop. Asfand had Naji talking to him in the village about the deal."

Naji was the second body from the left in the third row in that impromptu mortuary in the village square. So he didn't die in the shootout. Nor painlessly either. And that's why Schmidt didn't give the laptop to Langley; he didn't trust them to do the right thing with the information.

"I didn't need it either, but I didn't know that. Elena Weiss had already figured out that Volkov had the warheads and was trying to shop them to the Taliban."

A sudden horrifying thought popped into my mind. *Peter dies in San Francisco and Elena is almost killed in Istanbul… the only others to see parts of the puzzle forming.*

Riley sat quietly, looking thoughtful and watching the two of us. I wondered how much of this he knew about.

I said to Schmidt. "Was it hard to raise the other twenty-five million?"

"Yes and no. And I needed thirty-five, not twenty-five. Asfand wanted ten for his part in the project. I got all of it from a single individual, but it took me a while to find the right one and to work out the money transfers."

I remembered asking him, 'How are we funded?' *Dark corners of the CIA and a few individuals who believe in American exceptionalism …*

"So that night at the airstrip –"

"Everything had been set up by Naji when he made the twenty-five million deposit. The time, place … everything. Contingent only on the second twenty-five million being delivered. All that Volkov knew was that a party of Taliban would pick up the goods. All I had to do was to keep Nolan busy and out of the way."

It was about then that I began to ask myself the questions that I should have started worrying about twenty-hours earlier when Schmidt and I sat on the balcony talking openly about high crimes and treason.

Why is he telling me all this history? It is a violation of his personal code and threatens the mission. And why is Riley part of this mea culpa?

I also realized that there was no stopping for either of us; that some weird form of confessional momentum was at work. I didn't fully understand my own motives, let alone Schmidt's, but I did know that he had an ending already scripted, whatever it was. And so did I. Only time would tell which of the scripts would prevail.

I prompted him. "And everything was going like clockwork until Nolan showed up at the meeting place."

"I still don't know why he did,"

"I can help you with that. When his team intercepted the Taliban party that was on its way to the rendezvous, he found a box in the cab of the truck. It had a batch of radiation dosimeters and a Geiger counter."

Schmidt nodded. "I can see where that might get him a little bit excited. All he said to me was, 'I need to see what's on that plane.'"

I looked over at Riley. He was following the conversation closely. *He didn't know what we were going to find in that barn, and he doesn't know about that night at the airstrip either.*

Schmidt was paying no attention to Riley. He was intent on convincing me. *But of what? His innocence? The sheer rightness of what he intended to do?*

He leaned toward me, his eyes locked onto mine. "Even after Nolan showed up and all that shit hit the fan, I thought we were still OK. I convinced myself -- 'He's Special Ops ... seen all sorts of squirrelly stuff ... he won't say anything. Hell, maybe he didn't see anything except a lot of 155 HE rounds being unloaded. Then I thought he was dead and when he wasn't, I learned he wasn't talking about – or able to remember – what had happened. Especially when you tried at Bagram."

"Nolan stayed quiet a long time," I confirmed. "He finally told me about the box of nuclear instruments, but that was just two days ago, and that's all he knew."

That stopped him. "But ... then ... how did you –"

"You made two mistakes. First, you underestimated Elena Weiss. She's made a career out of tracking Volkov and those missing warheads. Between us, we figured out that he was personally delivering them on that night. Second, you and Asfand told different versions of what happened after Nolan showed up. You both lied to me, but you told different lies."

He waited. "You said the plane was an Ilyushin. But it was an Antonov. They're hard to confuse with one another. You said that Nolan was shot by a Taliban party that showed up unexpectedly ... that Asfand engaged in a running battle. Asfand said that Nolan was shot by somebody from the plane crew as soon as he showed up and that there never were any Taliban."

"Nolan got shot?"

Schmidt and I were so intent on our own little psychodrama that Riley's question startled both of us.

He was leaning forward, looking intently at Schmidt. When Schmidt didn't respond, he looked directly at me.

"Six AK-47 rounds in the back," I said. "The vest stopped all but one of them. He's OK now. On his way to the states." *At least I hope he is.* As I spoke, a new thought occurred to me. *Nolan said he got shot when he was walking up the ramp into the plane, away from Schmidt, according to Asfand. And Schmidt had told me before, "Asfand always carries an AK-47.'*

Riley wanted more. "And what does Nolan say about getting shot?"

"He didn't see the shooter. He was walking up the ramp to the interior of the plane." I didn't mention that both Asfand and Schmidt were standing behind him.

He looked back at Schmidt. "And Asfand got ten million for his part?"

Schmidt just stared at him.

Riley continued, more to himself than either of us. "So tomorrow or the next day, an ISG team gets an anonymous tip and 'discovers' this stash of WMD. And Bush gets to hold a press conference to announce that his war is now justified because of what's in that barn?"

"Riley." Schmidt's single word was freighted with the entire history of the last eighteen years ... all that Schmidt had told us to do, and all that we had done without questioning the 'why' of it. If fully translated, that one word would be the equivalent of a white paper on the role – or irrelevance -- of ethics in modern statecraft.

It had always worked, but this time it didn't. Riley said, "So Nolan was an unacceptable risk?   So you shot him in the back?   And Peter? He had to go because of what he found on the laptop?"

So Peter didn't get killed in some random street crime!

Our roles had switched.   I was now the observer. Schmidt and Riley were intent on one another, locked into an exchange where the old rules no longer applied, where asking and answering were fraught with new risks, where past decisions could be revisited and judgments altered.

Schmidt did not respond to any of Riley's accusations posed as questions.   He seemed more pensive than troubled, more disappointed than defensive.   And Riley did not press him.   I think he, like me, took Schmidt's silence as an indifferent form of confession.

Riley stood up. "Can we go now?" But Schmidt did not move. He looked at each of us in turn and said, "In a minute. First, I need to know that both of you will go along with the story."

We answered simultaneously, but I said, "No" and Riley, "I don't know." Schmidt nodded, unsurprised, and called out loudly, "Khan!"

Two Arab men in very faded fatigues came from an open doorway behind us. They looked familiar to me, probably from Asfand's militia, but they showed no sign of recognition, perhaps because most of my attention was focused on the pair of AK-47's they were pointing roughly in our direction. Riley and I looked at the M-16's, but they were leaning against the stone slab. Within easy reach, but they might as well have been back in Baghdad. *But we don't need them.*

I reached into the outside pocket of the vest I was wearing and pushed the large button on the face of the homing device that I was carrying. *Ibrahim said, 'Push it if you require assistance.'* As if by magic, the two men holding the AK-47s, collapsed as though struck by an ax and the gunshots reverberated from the encircling stone cliffs.

I moved to stand between Schmidt and the M-16s, but he was rooted in place, his arms still resting on the stone tabletop and his mouth open. And then it didn't matter because, within thirty seconds, there was a line of six very competent looking soldiers coming toward us with assault rifles aimed at us. Schmidt stared at their colorful shoulder patches.

"Bulgarians?"

"You're close. But they're actually Russians." The speaker and apparent leader of the group stepped out from behind the men, a much smaller figure and carrying only a sidearm. It was Monica Holst.

Strange Allies

I'd called her two days ago from Baghdad, after the series of visits from Riley, Nolan and Schmidt. She didn't believe me at first. Partly because of the instinctive mistrust that had accumulated over the years, not so surprising given our conflicting allegiances and the natural predisposition of spies toward doubt. But I suppose if you tell lies for a living, it's hard to accept even an obvious truth.

The first task was to find her. Russian counter-intelligence agents are not listed and their names and locations are guarded closely. However, Monica had a day job as a journalist, so she had a blog and a website and, on it, an email address. My message was simple. *This is Thomas Mahoney. I've missed you since Vladivostok and have more information to share with you about the 1991 theft. Please contact me ASAP.* She called seven hours later.

"Thomas."

"Hello again Monica. I'm glad you called. How are you doing in the new Russia?"

"Quite well, thank you. Rising oil prices and the American tendency to enmesh themselves in purely local wars on our borders have caused our FSB budget to double in two years."

"How's Vasili?"

Her voice changed slightly. "He's left the service for … how do you say, greener pastures? But you know all this, no? The CIA computers at Langley know our roster better than our Moscow apparatchiks."

But I'm not in the CIA. "They don't share such tidbits with personnel at my level."

Her voice shifted again, this time to the all-business register. "Is this phone line safe on your end?"

"Yes."

"Where are you?"

"In the Baghdad home of Tarik Aziz, ex-Foreign Minister of the Republic of Iraq. He's not here, however. I think he's scheduled to be hanged."

"Why are you calling me, Thomas? Have you found our missing ... devices?"

"No, but I will within the next two or three days. I'm pretty sure that they're somewhere in Iraq."

"Pretty sure ... such interesting phrasing."

I said nothing, knowing that she was not going to be put off by vocabulary at this point.

"Why are you telling me about this *pretty sure* discovery you're about to make? Have you decided to take me up on that offer I made to you in Vladivostok?"

To become a double agent? Not in the way that she intended, but I'm not sure that what I'm doing isn't an even worse form of treachery. "Not at all. But the ... devices ... belong to Russia, so I thought I'd give you the right of first refusal."

There was a long pause and when she spoke, I could hear the underlying thread of uncertainty. But she stuck to her script nevertheless. "You're lying to me, Thomas. We know where the devices are, and it's not in Iraq."

"You think that they're in Azerbaijan, in a warehouse in Baku on the Lake Baikal waterfront. And they were, but they're not there any more. Volkov sold them."

Aside from being a spy, Monica was the most direct woman I ever met, beginning when she said to me in Managua, "I want you to fuck me," to her "Get out of Russia" edict in Vladivostok. So she did not argue or ask about sources. There was a brief pause before she said, "Tell me more." We talked for another ten minutes. At the end, she said, "A man named Ibrahim will call on you at Mr. Aziz's home within twelve hours. He will give you some specialized equipment and further instructions."

"Monica. If you're not there when I find them, I can't help you after that." *Probably because I'll be dead if you don't show up.*

"I'll be there. Watch for a Bulgarian."

Rightful Owners

I worried about the decisions I'd made since Nolan turned up with his account of that night at the airstrip, followed in the next twenty-fours by first Riley and then Schmidt. Fortunately, I had very little time to worry about the forces I'd set in motion and where they might lead, although I did consume quite a lot of time trying to figure out if Elena would approve and finally gave up, mostly out of fear that I would conclude that she wouldn't.

There are psychological theories that suggest that one would suffer major feelings of regret or remorse once an important decision is made, and my decision to call Monica certainly seemed to qualify on that scale. But, instead, a curious calm settled on me. Actors would move of their own volition and there was little I could do to change the course of events.

The man named Ibrahim was there almost exactly twelve hours after my call to Monica. He gave me a miniaturized homing device that looked like a mobile phone and two simple instructions. "Turn it on when you start your trip" and "Press this button –" he pointed to the large button in the center of the gadget's aluminum face – "if you require assistance."

Which is why I was standing in the middle of an abandoned family compound near Tikrit with Monica Holst, watching three tactical nuclear weapons being disinterred from the rubble.

I said, "I thought we agreed. Nobody gets killed."

Monica looked at me with a faint smile. "Would you have preferred that I let those men with their AK-47's shoot you?"

They would have, of course. Schmidt had them there just for that purpose. He knew that I was not going to go along with his game to 'find' the warheads. But why did he bring Riley along? I have to think about that.

I didn't have to answer her, because of the noise of an MI-26 Soviet-era helicopter hovering and then landing next to the rusted shell of the pickup truck. Its twin rotors kicked up a dust cloud that took a long time to disperse in the still air. The machine had a very large Bulgarian flag painted on its side.

"Yours?" I asked Monica.

"Borrowed from Bulgaria. Russia is still on excellent terms with some of the so-called ex-Soviet Socialist Republics. But the helicopter is identical to the two that the Bulgarian army sent along with their three-hundred man contribution to Mr. Bush's invasion force, so we can move around without anybody getting excited."

"And your soldiers?" I pointed at the four men busy positioning one of the three large boxes to load into the cargo area of the MI-26. The other two men were watching Schmidt and Riley. The AK-47's and M-16's were lined up against the wall, well out of reach.

"FSB. Our version of your Special Ops people."

"What will happen to the weapons?"

She shrugged. "That's not up to me. We have a short flight to get out of Iraq and into Iranian air space. Then south to the Persian Gulf and a small freighter that's waiting just for us. That's the end of my part. But I suspect the plutonium will find a bigger and better use."

"You knew Volkov had the warheads?"

Another shrug. "We suspected. He cares far more about himself than his country, but he has powerful friends in the Kremlin. It was easier for us to pretend that we had truly lost them, and then to watch him. But we missed the warehouse in Baku. Until you called."

"What will happen to Volkov?" I pointed to the helicopter and the boxes being positioned and secured in its cargo space. "After this?"

"I will tell my superiors. It's up to them." After a few seconds, she added, "We shall see how powerful his friends are after I write my report."

"If it will help, tell your superiors that he was paid fifty million dollars for the weapons – twenty-five from the Taliban and twenty-five from the Americans."

She turned to look at me. "That is interesting. Anything else?"

"Volkov killed Chayka, but you already know that, I'm sure. You probably don't know that the Iranians were also interested in buying the warheads."

One of the soldiers in the cargo hold of the helicopter called out in Russian and Monica left me to talk with him. When she came back, she said, "The captain says that we're ready."   She looked over at Riley and Schmidt, clearly thinking. "Can I help you with those two?"

Help? As in shoot them? Or take them with her to that ship in the Persian Gulf? I wondered exactly how much latitude she had, whether she would honor our telephone agreement: "Just the warheads, Monica. No killing. No prisoners."

I kept my voice as neutral as I could, trying to sound like someone responding to a request for directions to the main highway. "No thanks. Just leave the M-16's with me."

She nodded and went to retrieve the two rifles. The helicopter's huge rotor blades were starting to spin and the engine noise was making it difficult to hear. She handed me the M-16's and turned to the helicopter, She stopped a few feet away, turned back and said, "Mahoney, why did you call me?"

Such a difficult question!

"The goods were stolen. All I ever wanted to do was return them to the rightful owner." *It's not an outright lie, but it's not an answer to her question either. That would require me to talk things I don't understand about myself — patriotism, self-disgust, remorse ...* But the engine noise was quite loud, and the dust was rising again. I'm not sure that she even heard me.

"They're in Iraqi air space for the next hour. We could probably find a standby Air Force F-16 to take them out. Be a great story ... a team of Russian commandos smuggling WMD out of Iraq ... Or maybe we could spin it so that they were bringing it in ... even better."

Schmidt knew that I wasn't interested and so he wasn't really trying very hard. He just couldn't help running last ditch rescue scenarios in his head. Then he asked me the same question as Monica. "Mahoney, why?" And Riley perked up and looked at me as well.

"Why let the Russians have the nukes? Maybe because they belong to Russia. It's like when the British Museum returned artifacts stolen from the pyramids to the Egyptian government. Or maybe because I don't know what else to do with them. I can't trust the CIA, who planted them in the first place. Or maybe because, this way, you" – I pointed at Schmidt – "no longer have a reason to kill us. All any of us have at this point is a fantastical story ... no real evidence. You have that precious thing called 'deniability.'"

It was a long and heated rant, and it would be a while before I learned how wrong some of it was. But Schmidt nodded as though to acknowledge its truth and neither of them responded. Schmidt looked bored and Riley thoughtful. I went on in a calmer tone. "Or maybe what you're really asking is why couldn't I just go along with the plan? Shut up and do what I was told, like always."

That is the important question. The one for which I have no answer. "I'm tired. I want to go home now." I stood up and walked away, unaware that – with that last phrase -- I had in fact answered the question as truthfully and exhaustively as if I had composed a ten-page affidavit.

Fallout

Schmidt dropped Riley and me off in front of the Tarik Aziz residence after a four-hour long and deathly silent return trip. His parting words were, "I'll see you in a week and we'll figure out how to shut down." Neither Riley nor I responded.

Abdul met us in the doorway and I asked, "Is there alcohol in the house?"

"Oh no, sir. It is against the Islamic law –"

"Of course. But Tarik Aziz was a very cosmopolitan diplomat who entertained frequently. Bring us something from his personal inventory." I walked past him before he could answer. Five minutes later, he found us in the library and he was carrying a cloth sack that clinked when he set it on the table.

I poured large glasses of whiskey for Riley and myself and we sat facing one another in a pair of enormous leather chairs, with a floor-to-ceiling backdrop of leather-bound books with Arabic titles. I wondered how many deals or treaties had been sealed – or violated – by men sitting in these same chairs.

Midway through the second glass, Riley said, "You know why Schmidt brought me along, don't you?"

I tried to make it easy for him. "Because he needed to make sure that you would support him. And he wasn't sure how much I had already told you."

He nodded, "That too. But that was only part of it."

"Riley, you don't need –"

"Yes, I do." He took a long sip and stared at the wall of books. "I was there to kill you. For being a traitor. He said it would be obvious before we were done. And I guess it was, wasn't it?"

I made another attempt to divert him. "He knew you wouldn't do it. That's why those two Afghanis were there with the AK-47's ... for both of us."

He shook his head. "No. They were backup, just in case I had last minute misgivings."

"Which you did." *Schmidt said, 'I need to know that both of you will go along' and Riley said 'I don't know.'*

He was paying no attention to me, far away in his own thoughts that had nothing to do with what transpired in that farmyard. "That day in the World Trade Center? When the planes hit? I was on the tenth floor in my office. A woman ... her name was Amanda ... was waiting for me at the viewing platform on the 107th floor. We were going to have coffee and talk about getting married and having kids. She said, 'This is a high point in my life, so we should be in a high place.'"

"Riley, I didn't know –"

"She was one of the jumpers."

I said nothing. There was nothing to say. But Riley needed to say more. "Schmidt told me that Benjamin and Peter had gone to the other side ... showed me what he said was proof. So I killed them."

I asked Schmidt, 'Can I quit?' and he said 'Of course.'

"Riley, it's late. I'll see you in the morning. I left him as he was reaching for the second bottle. I paid no attention to his muttered last words until later.

"Schmidt is not exempt."

The next morning, I left for Geneva. The trip took all day and I spent most of the time in a self-absorbed state. In one of my pseudo-lives as a spy, I had pretended to subscribe to the Twelve Steps of Alcoholic's Anonymous so that I could recruit an under-secretary of something or other in one of the lesser Balkan states. I could easily recite the fourth step -- 'Make a searching and fearless moral inventory of ourselves' – but I had never sought to try it for myself until that long day of travel from Baghdad to Kuwait City to Geneva. The result was as inconclusive as it was scathing, except that it left me feeling that alcohol or drugs might be preferable to such brutal introspection.

I called Elena from the Geneva terminal but got only her voice mail. I went to her apartment, but she did not answer her bell. I bribed the security guard/receptionist to let me wait in the lobby. During the ninety minutes before she came, I indulged fantasies about her showing up with a man, but she was alone, balancing a precarious stack of files under one arm as she reached for the elevator button.

When I came up behind her and said, "Elena," she whirled, scattering the files and then stepping on them to close the distance between us. It was only then that I realized how afraid I had been of being alone, of having forfeited the right to love or be loved.

It was about two in the morning before she asked the question. "What are you going to do now?"

"Stay here for a while, if you'll have me." I waited nervously because – for me – it was a question that I did not know the answer to, but she merely smiled. "Then try to disentangle myself from Schmidt. After that ..." I held my hands up in the classic 'que sera, sera' pose.

We made love again, slowly, with an attention to more nuanced sensory details, and then slept until the sun came through the tall windows in the opposite wall. We were having breakfast on her balcony when the phone rang.

"It's for you. A woman." She held the receiver out to me.

No one knows where I am. But, of course, I more than most people knew the reach of intelligence networks. I was not surprised when I heard the voice.

"I'm calling to say thank you. Your unexpected nd very generous gift to me has made me a rock star in our security services."

"Hello Monica. I gather you found your freighter in the Persian Gulf?"

She ignored me. "Please tell Elena Weiss that I'm sorry about her father. He was a good man and did not deserve what happened to him in Russia."

I looked at Elena, who was watching wide-eyed. I'm sure she had guessed who was calling. "I'll tell her. But she would prefer revenge to your sympathy. She is like you in that way."

"That speaks well of her. I think she is a woman of quality. As to revenge, that's part of my reason for calling. Our recent meeting in the countryside has made me curious, and I have used my new status in my firm to inquire into the activities of your Mr. Schmidt. I learned that our KGB and its successors have built up a substantial dossier. A member of our Swiss embassy staff will deliver a file to you by late this afternoon with some details of our research."

"Thank you, I think. And the quid pro quo?"

"I'm sorry. I don't understand Latin. We'll talk after you've had a chance to review the findings. Goodbye."

Elena was quiet much the morning, and I thought I knew why. We went for a walk along the Quai and she finally brought it up. "This woman, the one who called –"

"Her name is Monica Holst. She's a high-ranking member of Russia's secret service." *Recently promoted, thanks to me.*

"You gave her the warheads." It was not a question.

"Yes."

She did not ask, "Why?" Instead, "Can you trust her?"

Such a strange question to ask. Can I trust someone who is schooled to lie, to betray, to commit all manner of crimes ... a woman who uses sexual favors as leverage?   It was a surprisingly easy question for me to answer.

"Yes, for certain things. She is something rare in the business ... a person who actually puts their country ahead of everything else." *Like Schmidt must have been at some time in the past.*

"Was she ... is she ... *important* to you? This Monica Holst?"

That was also easy to answer. "No."

The promised file from Monica was quite thin, obviously redacted and only nine pages, but with a level of detail and an eye for truly unusual transactions. It spanned thirty years of a man's life, a man that existed at so many levels that reading the file was like experiencing an archeological 'dig' through a hitherto unknown culture.

I learned that Schmidt was rich ... rich as in billionaire, private jet, Forbes 400 rich. It was all carefully hidden, in many countries, under multiple pseudonyms and generated by diverse and mostly criminal activities. The CIA was his single most important source of business, but there were others. His customers/funders included governments, intelligence agencies, terrorist organizations, the Mafia and right-wing fellow billionaires from several countries. The only thing they had in common was their need for someone like Schmidt to do the things that ordinary people simply don't do. I found the thirty-five million he'd raised for the Volkov deal and noted that only two million was paid out to Asfand. So Schmidt's 'commission' for managing the purchase was eight million dollars.

So, he's rich, amoral and genuinely evil. Protected because he's very good at doing complicated things for other rich people who are frightened of what he knows about them. But do I care?

But I did care. Intensely. Because Monica had added a handwritten note – a single cryptic sentence – in the margin of the last page. It read, "V. contracted with S. to get rid of E.W. as a condition for getting the warheads." And suddenly I was recalling Elena's puzzled expression when the bullet struck the column a foot from her head and the tiny cloud of marble dust was settling onto the white tablecloth. *She was a threat to Volkov ... the kind of problem that Schmidt was good at solving.*

In any case, it turned out that I didn't have a choice about being involved. Monica's next call was pure business. "You saw the file?"

"Yes. It was ... interesting. But I'm no longer in that world. I've resigned."

"Not quite yet. I have one last proposal."

"No."

"Yes. I'll meet you at the Brunswick Monument in two hours." After thirty seconds of silence, she added, "Remember your deceased colleagues. The ones that thought they could quit." The phone went dead.

She's right. I don't have a choice.

The monument was only a twenty-minute walk from Elena's apartment. She wanted to come along and it was a marker of how far I had progressed in my withdrawal mode that I almost consented. I finally told her, "You do not want to be involved at this level. Trust me."

Monica was dressed in a severe pin-striped pants suit and had her hair pulled back into a bun with every hair in place. She looked forbidding, sexless; a caricature of Swiss probity. I gave her the file. "Here. I made no copies. It's quite a story, one that would sell a lot of newspapers if you wrote it up."

"I'm no longer a journalist. From now on, I will be running a significant part of our counter-intelligence programs, from Moscow. Monica Holst will disappear and a new person ... perhaps a woman named Nadya ... will appear. But only to a select few people."

So that's what happens to rock stars in the Russian secret services. Perhaps spies really can come in from the cold. Is that what I'm doing, only in the opposite direction?

She picked out a stone bench looking out over the park surrounding the monument and sat down. As soon as I sat down alongside her, she said, "We ... I ... need your help. And I can help you in return."

"And if I say no?"

"Just listen to me. You want out, and I can offer you a way – perhaps the only way – to make it work."

It isn't just Schmidt that I need to free myself from; it's all of them – the spies who build dossiers on other spies. "I'll listen. No guarantees, but I'll listen."

She leaned in close and began to talk. "There are two men ..."

London

Saddam Hussein stayed hidden for nine months, until he was discovered hiding in a hole in the ground near his hometown of Tikrit. During that same interval, coalition troops did find tens of thousands of old chemical weapons. The largest single batch consisted of artillery shells stacked floor to ceiling in an abandoned school building in the Anbar province. But all such munitions were simply leftovers from the Iran-Iraq War in the eighties and had been forgotten about by everybody, including the Iraqi military.

No trace of either biological or nuclear weapons was found and Bush's rationale for the war was being severely criticized in the world press. George Tenet, the CIA Director and his Director of Operations were being flailed by the political fallout and Congress was threatening to convene yet another inquiry into 'intelligence failures.'

I paid little attention. I was focused on the one last job, the one that I wasn't sure whether the client was Monica or me.

It took three months for all of the moving parts to align themselves. It took me that long to develop an identity as an up-and-coming British telecom entrepreneur named Brian Saxon who was interested in making a 'significant' investment in the Russian market. It was a very thin cover, existing almost entirely on paper, but this time I was only trying to fool a single and fairly gullible individual, not the security services of several countries.

London was looking more and more like a destination resort for Russian tourists, a testimonial to the power of raw capitalism to change both economies and lives. Riley was already there and we met in his hotel lobby. He looked nothing like the Riley I had last seen in Baghdad and we both laughed when I said, "Twenty years, three continents and all that training, and this is the first time that I've seen you in a disguise."

He was ten pounds heavier, with a beard and steel-rimmed glasses. His passport said that he was an Irish citizen named Patrick Doyle. He supposedly worked for me – rather, for Brian Saxon -- as a financial advisor. In my case, I didn't need a disguise. 'Brian Saxon' was an elaborate fictional and virtual creature whose only goal was to seduce Oleg Petrykin into inviting him to a meeting. When I last saw Petrykin, I was disguised as a Russian émigré named Mikhail Popov, so in a sense my real self was an effective disguise.

We'd been over the plan twenty times or more. Like most plans, it was elegant on paper and weak on the contingencies. But there was nothing more we could do except play it out and react in real time. So I was not surprised when Riley said, "Tell me again why we're doing this."

"Vladimir Putin is changing the lineup. Since becoming President, he's had an unholy alliance with the oligarchs – 'I'll make you ungodly rich in return for your support.' Now he thinks it's time to thin the ranks, to prune a little." *I'm channeling Monica, sitting on that bench at the Brunswick Memorial in Geneva.*

Riley nodded and said, "Particularly if the oligarch to be pruned is a stooge of the American CIA."

"Yes. That does simplify his choice."

"But why us? Putin has very competent specialists he can call on."

We've been over all this. Is he having second thoughts? He knew what I was thinking and quickly added, "I know, I know. Reciprocity. Deniability. Common interests. Volkov, stolen nukes, etc., etc."

The name 'Volkov' was suddenly there, seeming to echo in the air around us. He saw my sudden stillness for what it was and stood quietly, waiting for me to say it. *I didn't want this. I was reconciled to not knowing. To being grateful for what didn't happen. And this is not the time.* But he'd said the trigger word 'Volkov' and now he stood waiting, with those eyes, staring at me.

"Riley, I –"

"Schmidt needed the warheads. Volkov wanted Elena gone. It was the kind of favor you do to get a deal done."

"You don't need to –"

"And Schmidt had me, the fellow who kills whoever Schmidt points to. Even if they're on our side."

I gave up, knowing that his need for penance far outweighed my need to forget. I said, "It was an easy shot ... a couple hundred meters at most." *In those early days in Virginia, I watched you put ten rounds within a four-inch circle from that distance.*

"Yes, it was. But the boat was moving, and Elena ducked her head to pick up something."

"Yes. And you missed. I'm glad."

It was a dialogue that I would replay in my mind for a long time, but I never came up with a script that was adequate to the emotions that were in play or that would somehow convey what each of us wanted to say to the other. I choose to believe that each of us heard the unspoken words.

There was nothing I could tell him that he didn't already know, so I merely asked, "Are you ready? It's time."

It was a short walk to the Taj 51 Hotel, one of the favorites of the uber-rich Russians with its posh suites and St. James Square location near Buckingham Palace. Thanks to Monica's dossier, I knew that Schmidt and Oleg Petrykin had been meeting there once a quarter for the last couple of years. We had a meeting scheduled with them for eight o'clock – in our roles as Saxon and Doyle and supposedly to discuss telecom ventures in the St. Petersburg region.

Monica had told me, "This may be their last meeting. Petrykin is secure enough, and worried enough about Putin finding out about his American connections, that he wants to get rid of Schmidt, one way or another."

We went directly to the Petrykin suite and rang the bell. This is the part that worried Monica. *He'll have Vasili answer the door. You must be very careful with him. He's seen you before and he's very good. Petrykin has made him a very rich bodyguard but he still has excellent instincts. Do not take him lightly.*

When I shared her warnings with Riley, he smiled in a very tired way and said, "Mahoney. That's my department. I will deal with Vasili."

So when Vasili opened the door and immediately frowned when he saw me, Riley stepped forward, held a pistol with a long silencer to the bridge of Vasili's nose and used it to urge him inside. I followed them in and closed the door behind us. The floor plan showed the hallway running another thirty feet with bedrooms on both sides and a massive sitting room at the other end. We also knew that the closet to our left was a walk-in, so the two of us backed Vasili in there and again closed the door behind us. Riley kept the gun pointed at him while I extracted the pistol that Vasili kept in a shoulder holster.

This all happened within the first five seconds, but Vasili was processing furiously. He cursed in Russian and then started to say, "You clowns think –" Riley shot him twice in the middle of the chest and then caught him and lowered him gently to the floor. He was not in position to see Vasili's look of disbelief before it faded to the slack blankness unique to the dead.

We moved quickly, still following the choreography that we had reviewed so many times. Back into the hallway and moving fast. We were halfway to the end when Oleg Petrykin stepped into the opening at the far end and called out, "Vasili, who's –" He started backing up when he saw the two of us approaching with drawn guns. We were fully into the room before we saw Schmidt. He was sitting near the fireplace, pushing at the burning logs with an ornate poker. He turned and I saw the flash of surprise before it disappeared behind his usual bland expression. He stood up, still holding the poker.

He nodded at the elongated pistol that dangled loosely from Riley's right hand. "I thought I heard something. Those suppressor gadgets aren't all that quiet." When neither of us said anything, he said, "Vasili?" in a tone that suggested it wasn't really a question.

Petrykin had recovered from the initial shock and came toward us, stopping only when Riley raised the pistol. He looked angry more than frightened and I remembered my first meeting with him when he laid his pistol on the table before making his final offer to buy Boris's fleet of river barges. *I don't think he fully appreciates the situation just now.* I was surprised to find that I was looking forward to the next few minutes of Oleg Petrykin's education.

He turned to Schmidt. "These are your people?"

Schmidt said, "They were at one time, but not any more. I think they may have a new patron." He was looking at me while talking.

"Sit down, Oleg. I need to tell you something." *Monica had insisted on this. It's as meaningless as quoting Pushkin but I shall honor my commitment to her. She said, tell him 'Vy sovershili izmenu' and 'Vy ne nuzhny' before you kill him.*

Oleg sat at the glass table in front of the fireplace and poured himself a very large brandy. He had fully regained his characteristic arrogance. I think the combination of being a billionaire and a Russian in the highly civilized English city of London had dulled any sense of being subject to any will but his own. When I realized that, I looked forward even more to what was to be said.

"Vy ne nuzhny, Oleg." *You are unnecessary.*

The stark words and the way the two of us were staring at him as if he was a specimen on a glass slide seemed finally to penetrate. He put the brandy glass down and leaned back in his chair with crossed arms and his chin on his chest. It lasted perhaps three seconds.

"I am advisor to Putin –"

"It is Putin who said it, Oleg. Vy ne nuzhny."

"Nyet! My companies –"

"Were acquired by criminal acts, corruption, fraud … extortion of your fellow citizens."

"Schmidt!"   It was a plea, the first crack in his arrogance.

I moved two steps closer to him.   "Schmidt is a member of a foreign intelligence service that is opposed to Russian interests. Your relationship with him is disloyal to the state." I spoke Monica's other phrase.

"Vy sovershili izmenu." *You have committed treason.*

Petrykin was finally worried. The word 'treason' carried great weight in Kremlin circles and was never used lightly. He was looking left and right for help that wasn't there and his right hand had developed a noticeable tremor. When Riley looked at me, I nodded, and he raised the silenced pistol and fired a single muffled shot. A dime-sized red dot appeared in the middle of Petrykin's forehead and he fell in the same loose-limbed way that the two Afghanis had fallen in that Tikrit farmyard three months ago.

For perhaps a full minute, the only sound was the very faint sounds of London traffic and the crackling of the burning logs in the fireplace. Riley was the first to move. He held the pistol out for me to take, butt-first. I took it and handed him the semi-automatic that I had taken from Vasili. Schmidt watched the exchange without comment. Finally, he sat back down.

He said, "Putin is losing quite a few oligarchs recently."

I shrugged. "There's an infinite supply of volunteers. He will find others."

He nodded absently. "Why here? Why you? Why now? This –" he waved his hand at Petrykin – "will be a major international incident. In St. Petersburg, it would be a three-day story and Putin's message would be understood instantly by all the right people."

Typical Schmidt. He's imagining all the ways that the plan could have been improved, all the little changes that would perfect it. But he was starting from an incorrect premise, like a man giving impeccable directions to the wrong destination.

But he was getting there, one step at a time. "You said *izmenu...* treason ... a *foreign intelligence service* ... That's why it had to be now, and in London ... when he's in the act of meeting with the enemy. I had to be here."

He closed his eyes, trying to envision all the elements. But he wasn't quite there yet. "But Putin will be blamed for conducting an execution on British soil ... even worse."

I glanced at Riley. He was watching Schmidt working his way through the puzzle with an expression that seemed very much like fondness, as though Magda was here and we were in one of our sessions that would end with Schmidt sending us off to do whatever it was that he had worked out.

I could see the instant that he finally knew, when all the pieces came together. His entire body took on an absolute stillness and he closed his eyes for three or four seconds. I had an overwhelming need to know what he was thinking.

Schmidt looked first at Riley and then at me. "So you have another assignment. Not just Oleg."

Riley spoke before I could. "Yes," and it was as if all of the fondness was leached from his expression with that one word.

Schmidt nodded and asked, "Why?" and Riley answered, "Because that's what the client asked for." It was a cruel response and I began to see the depth of Riley's resentment for the last twenty years. *I wonder what will happen to him after this. I don't think he's going to do well.*

Schmidt looked at me, with that "Why?" question still hanging in the air. I said, "Because of the lies. The money. The reality that you would kill us for the sake of your miserable schemes. For Arthur, Roger, Peter, Alex, Benjamin." *And for Svetlana and Nolan and Elena ... and all the rest of the collateral damage.*

He did not react to my litany in any way other than nodding his head when I stopped. He asked, "Magda ... does she know?" When I shook my head, he said,

"Good," and I wondered what indictments she would add if given the chance ... and what punishment she would mete out.

He began, "All those times ... You know that I –"

Riley said, "Enough!" He raised his arm and fired two quick shots.

I wonder what he was about to say? Then I realized that I no longer cared.

We were back on the street within two minutes. Most of that time was spent arranging the scene so that the police could easily reach the conclusions that we'd scripted for them. The sound of Vasili's unsilenced gun had seemed extra loud to me, but the suites at the Taj 51 were designed for privacy in all its forms and there was no excitement in the hallway or lobby as we passed through.

We walked to Victoria Street, silent the entire time. When the light turned green, Riley said, "I'll leave you here. Say Hi to Magda for me." And he simply walked away. That's the last time I saw him.

I sent Monica -- I could not think of her as 'Nadja' --an email from Heathrow Airport consisting of seven words, using the address from her old website. "Done. Watch the news. Your turn."

The London police covered it up for almost twenty-four hours and even then released only the barest details. It was ten days before they shared their official version. It seems that Schmidt had shot Petrykin. The motive was probably related to their increasingly fractious business relationship. Then he and Vasili killed one another in the subsequent shootout. There was no mention of Petrykin's scheduled visit with Mr. Saxon and Mr. Doyle. The CIA was never mentioned.

Elena followed the story closely in the Swiss newspapers. One morning, she said, "It's curious that they pay so little attention to Schmidt." She read from the paper that was open before her. "He's described as 'a politically-connected American businessman with extensive financial investments in emerging market countries.'"

All of that is correct. It's what they don't say that is important. But none of the intelligence services involved – American, Russian or British – benefit from the truth.

In any case, the CIA had other problems. Congress announced the formation of a committee to investigate 'intelligence failures' in the run-up to the Iraq War, particularly concerning the existence of weapons of mass destruction. George Tenant, Director of the CIA, announced his retirement more or less simultaneously.

Elena's newspaper that morning also had an article about a car bombing at a mosque in Mosul that killed one-hundred and forty-eight Sunni worshippers. The writer quoted one of the government ministers saying, 'The resistance is only beginning. The Americans will never be able to leave."

A week later, there was a massive explosion at a warehouse in Baku, Azerbaijan. The explosion destroyed several hundred feet of waterfront properties and was large enough to register on seismographs throughout Europe. According to the news reports, the warehouse was owned by Boris Volkov, a Russian citizen and one of the world's foremost arms dealers. Volkov himself was killed in the explosion.

That same day, my inbox had an email from an unknown address. It read, 'Quid pro quo – An exchange in which one service is contingent on the other' and was signed simply 'Nadja.'

Oregon Coast

Even though he was dead, Schmidt still had games in play, and he would have enjoyed watching me deal with this last one. The call came while I was standing just inside the entrance of the First Class Lounge for Swiss Air. The caller ID read 'caller unknown.'

"Is this Mr. Mahoney?"

"Yes," in my angry why-are-you-bothering-me voice reserved for cold callers.

"Thomas Mahoney, the journalist?"

"Yes. What do you want? I'm –"

"Don't hang up. This is a quite serious and personal call. My name is Jerome Williams. I am a partner in a major international law firm and the executor for the last will and testament of Mr. Theodore Jacobs." He said all of this in a single breath and a rush that was designed to keep me on the phone.

"I don't know anybody named Theodore Jacobs."

"He said you would say that. He said, 'Just tell him it's Schmidt.'"

All of the ambient noise of the airport lounge went away and other people around me seemed to be moving in slow motion. I took a very deep breath and sat down. The caller sensed the change and was quiet as well. As an executor of wills, he probably was used to such transitions on calls like this. "Do you need a moment?" he asked.

"No, but, Mr. ..."

"Williams. Jerome Williams.   You may or may not know that Mr. Jacobs was quite wealthy. He has left you a very substantial bequest, subject only to a single condition.   There will be papers to sign and other formalities, but I will be happy to meet you at a time and place that you choose."

I asked, "What is the condition?" but I was seeing Schmidt in those last few seconds of his life... saying "All those times –" and for the first time since that night I wondered what he would have said if Riley hadn't cut him off so abruptly.

"Mr. Jacobs wants ... wanted ... to be buried in the town where he grew up, a small town on the Pacific coast of the United States. He has a sister there that will handle local arrangements, but he has designated you as the person to manage the physical transportation of his remains.   I gather that he anticipated that he might pass away in some remote spot, so he wanted to entrust this request to a person that he trusted."

"He's in London," I said. *What an inane comment!*

"Well then. That simplifies the paperwork. We have an office there. Will you accept this condition?"

When I didn't respond instantly, Mr. Williams jumped to the obvious conclusion. "Mr. Jacobs has provided an ample amount of money to cover transportation and funeral expenses. If you need to know the amount of your bequest –"

"No. That doesn't matter. And yes, I will honor Mr. Jacobs' request. I'm on my way to New York City right now.   Can we meet there sometime the day after tomorrow to discuss details?"

"Certainly. We have an office there as well. I'll send my contact information in an email."

"Good. One question: When was this will drawn up?"

There was a slight rustling of papers. "Ten years ago. It has not been modified since."

Magda and I followed the hearse in my rental car. The only other person from the chapel to continue with us was Schmidt's sister.   Our little three-vehicle procession went north on Highway One for about three miles and then turned away from the ocean and within a mile turned once more into an old-growth redwood grove that had a small and very old cemetery enclosed within a central clearing.   There was no graveside ceremony.   Schmidt's casket was simply lowered into the grave while three of us watched with our own thoughts. None of us talked and the sister left before the casket even completed its slow descent. When the winch stopped and the straps were retrieved from the grave, an indifferent worker in coveralls operated a small tractor to fill in the grave while Magda and I watched.

How very different from all those other hurried burials in far off places. All this ceremony and attention to detail. The polished casket, flowers and somber music. And no rocks to be stacked on top of the grave to keep the animals away, just the slow accumulation of pine needles over future decades.

We walked among the headstones in the late afternoon sunlight that filtered through the magnificent trees.

We found two other Jacobs. From the weathered inscriptions, we worked out that one of them was probably Schmidt's grandfather and another his father and that both of them had died in separate logging accidents a long time ago. The last burial in this cemetery —until today -- was more than thirty years ago.

Magda's car was back at the chapel, the lone car in the parking lot. Tendrils of incoming fog were beginning to seep through the cypress trees, muting the sunlight and dropping the temperature. When I stopped alongside her car and turned off the engine, she sat motionless, giving off an aura of immense melancholy with overtones of anger.

"Are you OK?"

She didn't answer directly. "It's his way of having the last word, isn't it? Making us witnesses to this. A clever form of posthumous revenge."

"We're alive. He's not. Revenge is sort of beside the point, I think. It's more about having a highly developed sense of irony." *And anyway, what exactly did we see? The burial of a man with no friends except those that could be bought and no legacy that could be talked about. Certainly nothing that would excite envy. This is not about revenge. It is a cautionary tale. But for whom?*

She wasn't listening. "Did he leave you money too? A lot of money?" I said, "Yes, quite a lot." *Seven zeroes and a bunch of properties.* For a while, I convinced myself that I would reject it, but Elena said, "We'll find a way to use it for something good."

Magda was still within her own head, talking to herself. "The lawyer said that the money was conditional on me attending the funeral. He wanted us to sit through this."

"Yes." *His way to convene one last meeting of the originals. Except for those who are dead, which is most of them. And Riley. Schmidt planned this reunion ten years ago, not because he wanted mourners or to have his life 'celebrated' in the modern fashion, but because he thought that we three had no one else except each other. He was wrong about that too.*

I knew the answer, but I asked anyway. "Have you heard from Riley?"

"No." I could read nothing from the word and she was looking away from me, out the window toward the ocean.

"I saw him in London. He said to tell you 'hi' for him." I listened to myself saying the words and thought that it was the bleakest sentence I had ever uttered to another person.

"Yes, he would do that." She reached for the door handle and seemed to gather herself, like a woman about to go from a warm house out into a arctic storm. I asked, "What are you going to do now? Where will you go?"

She said, "I don't know" and got out of the car. When I stopped at the entrance onto Highway One and looked back, she was standing at the entrance to the chapel, an alone and lonely figure not susceptible to either advice or compassion. I watched her fade into nothingness as the dense gray fog enveloped her and when she was no longer there, I turned onto the highway, heading south toward Elena along coastal bluffs still in bright sunlight.

Author's Note

My friends and relatives always ask, "How do you write your books?" which segues into a discussion of work habits (undisciplined), travel history (extensive) and all the minutiae of literary engineering (haphazard and self-taught). But the far more interesting question for me is "Why?" not "How?" In fairness, my (non-existent) psychoanalyst should answer that question, because it involves ancient maladies like compulsion, insecurity and arrogance; as well as more positive drives ... curiosity mostly, because I do not know where the story will take me and the only way to find out is to start writing and see where the characters decide to venture.

As to genre, I am drawn to the 'suspense/thriller' because of the way it permits colorful characters to inhabit a complex plot, while permitting me to upend the narrative and/or the protagonists with a stray bullet or a misplaced Top Secret file, sending it and them careening off toward yet another cliff edge. In the writing, however, I am increasingly troubled by the possibility ... likelihood? ... that my tales of morality come unglued, of corruption and malevolence, are not at all fictional; that such sinister forces are both real and barely contained. Perhaps such negativity is an occupational hazard for authors, but when readers ask "Where do you get your ideas?" my answer these days is disturbingly simple: I read the newspapers.

The Author

Thomas Hofstedt is engaged in approximately his fifth career, each of which is partially reflected in the plots and settings of his writing, including this book. In terms of vocations, he has worked as a professor in major universities, as a management consultant all over the globe, and as an advisor and board member for not-for-profit organizations. He is the product of a Scandinavian heritage, a Midwestern upbringing, and a Northern California value system. He lives in San Mateo, California with his wife and most diligent critic, Sharon.

He has authored nine other books of fiction, all of which are available in paperback or ebook formats from Amazon.com.

<u>Other Titles</u>

A Conspiracy of Patriots
A Convergence of Evils
The Hundred-Year Storm
They Call it Tinseltown
A Small War in a Far-Off Place
The House on Russian Hill
The Wisdom That Comes With Winters
A Lethal Intelligence
Fortunes of a Misbegotten War

⟨

www.ingramcontent.com/pod-product-compliance
Lightning Source LLC
Chambersburg PA
CBHW070615260626
47161CB00007B/2443